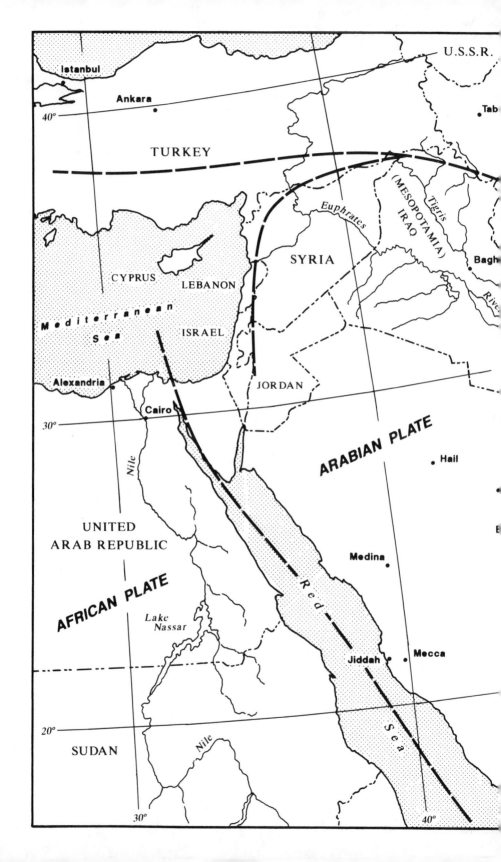

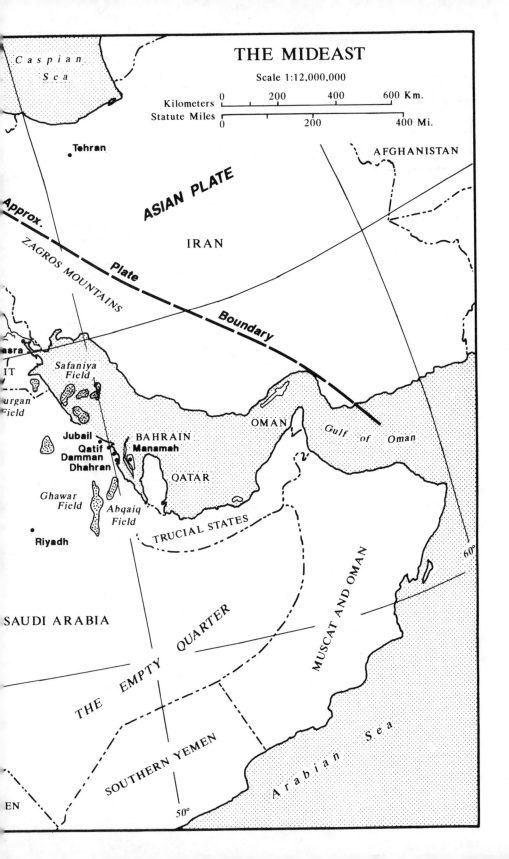

THE MIDEAST

Scale 1:12,000,000

Kilometers | 0   200   400   600 Km.
Statute Miles | 0   200   400 Mi.

Caspian Sea

• Tehran

AFGHANISTAN

ASIAN PLATE

IRAN

Approx.

ZAGROS MOUNTAINS

Plate

Boundary

asra

IT

Safaniya Field

urgan Field

Jubail

Qatif

Damman

Dhahran

BAHRAIN

Manamah

OMAN

Gulf *of* Oman

QATAR

Ghawar Field

Abqaiq Field

TRUCIAL STATES

• Riyadh

SAUDI ARABIA

THE EMPTY QUARTER

MUSCAT AND OMAN

60°

SOUTHERN YEMEN

50°

Arabian Sea

EN

THE ARABIAN LINK

JAMES WARNER

J'LEE BOOKS

The Arabian Link

Copyright © 1993 by James Warner

Cover Art by Howard Costner of Costner Graphics

Typography produced by Alpha Publishing Group

ISBN # 0-89896-304-4

J'LEE BOOKS

LARKSDALE

Printed in the United States of America

PREFACE

This book is fiction. Although based on factual incidents, it is basically a story of how it might have been in Saudi Arabia in the 1930's, and how it could be there in the late 1990's.

The story includes some real people, in particular, J. W. "Soak" Hoover, Bert Miller, and the other named geologists who worked for the very real Standard Oil Company of California, (SOCAL); and California Arabian Standard Oil Company (CASOC), that was formed in 1934 as a (SOCAL) subsidiary, and in 1944, became ARAMCO, Arabian American Oil Company. In 1937, CASOC acquired Texaco as a 50% interest participant; then in 1948, Standard Oil Company of New Jersey (later Exxon), and Socony-Vacuum Oil Company (later Mobil) acquired interests in ARAMCO. At that point, the ownership in ARAMCO was SOCAL 30%, Texaco 30%, Esso 30%, and Socony 10%. In the 1970's, Saudi Arabia acquired interests in ARAMCO leading finally to 100% Saudi ownership.

The locales, topographic features, ports, wells, history, travels, geologic and cultural features, and overall environment are real. Aircraft described are real; Imperial Airways is real; all air and other travel is fictitious, though based on real accommodations and means of transport.

All future geologic occurrences in the nineties are purely fiction, though based on sound geologic principles. Geologic references to faults, lithology, stratigraphy, structure, plate tectonics, earthquakes, reservoir fluids, sources, and dynamic petroleum entrapment, are mostly true and factual. Some specific geologic beds are fictitious, but the Arab D and major named strata are real.

There are no footnotes, but a Bibliography is listed by subject so that a reader may consult certain publications for more information. Acknowledgements are made when specific information is derived entirely from one publication.

The book would not have been possible without J. W. (Soak) Hoover, his diary and photographs, ARAMCO Public Relations, and personal interviews with several American and Saudi Arabian persons.

Special thanks are due Eddie Singer who triggered this story,

2

and to my wife, Lee, for her patience and encouragement.

The title, THE ARABIAN LINK, is derived from two facts:

The Arabian geologic sub-continental plate, is the plate that links the giant African and Asian continental plates.

Arab states are the major link to energy sufficiency for the entire world for the next several decades.

~~~~~~~~~~~~~~~

PROLOGUE

It was late evening in the *jebehl* or mountains east of Nafud Dunaylidhah and west of Riyadh in the Central Province of Saudi Arabia. Late fall, not so long after settlement of the Persian/Arabian Gulf crisis wrought by Iraq's Saddam Hussein in 1990. After sundown at this time of year, it was not uncommon to have temperatures below 50 degrees F even though temperatures in this arid region during the day often exceeded 90 degrees. This was a cool evening with long shadows cast by the rapidly sinking sun across the rocky crags that formed the *jabal* (mountain) crest.

The Saudi picked his way carefully across the rocky *wadi* astride his majestic black Arabian horse as he worked his way west up into the local pass through the *jabal* on an old abandoned camel road. Such roads, actually just vague trails, were clearly discernable only in those places where the rock walls or other natural impediment forced one to follow a particular path. Otherwise, pieces of trails were scattered across the terrain, all aiming in approximately the same direction. Some of these "roads" were thousands of years old, but now they were rarely used by anyone at all; all travelers choosing to use the paved highways that were now common all across the Kingdom. Such old camel roads carried the ghosts of the hundreds of caravans and nomadic herders; but now, nothing but the sounds of nature.

The horse, Wundeen, was accustomed to these outings. Rashid Ben Rimthan had picked his horse's name as a mixture of English and Arabic to indicate "all wise," because as a colt Wundeen had seemed to be quick to learn and had come from desert-wise parents. Besides, Rashid *wanted* him to be wise, naming him so might just help!

Rashid occasionally left his work place in Dhahran on the Arabian Gulf for a visit at his old home village just off the highway from Ushayqir on which one could drive south and east to Riyadh, the capital of Saudi Arabia. At Riyadh, a major east-west throughway connects Dhahran and Dammam on the east Arabian or Persian Gulf

Arabia. Through the mountains in the distance, Rashid could occasionally catch a glimpse of the major pipelines that carried oil from the fields of the Eastern Province to fill the never ending stream of tankers at Yanbu al Bahr on the Red Sea coast.

Rashid and Wundeen enjoyed these serene visits to the stark beauty and overwhelming quiet of these ancient mountains. Actually the mountains were quite old, being formed of rocks deposited over 100 million years ago during the Mesozoic period. In this environment, Khamis tried to capture the spirit of his heritage through the past centuries. This was enhanced by his visits with his mother and father, Amir Yahiya Ibn Rimthan, and their friends.

The trail dipped sharply, causing Wundeen to place his feet carefully among the rock rubble. Suddenly he jerked his head as he heard an unfamiliar gurgling sound just ahead in a dry wadi. These wadis served only as washes for water runoff after the brief, but sometimes very heavy, mountain rains. But now, unbelievably, this one was flowing water when there had been no rain in several days. Rashid dismounted and walked up the wadi toward a more pronounced gurgling, rushing sound. As he climbed up on a boulder and looked ahead, he saw a small geyser with water spurting a few inches into the air, and making a gurgling rushing sound. Springs were common in many topographically lower areas of Central Saudi Arabia, but Rashid knew of none in this high area. The water was coming from a fracture in the rock.

Then he lost his footing and began stumbling, having difficulty maintaining his balance as at the same time he became all too aware that the ground beneath his feet was trembling and heaving. He stumbled backward and steadied himself against a rock as he now observed the water flow had markedly increased. Also, the fracture from which the water gushed had widened to perhaps a half-inch, jaggedly cutting up across the now broken bedrock above the wadi. The rock layers were now vertically offset nearly a foot along this jagged fracture. Although not visible, the fracture extended as a rough plane in all directions through the bedrock.

In an instant, peace became chaos as the roar of rock slides overpowered all else, and Rashid's world became a whirling mass of rocks and rubble, water and the roar of nature adjusting its stresses. Rashid ran, stumbled, slid, and crawled his way back to Wundeen.

The horse had fallen, but had struggled back to his feet and now was terrified by this unknown. Rashid grabbed the horse's bridle, then his reins, and began working toward level ground. The shaking earth had now subsided, but slides continued and the water had become a roar as it rushed and tumbled down the wadi. From beginning to end, it had lasted only three minutes. But unknown to Rashid, there had already been two or three minor shocks earlier in the day, and there were several lesser aftershocks to come over the next few days.

Thus occurred a Richter 6 earthquake that was, unknown to Rashid, one of several earthquakes that were shortly to shock the world.

- - - - - - -

At the same time, across the world, a class was about to begin.

"Young scientists, you are about to hear all about Saudi Arabian geology." It was Dr. Martin Booth, head of the Geology Department. "Our speaker for today is Mr. James J. Burke, who was one of the early explorers there, and spent most of his professional career as a geologist working with that country."

Dr. Booth described JJ's background and family, then concluded, "and now, probably one of our best speakers for this fall, Mr. Burke."

It was a special seminar for science majors at Stephen F. Austin University in Nacogdoches, Texas, including a number who planned high school science teaching careers. This small university made a special effort to provide all around understanding for its students of the broad facets of their majors. To this end, there were several one-hour seminar courses for graduating seniors that incorporated frequent guest speakers. The class moderators were usually department heads, with one teaching professor heading each seminar class. Students were required to pay close attention. They were tested to confirm it. There were some geology students at this lecture, but most were otherwise.

JJ got out of his chair and slowly walked over to the lectern. He was still quite active, but as an octogenarian he was not prone to exactly bounce from place to place.

"Good morning, young ladies and gentlemen. I hope, I think,

you will find some of what I have to say to be interesting. I know it is important. Not only to Saudi Arabia, but perhaps even to you yourselves someday.

"The first thing you need to know is that the Saudis control a key part of the world's oil reserves. By far, most of the world's oil lies within a couple of hundred miles of the center of the Arabian, or Persian, Gulf. What caused it to be there, and what makes it available to us, is quite important to America. Today, in the hour allotted to me, I cannot address all the related topics. In fact, I'll do no more than touch the one thing I will address: key geologic features of Saudi Arabia."

JJ continued, "I'll use this overhead projector to show some things, and maybe do a little drawing on it now and then to help get my story across."

With that introduction, JJ then commenced his talk.

"Geologic field work in Saudi Arabia was started by Standard Oil of California, or SOCAL, then CASOC, an acronym for California Arabian Standard Oil Company, in 1933. Work that first season, plus the earlier broad brush geologic studies indicated that the mountains of the central and western provinces of Saudi Arabia were composed of older rocks ranging from pre-Cambrian granites, basalts, and other igneous and metamorphic rocks, in the western mountains or *jibehl*, to Paleozoic rocks along a northwest-southeast range just west of Riyadh."

JJ placed his first slide on the projector, a cross-section of rocks from the surface to about fifteen thousand feet. "The surface rocks grade from the old rocks in the west to much younger sediments on the east coast. Moving eastward from the western mountains, Paleozoic rocks lay on pre-Cambrian, then progressively upward above the Paleozoics, lie Mesozoic, Tertiary, and finally, Quaternary rocks at the coast.

"The Saudi Arabian part of the Arabian Peninsula might be thought of as a gigantic cake with many different kinds of layers, each layer laid down on the one below, then tilted easterly, and cut away on the top, or eroded, progressively more westerly away from the Arabian Gulf. At about the same time as the eastward tilt occurred, after all the layers had been laid down, the western part pushed together and crumpled up into the mountainous areas."

He slipped another slide in the projector. This one was a cross-section of the western mountains to the Red Sea.

"This pushing together was actually a part of the movement of the Arabian sub-plate, or a small part of the Earth's crust, against the African plate, a much larger part of the Earth's crust. These plate movements also produced the Red Sea which forms the west coast of Saudi Arabia."

JJ went back to the first slide and pointed with his pen to the surface as he talked.

"The erosion cut across the tilted layers forming Saudi Arabia, progressively more on the up-tilted western region until each layer lay exposed and terminated at the surface to the west, yet buried progressively deeper to the east. All this left the broad regional structure as it is today: The layers all tilted eastward with the eroded top of the earth being an irregular and gently eastward dipping surface, with the rocks underneath dipping in much the same direction, but at higher rates. In the Arabian Gulf, the pre-Cambrian basement rocks are up to about three miles deep."

He pointed to the surface area around Riyadh, the capital of Saudi Arabia, "Waters from the infrequent, though sometimes quite heavy, rains form the lifeblood of the Bedouin society, the main occupants of the eastern two-thirds of Saudi Arabia since at least biblical times. These waters, referred to as meteoric, collect in the topographic lows, and then either evaporate, drain off, or sink into the underlying porous rocks."

"While collected in the sometimes broad flat lows, the water gives life to the sparse vegetation, including the mineral-rich grass from which the sheep, goats, and camels of the Bedouins derive their sustenance. The water that drains off courses down the dry washes or wadis, until it evaporates or sinks into the underground. Little, if any, meteoric waters drain into the Gulf. "The water that sinks into the ground finds paths of permeability downward until it joins other water in some of the rock layers that are porous and permeable. These downward paths most often are provided simply by the outcrops of porous and permeable rock layers. The outcrops, or surface exposures, of these east-tilted layers were formed by surface erosion over the eons by rain and wind, and now stand ready to receive any water that flows across them in a wadi or other topographic low."

Now he pointed to a fault west of Riyadh, "Sometimes the water flows downward along fractures in the rocks, some of which fractures have displacements of the rocks on either side. When so displaced, the fracture is called a fault.

"As the water reaches a water laden porous rock, or aquifer, it collects in the aquifer up to a level called the water table, such as this." JJ placed his third slide, a three-dimensional block of earth showing the surface and part of the same earth section as on the first slide. He pointed to the top of a layer colored blue.

"When the water table rises above the level where gravity and other forces acting on the stored water are stable, the water will flow eastward by gravity down the east-dipping aquifer," he moved his pen eastward along the blue layer, "and will continue to flow if there is some way for the water to get out of the aquifer further downdip, such as this fault," he pointed to a fault. "If the forces again stablilize, the water will cease to flow. However, since the flow rate is very slow, perhaps only a few feet per year, flow will be rather continuous if there is a modest resupply from occasional rainfall.

"Faults often form outlets of this water to or near the surface which, at the more easterly position, is lower than the water table at the inlet source for the aquifer. Such faults form the many springs, and along with the aquifers become the water source for wells. For at least the past three thousand years, the Bedouins have known where these springs are located and, in many cases, have dug wells near the springs.

"Each year, the Bedouins form large encampments near these wells for the hot and dry summers, and then move out at the beginning of fall, wandering in search of grass for their herds.

"These Arabs of the desert are the originators of astronomy and named most of the visible stars and constellations formed by the stars, and also were the first to recognize the visible planets, or 'moving stars.'

"Among the many stars they named is Canopus, a bright star that sinks beneath the horizon in Saudi Arabia each spring, and is not visible at night until near the fall equinox, when days and nights are of the same length, then Canopus rises above the horizon for another cycle. The Bedouins used the rising of Canopus as a signal to move out to their unmarked and non-specific pastures. Thus the annual wandering begins.

"Although the rainy season, weak though it normally is, does not begin until some weeks later, and the days are still very hot, Canopus is their signal. Even though it is only the end of September, the nights are commonly cool and pleasant. In a desert, low humidity is routine. But in Saudi Arabia, expecially the eastern half, humidity is fairly normal, and near the Gulf, humidity often is relatively high and adds considerable discomfort to the heat."

During the last part of his presentation, JJ showed a number of photographs of the Bedouins, their camps, herds moving, camel trains, and other scenes.

"Well, future leaders, that's about all I can cover in my allotted time. I tried to give you a smattering of the culture and climate as well as general geology. If we're allowed to, I'll try to answer a few questions if you have any." As he made his last statement, JJ saw Dr. Booth get up and come over.

"We will certainly take the time for some questions," said Dr. Booth, "so if there are any, let's start!"

There were many questions by the interested students before it was finally cut off by Dr. Booth. There had been communication. From the old warrior to the new hope.

Later that afternoon, sitting in a lawn chair under an old pecan tree in his back yard, sipping a bourbon and water, the old man's mind drifted back to 1934...

~~~~~~~~~~~~~~~

BOOK ONE

THE EARLY YEARS

CHAPTER 1

West Texas

The pickup swerved on the ranch road to miss a jackrabbit as JJ started home for the last time from his mapping project near Sanderson in far west Texas. He never liked to hit these rather large rabbits because, first, he didn't like to unnecessarily kill other creatures, and second, he didn't like to clean the blood off his mule, as he called the sturdy Ford pickup. He was now about four miles from the Sanderson-Ft. Stockton gravel road, and then some fifty-three miles on into Ft. Stockton.

It was a hot and rather windy, and consequently dusty, afternoon in early August, 1934, and JJ was not at all unhappy to be leaving this country. JJ, or more formally, James Jonathon Burke, was kidded as he grew up because of the spelling of his name, but he was always careful to point out that his name was spelled Jonathon, not the more common Jonathan. His folks thought he was special, and needed a special name! By the time he got in high school, they were not still certain he was all that "special," but the name was fixed anyway. Later on, they decided he *was* "special," at least to them, after all. "JJ" was a natural and expected resultant nickname.

He had received a letter the previous week from Standard Oil headquarters in Midland, Texas, to wind up his surface geologic mapping and come in to the office for a new assignment. He was very curious what and where this new assignment would be. Especially since the office indicated it was unusual.

Although the trans-Pecos country was tough, and often trying, the geology was all laid out to be seen and mapped, and it was still quite beautiful in a rather harsh way. For example, during the summer in the field, with temperatures above 100 degrees F in the shade, there was no shade except to nestle under a three-foot greasewood, and sometimes one had to contest that shade with a rattlesnake that figured he had as much right to the shade as some interloping human. But once under the greasewood, and relaxed, the slight breezes with extremely low humidity created a rather comfortable place to view the rather stark, but dramatic canyons, buttes, mesas, and draws formed natural erosion over eons, leaving rock layers exposed for all to see.

But, all in all, he was ready to try something else!

JJ had been in the field now for nearly fourteen months. While he had not lost any of his 180 pounds spread out over his 6'1" height, his normally medium red-brown hair had been exposed to so much sun that it was bleached to a sandy brown. Quick, sharp, at times piercing, green eyes, though somewhat red-green color blind, enabled him to see movement, such as a snake rearing back, unusually well.

He had hired a local man to drive and otherwise assist him, and had a surveyor come down to assist when it was necessary to use a plane table and alidade. Most of his work was done with a Brunton compass, a small surveying instrument that could be used for many purposes, both geologic and surveying, and United States Geological Survey Topographic Sheets. Occasionally, he had to resort to county records to develop maps showing surveys and culture. Key information, such as magnetic declination, elevations, and survey markers were available on the USGS maps, Coast and Geodetic Markers, other surveyor stakes, etc.

The two men did much cross-country driving, dodging cholla cactus and the spindly spine-filled ocotilla tree-bushes. They learned early to not ignore the low innocuous lecheguilla plants with their thick succulent leaves. The end of each leaf had a sharp spine fully capable of penetrating pickup tires. All plants, including the abundant prickly pear, were adapted to discourage being eaten, being well covered with all manner of sharp thorns and spines.

The occasional leheguilla and rock-strewn landscapes commonly resulted in one or two flats daily, even though every effort was taken to avoid such hazards. Broken springs were another frequent malady of geologic field work.

But their business was making geologic maps, and vehicle damage was one of the expected costs.

On these maps, he marked geologic and other mapping data as necessary to record the culture and geology of the area. The field geology was interesting, and he had mapped an anticlinal structure in the Cretaceous surface rocks about 30 miles southeasterly from Ft. Stockton, near the Puckett ranch. More recently he found a large anticline some six miles northwest of Sanderson and this was very exciting. He lost the excitement though when he found the remains of a dry hole on the crest of the anticline that had been drilled several years earlier. Someone had already found that structure! And wasted a lot of money on it.

He reached the main road, a sparsely traveled caliche and gravel highway that wound its way through canyons and across the mesas from Sanderson to Ft. Stockton. He turned north, and about an hour later, just at the south edge of Ft. Stockton, turned left to go to his small apartment in the home of the elderly Carlisles on the southwest side of Ft. Stockton. As he came in the house, Mrs. Carlisle was waiting, "Well, you must have had another flat. I expected you'd try to get here a little earlier since you were goin' on to Midland today. Are you stayin' with that plan?"

"Yes ma'am. I've sure enjoyed staying here, and finding out what a good cook you are on those few occasions when you took pity on a poor lonesome geologist. But all things, including this stay, must eventually come to an end, so I guess I'd better gather my things, and set sail."

"Do you need any help?"

"No ma'am. I thought I'd wash my face, load up, and try to make Midland before I starve to death."

After goodbyes to these warm people with whom JJ had become good friends, and with no further delays, JJ did load up and started the three-hour drive to Midland.

After a short delay caused by a big sheep herd strung out for nearly two miles near Pecos, he pulled into the Scarborough Hotel nearly three and a half hours later. He checked in for the night, went upstairs to his room, and got busy washing off West Texas dust. He dressed, and literally ran downstairs to the coffee shop, absolutely starved. He had dinner, or supper as he had grown up to call it, and after reading the Midland Reporter-Telegram, went to bed.

The next morning, he reported to Standard's District office where Martin Rogers, the District Geologist had his orders.

Rogers said, "Welcome back to civilization. Maybe it would be nice now to sit in an office for a while to do your mapping, but the company has other plans."

The only thing JJ could think of to say was, "Oh?."

"How do you think you'd look wearing an Arab robe?"

JJ, somewhat startled, thought a few seconds, and, "You mean, like in Arabia?"

"None other," replied Rogers. "Here's your formal request letter."

Feeling a bit shocked, JJ sat down to read the letter. It was a request that he accept a transfer to Saudi Arabia for a two-year surface mapping program under the Oil and Gas Concession granted by King Ibn Sa'ud of Saudi Arabia to Standard Oil Company of California, better known as Socal, in 1933.

"You don't have to accept it, you know, but I think it might be the beginning of an exciting new operation," Rogers explained.

"Well," JJ came back, "It's a bit surprising, and I'd like to sleep on it, but off the cuff, I think that I'm at the right time of my life to do this sort of thing."

They discussed the overall job, the remoteness, the lack of any starting maps, the complications, the culture changes, and many more things associated with this big decision for any man. Then JJ left Roger's office to visit with some of his friends in the office. He talked to several of them and asked their opinions--which were varied, but all generally suggesting he ought to try it.

JJ spent an up and down night at the hotel as he kept awaking and immediately thinking about this project. Finally, he slept soundly, awakened, and the decision was clear: Go!

And go he did. He spent the day in the office going over his field maps with Rogers, most of which had already been furnished to the office essentially as done. Then, he called his folks to tell them he was coming for a delay-in-route vacation, took care of a few personal matters regarding his bank account and belongings, and wound up a very active day. He left Midland the next morning on the Texas & Pacific passenger train for Fort Worth where he boarded a bus for Nacogdoches, Texas, his home town.

~ ~ ~ ~ ~ ~ ~ ~ ~ ~ ~ ~ ~ ~ ~

CHAPTER 2

East Texas

What a way to wake up, thought JJ: The smell of frying bacon! He had arrived late the day before, had a supper of butter beans and ham, with cornbread, fresh spinach and potato salad, and hit the sack. Then to awaken to some more of his mother's East Texas cooking. He bounced out of bed, quickly slipped on a pair of pants and headed for the oversized kitchen which also served as the normal dining room. He ran in, grabbed his mother in a big hug, "You do know how to get a man out of bed!"

"Yes, I've had a few years practice learning how to get the attention of my family," replied Alma Burke, a slightly plump and still quite lovely blue-eyed and dark-haired lady of 47 years. They discussed JJ's new job and how it was similar, yet quite different from his recent work. Then after his breakfast of orange juice, grits, bacon, eggs, and toast, JJ took his cup of black coffee and headed out the back door. "Gonna take a little walk, Mom. Be back in a little while."

JJ walked out the back door, across the back yard and into the woodland trail that commenced at the back of the yard. Lordy, how many times have I walked this trail. Their home was on the outskirts of the city, where his father Charles Homer Burke had bought a small farm shortly after JJ was born 24 years earlier. Homer was a storeowner who had taken over his dad's general store and built it into a department store specializing in hardware and sporting goods. The store provided only a modest living in these depression years, but had been a good income source during the twenties and provided a good nest egg that Homer had built on with sound investments.

- - - - - - -

As their three children grew up, Homer and Alma always tried to encourage accomplishment and the discipline needed to do that. They did not attempt to force education, but were quite happy that their two girls and one boy took to learning so well.

His older sister by two years, Mary Jane, was a salutatorian of her high school graduating class, and went on to Stephen F. Austin College to get a degree in music so as to teach music and art. The other sister, Elizabeth Ann, was a real beauty, taking after her mother, but not a very good student. She was just finishing a stenographic course after high school and, at age 19, was about to go out into the world of business for a job.

JJ's education was not marked by consistently good grades until he reached the seventh grade and encountered Miss Myrtle McCardle who taught arithmetic and general science. This lady inspired anyone who had an interest in the how's and why's of math and nature, and JJ took to it like a duck to water.

In high school, JJ participated in several sports, and although fast with his hands and reflexes, he could not run faster than a little above average. Therefore, he became a football lineman. Because of his 6' 3" height, but only 168 pounds as a senior, he was assigned to end. JJ was no star, but with his good strength, plus his strong drive and desire, he was a steady and reliable performer.

By his senior year at age 17, he had become very interested in the earth and the stars, and took all the science and math available. He ended up graduating third in a class of 122 in 1928, and knew that he had to study much more to find his place in life.

Whatever else, JJ did not lack courage. He participated in a number of daring adventures. Once, when he was a sophomore in high school, he and Fred Johnston, a classmate, climbed a water tower and painted a girl friend's name there. While they did not get caught, there was enough suspicion that the sheriff called them in to tell them of the dangers of water towers.

But his courage was not always directed in just the right direction. Later that same sophomore year he got to meet the sheriff again, and this time it wasn't just for mischief.

One night not long after Christmas, while he, Fred and another friend, Jack LeRoy, were on their way home from a Boy Scout meeting, Jack said, "Hey men, you see that service station over there?" He pointed to a well-lit Humble service station.

The other boys looked and Fred said, "So?"

"Well, that candy box isn't locked!" Jack was speaking of a tall storage/display cabinet with glass-paned doors so that customers could see the candy inside. All kinds of good stuff!

"That's stupid," said JJ, "who would leave their candy box unlocked?"

Jack replied, "it's not *exactly* unlocked. It's just that you can stick a knife blade in there and pry it back. Then the door will open."

Jack was a very happy-go-lucky boy who never worried much about what was right or wrong. He laughed easily, always had a joke to tell, and never even tried to do much school work. Or any other kind of work for that matter. Unbeknownst to Fred and JJ, Jack had already had a talk or two with the sheriff regarding suspicion of petty theft. But he *was* a fun guy to be around!

Jack walked over to the cabinet, took out his pocketknife and proceeded to pry the latch back and open the door. There it was! Loads of candy of all kinds for three hungry boys!

They nervously grabbed a dozen or so bars each, quickly closed the cabinet door, and took off running. After a block, they slowed down to a walk, and excitedly laughed and talked about how easy it was! They parted company as they arrived at Jack's house another block away, then Fred and JJ continued on toward their home another half-mile away.

"You know," said Fred, "it's really not right to take that candy." His father had been a school principal before he died with pneumonia a few years earlier, and had always tried to instill responsibility in his children.

"I know," replied JJ, "but it ain't really so bad. How much did that candy cost that guy. Maybe a dollar?"

"I guess so. But still, I don't feel exactly right about it."

A week later, on their way home from the scout meeting, they helped themselves to the candy again, but took less, so that it wouldn't be missed. Then, two weeks later, still again. They had a good thing going, and Fred and JJ overcame their conscience, concluding that the station owner probably didn't even miss the amounts they took.

One night, as they approached the candy cabinet, something was different: It had a locked chain around it. Jack looked it over, and said, "hey...this ain't so tight. Look, I can slip it off over the top!"

Sure enough, with a little help from JJ, they worked the chain off over the top. Then Jack open the lock with his knife and they swung the door open. Suddenly they heard an engine roar and turned toward the sound about a half block away across the street.

A car was accelerating rapidly away from the curb and headed straight toward them, with all three of the boys nearly blinded by the bright headlights aimed directly at them! The car screeched to a stop in the station bay, and a large man jumped out.

At a glance, the boys saw that it was the owner, and that he had his wife in the car with him. She was one of the boys' teachers. They were scared, angry, and worried all at once. The owner let them all go after angrily and harshly explaining to them the error of their way. He remembered who they were. And told the sheriff. Who called them in one by one over the next two weeks.

Jack was called in first. What the sheriff had to say wasn't overly important to him, but he maintained a polite and submissive demeanor. Just like he thought the sheriff would like to see. The sheriff delayed his call for Fred and JJ for several days so as to let the pressure grow! Then he called Fred. Then JJ.

By the time it was all over, the main things Fred and JJ felt were shame and embarrassment. Especially after the sheriff pointed out to them how they had embarrassed their families. Their parents made the boys take their own little savings, and work until they made enough money to pay the station owner back for all of the candy. Doubled. Except Jack. His husbandless mother failed in her attempt to make Jack meet all of his responsibility.

Another time, when JJ was fifteen, early on a winter morning he saw smoke boiling into the air about a block from his home, and he ran over to see that it was the home of a young couple he knew who had a small child. The father had already gone to work, and the mother was in front of the blazing cottage screaming, "Ricky's in there! Ricky's in there! Oh, God somebody help me."

At that time, the fire truck had just pulled up and the firemen were running to get water connected. JJ ran up to the truck, grabbed a fireman's coat and shouted, "Get water on me!" and ran for the house. He slammed through the partly closed front door, and ran through the small five-room house shouting, "Ricky, Ricky." He kicked open a door which turned out to be a bedroom, and saw the boy, three years old, cringing behind a bed and stiffened with panic.

The smoke at this time hung heavy in the air about three feet off the floor, and JJ had run in a crouch. He grabbed Ricky and sprinted back out the front door into a heavy wall of water from the fire hose in spray pattern. His only injuries were a burn on one hand from the iron bedstead and singed eyebrows and hair. He was in and out in a bit less than a minute. For this he got a mention in the newspaper and a medal. And a little appreciation from Ricky's mother.

By the time he reached his senior year in high school, family and friends had made it abundantly clear that he had two characteristics that needed control. First was his temper.

Although JJ's temper never got him into any really bad situations, it led to a few fistfights and little embarrassments now and then. After learning that temper flaring only made things worse, he would literally bite his tongue, close his eyes momentarily, and then lash out! But, he hoped it was improving! He constantly reminded himself of his mother's admonishment, "Keep you temper, Jonathon, nobody else wants it!"

His second problem was impatience, and this seemed to be getting worse! Again, by the time he finished high school, he knew this was a problem and was trying to learn how to be more patient. Another family maxim, this one from his father, helped: "Patience creates, impatience destroys."

After high school, JJ worked in the family store as usual during the summer, and then was accepted into Texas A&M College that fall. At Texas A&M, JJ thought he would study civil engineering with side courses in geology. He found that he could not take any geology the first year; all engineering students took the same basic curriculum. He also found that while he had been a top student in high school, this was another place, where, evidently, the main objective seemed to be to flunk out all possible. As a result, he had to study harder than he thought possible, yet still could only muster a high "C" average.

The next summer he worked again at the family store, and visited with family and friends about a best course of study. That fall, he decided to switch to geological engineering, and started his first geology courses. Also, he was "running scared" and was determined to improve his grades. He did. He posted a low "A" average the first semester, won Distinguished Student honors, and never looked back after that; winning DS honors all the remaining semesters at A&M.

In his senior year, and the following summer, he took an extra field mapping course and two graduate courses. As a result, he had a good understanding of geologic field instruments and how to use them, as well as subsurface mapping techniques, using the new Schlumberger electric logs as well as driller's and sample logs on boreholes. This was later noticed in job interviews, and because of his outstanding grades and extra study, he was accepted as well as many geologists with Master's degrees even though he had only a Bachelor degree.

He started to work for a Texas subsidiary of Standard Oil of California, Socal, shortly after his birthday in September, 1932. After a few months of office and field training, JJ was assigned to field mapping and, before his second year was finished, he had been assigned to his first field mapping project on his own.

The days of visiting, fishing, reading, and eating, ended all too soon and it was time to leave for San Francisco. Besides, one of the main attractions in Nacogdoches, Ruthanne Cook, was not there. She had already left for The University of Texas at Austin for her junior year. When JJ finished high school, he hadn't paid much attention to Ruthanne, since she was only fourteen then. But how things change! Last Christmas when he was home, he saw Ruthanne at a Christmas party and did not recognize her until she spoke to him.

He had been temporarily confused by this lovely auburn-haired, green-eyed beauty walking up to him with an outgoing greeting. After a little recovery, they had talked more, and had since corresponded a number of times. He had one date with her in Austin the previous May, but had not managed another meeting since. JJ intended and hoped to see more of Ruthanne, but not at this time.

She was determined to graduate before getting serious with any man, and he had to make a bit more of himself before he was ready to take on the responsibility of a wife. And there was no doubt Ruthanne was just the sort of girl that he wouldn't date too much before things could easily get very serious as far as he was concerned. So, all in all, it was best Ruthanne had other irons in the fire for the time being. And he was free to survey the field!

- - - - - - -

It was a typically hot August 24 when JJ boarded a bus for Houston where he would take the Sunset Limited to Los Angeles, then bus again up to San Francisco and Socal offices. The Limited took a little over two days to Los Angeles. It was a pleasant, interesting trip;

especially since someone else was picking up the fare! The food in the dining car was quite good, though to him also quite expensive, and his made-down bed was quite comfortable. He had never been west of West Texas, and the often barren and arid lands of New Mexico, Arizona, and California created an ongoing picture of serene, though harsh, beauty that was new to him.

As the clickity-clack of the rails marked the ever-increasing miles from home, JJ found his mind wandering over many subjects: The beginning of a new and unusual adventure, leaving the familiarity and warmth of home and East Texas, his family and friends, but most of all, what lay ahead. He wondered why they had asked him to take this assignment when there were many other field geologists with as much and more experience.

He had no knowledge that he had been picked because it had been noticed that his field notes and observations showed that he had a knack for seeing and comprehending vague geological clues to petroleum entrapment that often were overlooked by others. Actually, most of what a field geologist did was to map the layers of sediments and rocks, or strata, exposed at the surface, take elevations on those beds, then contour those elevations so as to produce a picture of how the rocks were bowed and shaped. The "hills," or highs, are called anticlines, while the "valleys," or lows, are called synclines. A round anticline is a dome, an anticline with one steep and one gentle flank is an asymmetric anticline.

Since oil and gas are lighter than water, both these fluids will pass up through water in porous and permeable layers and float on the water. So, in reverse to the normal expectancy that lows fill up, and highs drain off, in the subsurface, oil or gas lies on water in porous rock or sediments, and is trapped and accumulates in the highs or anticlines. All this was second nature to JJ and he knew how to spot the slightest hint of strata that was dipping, that is, not flat. Then, like a detective story, with Mother Nature providing the clues, a picture of the shape of the surface strata could be developed.

After the surface structure was developed as best possible with the available rock exposures, or outcrops, JJ and other geologists sometimes employed core drilling rigs to drill holes ten to a few hundred feet deep in order to find the subsurface position of rocks that lay beneath the surface, and then use those points to better define the structure. When an anticline was mapped, it was probable that this surface and near-surface structure also existed several thousand feet below in older rocks and sediments where oil and gas occur. Thus, surface geology was used to find oil and gas.

JJ wondered if such simple things as survey boundaries and topographic elevations would be available in Saudi Arabia. In that dry place, what did the field geologist do for water. What did they eat? Would the people be friendly or hostile? Time would answer these questions, and answer a host more that JJ did not know to ask.

In Los Angeles, he changed trains for San Francisco. The trip north to San Francisco was uneventful but profoundly interesting to JJ. He had seen the Gulf of Mexico, but the occasional glimpses of the ocean he saw on this leg of his trip was different. This was the great Pacific! He studied the hills, the terrain, as the train rolled along, and became impressed with several conditions that were new to him.

Here and there he could make out faults and sharply dipping layers in road cuts. He also noticed that most of the layers seemed to be clastics, that is, sandstones and shales. The terrain was striking in places, and the vegetation beautiful. But another situation also caught his eye. He thought that sharp bluffs and shaley rocks presented optimum conditions in some places for landslides to occur. And, though he didn't know it, such was indeed the case.

~ ~ ~ ~ ~ ~ ~ ~ ~ ~ ~ ~ ~ ~

CHAPTER 3

The Trip

It was a little after 6 PM when JJ got off the train in San Francisco. He got his bag, then took a cab to the Clift Hotel where he had a reservation, and checked in. He had dinner, bought a newspaper and went back to his room.

The headlines had to do with demonstrations about jobs, the high unemployment, and the developing dust bowl in Oklahoma and other central states. This was mostly rather distressing, but did have the effect of making JJ realize how fortunate he was to have a good job, and not only a job, but one with great excitement in store.

He turned to the sports to read about the early season football and late season baseball games, and was happy to see that Texas A&M was not too bad according to the small three-line item on page three of the sports section. With that, he turned out the lights, thought a bit of the morrow, and went to sleep.

The 6 AM call seemed mighty early, but JJ bounded out of bed and headed for the shower. While briskly rubbing down with the rough towel, JJ began to think of all the questions he wanted to ask, and realized that he had better take a few quiet minutes to think of all the things he needed to know. Then, off to breakfast, back, brush teeth, and start the walk to the office at 225 Bush Street.

JJ went to the receptionist and asked for Bill Stroud at the Standard Oil Company of California, or Socal, later to be called Casoc in Saudi Arabia. Bill was the Field Coordinating Geologist for the Saudi operations. Bill explained to JJ that he would be in San Francisco about a week, during which time he would be briefed on the geology, people, and customs of Saudi Arabia, as best known to Casoc, get a passport, and do some shopping for personal things. Also, he would have a visit with Bill's boss, Doc Nomland, Chief Geologist, regarding the work and the concession and its terms. The first thing on the agenda that morning was to get passport photographs as guided by Stroud.

During these briefings, JJ learned a great deal that tended to build his excitement ever more. He would be going to the Persian Gulf as the Brits called it, (Arabian Gulf to the Arabs). The British did nearly all early oil exploration, felt they had a special niche, and thought Americans would have a tough time making any deals.

This was to be expected because the British had held sway in political and commercial matters for at least fifty years, and considerable influence for the preceding one hundred years. The Royal Navy was the dominant military force and acted as an enforcing agent for the treaties and agreements. As an example of British control, in 1892, Zaid ibn Khalifa, Abu Dhabi Chieftain, signed an agreement with Britain binding himself and his heirs forever to Britain. In this agreement, Zaid agreed to such extremes as to never allow residence of any foreigner seeking deals unless specifically approved by Britain. In 1933, the British were very surprised when Saudi Arabia made a petroleum concession to a U.S. company.

In 1933, British companies were already active in Persian (Iranian) petroleum exploration, and had concessions from Iran, Iraq, Kuwait, Qatar, and the Trucial Coast. It was a two-way street, of course. In exchange for the British monopoly, the Royal Navy maintained peace and British subjects added to the welfare of the people by creating work, industry, and an improved life in general.

The Anglo-Persian Oil Company, forerunner of British Petroleum, was half owned by the British Government, and had the Royal Navy as a major customer. This company, either alone or with other companies, had considerable oil production in Iran and Iraq in 1933. However, starting in 1922, a New Zealander by the name of Frank Holmes managed, after exhausting effort, but finally with British approval, to get an oil concession from the Sheik of Bahrain, an independent emirate or sheikhdom, in 1925, for exploration on that Arabian Gulf island just off Saudi Arabia's east coast.

The result: a classic domal anticline mapped by Ralph Rhoades, a Gulf Oil Co. geologist, after Gulf bought the concession. Bahrain proved to be a critical step in Saudi development.

After study, Gulf decided to not explore Bahrain, largely because of nigh unsolvable political problems involving the British, but also because the Tertiary formations then productive in Iran and Iraq, were not present at Bahrain, and only deeper and older sediments, with completely unknown potential, were available to explore.

Gulf sold out to Standard Oil of California, who had

monumental struggles satisfying British political requirements aimed at their retaining a strong measure of control. A syndicate operated by Socal made a final agreement with The Sheikh of Bahrain in 1930. A Socal Canadian subsidiary, Bahrain Petroleum Company, represented locally by none other than the intrepid Major Frank Holmes, finally got to the business of testing the large structure later that year.

In May 1930, the first Socal geologist, Fred Davies, came to Bahrain. He located the first test well shortly thereafter, and that well, Jabal Dukhan No. 1, finally started drilling, or spudded, in October 1931. It was completed in June, 1932 as a major oil discovery from Cretaceous rocks, much older and deeper than the lower Tertiary limestones thought to be the main pay objectives.

This was the discovery of Bahrain Field. During all this time from 1930 through the summer of 1932, Socal had been making a effort to secure an exploration concession from Saudi Arabia, based on broad reconnaissance work done largely by Major Holmes and Karl Twitchell some years earlier. Nothing was really known about the geology in the vast arid lands of the Saudi Arabian kingdom.

It was felt that if significant oil occurred in Bahrain, it should also exist on the Arabian mainland. And the general appearance of rocks sloping eastward across central and eastern Saudi Arabia from the known basement rocks in the Western Province, seemed to establish broadly favorable conditions for petroleum accumulations.

In July, 1933, Socal finally reached a Concession Agreement with representatives of King Ibn Sa'ud. In view of the seemingly insurmountable problems, it was nearly a miracle that all the forces and personalities could voluntarily reach such a complex agreement. But reach it they did, and with Bahrain as a feather in their cap, Socal was ready to attack the exciting and major potential of the mainland.

After the first day of instructions, JJ felt as if he had been crammed to overflowing with information, and much more was to come. That evening, Bill Stroud joined him after work for a couple of beers, then JJ returned to the hotel for dinner and a review of the several booklets and papers he had been furnished. He noted that much of the data concerned Saudi history, customs, and terms of the concession. He could see that much reading lay ahead.

For the next four days, JJ attended several meetings with

Stroud, one with Doc Nomland, and several with other Socal people. He learned a great deal more about Saudi Arabia, the people, and the concession, but most of all he learned the broad geological parameters and why it seemed an attractive place for large petroleum accumulations.

Interspersed with the technical and business meetings, JJ undertook sightseeing and personal shopping.

Stroud had suggested that one thing he might have difficulty finding in Arabia was a simple sturdy canteen for water. By this time JJ knew that the normal water containers in Arabia were the sewn skins of small animals, which often imparted an undesirable odor and taste to the water. While it would best suit the Arabians to use the same thing they used, JJ thought it wouldn't hurt to have his own half-gallon canteen.

While exploring the city, he found and bought his canteen, a camera, several articles of clothing, mostly underwear and socks, a small notebook, a slide rule, a large travel bag, a book on astronomy, and a book on surveying under remote conditions. He also had in mind several other items, but decided to get them in Paris in order to have less to carry to that point. Also, he picked up his passport which was now ready.

During these few days, JJ enjoyed the many different sights of San Francisco. Of particular interest was the cable cars and how they functioned. It was fun riding them, but it was also interesting to find out how the cars could couple and disengage as needed. Then there was the old fort, the beautiful gardens, the profound variations of excellent food in the many restaurants. JJ steered clear of the expensive places, but even so, he found plenty of good eating. Then there was Golden Gate.

One evening, JJ took a taxicab into Chinatown to try the Chinese food and atmosphere. He was not particularly impressed with the food: it differed a bit too much from his "meat and potatoes" background. But while in the taxi, he noted these monster towers in the distance and was told by the driver that what he was seeing was the Golden Gate bridge, then under construction. The next day, JJ took another cab to that area and was awestruck by the magnitude of this immense construction. The bridge across the Golden Gate was started the previous year, and now, only the towers were readily obvious. But it was of such interest to JJ that he visited with one man near the work area, then another, until he met one who was willing to show the basic plans to a fellow engineer. It was some three years away from being finished, but was obviously to be a bridge like nothing anywhere else in the world.

On his last day in San Francisco, he borrowed Stroud's car, took the ferry over to Oakland, visited there, then back on the ferry, to another ferry north to Muir Woods. He took the coast road after Muir Woods, and finally back to the ferry and San Francisco. It was a long and tiring, but exciting and inspiring day. Capped that evening by dinner with the Strouds.

That evening he packed for the trip ahead, wrote letters to home, to Ruthanne, to Martin Rogers in Midland, and turned in for the next day's early start. As he crawled into bed that night, JJ marked this as a most memorable day of visiting and seeing; it was to him the most interesting and beautiful area overall that he had to this time witnessed. He would never forget the mammoth Golden Gate bridge that was being built. What a wonder of the world this would be when it was finished...stretching so far over open water, over four thousand feet of free-hanging suspension, and high enough for the largest ships to easily glide beneath!

Saturday, September 1, 1934: JJ found himself awake at 5:30 AM, even though his call was for 6:30. He tried to go back to sleep, but after about thirty minutes, he gave up and got up. Since he did not board the train until evening, he had a full day to kill. After showering and breakfasting, he thought it would be good to just see what this city was like for a few hours.

So, off he went walking. He walked down to Fisherman's Wharf, walked all along the bay shore on the north side, looked across at Alcatraz and wondered how anyone could possibly escape from that prison across the cold bay waters, and understood why it was called escape-proof.

Near noon he found himself near a Chinese cafe and that is where he lunched, finding the Chinese food still rather strange to his East Texas taste, yet rather good this time, especially the egg rolls and the stir fried chicken and chopped vegetable main course which had a local name he couldn't remember.

JJ returned to his hotel room for a quick perusal of his

sizeable stack of literature. It was apparent that much reading and studying time would be required, and fortunately, the next few weeks should provide a good deal of available time. He checked out of the Clift a little after 2 PM, then boarded a bus for a ferry ride to Oakland and the train depot. He waved goodbye to the bay area and boarded the New York bound "Overland" at 6:45 PM.

The next morning he awoke in the desert wilderness of eastern Nevada and rode all that day through rather uninspiring country unless one was inspired by dry and barren land denuded of almost all vegetation except for scattered grass, cactus, and eighteen-inch straggly bushes. Some of the land was very similar to part of the west Texas country he had left: Rocky, sandy soils, with occotilla, cholla, and lecheguilla cactus mixed in with the greasewood, scattered mineral-laden grasses, and the dwarf oak bushes commonly called chinnere.

That afternoon, they crossed the Great Salt Lake and its remarkable flatness. JJ took a snapshot of that with his new 35-mm camera. He was impressed with the work that had gone into building this railroad across the many miles of that old lake that time had turned into nothing but the salts from the waters that were trapped in it and evaporated.

After a brief stop in Ogden, Utah, the Overland continued its eastward journey into the evening shadows. Again, the dining car was a popular place, and the train crew took great pride in serving excellent food in an elegant manner. JJ turned in early on this, another memorable and interesting day.

Monday, September 3, 1934. Sunlight reflecting off the window frame awakened JJ to another day of travel. They were stopped in Cheyenne, Wyoming. He got up, dressed quickly, and got off for a brief walk around this bit of the Old West. He imagined the numerous old board buildings, though not alone in this western outpost, little unchanged from the time they were built some five to seven decades earlier. He could almost hear the sounds of cattle, cowboys, and miners in this preserved part of the Old West.

Back on the train, and on eastward they moved, with the clickity-clack making a melodious and rhythmic accompaniment to the slight sway of the cars.

On across eastern Wyoming, then into Nebraska and Omaha

at dusk. The train was stopped again for about fifteen minutes, and JJ again got off with the many other passengers for a chance to stretch their legs. The main thing JJ did was to walk briskly around and around the depot, taking in the scene as he walked.   S h o r t l y thereafter, JJ went to the dining car for dinner and noticed a rather lovely lady who had gotten on at Omaha. Her dark brown hair was cutely bobbed and curved back under her ears so as to frame her softly white face and delicate features. She was alone. It didn't seem right that such an attractive young lady should have to bear such loneliness and JJ was the very man to come to her rescue.

He walked up, "anyone sitting here?" She looked up, and displayed her clear violet eyes, "Not to my knowledge." "May I join you?"

"Why not?" So, he did, and a wonderful evening started. They dined together, then walked back to the observation car and looked into the night together. JJ found that this was Suzanne Stuart, from Omaha, bound to New York and a new job as linguist for an exporting firm.

She had studied language at the University of Nebraska, and was a specialist in the romantic languages, particularly French. She expected to travel from time to time with the company sales representatives. Among other export items, the firm handled some American automobiles, mainly Fords.

She was just as interested in JJ's work as he was in her's. Each had a rather unusual specific occupation for such depressed times. They found much to talk about the rest of the night well into the wee hours. Finally they parted with the agreement to meet for breakfast at 8AM.

JJ was awakened by the train lurching a bit, raised his window shade and looked out on a large city. He thought a bit and realized this must be Chicago, and so it was. He looked at his watch and found he had hardly twenty minutes to get to the dining car.

With quick agility, he pulled on his trousers, jumped from the bunk, and headed for the men's room, hoping there would be no delay in draining his bladder before it burst, and then getting a very fast shave. He was lucky. No one was there. He made it to the dining car at 8:02 AM. And there she was, this alert and attractive traveling companion.

"How's Suzy, and how did she sleep?"

"Well JJ, Suzy is fine, but Suzy did not sleep as well as she would in her own bed. I kept waking up every time the train wobbled, but did go back to sleep, and got enough."

"No problem with me. If the train hadn't lurched as it came into the Chicago yards, I'd still be asleep and you'd think I was just another fly-by-night." Then JJ noticed Suzanne seemed nervous. "What's bothering you, Suzy. You seem a little taut." She looked up, "it's not every day that a girl goes to her first job, JJ, and it's only one more day 'til I meet my boss at Penn Station tomorrow morning. And I'm a mix of excitement and concern about the outcome."

"With someone as alert and as attractive as you, I don't see how any normal man could be anything other than swept off his feet by you, so you have absolutely no reason to be concerned. Besides, just remember, a cowardly lady dies a thousand deaths, a brave one dies but once! So, just do your best, and I guarantee, everything will work out fine!"

They continued to discuss her job, his, and their voyage into the unknown. Also, they exchanged addresses, both temporary and permanent, and reviewed ways to contact each other in the future. But at the moment there was something much more pertinent: They had to change to the Pennsylvania Railroad. By 10:30 AM, they were on their way east.

Suzanne and JJ were together most of the day as they passed through the rest of Illinois, then Indiana, Ohio, and into Pennsylvania, arriving at Pittsburgh shortly after their dinner together that evening. It was a dark and rainy night, but this was of no concern to them; the train was quite dry and comfortable, and they found they had a great deal to talk about. Again, they talked later than planned, but finally went to their respective bunks after a warm, but not passionate, goodnight kiss.

They arrived at Penn Station in New York at 8:30 AM, September 5, 1934. JJ and Suzy hardly had a chance to greet each other before she was met by her new boss. She got her luggage, hugged JJ and left with her boss.

He already felt a little lonely for this charming woman. But, he had other things to pursue and his mind moved to those matters. He got his luggage and took a cab to the New Yorker Hotel where he had a reservation. He checked in, unpacked some of his things, and went back out to see New York.

He spent most of the day on Manhattan, but by ferry or cab visited several of the well known attractions of greater New York. He did find out that when possible, take the subway or a bus; the cabs would break him if he kept using them.

The next day, he was able to contact Suzanne who that evening at six, met him at his hotel and off they went for dinner at Childs Restaurant on Staten Island. They again had a splendid evening together, and again had a warm, though perhaps bordering on passionate, kiss goodnight when he put her in her cab to her newfound apartment. JJ thought, "Much more of this lass and I might have just a wee bit of a problem sailing away!"

JJ spent the next two days shopping, visiting, calling two friends who lived in the area--then joining them for drinks, and several calls to Suzy. He bought an excellent map of Europe, and two more maps that together fairly well demonstrated the eastern Mediterranean and Arabian Gulf areas.

At 9 PM on the ninth, he boarded the S. S. Rotterdam bound for Plymouth, Great Britain. This was JJ's first ocean voyage, and he was interested and curious about just about everything. By their sailing time at midnight, he had walked all over the ship and gotten a good idea where the food, engines, games, dining, lounging, and most other things were located.

For the next eight days, JJ learned a little about ocean travel. First, he found the food to be ample and tasty, and in the evening, most elegantly served. The ladies were plentiful, lovely, and charming. And nearly all married.

By the second day he had one rather bad spell of seasickness during some stormy weather that caused the ship to roll and pitch at the same time. The pitch was not strong, but the rolls were very slow and as much as 30 degrees. All this left him with a faint nausea much of the time, but really seasick only occasionally. And he found that frequently eating simple food without much seasoning was helpful in reducing nausea.

He thought, "This may be psychological, this business of eating to feel well, but it works for me and I'm gonna keep it up." And so he did, even though some others got sick at the sight of food.

He met the ship's doctor from North Carolina, the Captain from Holland, and two of the entertainers, one American and one Dutch. The ship displaced nearly 35,000 tons, but had only 90 passengers. This resulted in unusually good service and an excellent shipboard environment.

All but eleven of the passengers were Dutch, most returning from vacations and family visits in the United States, though some were on business trips. The non-Dutch consisted of one charming red-haired English girl, Miss Mercado; a British couple, the Coles; two Javanese; three French; and three Americans, including one James Jonathon Burke.

In the evenings, he watched silent movies and played bridge when he was not watching the shows put on by the entertainers. The shows consisted of what to JJ was very good dancing, some slapstick, and very good musical solos. The Dutch were very jovial bridge participants, and all in all fine travel companions. The two Javanese, a young couple, were very entertaining dancers, and mean shuffleboard players!

During the day, JJ spent most of his time reading or playing deck games, including one shuffleboard tournament in which he lost out in the first round...there were experts aboard! He also played ping pong at which he had some skill and outperformed all but one Dutchman who beat him consistently. He also found that the ship was well stocked with wines, brandies, beers, Scotch, and several other whiskeys, of which he tried several--to his dismay on the fourth night out.

After a drinking contest with the Dutch in the evening, which he lost, he slowly found his way back to his cabin, worked his way over to his bed and found that the damn thing wouldn't stand still. It seemed that there were some large but smooth sea swells that caused the floor to tilt slowly one way, then the other. This unstable floor business along with his unstable head resulted in one hell of a job just to sit down. He finally made it. Just in time to have to get up and run, rather stumble/fall, his way to the commode to unload all the excess alcohol. After about two hours of varying misery, JJ finally got to sleep. And awakened with a roaring headache. One thing he learned: Don't try to outdrink the Dutch!

The last two mornings, JJ had breakfast in his cabin. That, to him, was real luxury, and he thoroughly enjoyed it. He enjoyed the deck games, even the miniature golf at which he also held his own pretty well. It was also nice just to lounge and watch the sea. He spent several hours most days doing this or reading while lounging.

On the evening of the fifteenth, they saw the Coles and Miss Mercado, the redhead, off at Plymouth, then undertook another partying session with B. A. Ten Cate and some of his Dutch friends, for Ten Cate's 30th birthday party, but JJ didn't need reminding about the evils of alcohol, so he drank well, but lightly. And mixed some good food with it this time. It was another most pleasant evening for all.

JJ arose early on the sixteenth, had an early breakfast in his cabin, finished packing, and disembarked at Boulogne, France. Here he saw a city unlike any he knew, but rather similar to more that he would see in the next few days.

The streets were narrow, the buildings mostly three and four stories off the ground and attractive, there were no front yards, and everywhere he turned, he saw differences from the United States and most certainly, East Texas. Not better or worse; just different and interesting.

He followed his trip plan, along with a little help from the police, found the train station and boarded a train for Paris.

Now JJ really saw the beauty of France. The rolling green hills, and carefully nurtured fields and gardens, with flowers of every color seemingly everywhere, the neat and well kept homes, the vineyards. It was quite unlike East Texas. The main difference was the density of fields, villages, orchards, homes, and all evidences of human habitation; along with the orderliness of all these manifestations of humanity.

Again, it was not better or worse, just beautiful in a different way. While East Texas is beautiful largely because of Nature augmented with human effort, France is beautiful because of a loving people working intensively with Nature.

It seemed that this trip was one memorable occasion after another. And the train from the coast to Paris was no exception. Nor was JJ's impression of Paris. He arrived in Paris, collected his baggage and taxied to the Continental Hotel where he checked in for his wait on the Orient Express. But he jolly well planned to use this "wait" well.

For the next four days, JJ saw Paris and its environs. Champs Elysees, Notre Dame Cathedral with its inventive flying buttresses, the Louvre, Eiffel Tower, Arc de Triomphe, Versailles, Trocadero, Harry's Bar, and on and on. He also found occasions to meet and visit with several young ladies and a couple of men, and to do a little final shopping.

He bought film, filters, and sunshade for his camera, a few more clothes, and another Arabian-Mid East map, and had his first two rolls of film developed and printed. His impressions of Paris were so extensive that a book could be written on his visit, and one day he might try. But as on so many occasions on this trip, he had to move on.

September 21, 1934. JJ collected his film and photographs, bought one or two additional items, and boarded the Orient Express at 8:10 PM that evening. His compartment was shared with Joseph Hinson, British construction engineer for Anglo-Persian Oil Company, the driving force behind Iranian petroleum.

The next few days seemed like a dream. Never had JJ seen so many changes so fast. First there was the rolling hills and green hills, often accented with the yellow flax fields, of France, then the strikingly beautiful mountains, lakes and tunnels of Switzerland, followed by the same eye-catching mountains of northern Italy, grading into the plains of Lombardy; to Milan, to Trieste, then Yugoslavia, on to Belgrade, then to Istanbul, Turkey, where the Orient Express ended.

After a train change, he continued on into the heartland of Turkey. As the train moved east, and then south, it seemed that the people and their surroundings sort of matched the natural terrain: There were only a few of the vivid greens, yellows, and blues with their many hues adorning the pastures and hillsides; instead there were mostly stark grays and browns of rock and sand. The clothing, the homes and buildings, the roadways, the culture, bespoke widespread poverty and lives devoted more to basics with little time for fun and games.

He finally reached rails end at a dusty destination in Tall Kushik in Syria near the Iraq border on September 26. From there the passengers boarded large Rolls Royce cars bound for Baghdad, in Iraq, where rail transportation elsewhere was available. It was a long dusty ride through the ancient birthplace of so much of civilization, writing, mathematics, and philosophy. JJ could not but wonder at this land that nurtured so much yet now foundered in poverty and ignorance of so much that grew from its primeval roots.

At least, now JJ had seen and could see the descendants of the creators of the cipher, the Arabs. Without their cipher, we might still be trying to handle large numbers with Roman letters. He knew that these were a different people and he was to learn still much more. He had a built-in admiration and curiosity about these Arabs, and looked forward to their unusual mix of high intelligence and profound ignorance.

The Rolls Royce cars pulled into Baghdad well disguised with the mask of dust derived from nearly two days of unpaved roads. The passengers were also similarly disguised, and wished for time to bathe and re-clothe, but such was not to be for JJ. He left the Rolls, and was taken by much poorer automotive transport to the train station for his train from Baghdad to Basra.

Finally, early in the morning of Saturday, September 29, 1934, JJ arrived in Basra. Even though he felt filthy with dust and sweat as he got off the train, JJ could not help but feel rather awed by this drab and poor city that lay on Shatt al-Arab, the broad river-bay caused by the confluence of the Tigris and Euphrates rivers about 100 km from the northern edge of the Arabian, or Persian, Gulf.

The Iranians felt that this gulf that bordered their ancient Persia was the Persian Gulf. The Arabs of the equally ancient Arabian peninsula and Iraq called it the Arabian Gulf. JJ knew that, even though his surroundings painted a picture of poverty and grubby existence for most, the spirits of the past were abundant and powerful.

This was Mesopotamia. This was Babylonia. This was where the inhabitants recorded their transactions and trade in cuneiform writing in clay in the millennium before the first Egyptian Pharaoh. Where by the ninth millennium B.C. they raised sheep and goats, wheat and barley, while residents of the land of what was to be Egypt were still mainly hunters and gatherers; while most Europeans were hunter-gatherers and lived in caves or primitive dwellings, and fought the cold of the long winters of the receding continental glaciers. By the sixth millennium B.C., these people were using crop irrigation.

Yes, thought JJ, this may look sorry now, and the culture may be far behind much of the world, but this is *the* cradle of agriculture, commerce, trade, science and mathematics, and we must never forget it.

JJ had learned that his steamer was to leave at 11:00 AM and it was now seven, so he had to hustle. He rushed off the train, took nearly thirty minutes to get his luggage, then was rushed by the Station Agent in an old touring car of unknown vintage and brand to the agent in the city to exchange his American Express order for a ticket, then to the dock where his ship, the SS Baroda, awaited. He hurriedly boarded with his belongings and got settled in a small cabin a full hour before sailing at eleven!

JJ estimated that this ship was about the length of a football field and maybe fifty feet or so wide. It was a bit rusty here and there, but overall rather clean and neat, and not a bad way to travel. It wasn't near the luxury of the Dutch ship, but one helluva lot better than a rowboat! Since he was one of the two or three firstclass passengers on this cargo vessel, he was well treated by the crew, and found the food to be quite different, but clean and tasty. He found that there were about thirty passengers aboard, all Arabs except for him and a British salesman headed, as he was, for Bahrain.

That afternoon, they sailed past a very large British-owned oil refinery on the Persian side of Shatt al-Arab, then dropped anchor off Kuwait before daylight the next morning. Later that day, the Baroda proceeded on to Bushehr or the Persian coast, then on to Bahrain the next morning, Tuesday.

Aboard ship, JJ noticed two firsts: An Arab with a harem, and one with a hunting falcon. He was later to see few harems, but many falcons. The four ladies in the harem did not appear as JJ thought harem women should appear: In flowing silks, with multiple layers fine and translucent to vaguely reveal parts of the feminine body. Instead, they were clothed in the typical Arabian woman black head-to-foot dress, commonly called a *chaddor*, along with a veil, all made out of what appeared to be cotton, maybe wool, and not even an ankle was revealed.

But the falcon was everything it was supposed to be: Sitting on a leather wrist sleeve of its human partner, not master, with head upright, viewing the world and all its contents with assurance and a touch of disdain for those less important. And most other life forms were indeed less important. These were hunting birds of significant value and traded with great pride amongst the Arabs who thought of themselves as the owners of such majestic flyers.

October 2, 1934: Bahrain Island, an independent Sheikhdom, with an ancient city thereon now also called Bahrain. On the Arabian Gulf voyage, JJ had seen two British warships, and now saw four such destroyers at anchor near the docks where he landed. These ships and others like them were one of the reasons for both the British influence in the region and one of the needs of nearby oil refineries. As JJ walked off the ship, he looked both ways, saw nothing, and was about to wonder where he should go when a booming deep voice sounded: "Well, Mr. Burke, you have found the right place."

Turning to his left rear, JJ saw a red-haired man about six feet three inches tall and weighing perhaps 220 pounds, and about his age, with a smile on his face and a huge right hand stuck out. "You catch me by surprise, and have the advantage," said JJ.

"I'm Huey L. Larsh, your partner for the next two years! Take a good look, I don't get any better with time, but I'm a helluva lot better than no partner at all. And, in case you're curious, the L in my name stands for Lyman. Huey Lyman Larsh, that's all!"

"Well, I'll be damned," says JJ, "I knew your name from the San Francisco briefing, but they didn't give me a photo so I had no idea what you looked like. Anyway, I'm mighty happy you're here and I don't hafta find out where I go from here all by myself."

Huey laughed easily, "JJ, it's not too bad. I was met by one of the crew from our field office at Jubail on the Saudi coast when I arrived here nearly two weeks ago, and they sent me to get you. As you'll see, things ain't too fancy, but it could be a lot worse." With that they climbed into a company vehicle, a Ford touring car, and headed for the company camp for the large oil field on Bahrain.

In about twenty minutes, Huey pulled up at a group of frame buildings and parked. "This is it," said Huey. "Over there is the bunk house you and I will be in tonight, and that long building down there is the mess hall where the Bapco manager, Dale Nix, will host some British naval officers tonight, and they can tell us all about their operations."

JJ turned quickly back to Huey: "Bapco. Is that the Canadian subsidiary of Socal that operates this field?"

"That's it. Actually, the field is not owned 100% by Socal, but they operate it, and have developed enough production to have regular tanker runs out of here. As you probably learned in your briefing, the production is from Cretaceous rocks, not the overlying Tertiary beds productive in most of the Arabian Gulf area."

"Yeah," JJ returned, "I remember that, the discovery well was the No.1 Jabal Dukhan, right?"

"Yep, that's right. And it stirred up a lot of interest in this region. Now, the idea is to extend the production onto the mainland."

JJ got settled, then Huey took him to the town shops, the bazaar, to find Arab clothes. Although was not required, it was felt that the Saudis would accept them better if they dressed in the traditional Arab *thobe*, a long shirtlike garment, and *ghutra*, or headdress, held on with an *aghal*, a double headcord to hold the headdress.

Most of the geologists found that no problem. Huey explained that nearly all supplies for their mainland operation came through the Bahrain facilities, and that the only shopping and medical facilities available to them were now on Bahrain.

On the mainland, there were no such things as electricity, hospitals, large stores, schools, service stations, and the other trappings of Western civilization, except in limited amounts in the capital of Riyadh, and more in the western port city of Jiddah. But the British and Socal had brought some of these things to Bahrain, and so this was in, effect, a staging area for the mainland operations.

Also, the only docks that could service anything other than a shallow-draft dhow or smaller boats, were on Bahrain. But, before Socal, there had been little need for much trading into the small villages on the Saudi east coast, and the absence of Saudi docks for oceangoing vessels caused no problems for the Saudis. The only commerce out of the Saudi coastal villages was fishing and pearl diving, and for those endeavors, nothing massive was needed. In fact, when the Americans first arrived, they literally stepped from their dhow onto the Saudi beach.

On that first evening, JJ and Huey joined the manager and the British officers for a pleasant dinner, even if the table and surroundings were rather plain. Then they learned from the British that the Arabian Gulf, or Persian Gulf as they called it, was important to Britain in more ways than JJ thought. The oil was very important because it was the only meaningful source for the British Empire. Also, the nearby British-owned refineries, and other businesses were a part of the Empire along with their many interests in Persia and Egypt and thus, important to the overall British economy. This warranted the presence of their naval vessels.

The next few days, JJ shopped a bit more, visited the new rather crude golf course where he and Huey demonstrated their ineptness at that sport, visited the active oil field and observed the kinds of equipment being used, and studied copies of the measured geologic sections from the mainland.

They saw that the well equipment was about the same as they had in west Texas; most of it had been shipped from the United States, but the rig crews were a more motley bunch: Some Arabs, but mostly Americans, some from South America, and a few Europeans.

They also found time to visit some of the ancient tombs and ruins on the island that attested to a long and, at times, prosperous civilization.

On October 5, they took JJ's luggage, including his new Arab clothes that he was not wearing, and boarded the dhow for the mainland. In their Arab clothes, they would have passed fairly well for Arabs except for the absence of beards. Which they would correct in time. This dhow was operated by Salamon Asiri, who had contracted to transport people, small equipment and other items between Bahrain and Ojair, a village on the Saudi coast.

Asiri's dhow was much like many others, with a triangular, spinnaker-like...but smaller and less billowing, sail referred to as a lateen sail. The vessel had no fixed mast or booms and thus most of the deck area was often available for storage. Also, the prow overhangs and extends beyond the water contact, thus often allowing one access from the very front of the vessel downward to the beach sand below after the vessel had reached a shore with no dock. The vessel had a poop deck aft and an open waist to accommodate loading and unloading. It was an efficient vessel developed over thousands of years, and had not changed much since biblical times.

They sailed in mid-morning and after a lunch of canned peaches, bread and cheese, both JJ and Huey found themselves in need of a place to relieve themselves. They searched and found none. Now, they were getting desperate, especially JJ, so they asked Salamon who wordlessly pointed to a board extending aft of the vessel.

Huey said, "Go ahead, JJ. I'll wait for you to show me how."

JJ moved ahead, "Desperation breeds boldness." And he proceeded to demonstrate to Huey how to use the board. They managed to use it only twice by the end of the voyage the next morning.

They slept that night on the open deck and found it quite chilly, so they pulled their Arab robes quite close and found some sacked cargo to snuggle up to. They drifted into sleep to the sounds of the water slapping the hull as an accompaniment to the haunting Arab singing.

Singing and sun awoke JJ and Huey on the cool crisp morning, and they were proffered coffee, or *ghawa*, to start the day. This was Arab coffee, a beverage used very often in this land where alcohol was forbidden. And it was not American coffee. It was a thick, heavily sweetened, black, cardamon tasting drink that took some getting used to. It was served in small cups which Arabs emptied in only a few swallows, and usually had several cups. JJ could take only one; Huey managed two.

Shortly thereafter, the dhow landed at the beach of Ojair. The craft maneuvered alongside a crude pier built of rocks, then a heavy board was laid down as a gangplank to unload. Huey led off, with part of JJ's luggage. JJ followed with the rest. Just as they stepped off, they were met by Robert P. (Bert) Miller, District Geologist, and Hughey Burchfiel.

"Hello, Huey, I see you got our other rookie here safely," spoke Bert. "And to you, James Jonathon Burke," with his hand extended, "welcome to Saudi Arabia."

With that, they shook hands around, got in the Ford touring car and headed for camp. The trip was complete. Looking back, JJ saw that the dhow crew with local help had pulled the dhow up on the sand where it lay on its side.

[J. W. (Soak) Hoover, Aramco geologist, made a similar trip in 1934.]

CHAPTER 4

Jubail to Al Habl

"We'll get right on the highway for Jubail," said Bert Miller, "it's only about a hundred yards, or as we say over here, meters."

JJ knew that he'd have to become accustomed to the metric system and it would take a little practice. Actually, the metrics were much easier to relate than English measurements, but it would still take some time to think in terms of a meter, 39 inches, or a kilometer, or km, approximately 62/100 of a mile. But he didn't see any highway, and knew that there probably was none, "Is it divided, or just a two-lane?" Bert, laughing: "Hell, it's divided, many times, you're on it. Can't you see the heavy work that went into this paved marvel? Highways over here are where you make them, and you'll make several every day. There are no normal roads where we work, paved or unpaved. Zip. None. What are called roads over here are what you'd call ranch trails in west Texas, just braided trails made by domestic animals moving from one place to another."

They drove north along a faintly marked trail over the occasional low, relatively firm dunes scattered along and interspersed with beach sands and gravel, along with the hardpan and salt flats known as sabkhas. JJ noticed wavy trees in the distance that abruptly disappeared upon closer approach: A mirage; common to the sabkha.

The trip covered about 80 km and took the better part of two hours. They arrived at an encampment near the coastal pearling town of Jubail that was similar to the one JJ had seen on Bahrain.

Huey had already been placed in a bunkhouse and knew the camp details, so he undertook to set JJ up with a bed and storage cabinet, after which he showed him the equipment building and its contents. JJ was quite familiar with all the equipment. It consisted of aneroid barometers, plane tables and alidades, stadia boards, two transits, steel measuring tapes, hand levels, Brunton compasses, chronometers, sketch boards, and many rolls of sketch paper.

Huey pointed out to JJ that there were no useful base maps; the geologists had to make them as they went, including bringing in elevations from high tide by transit to base stations. To make maps, they had to lay out long base lines, usually by transit, then map in key geologic data with plane tables and alidades.

During the first field year, October, 1933 to July, 1934, the two initial CASOC geological teams mainly mapped by drawing and marking on rolls of sketching paper, and using automobile odometer readings roughly scale out the map positions of various features. The plan was to first do reconnaissance mapping to locate structural anomalies, then detail the anomalous areas later with an aneroid barometer for approximate elevations. Or plane table and alidade if needed for more precision. Then further establish the elevations of key rock layers below the surface by drilling shallow holes with small portable drilling rigs as might be desired.

A transit is designed mainly to measure angles and establish lines, with the distances between transit stations measured by "chains" which were actually steel tapes usually 100' long.

The alidade is a transit-like instrument that slides around on a leveled plane table board about two feet square, and sightings are marked as lines on a heavy paper map attached to the board.

Both the transit and the alidade have target bubbles so the instrument can be leveled in all directions, and each has a magnetic compass so that it can be oriented in reference to north.

North as measured by a compass, is magnetic north, which has a declination from true north according to the location of the measurement. In the United States, this declination is known for most areas and is marked on topographic maps. But in Saudi Arabia, an accurate declination was not known.

In order to establish this declination in this area, the geologists set up a transit at night and shot the North Star to establish the direction of true north, then rotated the transit horizontally until the magnetic needle showed magnetic north, and read the angle in between. Latitude and longitude were determined by shooting stars at specific times per a chronometer and comparing the angles read to charts and tables.

As used by the geologists, the alidade can be rotated vertically to measure vertical angles, and is aimed at a stadia board or rod held by another individual at some distant point, and measures both direction and distance. The stadia board is commonly 16 feet long, folded on a hinge in the middle for ease of carrying, and marked with various patterns one-tenth of a foot apart, so that the distance between these markers can be measured by the crosshairs in the alidade telescope.

Those measured distances on the stadia board are proportionate to the distance on the ground between the alidade and the stadia, and thus the distance on the ground can be computed and then marked on an imaginary line drawn along the ruled base edge of the alidade on the map on the board. Thus, a map with specific objects, markers, and elevations as desired is made of selected areas.

JJ spent the following two days studying work from the first season, plus the earlier broad brush geologic writings. These indicated that the mountains of the central and western provinces of Saudi Arabia were composed of older rocks ranging from pre-Cambrian granites, basalts, and other igneous and metamorphic rocks in the western mountains or *jibehl*, to Paleozoic rocks along a northwest-southeast range just west of Riyadh.

He learned that these surface rocks grade from the pre-Cambrian basement in the west to Quaternary sediments on the east coast. The whole geologic section was tilted easterly, with the pre-Cambrian lying at an unknown great depth under the Arabian Gulf.

Mealtimes proved to be very educational to JJ. The other geologists that had been in Saudi Arabia for over a year now, told him about a few key facts of life in this country. The primary control to all life was water. Plain water.

Occasional rains during the so-called rainy season produced sparse, mineral-rich grass and other vegetation in the low-lying areas. This is where the Bedouins congregate with their usually small herds of sheep, goats, and camels. Some of this water sinks into the subsurface. Some evaporates.

He was advised that there are no perennial streams, no rivers. The water either goes into the ground, or back into the air. Practically none ever drains into the Arabian Gulf. JJ learned that the accepted theory amongst the Americans was that the various well-known springs derived their water from underground aquifers supplied by the meteoric water. With fractures and faults providing the conduits both into and out of the subsurface.

During this indoctrination period, Huey and JJ took one of the Ford touring sedans out for a day of cultural observation. They saw three small groups of Bedouins during the day. Two were encamped, one was moving. The encamped families were ensconced in and near their tents, while the animals grazed on the available scattered clumps and patches of grass.

It was October, and these nomads had left their base camps near wells and springs several weeks ago. These desert people had left their base camps when so advised by Canopus, the equinox signal star to the Bedouins. To them, that star rising low on the horizon marked the fall equinox, the time to leave their base camps. Its sinking below the horizon in the spring marked the vernal equinox, the time to return to base camps to wait out the desert heat of the summer. The Arabs knew that the "rainy season" normally began after several more weeks of hot weather, but they were ready to do something different and the rising of Canopus was a welcome signal.

The American explorationists had experienced their first rain shower of the "rainy season" only last week. It had a pleasing effect on people, animals and vegetation, but it had one bad side effect: increased humidity. And it was already humid enough here near the coast. But the nights were mostly pleasantly cool, and rain was always a welcome relief from the dusty, sandy life.

For the next two days, Huey and JJ continued to study past reports, especially about Dammam Dome, a rather circular anticline, or upfolding of the layers of sediments.

J. W. (Soak) Hoover and Schuyler B. (Krug) Henry had loosely mapped the obvious structure the year before, followed up with detail mapping earlier in 1934, and picked the location for the first well in June.

Preparatory to the spudding of the well, planned for early 1935, and the subsequent drilling, it had been decided that Huey and JJ should measure some sections to give a better idea of the section the well would penetrate. To do this, they needed to review the earlier measured sections, then try to add to them in the Dammam area, then move to other *jibehl* to the west to get older sediments than present in the Dammam *jabal*.

JJ and Huey moved from the Jubail camp south to a camp at Dammam, near where they had landed on the coast a few days earlier. Using existing field notes, and photos from the special Fairchild 71 high wing monoplane shipped in early that year, they found three small outcrops of sediments older than previously measured in the Dammam area and proceeded to measure and describe the outcropping sediments.

All layers of the sedimentary rocks, whether sands, sandstones, clays or shales, gypsum, or carbonates such as limestone, were laid down, one atop another, with progressively older beds beneath.

Then, with time, some layers were uplifted by tectonic forces, some sank into synclinal lows, wind and rain with heat and cold broke and eroded the upper layers, sometimes cutting ravines or creating slides or otherwise exposing the bedrock. Thus, by careful measurement and description at a number of selected exposures, the surface geologists could measure hundreds of meters of sediments.

They measured the Dammam sections, then JJ and Huey worked westward measuring more where they could find workable outcrop exposures.

After the few days in Dammam camp, JJ began to learn more about the scarcity of fresh water. Near the east coast, there were few wells or springs to provide fresh water and the natives were well accustomed to conservation. They rarely bathed except for sponging their bottoms and once in a while their hands and face. Little water was used for cleaning utensils or anything else.

Fresh water was used mostly for cooking and drinking, and

occasionally washing clothes. However, when several *ghirbas* of water were available, it was not uncommon to see them waste water with excessive personal washing. But they knew how to conserve when necessary. To construct a *ghirba*, one most often used camel skin that had been usually, but not always, carefully scraped of fat, then sewn together, with as little sewing as possible, to form a bag with a neck that could be tied shut.

All the geologists were first astounded, then quite interested in one unique source of fresh water: Underwater springs on the bottom, beneath the salty sea water of the Arabian Gulf. In the western gulf, sometimes even on the mud flats at low tide, there are springs that constantly flow, some at fairly good rates.

The water from the springs is variable in quality, sometimes more or less brackish, or salty, but nearly always sufficiently fresh for all normal needs. The pearl divers routinely used these springs for their fresh water supply. One would dive down with a *ghirba*, put the neck over the spring, and let the fresh water flow into it. Usually it took two or three dives by two divers to fill the *ghirba*. Most of these springs that were used were in water depths of less than about 12 meters.

The interesting part of these springs to the Americans was the source for the fresh water. Obviously, the water came from aquifers, up fractures, small faults, or other permeability channels. But why would any fresh water aquifer occur under the Gulf with no catchment area for the aquifer anywhere to be seen? Could it come from the outcrops in the mountains over 200 km to the west, where most of the rainfall occurred?

They could develop no sure theory, but the best bet was a fairly distant source, with the aquifer water flowing slowly over the years downdip easterly, then at any upward outlet, such as a fault, with its surface contact lower than the catchment area, the water would tend to flow upward and form a spring.

After a few drinks from a *ghirba*, JJ was happy to have his large canteen that he had brought all this distance. They tried to boil their drinking water when possible, but sometimes they had to take what was available, dirty though it might be. JJ had learned long ago, while on a brief mapping stint in Mexico, that care with water could prevent a lot of misery. And the purification pills they had to put in the water didn't always seem to work. So, when possible, JJ got boiled water for his drinking.

In any case, water from his canteen tasted better than direct from a *ghirba* that often imparted a dead meat, fatty, taste. He received a lot of kidding about his water persnicketiness and canteen, but he seemed to have less toss and trots than most of the other men.

By carefully studying aerial photos taken by the Fairchild and existing sketchy field notes, they found a few outcrops starting just a few kilometers west of Dammam, and then more on toward the town of Abqaiq, about 60 km southwest.

After measuring all the outcrops they could find within about 30 km of Dammam, they moved to a new camp they called Al Habl, north of Abqaiq, from which they could measure a number of sections within a radius of about 35 km from that camp.

They were introduced to three key members of their camp entourage; the soldier chief, or *Amir*, Ajab Ben Thanian, guide Yahiya Ibn Rimthan, and driver and servant Abdul Jamban. The Amir was about forty years old, tall, and charismatic. Yahiya was about twenty-eight, could speak some English, and was amazing in his knowledge of terrain and geography. Abdul was perhaps eighteen, and could also speak some English.

"Huey, did you know how involved this camping out would be?" asked JJ on the morning of their move to Al Habl.

"Even though they told me some about this," returned Huey, "I never had any idea it would take fifteen soldiers, an *Amir* for the soldiers, plus three cooks and helpers, guide, two servants, two camel drovers, a driver, four big tents, several tons of supplies, along with a drove of camels as packanimals. Hell, when I mapped in California and Nevada, it was just me and a pickup with some local hire for field help."

"Yeah, it was the same with me in West Texas. And the cost. I understand we pay $688.00 a month for the soldiers, $72.00 a month for each of the other hands, and $150.00 a month for the ticky camels. They never had so much money in their lives! Do you reckon they have all these soldiers to protect us from bandits? If not, maybe it's to protect the people from us!"

"Well, they're here to protect us from something, or at least the King worries about it or they wouldn't be here." With that, Huey turned to the business of unloading equipment and supplies from the car. "Did you check for the replacement parts for the car?"

JJ: "Yep. Did you use these kinds of cars in your field work? I used a pickup."

Huey: "I used a pickup mostly, but got one of these one time and liked it a lot better...seemed to have better traction cross-country, and you could keep the top up or down. Besides, I never had much in the pickup and found the car to be plenty roomy for equipment."

The car they used was a Ford touring car, same as the other crews. They had three available, plus a pickup truck. When they first delivered the cars, they had normal large tires, plus reinforced front ends, and extra heavy springs. Shortly before they left Jubail, new 9:00X18" balloon tires had been installed and the problems of sticking in the loose dune sands was largely overcome, although getting stuck in soft spots was still common. Breaking springs was a common event and replacement springs, as well as some other parts, were normally kept in the cars for replacement at any time.

The cars were convertible, with a heavy canvass top storable along with a collapsible rear frame in a pocket behind the rear passenger seat. Also stored in the rear were side panels of similar canvass, with windows sewn in, that could be attached to the tops of the doors, the windshield frame, and the top in inclement weather. The side panels were easily installed by fitting metal eyelets over metal buttons that could be turned to lock over the eyelet. JJ and Huey rarely used the side panels, but almost always kept the roof up to reduce the blasting heat from the sun.

One day in late October, they caught their first glimpse of the Arabian gazelle, a variety of antelope. They were driving across a *sabkha*, a low-lying sand flat, surrounded by a slightly higher *dikaka*, a terrain marked by scattered hummocks of sand held in place by small desert shrubs. They were heading for the low hills ahead that marked the beginning of an upland where they hoped to find the outcrop indicated by an air photo.

A slight movement off to the left front caught Huey's eyes. "Hey...look!" he said as he pointed. There stood three gazelles gazing at this strange apparition coming toward them, while a fourth had started trotting away. Their driver, Abdul Janban, got excited and wanted to kill the animals for food, but since they had no gun and JJ preferred to eat other things, they decided instead to see how fast the gazelles could run.

Even though the *dikaka* where the gazelles stood was higher than the *sabkha* on which they drove, it was only a few feet higher, and as long as one dodged the shrub mounds, the terrain provided excellent ground for fast travel. But, in order to get to the vicinity of the antelope-like creatures faster, Abdul continued to drive on the *sabkha*, approaching somewhat to the right of the animals. As they approached them, the animals started running, somewhat parallel to the car's path on the *sabkha,* and became determined to run from left to right across the path of the vehicle.

The gazelles gained on the Ford, then cut across its path. Abdul floored the accelerator to gain maximum speed, and began to close on the gazelles. A few moments of this passed when the gazelles decided it was time to really shag out, and they did; with the Ford now roaring along with the speedometer needle waving wildly between fifty and sixty miles per hour and everybody hanging on over the occasional bounces.

The gazelles figured this thing is after us, so they shifted into high gear. The Ford couldn't close the distance between them, about 300 or 400 meters, for about a minute, but then it began to close the gap. As close as a car length from the nearest animal. After another half-minute or so with the bouncing speedometer needle indicating nearly sixty miles per hour, the gazelles began to slow down measurably, except for one large buck who held up pretty well, and he led them off in another direction to the right of their path. At this point, JJ said, "look at their tongues...their tongues!"

The two nearest doe had their tongues hanging out, flapping with each long graceful leap, and clearly, they could not keep this up or they would collapse. Huey called out, "OK, let 'em go...slow down."

JJ: "Man, did you know that we were up to over 60 miles per hour there? Those guys apparently are good for at least 60 mph sprints, but they can't hold that high speed long."

"No," answered Huey, "but when you think about how much energy they consume for those speeds, it's understandable. After all, how long can a man run at full speed? Fifteen seconds? Twenty? Not very long in any case. So, I suppose gazelles have the same problem."

It had been an exciting chase they would always remember. And the "they" included the gazelles.

The men returned to their Al Habl camp which had been selected with several things in mind. First, they wanted to be near a water supply to fill their *ghirba* and two barrels. The *ghirba* water was used for drinking and cooking; the barrel water was used for washing: the occasional baths, the tables, and a few other items. The barrels could be filled only when the pickup was available to haul them with the consequence that, for frequent periods, only *ghirba* water was available. This bagged water could be hauled by camels, car, or horse, and was used exclusively by the soldiers who rarely bathed their bodies, but frequently washed their hands.

After a water supply, the next criteria for a camp was protection from the frequent high winds that usually were laden with dust, sand, and brush. Although such protection was not always available, the Al Habl camp did have it. The large, low, open tents were pitched near a rock shelf formed by outcrops of Miocene-Pliocene (Tertiary) shell-laden, or fossiliferous, shaley limestones called marls.

The shelf rose about twenty feet above the surrounding terrain and formed a barrier to deflect the prevailing north winds above the tents. There was a low supply tent, a large peaked kitchen and dining tent where all the camp members routinely ate, a very large low tent for the soldiers, a work tent for the geologists, and two bedroom tents, one for the camp personnel and the other for the geologists.

Sand, or more appropriately, dust, storms were an ongoing discomfort in many ways, but worst in the so-called spring. Actually, in this area, spring was subdued and one had to search for its signs in most locales. But it was much like spring elsewhere: a time of new vegetation, though only in limited areas, usually a *wadi* (a dry wash with occasional flowing water), or low area, and changing temperatures. And wind. With winds, came dust and sand, and fragments of bushes and shrubs.

JJ noticed that these storms were very much like those that he had seen in trans-Pecos Texas, especially in the Midland area: The first evidence was a dark cloud on the horizon, which rose in the sky as it approached, gradually changing from darker to lighter browns as it grew in height and blew closer.

Then, with a blinding blast, it hit! Dust and sand and fragments permeating everything that was not water tight; tents, folders, books, lockers, vehicles, instrument cases, clothes; everything. Instruments were often wrapped in cloth inside cases to avoid damage.

Arab dress was most appropriate for such conditions, and this was one reason the Americans adapted to it. Arabs had long since learned to cope with dust and sand, with every inch of the body except for the eyes covered. And for the eyes, only slits between cloth folds; and in the worst times, one covered eyes also, thus now 100 percent of the body being covered.

"Restroom" facilities consisted of a designated area for all personnel to use, where feces was usually covered and urine helped supply water for the sparse vegetation that welcomed moisture in any form. Another area was designated for the "bathroom."

This consisted of a few boards forming a vertical frame on which canvas was draped on three sides, with overhead boards serving to hold a bucket which could be tilted by pulling a rope, thus pouring water on the bather. So, to take a bath, one filled a bucket with water from a barrel, or *ghirba* if the barrel was empty, took the bucket to the "bathroom," suspended it with the rope harness, then pulled the rope to get enough water to soap up, then pull again to wash the soap off.

Thus one could get a good bath with about a gallon of water. In times of short supply, there was less bathing and skimpy showers. Bathing was infrequent at best and the Americans sometimes went for weeks without more than a "whore's" or sponge bath.

A sustained effort was made to catch the occasional rainwater, by tilting a tent edge toward a *ghirba* hung at the low end. This way, good quality soft water was sometimes available.

Cooking at Al Habl was over an open fire made from any fuel available, the most common being camel dung. Brush and some garbage was another fuel source, even gasoline was sometimes used. Food was normally prepared from canned vegetables and canned chipped beef and other canned beef or fish, along with bags of rice, pasta, dumplings and bread, augmented with occasional fresh breads and fresh meat from chickens, domestic camels and hunting. A frequent hunted food was the gazelle which, when available, was an occasion for celebration.

A large lizard, the *dabb*, often over a foot and a half long, provided a chicken-like light-colored meat enjoyed by the Arab camp members, and tolerated by the Americans. A hunted food enjoyed by all was the bustard called *hubara*, a bird not unlike a pheasant in taste. Even though the water from the *ghirba* often tasted greasy, it was still very good when none other was available. In coffee it was better. Much coffee and tea was consumed. Alcohol was forbidden, and none was available. Occasionally, the cook served what they called *Jerboa*, a rat-like rodent with a long tail enlarged at the tip, and with long rear legs and very short front ones. Tasted good. For a rat.

The Americans slept on cots at Al Habl; the soldiers and Arab members commonly slept on blankets on the ground. All members had to stay alert for night insects such as the black fat-tailed scorpion which when brushed, often resulted in the sudden feel of a white-hot poker from the sting of its tail. The sting was very painful, usually resulted in swelling, but sometimes responded to baking soda or vinegar, and was never very long-lived unless it became infected, in which case severe illness resulted. Both JJ and Huey only had to have one sting before learning to empty boots in the mornings and not walk barefoot at night.

The only other frightening night creature that all learned to avoid, was the hairy *shabath*, or camel spider, which looked much like a West Texas tarantula and was equally dangerous: That is, not at all, unless one hurt themselves getting away from this aggressive arachnid, commonly up to six inches in diameter.

The most annoying creatures were common flies which seemed to go wherever humans and camels went. There was no way to avoid the flies. They were around the camels, in the food, in a man's face, and a distinct nuisance with no solution in an open camp. Fortunately, their abundance diminished in the desert camps, and one learned how to live with them. Mosquitoes were an occasional nuisance, and were a serious source of malaria; but in the dry desert camps, were not routinely a major concern.

JJ and Huey used sleeping nets on their cots to keep the insects off during their sleep. These nets hung from a light frame extending about 30 inches above the cots and were tucked in under the light sleeping mattress.

A few days after the gazelle chase, after considerable outcrop search, some sketching of terrain and outcrops, and three more outcrop measurements involving a total of 23 meters of section, JJ and Huey found something that did not fit the regional pattern.

They were driving across a *dikaka* just north of Abqaiq when Huey commented, "Boy! Except for a little bush dodging now and then, this is like driving on a highway!"

JJ: "Sure is...hey...wait, Huey, we're driving on an exposed bed!"

They told Abdul to stop, then they got out and looked around. "Looks like recent winds have blown all the sand off this bed for the time being," said JJ. "Let's take a dip." With that, he pulled out his Brunton compass, laid it in various positions on the hardpan until he established the direction in which the relatively flat bed was level, then turned the Brunton at right angles on the bed and read a little over two degrees northwest dip.

Huey: "If that's right, we've got something."

JJ: "OK, let's check it a little closer." He took his hand level out of its belt case, and looked through it at Huey's face while they stood next to each other. He found that his eye was level with the bottom of Huey's nose. "Huey, go over there and let's find out for sure what the strike of this bed is." The strike of the bed would be the direction in which the bed is flat or level, and the direction at right angles to that is the dip, either updip, or downdip.

"OK, Huey, that's about it," after JJ had moved around until his eye was level with Huey's nose while Huey was some fifteen steps away. Then they both walked to new positions where Huey now stood some twenty steps northwest of the strike line they had established, while JJ moved to a position where their new line of direction was at right angles to the strike line, and took another level shot. The level line was about two inches above Huey's head.

JJ: "We got a clearcut northwest dip, at least on this area of this bed. Pretty close to that two degrees the Brunton showed on one spot. Purty excitin', huh?"

Huey: "Yep. Let's get the alidade and check this before the wind covers it with sand again."

They took their hammers and broke off flakes and chips of the bed, then viewed these with their hand lenses to see the rock character. It was a hard calcareous clay material, called a marl, and contained numerous shells, that looked much like oyster shells. These shells were actually fossil pelecypods.

Huey: "This isn't the same marl we saw in the Dammam sections. And the marl there was beneath the gravel and sandy lime beds, and the shells were ostracods, not pelecypods. Although we can't prove it, I think this is older rock, and probably uplifted a bit."

JJ: "With northwest dip."

The reason for their excitement was that the northwest dip was counter to the normal east dip, and thus indicated a possible anticline that would dip in all directions away from a crestal area. And, the presence of possible older rocks was also indicative of an uplift.

An anticline here could contain an oil treasure greater than the greatest gold field ever found in California in the 1849 gold rush.

For the next several days, all they could think of was this possible structure, and they were out ten hours or more each day trying to find more evidence of an anticline. Larsh and Burke correlated their measured sections with others done earlier by one of the two initial teams, J. W. (Soak) Hoover, and Schuyler B. (Krug) Henry.

From this, they were able to determine that the outcrop they plane-tabled was Miocene and indeed older than the coastal Pliocene (Tertiary) and Pleistocene (Quaternary) rocks. But confirmation was difficult. The rock outcrops were sparse and, when present, exposed just enough to serve as a tease. They found a few outcrops that were measured with Brunton for dips, but most outcrops were so small, and the dips so low, that the dips could not be considered reliable.

It was now early November, 1934; Thursday, the eighth, to be exact.

"Dammit, JJ, what we need is a core drill," spouted a frustrated Huey. "And they ain't gettin' their money's worth either, payin' me $234.00 a month to do one hell of a lot of pure guessin'."

JJ: "First off, Huey, Peasant, be advised that I am paid more than you. I suppose they recognize my superior talents and my profoundly greater experience, three months I believe, and that's why they pay me $241.00 per month. Well, someday you too may achieve greater recognition...as to the core drill, I agree, but we ain't got it.

Let's try to get one. These rocks are too hard to use a hand auger, if we even had that." (Hand auger: a man-operated earth drill designed to drill a hole about fifty feet deep in relatively soft sediments.)

A hand auger could be shipped in without much trouble, but a core drill, or structure drill, unit was another thing. This was a very new technology, cumbersome truck-mounted small drilling rig, operated by a crew of three men and requiring considerable support equipment and supplies. It was a modification of the shot-hole rigs now being used to drill holes for explosive placement in seismic surveying. They were available in the United States, but not easily available elsewhere.

Without any way to map the rocks just beneath the surface, their surface geology only pointed out an anomalous area; one that had to be further explored, but that could not be confirmed as a place to drill at this time.

> (The time was to come when this ghostly structure would be proved and a major discovery, Abqaiq Field, worth far more than all of King Solomon's treasures, would be developed.)

~ ~ ~ ~ ~ ~ ~ ~ ~ ~ ~ ~ ~ ~

CHAPTER 5

Hofuf

"Watch out, JJ! OOOoooo, here we go!" yelled Huey.

JJ returned, "I'm watchin', I'm watch it..." And with that cutoff statement, the car came to a sudden stop with both front wheels hanging over the downwind sharp slope of a crested sand dune. Huey saw it coming a little ahead of JJ, who, with mixed emotion, had slammed on the brakes, knowing full well that such action was bad news when trying to drive across one of these dunes of loose sand.

They had seen the large dune ahead and, as usual, had speeded up a little in order to hit the dune traveling pretty fast. This sometimes resulted in things flying around in the car, but it also resulted in getting across the loose sand as long as speed was fairly well maintained. Except this time, they were approaching what amounted to a cliff and it wasn't the best thing in the world to go flying off that into the unknown of the sharp dropoff on the other side. So, when JJ locked the brakes, the car slowed, then as the front wheels dropped off the crest, they bottomed out on the sand and abruptly stopped.

"Well, coach, what do we do now?"

JJ sat still for a few seconds trying to realize what happened, then, "We get out," he said lamely.

They got out and reviewed the situation. Clearly, this was going to take some time, it was nearly dark, and they were both tired, hungry, and nearly out of water. But, it was either start digging, or start trudging across the sand toward camp. Since camp was about eight miles away, digging seemed best. So they broke out the shovel and alternately dug. And jacked. Jack up one rear wheel at a time, dig out under the car and throw the sand under the rear wheel, jack some more, dig and toss sand some more, and on and on. Finally, they got the rear elevated enough that the lowered front tires were on sand and the car bottom was barely clear of sand. Of course by this time, the car was resting at a rather racy angle, maybe 30 degrees off horizontal, but aimed downhill.

"Huey, you can stand and watch, or ride; but if you choose to ride, don't get upset if the car turns over when I have to turn sharp at the bottom of the dune. That's a joke, son; upset...see?

"Yeah. Great joke. Okay, I'll watch. Not because of your wildness, but because you need a push to get started." So he got in position and pushed. After a little wheel spinning, the car started forward. Then, faster and faster down the several hundred feet of steep slope, with JJ turning as the car approached the dune bottom to keep from slamming into the hard earth where the dune base contacted the underlying earth at a sharp angle. The car sloughed sideways, rising briefly up on the two outside wheels, then slammed back down on the other two wheels.

Huey came jumping and sliding down the slope. "Okay, JJ, that's enough excitement for this day; let's see if we can make it in for a late supper without more thrills."

"I hate to say this, Huey, but we may have to sorta limp in...you see, I think that last maneuver broke the right front spring."

Huey looked under the fender. "It did. But I'm too tired to care. Let's limp in."

And so ended another day of measuring sections of Arabian rocks.

The following morning in Al Habl camp, their first job was to repair the broken spring. This was no major job; they had done it often, and they had the parts in supply. The rest of that day, they worked in camp on their maps, notes, and sketches, laying out what they were sure were the elements of a large anticlinal structure. They could not fix the crest, nor prove several elements, but there was no doubt that this structure near Abqaiq was a large anticline where core drilling was needed, and they would so recommend.

The next day, the camp was very active just after dawn. The soldiers and camp personnel were striking tents, packing and loading camels, and the geologists were busy packing and loading maps, instruments, stadia board, plane tables, and other gear. Al Habl camp was to be abandoned, and a new camp set up farther southwest, about 30 kilometers west of Hofuf. The object was to get all loading done in time to get some of the gear to the next site and at least one tent set up before dark.

Actually, JJ and Huey had packed most of their gear the night before. They now had to pack only one tent, before they could leave. Their plan was to make one trip with the car, unload, leave Abdul there with an assistant cook, then return for another load, the soldier's Amir and a cook.

The next two days were spent moving the camp a little over sixty kilometers, or thirty-six miles, and to Huey and JJ it seemed that the new camp might never be set up because of the recurring delays.

They called the new site Camp Udayliyah, after the nearby village of low mudbrick buildings that blended in with the surrounding grays and browns of the desert terrain on the eastern margin of the great interior desert, *Nafud ad Dahna*. They often referred to this work area as the Hofuf area because a good part of the work area lay to the east of the camp back toward the old walled city of Hofuf.

Regardless of the camp name, frustration was the name of the Americans. It was near impossible to get any of the camp personnel to work at any job other than their specialty. Cooks looked upon tent work with disdain, as did the soldiers; and the camel drivers would do nothing except drive camels. Even in the face of chaos, the common comment was *"Insha Allah,"* "as God wills." Even if a tent was falling over on a soldier, the soldier would normally just push it away or get out of the way, but do little or nothing to help get it set up. His job was soldiering, not tent man or servant.

Then, the work pace itself was exasperatingly slow to the Americans. It was the nature of the Saudis to study and think about the job, then slowly and methodically proceed with it. And rarely could anyone be hurried.

Of course, the five daily prayers of all faithful Muslims delayed activity, not only for the prayers, but also for the time getting ready for prayers, and the time getting ready to go back to work. Prayers were routinely held at dawn, midday, mid-afternoon, sundown, and evening. JJ and Huey knew that they were guests of the Saudis and it was their place to do or say nothing that in any way conflicted with Saudi custom or religion. Instead, they themselves were to adjust. But it wasn't easy. The dawn and evening prayers caused no conflict for the geologists, but the three daytime prayers did sometimes cause them to adjust their schedules.

It took nearly a week to get the camp completely moved, set up and functioning as before the move. During this time, little geology was done; instead, much housekeeping, rebuilding, organizing, and waiting, and waiting, and waiting, were the daily events. But finally,

Insha Allah, it was done, and the purpose of the camp could again be undertaken.

The next three weeks in November and December, 1934 were spent locating rock outcrops, using mainly the air photos that were taken in long strips of overlapping photographs. The geologists spent day after day driving, walking, climbing, and sketching the positions of the outcrops of ancient rock layers indicated by the air photos. These were placed on roll maps and tied to latitude and longitude as best they could measure by the positions of the sun and stars for the date.

Then they went back to the best rock exposures to measure sections. This way, they would get a small thickness of the sedimentary rock layers at one place, part at another, more at another, until they had many measurements and descriptions of rocks at a number of outcrops. These descriptions were then correlated to find out which layers were common at more than one outcrop. Correlation was done by comparing the detail descriptions, such as 'the brown ostracod marl just below a gray sandstone bed, and above a red-brown shaley sandstone bed,' until finally, all of the measured sections could be combined to form a stratigraphic section of the rock layers near and at the surface of the earth.

Comparing the stratigraphic sections thus obtained with others farther away, it was finally possible for the geologists to go to a certain outcrop, examine the rocks, and know immediately where this exposure fit in the overall section. The layers of rock in Saudi Arabia become older to the west away from the coast, and occasionally the geologists would find an outcrop of older rock layers within an area surrounded by outcrops of only younger layers. Such older rocks outcrop is called an *inlier*. When this occurred, it was exciting because this was an indication of an uplift, such as an anticline or dome, that could mark a place where oil would be trapped thousands of feet below.

One Thursday in mid-December, Huey and JJ combined a trip into Hofuf for water with a break from their seven-day work weeks. They planned to spend the night, and after much discussion with the camp Amir, Ajab bin Thanian, they were allowed to go but had to take two soldiers along. So, just after the noon meal, off they went. With Abdul Jamban driving and two soldiers, they had a car full. They drove into Hofuf and found a place to park the car near a *soukh*, or bazaar, within the old city. After some delay caused by the swarm of Saudis who had to inspect this strange sight of a rarely seen automobile with foreigners and soldiers, Abdul stayed with the car while JJ and Huey, along with the soldiers, started exploring.

Hofuf was an old city, dating at least to Roman times, with the remnants of three walls still visible on three sides of the city. Streets consisted of little more than narrow alleys, usually no more than some eight feet, or two-and-a-half meters, wide, sometimes appearing as tunnels between buildings that extended across the street some eight or ten feet above the cobble-paved or unpaved surface. The city had changed little, if any, in the past two thousand years. The Saudis used kerosene lamps now that were a vast improvement over the lighting a few decades earlier, and a few buildings and homes had improved sanitation facilities in recent years. But to a casual observer, whether ancient Roman or modern American, it all looked about the same.

The buildings were constructed of solid mudbrick walls, often plastered to a finished surface, and roofed with clay tiles. There were no hotels, bars, restaurants, service stations, highways, trains, public transportation, or other service facilities common to Americans. It was possible to find a facility that might be called an inn to sleep overnight, and limited foodstuffs were sold at shops and off carpets laid on the ground at the *soukh*.

But there was one thing of particular note: There were hot springs at Hofuf, and these, along with other normal springs, were the main reason the city had existed for eons. All these springs denoted the presence of rock fractures associated with faults, which formed conduits to the surface from aquifers at considerable depth. Waters came up these conduits. Hot waters came from greater depths, perhaps thousands of feet. These waters came into these aquifers from sources to the west where those beds were much shallower and outcropped or were connected to the surface by similar fault fractures. In either case, rain waters fed wadis and shallow catchment areas which in turn drained into the aquifers which transported the water downdip to other fractures connected to an earth surface lower than the source area, with resultant upflow of the waters back to the surface.

JJ and Huey visited the *soukh*, bought a few items, including some tasty dates, studied the old walls, and returned to the car in late afternoon. After a brief evening meal of rice and canned beef prepared by Abdul, topped off with dates and coffee, the Americans set out for a brief examination of one of the unlighted "tunnel streets" before it got completely dark. Since they would only be gone a few minutes, the soldiers decided to stay at the car. That was a mistake.

About ten minutes walk from the car, Huey sighted what they called a tunnel street, and they walked there to look it over. As they entered the covered area, they saw a young woman a few doors ahead come out, walk across the street, open a door and go in. Then she came back out and started across the street to her original door and stumbled on a street cobble just as JJ and Huey came abreast of her.

Instinctively, JJ reached out to grab her as she fell and did so; one hand brushing her soft breast as he caught her shoulder. Just as the girl was in his grasp, the door opened and an older man stepped out, seeing JJ holding the girl.

She had stepped out of her home for just a moment to get something at her aunt's home, and did not have on the traditional black veil and *chador*, or full-length, loose, black, hooded robe-dress. Instead, she was dressed in a dark ankle-length dress with nothing on her head, revealing her beautiful tan-skinned
features, long flowing black hair, and eighteen to twenty years age. JJ and Huey were taken aback by this momentary flash of beauty, but things changed rather quickly.

With their bare understanding of Arabic, JJ and Huey were unable to quickly converse with the man, but they were able to understand enough from his shouting to comprehend that he was the father of the unmarried girl and that JJ had violated Islamic law by gazing upon and touching his daughter, and may have destroyed her worthiness for a proper husband.

Also, since Huey had also similarly gazed, he too was guilty of violation. By this time many doors were open, a crowd of men surrounded them, and it appeared that JJ and Huey were in danger of violence. Attracted by the commotion, a local *askaree*, or policeman-soldier, hurried up, and took control. He learned the violation and looked scornfully at the Americans. Recognizing that the violators were foreigners and infidels, he had little sympathy for them, especially since neither JJ nor Huey could adequately explain anything.

Back at the car, out of earshot, neither Abdul nor the soldiers had any idea of the trouble brewing. JJ and Huey were on their own.

The *askaree* took them to the local jail for safekeeping until he could speak with his superiors about this violation.

A bad situation had now become serious. The Americans knew that Saudi punishment was swift and often harsh, and that a lot depended on how the local *qadi* (both legal and religious, Islamic, judge) interpreted the Koran which was the written law from which personal affairs judgments were made. They knew that they might suffer some physical punishment, perhaps caning, or possibly might have an eye put out. And the physical conditions of their incarceration augmented their despair.

They were put in a large holding room or bullpen with a number of other prisoners, some of whom had already gone to bed on their blankets on the floor. "JJ, I think we need to get word to Abdul somehow."

"I agree, but since telephones are scarce and he is over a half mile away, there's no need to yell." Then JJ noticed a doorway into a dark room behind their jail from which a foul, overpowering odor emitted. "Catch that odor, buddy?"

"How could I miss it? I reckon the toilet doesn't flush too well. Just hope we get out before we have to use it!"

"Toilet hell, you know what's happened. Not enough water to wash away the crap." And, indeed, so it was. Even though he tried mightily not to, Huey later had to go to that room. He tied his handkerchief around his nose and went in. He found a large pile of human excrement in, on, and around the hole in the floor used for relief. The normal practice was to dump water in the hole and sewer drain after use, but with inadequate water, it just piled up. Huey found a place nearby.

Although in there only a minute or so, Huey nearly passed out. He came out gasping, and hurried over to JJ who had already gotten in position to stay as far across the bullpen as possible from the "restroom." "Larsh, we're in trouble...especially if Abdul and the soldiers don't decide to start looking for us. You'll finally have to go in there, and you won't make it!"

"I know, I know," said JJ. "But I hope and guess they are looking for us right now, and maybe something will happen before too long."

Actually, Abdul and the soldiers already *were* looking, and had found a man who had heard commotion near the covered street where the foreigners had encountered the pretty young woman. Following this lead, Abdul then went to that area and started knocking on doors. The second door opened and after conversation with that man, Abdul and the soldiers learned what had happened. They decided that the soldiers would go to the jail and see if they could get the Americans released, while Abdul went back to camp for the Amir and more men in case the jailer was not cooperative.

"Hey, J square, something is happening." They could hear voices in the outer room and by getting in the far outside corner of the bullpen, they could see into the outer room. "It's the soldiers!"

Then both Americans started yelling and one of the soldiers came back in the hall near the bullpen door and signaled them he knew where they were. Then he went back in the outer office and much loud conversation took place. Later, they learned that the soldiers told the jailer that these men were under the protection of King Sa'ud, and that if he did not wish to incur the wrath of said King, he had better release the Americans.

The jailer complained that he could not release them or he would surely be severely punished. The soldiers then explained that additional soldiers and their Amir bin Thanian, acting under orders of the King, would be arriving soon and that something better happen soon.

With that bit of advice, the frightened jailer asked the soldiers to wait while he ran to find the Amir of the *askaree*. In about a half hour, the jailer, an *askaree*, and another man came in the jail outer room. The new man was tall, rather slender, and wearing a white *kafiya*, or headdress, with golden *aghal*, or headdress cords. His *thobe*, or robe-shirt garment, was bordered in similar color. This man walked with a sense of authority, and the soldiers immediately recognized a man of some importance, and wished for their Amir. In fact, he was the local *qadi* that the *askaree* had already sought out before the jailer found him. The *askaree* knew that these foreigners were unusual and that he needed more authority on what action to take.

This *qadi* was also the same man who would have to pass

judgment on the foreigners, and normally would never have come to the jail at night, but as the story unfolded to him from the *askaree*, he too knew that an unusual situation might exist.

Discussion continued in the outer room for some time. Finally, the *qadi* came back to the bullpen door and spoke. The Americans had difficulty understanding his meaning, so JJ spoke back in his limited Arabic, "We are Americans. We search for oil...papers from King Sa'ud."

The *qadi* listened, then walked back to the outer room and continued discussion with the others. The soldiers later explained that the *qadi* had no grounds to act other than under the law of Islam as outlined in the Koran, and unless something else were forthcoming, he could do nothing until direct word was received from the King. The soldiers told him that their Amir might be arriving shortly and could give him such word. So all waited.

The two geologists had been arrested about 6 PM, and had now been in the jail several hours. At 9:40 PM, the outer door opened and in strode the soldier's Amir Ahab Ben Thanian with four more soldiers and Abdul Jamban. Much additional conversation took place, mainly between the Amir and the *qadi*. The Amir pointed out that the Americans were under special orders from the King and that they were not to be subjected to arrest without his specific approval. The *qadi* demurred. Then the Amir asked if the *qadi* remembered the story of the Englishmen and the fierce Saudi Arabian Ikhwan soldiers just before the fall of Medina in December, 1925. He did not.

So Amir bin Thanian pulled up to his full height of about six feet, two inches, and proceeded to relate the story about the two Ikhwan soldiers who berated and cursed Gilbert Clayton and his associate George Antonius, while they were near the King's camp near Medina. Later, Clayton started to apologize to the King for what he thought was his own improper conduct, and he was abruptly stopped. King ibn Sa'ud Abdul Aziz then summoned the two Ikhwan soldiers, had them caned then and there, after which they were sent to prison in Mecca for time to consider their discourtesy to the King's guests.

This alone did not convince the *qadi*, but he recognized the danger of discourtesy to the Americans and, along with all else, agreed that the Americans could be released. And so they were, before Burke had to use the restroom, *Allah Akbar!* (God is Great!)

Over the next few days in the third week of December, there were many messages back and forth with Jubail, as well as other contacts and fence-mending with the *qadi* of Hofuf over the girl-catching act.

And the Amir never let the Americans forget this incident, though only in jest. In any case, JJ and Huey thereafter were careful to stay well away from any Saudi women.

In these messages with Jubail they did learn that they were now Aramco, and no longer Casoc. Also, they learned that another heavily experienced geologist, Max Steineke, and his partner Tom Koch were now in the field, and using the outstanding guide, Khamis ibn Rimthan, who had helped several of the field crews, including Burke and Larsh.

The guide for Burke and Larsh, Yahiya Ibn Rimthan, was the slightly younger brother of Khamis.

Later, after the girl-catching incident had died down a bit, JJ thought he should advise Huey that the catch was not totally without some value, and that after all, there had been a little advance compensation for the jail distress.

JJ told Huey about the slight breast-feeling he got as he held the girl. Huey stormed back, "Goddam you Burke, we, especially me, went through all that misery and uncertainty over your attempt at being a bosom buddy to forbidden fruit if there ever was any, and I didn't even get a good look, much less a feel! You should have at least had the manners to break it to me gently! But, then, I guess, better one accidental bosom buddy than none..."

~ ~ ~ ~ ~ ~ ~ ~ ~ ~ ~ ~ ~ ~ ~

CHAPTER 6

Udayliyah

Shortly after returning to Camp Udayliyah from Hofuf, the Americans learned that a pier had been completed at Khobar, near Dammam on the east coast. This would greatly expedite movement of men and materials compared to the prior procedure of "make do" with the boat grounded in shallow water. With the pending well to be drilled at Dammam dome, and absolutely every item therefor having to be brought in, such a pier was a necessity.

Letters from home described the Depression for all the Americans in Saudi Arabia. They were grateful to have good jobs when the unemployment back home was hovering around twenty percent. JJ was carrying on a regular correspondence with Ruthanne who, among other things, gave a running description of the Depression in East Texas.

The main evidence she discussed were the homeless men. Once or twice each week, a man would knock on the door asking for a job to earn a sandwich and a glass of water. Hitchhiking and hoboing became a common way to travel in search of the scarce jobs. And to make things more difficult, a drought was developing in the central plains country, particularly Oklahoma, and crop failures were common. So, all in all, the Americans in Saudi Arabia in the mid-thirties were pretty well off, even with the lack of comfort and multiple problems with which to cope.

Christmas, 1934 was not far away and the geologists began to feel the absence from family, especially knowing that they would work right through Christmas, except maybe for a particularly good meal that day. And in order to make that happen, they decided to help things along. What they needed were fresh *hubara*, and the best way to get those tasty birds was with falcons. And the soldier's Amir Ajab Ben Thanian was just the man. He had a falcon. So developed the great Falcon Hunt.

Wheeling through the sky in great soaring circles, Ajab's falcon searched for targets. He wasn't overly particular. His first victim was an innocent wren-like bird with black head, face and beak, adorned with a white ring around its neck and the black extending down across its chest, and intermixed with white on its wings but red and white on its body. The geologists had seen these small birds several times, and had earlier found one with a broken wing, which they had nursed back to health and released. It was a pity to kill such a bird, but the falcon had his own mind and could not be controlled in the air. Normally, the falcon would have nothing to do with such a small bird, but he was hungry, had not been allowed to hunt in several weeks, and was ready to attack anything in the skies.

Most of the Saudi hunting falcons were birds of prey called kestrels and had wingspreads of fifteen to twenty-eight inches. But this hunter was a different, larger variety, the size of a small hen, with a wingspread near three feet. He was impressive, both in camp and in the sky. The geologists had seen him make a pass at a fairly large bird they called a *hudhud*, a black-and-white-striped bird that reminded JJ of a Texas crow, and which the Arabs ate, but had never seen a kill. Huey talked JJ into the idea of the overnight hunt, and the two of them together convinced Ajab that it was the thing to do. Especially with that fine hunting bird.

Their plan was to go out well before sunset to a nearby *wadi* flat which had caught water recently and had produced a good crop of grass seed in the past month or so. They would hunt until after sunset, then bed down on blankets with a sand mattress for the night, then arise just before dawn for another hunt. They took along a few cans of meat and beans and some bread for supper and breakfast. Water was the drink. The plan proved workably simple, and the results were quite satisfactory.

The first evening, the falcon, who seemed to respond to a call that sounded like, "Askra, Askra," which the geologists assumed was a command or the bird's name. Anyway, when the bird had hit his prey, Ajab would call "Askra, Askra," maybe two or three times, and blow a whistle he had, and the falcon would return and drop his prey. It was pretty apparent that he was quite content to come back with the prey because Ajab always gave him a piece of meat that to "Askra" must have been a real goodie. Later, they learned from Ajab that "Askra" was indeed the falcon's name, and meant "Soldier." Ajab felt that Askra was so obedient and performed so well that he was a real little soldier, and so he was called.

After the small-bird fiasco on the first afternoon, Askra settled down to that for which he was trained: To search for and capture edible birds, which to Askra was only the *hubara* and the *hudhud*. What they really wanted was the pheasant-like *hubara*. The first evening was a total loss. Though Askra searched far and wide, none of the game birds came to check out the newly prepared seed supply. So at sundown, the men walked the few hundred yards back to their camp and bedded down after a cold meal of canned meat and beans.

Ajab shook the geologists awake, and JJ responded, "Hey, it's the middle of the night."

"We must eat and go before our bird sits down to dine," said Ajab in his Arab/English lingo which, with their similar lingo, the Americans communicated.

So, the four men in the hunting party prepared to leave. The Americans walked away from camp to relieve their complaining bladders, then returned and stole a handful of water to wash their hands and face. Then, after a hearty breakfast of cold canned peaches and leftover meat, all four, Abdul, Ajab, Huey, and JJ, left for the hunt. They were in position by dawn.

Falcon hunting consists of periods of extreme boredom occasionally interspersed with moments of extreme excitement as the falcon begins and finishes his attack. The men had settled down near a rock ledge overlooking the grassy *wadi*, or draw, as JJ would call it, and waited to see if *hubara* were interested in the food supply there and waiting. Indeed they were.

Askra was wheeling through the sky perhaps 700 or 800 feet above the ground, and three *hubara* came in just above the ground, completely unaware of the menace above them. Just as they started to settle in, Askra silently turned over and started down in a power dive toward the large tailing hen. She probably never knew what hit her. Askra made contact about twenty feet in the air and he and the hen went on to the ground with Askra rapidly beating his great wings so as to reduce the crash. He succeeded somewhat, but the two birds still struck the ground with an impact that sent feathers flying from the hen; Askra was atop her with his claws firmly affixed to her back. The falcon quickly struck the hen in the head, then dropped her in order to leave in a rush of beating wings after one of the two departing birds. After a short flight, Askra overtook another *hubara* and took him down.

For the next hour or so, there were repeated flights of incoming *hubara*, with attacks by Askra. Finally, after getting four birds, Ajab decided the hunt was over. Askra was clearly slowing down from exhaustion, and needed rest. Besides, they had enough for the planned Christmas dinner, and it was proper to leave some *hubara* to raise more *hubara*!

Thursday, January 3, 1935. It was cold and JJ pulled the blanket over his head to keep warm. He had just crawled back in his bunk after a dawn call to empty his bladder. The temperature must be in the thirties, he thought, as he dozed off. About an hour later he was rudely awakened by an insistent Huey: "Come on, JJ, get up, we got visitors!"

Huey had gotten his morning bladder call shortly after sunrise and, while out, noticed horsemen working their way down the sharp hill behind their Udayliyah camp. This was unusual enough to see what JJ thought.

The two Americans watched as the horsemen worked their way in a curving arc down the hill toward their camp and, after reaching the trail at the base of the hill, broke into a canter toward the group of tents that formed Camp Udayliyah. By this time, Amir Ajab and a few other men had strolled up near the geologists just as the two horsemen arrived. One, the older man, was wearing a near-white *kafiya*, or headdress, with golden *aghal*, the double headdress cords that holds the *kafiya* in place. The men were obviously Bedouins, and the older man, with a grey, but not white, beard, had the bearing and carriage of a leader.

The older man walked up to Ajab, and introduced himself as Sheik Zaki Ahmed Khaled, of Harad, a town some one hundred kilometers to the south, and now in this area for pasturage for their animals. The Sheik introduced the other man as his brother. They had ridden over from their pasturage encampment of several Bedouin families a few kilometers to the west of Camp Udayliyah. After exchange of pleasantries with the Amir, the Sheik carried on a brief conversation with Ajab, at one time motioning to the Americans.

The Amir turned to the geologists, and said, "Sheik Khaled has a sick girl and hears that you know medicine."

After additional slow and stumbling conversation mixing Arab and English, the Americans learned the story. It had become known to the Arabs in camp, and then the word spread into nearby villages that the Americans had medicines, and knew something about the treatment of illnesses. Huey and JJ never tried to pass themselves off as medical doctors and, in fact, preferred not to treat any ill people in case of their treatment backfiring. But to the Bedouin nomads, who rarely saw anyone trained in medicine at all, the Americans were medical experts and they often requested help from them.

This was especially true of the soldiers and other camp personnel. A common problem was camel ticks. The ticks would drop off the camels, then get in the tents and somehow end up in the men's groins, underarms, scalps, and ears, as well as elsewhere. Infections from tick bites were very common, and JJ in particular got pretty adept at getting such ticks out of a man's ear and treating the bite to minimize infection. He simply poured diluted peroxide into the ear and most often that made the tick release and, at the same time, kill bacteria. Sometimes he employed tweezers, and occasionally alcohol swabs, but found the peroxide most effective.

JJ agreed to go with the Sheik and his brother back to their camp and see if he could help. They had a good deal of map posting to do anyway, and Huey could work on that while JJ was gone.

It was agreed that JJ and the visitors would drive the car to the Khaled camp, and bring the men back for their horses when he returned. After a brief drive under their direction, JJ arrived at the Khaled camp, which consisted of five large, low, dark woven goat-hair tents, plus several smaller tents, one of which appeared to be an old military canvas tent.

The Arabs lived in the large tents, up to twenty-five-feet across, and air circulation was provided by the simple device of not tying the tents to the ground except at selected positions. Thus the perimeter of the tents during warm or hot weather was one to four feet off the ground around most of the tent. With little rainfall, the design was mostly to provide shade. However, in this cold period, the tents were snubbed down pretty well to keep the cold air out. More than one family might live in one large tent.

The Sheik took JJ to one of the large tents and called out as he approached. A woman wearing the typical black head to foot dress, came out and then led JJ back into the tent. There were large sheet-like cloths that served to divide parts of the tent into "rooms." In one of these rooms, JJ was shown the sick girl lying on a bed of two or three rugs. She appeared to be about twelve years old. He heard the woman address the girl as *Sukkar*, which he knew to be "sugar," so to him, she was "Sugar." He knelt beside her and spoke, "Here, Sugar, let me see what is wrong."

She felt normal, but she tearfully pointed to her leg. JJ looked down and saw that her leg was badly swollen from her foot to her knee. Then he saw a wound on her foot that had become infected, with two red streaks extending over two inches from the wound. There was no doubt that the foot was infected and very painful. To heal, it was necessary to get more blood to the wound. Also, the foot was dirty, had not been washed, and was probably reinfected. He had brought their medicine kit and proceeded to administer aspirin, wash the lower leg in warm water, with soap he had brought, then treat the wound, first with peroxide, then with disinfectant. Sugar cried out when he put the merthiolate on the wound, so JJ held her hand and spoke soothingly. After a bit, the sting from the merthiolate subsided, and she relaxed. Then he formed a pillow out of two rugs and put this under her leg to elevate it.

He laboriously described to the Sheik to wash the leg in warm water morning and night, keep it elevated, use the aspirin three or four times daily, and use the small bottles of peroxide and merthiolate after each washing. He also suggested several feedings each day of sweet hot tea and broths. He knew that the aspirin would help on the pain and get more blood to the wound, and that raising the leg would enhance blood flow. The rest was to reduce infection and reinfection. He also knew that "blood poisoning" was likely, and could finally require amputation. Beyond that, he could help little. He asked to see her again in about three days, so as to see if they could get her to a hospital somewhere if they could.

The two Arabs joined JJ and they all returned to Camp Udayliyah, where the Arabs got their horses, thanked JJ, and left.

Three days later, JJ visited Sugar and found her much improved and on the road to recovery. The Sheik and his wife, as well as Sugar, were very pleased with the results and let JJ know that they were available if ever he needed their help. Also, they invited JJ and Huey to come over to their camp for a feast the next week.

During this period, the geologists were measuring sections in the scattered rock outcrop exposures in the *jibehl*, or hills, that trended north-south within their camp mapping area of about 15 to 20 kilometers radius. At this time, they were not mapping in the outcrops, just sketching their location on the long rolls of sketch paper they carried, then describing and measuring the thickness of the rock outcrops. At this time, it seemed curious to them that at nearly all the outcrops, the rocks were dipping westerly, when regional dip was easterly. They saw such dips so much that they became relatively sure that the anomalous dips over such a large area probably meant nothing particularly prospective. How wrong that turned out to be.

The Bedouins employ the Islamic Calendar and, to them, the Western year 1935 was the Islamic year 1354. And to make things a bit more complex, the Islamic year consists of twelve lunar months, a new month with each new moon, and about 354.33 days long, or a little over 10 days shorter than the Western calendar. This creates the situation where the Islamic month of *Rajab* of one year is in the dead of winter, and about seventeen years later, it is in the middle of summer. Then on a cycle of about 33 years, the year equivalents change. For example the Islamic year of 1354 is Western year 1935, or 581 years difference, so one would think that the Islamic Year 1364 should be 1945. It is not; it is 1944. For this reason, the Americans communicated best with the Arabs by referring to a recent Islamic lunar month such as *Ramadhan*, the month of Islamic fasting.

During Ramadhan the good Muslim does not eat or drink from dawn to sunset. However, this does not prevent eating at night, and they do; but even then the good Muslim follows the orders of the Koran regarding excesses. During Ramadhan, which may be in summer or winter or anywhere in between, Bedouins sleep a lot during the day, especially in the mornings. A common sight at a Bedouin camp on a morning during Ramadhan, are people lying on rugs in and near tents or other protection from the sun, apparently asleep. Such sleeping is also common during the hot summer months.

Regardless of calendar differences, both Bedouins and Americans felt the same toward cold or hot weather, and they both knew this was the best time of year. Night temperatures were typically in the forty degrees range, and day temperatures in the seventies. And even though it might all come in one or two downpours, this was the "rainy" season that brought on the desert-acclimated vegetation and grasses so important to the Bedouins and their cattle. Thus, when the winds were calm, this was a beautiful time of year in the Arabian desert. It was a perfect time for an evening feast and philosophic conversations between different cultures.

A few days after JJ's second visit with Sugar, he and Huey, along with driver Abdul Jamban to act as translator, headed out to the Bedouins camp. Abdul was by no means eloquent in English, but he was the best in camp at being bi-lingual, so with him along, the Americans felt they could communicate better. They arrived at Sheik Zaki Ahmed Khaled's camp about an hour before sundown, and after the normal *salaam*, or peaceful greetings, all settled down for the traditional Arab coffee and conversation. After about six of the small cups of very sweet, scented, and flavored coffee, they all partook of the feast.

The main dish was roasted goat and mutton, cooked to excellent taste. By this time the Americans had learned the proper Arab way of eating and joined the Sheik and the nine other male members of his family group in tearing off strips of meat with their right hand and holding it in that hand while eating. Occasionally, one would lay the meat down, then with the right hand alone, ball up the slightly sticky rice and transfer the ball to the mouth with the right hand. One was careful to never touch food with the left hand, nor to pass anything to anyone else with the left hand.

This custom developed along with the custom to clean one's bottom only with the left hand, and in the desert, often with no water or substance other than sand or rough shrub-bush with which to clean, that hand might not be altogether clean. The Bedouin does not hand anything to another with the left hand unless it is desired to show disdain or rudeness to the other party.

The feast was much enjoyed by the Americans, and was topped off with delicious dates and another fruit they could not identify, along with small cakes and the heavy, but tasty, Arab coffee. All the men now felt quite comfortable sitting on rugs around the rug on which the food was served, all of which rested on the desert sand. By this time, the sky had become dark and filled with stars with a brilliance as only can be found in a clear desert atmosphere. Soft light drifted out from the few lanterns in the nearby tents.

Since the geologists used some of the stars for their map

positioning, and also because JJ was an ex-Boy Scout Astronomy Merit Badge instructor, they had more than passing knowledge of the heavens. The Bedouins were also quite familiar with the heavens because they too used them for positioning, and from knowledge passed down over the generations, were quite authoritative in some areas of astronomy. Many of the Western names of stars and constellations are derived from ancient Arab sources. These people were the first to formally recognize the patterns of the stars, the wandering of the planets and the recurring relationships between them and the Earth, Moon, and Sun. Arabs are the prime source for the science of Astronomy. The conversation was not smooth, but with the help of Abdul, reasonable communication was achieved.

With the delays, stammering, poor grammar and other difficulties of communication removed, the following conversation was rather enlightening to the Americans:

Sheik Zaki: "You know that bright star over there?"

"Yes, that is Venus, one of the seven planets," replied Huey. "Would you like to see it through our transit telescope?"

"That would be a marvel," said Zaki, "I have never looked at anything with such a thing. Since you have seen this Venus, then you must know it acts like the moon?"

JJ: "I do not understand. Venus does act like the moon; it has phases, and at times it appears like a half-moon in the telescope. But how could you know that?"

"Ah," answered Zaki, "Those among our people with eyes like the falcon have known it to be so since long before the time of Mohammed. As a young man, with help from my father, and by looking just to the side of Venus, I myself saw the half-moon appearance."

Having recently learned that Mohammed was born in Mecca in 571 AD, long before the development of the first telescope in the 16th century, the geologists were amazed at such knowledge. And they were to be further amazed.

Zaki continued: "For ages, the Bedouin has lived by the stars, and know of the strange cloud in that area," as he pointed toward the constellation of Andromeda, "and the similar cloud in that area near one of our stars, Betelgeuse," As he pointed toward the area beneath the belt of the constellation Orion.

Neither Larsh nor Burke had ever known of the Orion Nebula and the Andromeda Galaxy until someone had shown them with binoculars. It seemed unbelievable that these Saudis could have known about such things for so long. As the evening wore on, they learned much more.

Although he had no formal education, Sheik Zaki Ahmed Khaled was an unusual man. As a child he had become interested in the Arabic numerals invented by his forbearers, and by the night sky. His ancestors had known for centuries, just as did the ancient Greeks, that the only way to explain our surroundings and the sky would be for the Earth to be like a ball, not flat, and that some of the "stars" were wanderers, with no fixed place, except that over periods of time, some of these wanderers, the planets, came back to a position against the stars similar to times far past.

As Zaki grew older, he learned to read and was furnished books by his family. From these, he learned much more about the history of his country and the world in general, as well as a great deal more about mathematics and astronomy, both natural fields for Arabs. Also, he read the Koran and other works on Islam and became very knowledgeable of Islamic laws and guides.

At this visit and several more to follow over the next few months, the Americans learned a great deal about Islamic law, the history of Saudi Arabia, and the five or six principal cities of Saudi Arabia. Sheik Zaki was a good teacher. He, in turn, was quite interested in America, Western history, and mostly, in geology and its application to the Saudi environment and the search for oil.

Finally, as the moon rose near midnight, the thoroughly fascinated geologists had to leave. Tomorrow was a workday. With fond farewells to this new Arab friend, they drove out into the darkness toward Udayliyah.

This was an enjoyable time for James Jonathon Burke and his partner, Huey Lyman Larsh. The weather was mostly pleasant, they had seen two rains, the work was becoming more and more interesting, and there was the hunting. They went on two more falcon hunts, one of them with Sheik Zaki as they called him. Zaki had two falcons who had been trained to work together, and their hunting was fascinating to watch. One would follow behind while the other dove on a game bird, then if the first failed, the second falcon would hit before the game bird had a chance to recover. The result was that if a game bird came within sight, it was apt to end up on the dining rug.

Also, the Americans were very happy over their gazelle hunt with Zaki, Amir Ajab, Abdul Jamban, and their guide Yahiya Ibn Rimthan. Zaki, Ajab, and Yahiya had old rifles, that to the Americans appeared to be British Enfields left over from the World War military actions in Saudi Arabia.

Late one afternoon, they drove out to the same wadi where they had hunted with falcons, because gazelle had been seen in that grassy area. Just before reaching the wadi, they jumped a small herd, and gave chase. Both Americans were allowed to fire the rifles at the fleeing targets from the moving car. Both missed. But later on, they decided to leave the car as they approached a *jabal*, and try to sneak up on gazelle on the other side. This succeeded. After a ten minute walk, they carefully worked their way to the crest, and about a hundred yards away were eight gazelle. They picked out the bucks and Zaki, JJ and Huey fired first. Two bucks ran a few steps and dropped. The rifles were hurriedly handed to Ajab and Yahiya, who with Zaki, got off one more round each at the flushed gazelle who were rapidly abandoning the area. Two more dropped.

All, including the remainder of the Camp personnel and Zaki's family group, enjoyed the fresh gazelle feast that followed.

The geologists continued their section measuring, with a little map sketching. The primary need at this time was to learn the geologic section, that is, what layers of what kinds of rocks were above and below other layers. By use of the fossils found in the sparse shale, sandstone and marl outcrops, they were able to keep a rough idea of the general Miocene age of the beds.

On one section not far from the village of Udayliyah, they were startled to find in a rather deep wadi, limestone ledges with mollusk (shellfish) fossils known as *Nummulites*, clearly older than the Miocene beds they were describing and measuring. At the time, they were puzzled by this apparent inlier (older rock outcrop, or exposure, surrounded by younger rocks). Later, after much mapping yet to be done, they would understand the significance of this find.

One morning in late April, just at dawn, Camp Udayliyah was abruptly awakened by gunfire and the thunder of horses. The startled Americans, along with the entire entourage, rushed from their tents to come face to face with a band of Bedouin horsemen who were rapidly dismounting, firing their rifles, and running to surround the soldier's tent while they kept all others at bay with leveled rifles. This was something that was not supposed to happen. It was general knowledge that the Americans were in Saudi Arabia as guests of the King, and that they were to be treated at all times as guests. Of course, the King had supplied the soldiers just in case someone forgot.

But, as it turned out, this was a band of Ikhwan Bedouin tribesmen led by one of the King's old allies back during the conquering of Arabia. The Ikhwan allies turned enemy during the late 1920's when they strongly disagreed with King Sa'ud Abdul Aziz in his interpretation and application of Islamic teachings. About six years earlier the King had met and defeated the Ikhwan and his old brothers in arms, Faisal al Daweesh and Ibn Bijad, in a massive battle near the town of al Artawiya, some 240 kilometers northwest of Riyadh, in north central Saudi Arabia. The battle is known as Sabillah, for the plain on which it was fought. The King's forces outnumbered those of al Daweesh over two to one, and he used tactics unexpected by the Ikhwan. The battle was short and bloody and left the Ikhwan survivors with a taste for revenge.

These disgruntled Ikhwans were doing nothing more than what had been a Bedouin custom for centuries: *Ghazzu*. This was a game, albeit serious and dangerous, amongst Bedouins in which most young men participated. It consisted of raiding another tribe's area, to capture their animals and other valuables, while avoiding killing if at all possible, and never touching women or children. In turn, the robbed would respond with a *ghazzu* against the raiders, or some other tribe. This raid on Camp Udayliyah was aimed at capturing and exchanging the Americans for ransom. And at the same time, slapping King Sa'ud, who had forbidden such raids after he consolidated Saudi Arabia in the late 1920's. The Ikhwans felt the King had no right to curtail *ghazzu*, there was no Islamic law to prevent it, and that was the only law they respected.

In a businesslike fashion, the Ikhwans took the two Americans, all the camels in sight, and food supplies, and after shooting out the tires on the car and pickup, left camp in a hurry. The entire operation was done in less than fifteen minutes, with very little conversation at all. They knew the soldiers would be on their tails as soon as possible, but hoped to make it into Iraq to the north before help could arrive. But they did not reckon with Ben Thanian.

Within minutes, he was on the wireless radio for help and requesting transportation. The Ikhwan knew nothing of the radio or they would have destroyed or taken it. Also, they did not know of the five camels that had been placed for foraging in the brushy area behind the hill beside the camp. To avoid loss of contact, the Amir immediately dispatched four of his soldiers in teams of two aboard two of the remaining camels so that they could continuously keep track of the Ikhwan location, and one team report back daily to the following soldiers. Then, using spare tires and stripping the car, he got enough tires to equip the pickup, and within two hours was underway with a load of five soldiers, Yahiya and Abdul. And, by this time motorized soldiers were underway from Jubail, and, anticipating the Ikhwan objective, headed northwest so as to cut the Ikhwan off before they reached the Iraqi border.

But the Ikhwan also had a trick or two up their sleeve. After heading north from Camp Udayliyah until they got out of sight, they veered due west toward the great Dhana desert. They had planned on motorized intercept out of Jubail, so had brought extra food and water for a desert flight. The food they had taken from the camp just augmented their supply. After riding to the vicinity of al Artawiya, it was their plan to then swing north for a 300 kilometer ride to the Iraqi border. The whole trip would take them about eight to ten days.

Again, the main problem was that the Ikhwans had not properly allowed for Ben Thanian. He was now underway in the pickup with six armed soldiers including himself, had extra tires, springs, and gasoline, and had five more soldiers following afoot, with guns and supplies aboard the two remaining camels. And he had a radio to keep contact with Jubail. Guide Mohammed was in the seat of the pickup, with his rifle, and Abdul was driving.

Within two hours after leaving camp, the pickup met one of the scouting soldiers reporting the change in direction of the Ikhwan trail. Ajab knew that he could catch the fleeing Ikhwans before sundown, but he was outnumbered at least two to one, and he feared for the Americans in a firefight. All he could do was to keep track and follow, with radioed instructions of the Ikhwan's location to Jubail.

Meanwhile, Burke and Larsh were getting saddle sores from their unexpected riding, but were not about to try to make a break. They traveled on and stopped near a rocky ridge for overnite camp. The raiders set out guards some distance from camp. The hostages were given bread, dates, and water for an evening meal.

For the next two days, the raiders kept on their planned route, with Ajab following as he planned. On the morning of the third day, the Ikhwan outposts spotted Ajab's scout and exchanged a few rounds of rifle fire. The Ikhwans quickly struck camp and departed at a pace as fast as they felt the horses could sustain. The chase continued during the day, with both parties aware of the other, and also aware that the hostages prevented a firefight. As usual, the raiders stopped for camp at sundown.

Huey could understand Arab speech better than JJ, and while the two were riding along side by side, said, "Did you get the drift of that last conversation before we got aboard the horses?"

"I caught something about leaving early tomorrow and changing direction," replied JJ.

"Well, I caught 'midnight' and 'south,' and assume that means they intend to leave our next camp at midnight and change direction to the south. I'll bet they also intend to lay a trap for the Amir's scouts."

"Seems to me tonight is the time to make a break."

"Yeah, but how?"

"Mr. Larsh, if they plan a midnight takeoff, there's a fair chance they'll try to get some good sleep in before takeoff, so maybe we'll have a bunch of sacked out raiders around ten or eleven o'clock, and could sneak out."

"Such as very quietly if we just sorta bedded down a bit closer to the edge of the crowd than before?"

"Yeah. You got it!"

So, after the evening repast, the geologists carefully checked their pockets and clothes for anything that could make a noise, and with a little changing around had no sound-makers. They then removed their boots and crawled under the blanket on their bed rug, which they had earlier just happened to place near the edge of the sleeping area.

It seemed that the Ikhwans would never get bedded down but,

as expected, they did bed down earlier than normal and the camp was apparently fast asleep by ten P. M. The geologists had touch signals worked out: Danger, stop: Two touches; Continue: Three touches; etc. Shortly before eleven, they rolled out of their bedding, quietly pushed in sand to make mounds under the blanket, then left their boots and hats in place at the ends of the mounds. They then started crawling ever so slowly through the sand toward the three-foot gap between two sleeping Ikhwans at the perimeter of the area.

After two false danger stops, and a lot of held breath, the two finally cleared the perimeter. They kept crawling very slowly and quietly for another ten minutes, then got up and quietly walked at a direction perpendicular to the two outpost guards, one of whom was nodding, half-asleep. They were careful to leave their trail in the sand for easy tracking, because as soon as they got to the nearby rocky slope, they would change direction. And they did. Once they got on the hard rock with no tracks, they ran as best they could, in a direction near one of the outposts, with the idea in mind that no one would expect them to do such a foolish thing. Then, the plan was that as soon as the man left his post after the coming escape alarm, they would occupy that position and try to hide among the brush and rocks.

They got in a place to await further action, and sat down among some brush. After a while, they noticed the camp stirring, and shortly after that, a shout rang out and they picked up the word, "...*yimshee*..." (...go away...). Then two shots rang out as someone excitedly shot at an escapee shadow, fortunately nowhere near the Americans. The Ikhwan quickly saddled their horses, called in the guards, and moved off in the direction of the geologist's trail. After a while, they circled back and began a systematic search of the whole area.

By now, the geologists had moved into the guard's abandoned position and, as hoped, the thundering horses did not come closer than thirty or forty yards to the two Americans crouched in a small slump of brush. In their field khaki clothes, they blended in very well with the sand and rock. Still, it was surprising how small these two big men could make themselves under and in a three-foot bush when they thought their lives depended on it. For good measure, they had dragged loose brush up close, like it was naturally from windblown trapping. Also, by getting on the downwind side of the bushes, they were able to scoop out some of the windblown sand naturally trapped there, so as to be partly hidden by the sand pile.

Meanwhile, the Amir's scout had heard the gunfire, checked to see all the commotion, and had his partner immediately ride for the Amir. Since the Amir and his main force was only a kilometer or two behind the scouts, that took little time. A little over twenty minutes after the shots were heard, the Amir and soldiers were running for the pickup, and it took them another six or seven minutes including loading time to get close enough to the Ikhwan camp to stop and listen. The Ikhwans were using flares and lanterns in the dark night to try to find the geologists, so the Ikhwan were visible to the Amir, but the Amir and his soldiers were not visible to the Ikhwans. This helped considerably.

Ajab puzzled for a while over what all the commotion was about, but finally reasoned out that most likely the only thing that would cause this would be an escape attempt by the hostage Americans. He decided to gamble on that reasoning. He explained his plan to his soldiers and they set it in motion.

The soldiers spread out in a line of skirmishers and, upon the Amir's signal, began a slow deliberate walking advance toward the Ikhwan. By this time, the Ikhwan had broken their force of some forty horsemen into three groups who were combing the area, still on horseback. One of these three groups rode toward the advancing soldiers, whereupon, when they got within about a hundred yards, the soldiers knelt and opened fire. Three Ikhwan riders fell. The others wheeled their mounts and headed back to their comrades.

As the Ikhwan regrouped to face the new challenge, the two geologists, who were on the left flank of the advancing soldiers, broke out of the brush cover and started running across the rocky and sandy plain on which the entire operation was taking place.

"Ajab, Ajab...ouch.. Ajab, damn it.. it's Burke and Larsh..ouch!" cried Burke, as they banged and bruised their bare feet on the rocks as they ran.

After about two hundred yards, Huey sounded off: "Burke, these...damn it...damn rocks, are tearing...ouch!...my feet...they see us, let's...ouch!...stop!"

"OK, you got it," replied JJ and they stopped running and

began to pick their way carefully toward the soldiers, one of whom, a large Negro Arab named Suleiman, ran to meet them.

When the Americans jumped from cover and started running, the Ikhwan immediately started after them, but rifle fire from the kneeling soldiers stopped that in a hurry. So the raiders pulled back to plan their next action. By this time the JJ and Huey were safe with the soldiers and describing the Ikhwan force to Ajab.

The Ikhwan knew they outnumbered the soldiers, but they did not know whether the soldiers had a machine gun, that was their downfall at the battle of Sabillah. And Ajab was not about to tell them. Ajab walked out on a sand dune and called out for a talk.

After a few minutes, five Ikhwan horsemen rode out of their group toward the Amir who was heading their way. Three of the Ikhwan broke off and went to recover their downed comrades. The other two continued toward the soldiers. They greeted the Amir with normal Arab courtesy, and the Amir responded similarly. Then they talked.

Amir Ben Thanian explained to the Ikhwan that they could not get the geologists without a fight and that many would die if they forced the issue. Also, he explained that a large motorized armed force was on its way from the east and would arrive at their location the next morning.

He further explained that even if the Ikhwan recaptured the Americans, another motorized force was moving to cut them off before they could make the Iraqi border. The Ikhwan horsemen listened, then rode off, back to their comrades. After a few minutes, the entire Ikhwan force, silhouetted against the faintly lit sky by a rising quarter moon, rode off to the northwest. They decided that their plan for ransom was hopeless.

They did not return the camels or food they took. The Amir recognized this, but decided that to let them have some success for their *ghazzu* would help prevent a battle. Evidently, it did.

The Americans learned later that the Ikhwan force had broken up and returned to their respective tribes. The Saudi government elected to not punish them other than to demand cessation of *ghazzu*; evidently feeling that since only the Ikhwan suffered casualties from the raid, peace and harmony was best served by leniency.

Burke and Larsh were just glad to be back in camp in one

piece, even if their feet were so bruised, cut, and sore that they did little walking for several days.

~ ~ ~ ~ ~ ~ ~ ~ ~ ~ ~ ~ ~ ~ ~

CHAPTER 7

Field Test

For the first few days after the Americans got back in camp, their main concern was to heal their sore and bruised feet, and each of them had a few thorn wounds to boot. The desert soil over which they had run from the Ikhwan was surely not intended for bare feet unless the feet were quite tough and, even then, injury was certain sooner or later.

During this time JJ and Huey consulted their small library to try to learn more about these bandit Ikhwan Arabs. And while they were at it, they found out more about Arabia in general.

They had a small encyclopedia on both Arabia and the Muslim religion, plus books by R. E. Cheesman 1926, Charles M. Doughty 1921, Alois Musil 1927, and H. St. J. B. Philby 1922 and 1928. The interesting thing about their accumulation of books before leaving the United States was how little had been written on this ancient land, and how practically nothing written before the last dozen years could be found.

Of course, their baggage limitations also restricted their library. But they did have the 1921 paper by R. B. Newton on central Arabia fossils which, with the Philby books, was all they had on background geology. Although not a geologist, Philby had written much about the Arabian lands, its people, and made numerous references to geologic information.

Arabia of 1935, constituting the southwestern part of Asia, consists of several Protectorates and sheikdoms, mostly with indefinite boundaries which, along with Saudi Arabia, formed the largest peninsula in the world. The occasionally deep wadis suggest more rainfall in the past than now, perhaps during Pleistocene glacial cycles over the last few hundred thousand years, with the latest rainy age perhaps as recent as six to nine thousand years ago. The highest mountains are in the southern part of the peninsula with the highest Saudi mountains peaking about 9000 feet, or approximately 2770 meters, a few hundred kilometers southeast of Mecca on the west coast of Saudi Arabia.

The central region of the Kingdom is a mountainous and topographically irregular plateau, with more relatively high mountains near the Jordan border and the Red Sea.

Most information about Arabia comes from writings after 1885, before which little was written after Greek and Roman authors. The earliest notable western visitations to this historic region occurred less than a hundred years before these geologists arived, prior to which, for the written record, little but the historical development of Islam broke the long gap between Roman and recent times.

Parts of Saudi Arabia, mainly on the two coasts and the northern corners, were well known and traveled long before Christ. Quite possibly, the Bedouin ancestors were in place as early as 5000 BC. They were surely there to greet Greek and Roman explorers and builders, as well as much earlier Babylonians and 1st Dynasty Egyptians. These ancestors in turn probably developed from stone age hunter-gatherers who occupied some Arabian areas during much earlier rainy periods. Of most importance to all of Arabia was the seventh century AD.

Mohammed was born about 570 AD in Mecca, and died in Medina in 632. He came to be recognized by his contemporaries as the greatest of the long string of Prophets dating back for centuries, perhaps millennia. Before 700 AD, Mohammed's followers compiled the Koran which was accepted not only as the bible, but also as the base for all laws of conduct and human interrelationship for Muslims.

Based on the Koran, the Ikhwan sect

developed in the tenth century and from their center in Basra, now Iraq, compiled scholarly papers mainly on mathematics and astronomy, but also other disciplines. They were quite aware of some Greek and Roman philosophers and scholars, and developed their own Koran-guided philosophy for their people. It was from these strict people that the current Bedouin tribes of the Ikhwan sect developed. The Ikhwan took a very dim view of any non-believers, especially such as the Americans. This may have partly explained their kidnapping and poor treatment of the geologists.

Of course, there were several other competing sects of Islam, such as the tenth century Qarmatians, the eighteenth century Wahhabis, the Persian Shiites, and Sunnis who accept the Sunna as a supplement to the Koran. While the Shiite and Sunni sects are the major branches of Islam, the land of King Sa'ud, as well as the Wahhabi branch of Sunni, center at Riyadh. In 1935, the Wahhabis numbered no more than 30,000 but, most important, included the royal family of Sa'ud.

"JJ," said Huey one windy and very dusty day while they were still in the foot-healing business, "did you realize that the only real cities of all the eastern half of Saudi Arabia are Riyadh, population maybe 30,000, and old Hofuf which we have visited?"

"Well, now that you mention it, I suppose I might have guessed that, and also that both of them are there because of large fault-fed springs and water supply."

And, indeed it was so. Both cities were little more than a collection of grey-brown low mud-brick buildings, with little color except for the locally beautiful green and colorful gardens and groves. Around and in these oases that developed were townspeople, the craftsmen, the shopkeepers, all those who form a center for the traveler and surrounding herdsmen. Riyadh was an oasis on the Iraq-Mecca trail; Hofuf, just a large natural oasis that formed a center for the coastal area herdsmen and travelers. Riyadh was also the family home of the royal family, as well as the capital of Nejd Province and Saudi Arabia.

Neither city had any significant manufacturing, mineral or export businesses other than those that furnished the needs of the local population. Except for dates. Arabian dates were grown and shipped widely since biblical times. Also, at times, both mineral and olive oils had been traded, but neither constituted a major industry. Both had ancient origins, and some Arabs felt that Abraham himself came out of Arab lands to the ancient Babylonian city of Ur.

Jubail, company field headquarters, was just a small fishing village. Dhahran was the same. Some inland named locations, such as Abqaiq and Harad, were often little more than one- to ten-family collections of mud-brick homes, often supplemented with camel-hair tents; sometimes a few wells; rarely any shops.

Saudi Arabia had been partly occupied by Babylonians, Greeks, Romans, Ottomans, and numerous Arabian groups, prior to the development of the adjacent British protectorates on the Arabian Gulf coast before and as a result of the World War.

Twelve to fourteen miles off the east coast, Bahrain, an archipelago with one large main island, long occupied by successive groups of humankind, forms one of the main British protectorates under an 1820 Friendship Treaty that was developed in an effort to maintain British commerce and reduce the theretofore rampant piracy and slave trade in that area of the Gulf. It was well known to the ancients, as Tylos to some, and there are both Greek and Roman chronicles of activity on Bahrain, or Tylos. Even those ancient authors referred to still more ancient chronicles; especially of the excellent pearls from that region of the Gulf.

Possibly, the high-quality pearls of this part of the Gulf may be associated with the underwater springs of fresh water that coincidentally occupy the same overall areas. These springs are probably fault-fed from deep aquifers that derive their supply from the distant highlands to the west in central Saudi Arabia.

Such aquifers, if forming a reservoir for oil, would result in dynamic, not static, oil accumulations. Such moving water would tend to cause an oil accumulation to move to a position not centered on the crest of a structure, with the oil movement in the direction of the water flow. If the rate of water flow changed, the oil would tend to move in the direction of the change; further off structure if the water flow rate increased, or back toward the structure crest if the flow rate decreased. Such shifting of the oil accumulation off center from the crest can occur with water flow rates of only a few feet per year.

- - - - - - -

Within a week after the Ikhwan kidnapping, Huey and JJ recovered adequately to go back to their sketching and measuring, and took to the field in search of one last outcrop hopefully in contact with the possibly pre-Miocene Nummulites limestone layer they had found in a topographic low shortly before the Ikhwan raid. Their next move, to *Camp Yabrin*, about 70 kilometers south of the village of Haradh, was scheduled before the end of May.

They learned that the first well on the Dammam dome, Dammam #1, had spudded (started drilling) April 30, and with that event there was a great deal of excitement throughout the Aramco organization, including San Francisco.

Bert Miller, District Geologist in Jubail, kept the field geologists informed as to progress of the well. And described the unusual problems and solutions involved. It was an exciting time for all, but often the excitement was intermixed with pure drudgery and difficult work. Dispatches, though erratic, were informative.

Work had been exceedingly slow on Dammam #1. Shipment of rig timbers and other equipment had been underway for months, and just getting the drill collar set at the surface required special effort. Even the requisite shallow hole needed for the drilling rig to commence operations was a problem. The surface limestone rock defeated hole making efforts with all available tools, so the crew flaked away a small starter hole by alternately heating and cooling the rock with water!

Then, the company had no regular rig building crew such as were available in the United States, so they made shift with all available to build the heavy timbered derrick, most of the timbers were two to three inches thick and eight to twelve inches wide. Some parts of the rig, such as the legs, were constructed using several planks.

Finally the rig was completed. It stood about 74 feet tall including the crown block that consisted of several heavy steel pulleys, and was about twenty feet square at the base. the bull and calf wheels, walking beam assembly, sand reel, steam boiler and steam engine of about 30 horsepower, and other equipment were moved into position and the cable tool drilling got under way.

- - - - - - -

In this year 1935, cable tool rigs in the United States had been largely supplanted with rotary rigs, but were still preferred in remote areas because of the lighter and simpler components, and smaller crew. Also, such a rig was more effective when drilling cavernous or fractured rocks through which rotary rigs with circulating drilling fluids tended to lose such fluids into caverns or fractures, thus achieving the common oil field expression of "lost circulation." Much of the time, a cable tool rig could be operated by one man, the driller, even though three men constituted the normal crew. But in most rocks it was much slower than a rotary rig. For example, in many sand and shale sections above 4000' depth, a cable tool rig might average four feet per hour, where a rotary rig would average 75 feet per hour.

A cable tool rig is drilled by raising and dropping a steel bit often similar in appearance to a massive star drill, with uphole attached segments or tools to give weight and force to the falling bit. Many different kinds of bits were available for different kinds of rocks. Often, especially in softer rocks, a double linked tool called drilling jars is attached above the drill stem which in turn is attached to the bit. The jars were installed in one or more pairs. A set of jars resembled two great links of a chain and were constructed to slide over each other in telescope fashion. The falling jars might give a second blow to the falling bit after the bit hit bottom, with a KA-WHAM effect, that is, a second heavy blow a split second after the first. However, the main purpose of the jars is to hammer the bit loose from the bottom of the hole in which it might be stuck, when the cable to which the entire drilling assembly is attached is pulled back uphole. In hard rocks, jars are commonly omitted. The total drilling assembly weighs 4000 to 6000 pounds.

From bottom up, the drilling assembly was bit, drill stem usually 20 to 40 feet long for weight, jars, rope socket, and 2-1/2" manila drilling cable. The manila, or sometimes hemp, cable was more flexible than steel cable down to about 1500 feet depth, and was for that reason preferred in drilling above that depth. The steel parts of the assembly were connected with tool joints, and the top of the assembly to the cable by a rope socket. At the top, the drilling cable was attached to a turnbuckle-like device called a temper screw, that in turn was attached to the walking beam. While drilling, the temper screw supports the weight of drilling cable and drilling assembly. From the temper screw, the drilling cable runs up to the crown pulley at the top of the derrick and then to the heavy wooden bull wheel, seven or eight feet in diameter.

The walking beam is a very heavy built-up wooden beam about twenty feet long that rests on a vertical sampson post, is restrained on the downstroke by a vertical "headache" post, and operated on the power end by a moving crank timber called a pitman. The pitman is attached off center to the band wheel which is turned by the steam or other engine.

The driller uses the walking beam to raise and lower the cable and bit assembly to shatter the rock on bottom for several blows, then turns the temper screw to lower the bit, followed by continued raising and lowering the cable and bit for additional blows on bottom by the bit. After thus drilling, or "making hole" for a few feet, the driller releases the cable from the temper screw and then uses the bull wheel, actually two, six to eight foot heavy wood wheels mounted on either end of a 16-inch circular oak shaft about 14 feet long, to reel up the bit assembly out of the hole. The outer surface of one of the two wheels is faced with a metal rim or band about ten inches wide against which a pad could be pressed to allow for friction braking when lowering the cable into the hole.

After reeling the drilling cable and assembly out of the hole, the driller uses the sand reel to roll the sand line in the hole with an attached bailer to retrieve the rock cuttings. The bailer has a valve at the bottom so that it can be dropped on the cuttings at hole bottom several times so as to fill the bailer. To aid in drilling and bailing, some ten to one hundred feet of water and mud are kept in the bottom of the hole.

The temper screw is a heavy steel turnbuckle-like device a few feet long and weighs about 400 pounds. The driller senses how to turn the temper screw and lower the drilling assembly by the sound of the drilling assembly downhole and the tension in the drilling cable. Such drilling thus has a bit of art to it.

During the spudding operation, until the hole is deep enough to hold the 40 feet of drilling assembly plus the eight to ten foot stroke of the walking beam, a different surface system eliminating the walking beam is used. While spudding, the drilling assembly is considerably shortened and a temporary jerk line from a spudding shoe, attached to the drilling line that runs over the crown block to the prime mover crank, is used. The prime mover for the entire rig is a steam or internal combustion engine with usually 30 to 50 horsepower.

When needed to keep the hole from caving, casing is suspended in the hole by a calf line, usually

1" steel, that runs from the calf wheel, usually smaller but sturdier than the bull wheel, over the crown block through a block and tackle system to a hoisting block from which the casing is suspended. Sometimes, the calf wheel assembly is omitted and the casing is handled by the bull wheel assembly.

Regardless of tools and rig system, in hard rocks, a typical rig would make only a few feet a day. Also, a cable tool rig was very unsatisfactory in drilling unconsolidated sediments such as geologically young sands and shales. Another major drawback to this rig was the high probability of losing control of the hole if a pressured reservoir was encountered by the bit.

Cable tool drilling was used by the Chinese, in a much more simple manner, at least a thousand years ago. On the other hand, the faster and safer rotary drilling method was first used on a large scale at Spindletop, near Beaumont, Texas in 1901.

- - - - - - -

As May, 1935 wore on, the geologists grew progressively more disenchanted with surface geologic mapping in Saudi Arabia because of the incessant wind and frequent dust storms that accompanied the increasing heat and surprisingly high humidity in this desert area. Day after day, the first thing to do before leaving for the field was to remove the canvas and other covers they had improvised to keep the touring car, maps, sketches, and other gear from being layered with dust.

Also, to aid in sleep, JJ and Huey rigged cloths around their sleeping cots to shield them from the dust and sand that often blew through their tent at night. Sometimes they wet these cloths to better cut the dust. They often pulled neckerchiefs up over their nose, and sometimes slept with these on dusty nights. The really unpleasant weather started in early April and there seemed to be no end to the ever-increasing heat. The one main blessing was that the winds usually died down by midnight and though still warm, the latter half of the night and on up until a hour or so after dawn could be rather pleasant. Another blessing was the position of their tent just downwind from an overlooking bluff about fifteen feet high, which shielded them from much of the blowing sand.

JJ Burke and Huey Larsh were good friends, but both were fairly quick tempered, and this, along with the conditions did lead to flare ups. But they both knew they were stuck together for the duration, and dam' glad neither was alone, so they always managed to get over huffs within a day. Ususally less.

Huey was the better diplomat. And he was easier to laugh, and generally easier going, yet still quite intelligent. Perhaps some of his demeanor came from his parents. His mother was part of a very wealthy steel manufacturing family from Pennsylvania, and his father came from a professional family in Tulsa, Oklahoma. His father was at this time a senior vice-president of a major oil company. Huey was a rich kid who really never had to work if he didn't want to, but he was determined to prove to the world, especially his family, that he could make his own wealth.

Though their family backgrounds were quite different, both men were ambitious, smart, quite capable, and hard working. Most of all, they were honest and reliable.

Still, their working conditions would try the patience of a saint, and neither of them pretended to be even a preacher, much less a saint!

Afternoons were the most miserable, and the wise Bedouins did a lot of sleeping during this period. The Americans had to learn the hard way. They did. By mid-May, the geologists were up and out by dawn, and back into camp by early afternoon. They tried to do as much measuring and rough describing as possible during the mornings before ten o'clock, then rough sketching in the field, then back to camp and the shade of their open tent to try to improve on their notes and sketches for the later final compilation work to be done at Jubail.

They transferred elevations from one area to the next by use of their aneroid barometer, or altimeter, graduated in feet. This instrument was calibrated to use the lessening air pressure for higher altitudes to measure elevation changes in feet between locations. It was not used for precise elevations and, when such were critical, the elevations were obtained by alidade or transit. However, the altimeter was a fast method of getting approximate elevations, and when closely controlled, could obtain elevations with a reliability of about twenty-five feet.

It was most reliable during the mornings before the diurnal air pressure changes became high and erratic. In order to correct for such pressure changes, it was necessary to take the altimeter back to a base station every half hour or so to measure and correct for the ever-changing air pressure. If a second altimeter was available, it could remain at the base station and continuously measure the pressure changes, thus resulting in more reliable corrections and elevations for the roaming altimeter. Since time was one of the correcting parameters, one altimeter surveying required rapid movement from base to new station and back. This sometimes resulted in more tire and spring damage to the car.

They completed their Camp Udayliyah area mapping in late May, then commenced the time-consuming and unpleasant, though necessary, move to their next camp which would conclude the mapping for this field season.

What with soldiers, camp personnel, tents, camels, the touring car and a temporary pickup, and a mountain of gear and supplies, it took three full days to get the camp moved and set up in the rather pleasant new camp they dubbed *Camp Yabrin*. The camp was set up near the east end of an irregularly high area marked by several low *jibehl* through which a rather wide and typically rocky dry wadi worked its way northeasterly to the great *Wadi As Sahba*.

Perhaps as recently as six thousand years ago, *Wadi As Sahba* had more or less perennially flowed water toward the Arabian Gulf although, even then, the water probably never made it all the way before it was swallowed up by the underlying sands, rocks, and fissures.

Part of the camp transfer procedure was the business of determining the location and elevation of the next camp in relation to the old camp. For initial efforts, subject to later careful surveying when needed, the geologists used the car odometer along with their Brunton compass to areally locate their new camp. An altimeter was used to transfer the elevation. Thus a new base station was established and marked by a pile of rocks with a letter and number painted on the top rock. Based on prior stations, a latitude and longitude position was computed for this new station, and then checked for accuracy against the stars and their star charts. Such checks often resulted in re-checking some of the ground measurements, and averaging differences.

As was their custom, the Americans set up the tents downwind to small bluffs. Of course, the wind didn't always blow as they hoped, but with the aid of their ever-knowledgeable guide, Yahiya, it usually worked pretty well. On a quiet evening, looking southwesterly, the desert presented a striking and harshly beautiful scene, with multi-hued reds and yellows of sunset sometimes extending from the western horizon across the sky past the meridian. It was by no means all bad. And when these times were added to the almost daily excitement of finding some new geologic secret, it was pretty good duty. Of course, it would be better without quite so much wind, dust, and heat!

For the next three weeks, Burke and Larsh worked mostly to the north and west of their camp where they had found some anomalous southerly dips in one small rock exposure. This was quite anomalous since regional dip was easterly, and it could mean a structure lying to the north toward the village of Harad. With much searching, and using the few air photos from the Fairchild, they found several exposures, most only a few feet thick. Sometimes they could improve the exposures by getting some of the camp personnel to come out with shovels and help them dig small holes in the rocky and sandy soil.

During the course of this period of sketching and section measuring along with all the dips they could measure in the usually small outcrops, they did indeed establish a rather broad area of southerly dips in the area just south of Harad, suggesting that older rocks might be found on the surface to the north near or beyond Harad. In time, this was to become part of the base for a very exciting geologic chase.

- - - - - - -

Time: Eleven A.M. Wednesday. A typically hot, dry, dusty, clear-skyed day in late June, 1935, at the eastern edge of a broad, flat, rocky desert area located southeast of Haradh. This blast furnace lay just east of the great sand dune country of Ad Dhana, and is part of that arid, rocky, occasionally hilly country marked by *jibehl* and wadis, and in particular, Wadi as Sahbi, where JJ was now situated.

This rather warped Garden of Eden, populated by hardy lizards, the hairy shabath spider, the sun or camel spider which grows up to six inches in diameter, scorpions such as the black fat-tailed scorpion, numerous varieties of birds, and a fair representation of hidden rodents, snakes, and insects, formed the backdrop for JJ's sweat-streaked body as he methodically attempted to pry loose the damned stuck car.

The 1933 Ford touring car, with its top down as the geologists usually drove them, was sitting at a ridiculous angle, with the left front wheel firmly wedged between two boulders, where it had dropped when JJ had attempted to negotiate this particular stretch of dry wadi. One rear wheel was hanging in the air about three inches off the ground. The other two wheels contacted the loose wash rubble. Looking somewhat like a wounded beast, the Ford rested there, as if to defy any mere human with a shovel and three-foot tire tool to disengage the wedged wheel.

And to add further slight complication to the situation, the location was some 15 kilometers from the nearest regular camel road, actually just a barely discernible trail across the shifting sands and rubble that topped the underlying Miocene deposits. A tumbleweed-like bush and sparse, short, wiry grass formed nature's vegetative offering of shade.

Although occasional traffic on the camel trail offered distant aid, nothing closer would provide any help. The last vestige of a trail lay several miles back where JJ had struck off cross-country, and he knew for a fact the nearest household was in the barren three buildings occupied by a single Arab family at the tiny village about 20 km to the northeast which, in turn, was situated over 35 kilometers east of Haradh. All in all, one could say the location was a bit remote.

Well, thought JJ, this situation is beginning to get kinda' funny, it's so ridiculous. Huey must have had six varieties of fits by now, since he was expecting me as usual about sundown yesterday. Probably has the soldiers out looking for me, but they'll look where I was supposed to be, near Soak Hoover's Harmaliyah camp, about 50 km north of the village. Why in the devil did I ever take a notion to check that cockeyed outcrop east of the mapping area in the first place? If I hadn't done that, I wouldn't have tried the fool stunt of attempting a short cut to the Harmaliyah camp.

And to make matters worse, I should never have violated our cardinal rule in this strange country: Never travel alone. Period. It seemed such a little thing to make a short side trip off the trail on my way to Harmaliyah for a few bags of water and other supplies. Never again will I break that rule for any reason. If I get outa this in one piece.

JJ had been in the field now for over three years as a surface geologist for Calco, the last nine months in Saudi Arabia, so he knew pretty well how to operate. He had extra water, spare tires, first aid equipment, and extra gas, but a clean-up of the car a few days before accounted for the lack of some of the tools that were normally kept in the car. He hadn't struck out afoot for any place yet, because he knew it would take at least eight hours of walking through rough terrain and, with just a little bad luck, such as a sand storm, sprained ankle, or getting lost, he might not be found until his bones joined those bleached ones lying here and there that formerly belonged to camels and horses.

No, JJ knew that his best bet was to stick with the Ford and attempt to free it, at least until sundown. Then he could load himself with the water and a little other gear, trust to the cool of night for less exhausting travel, and attempt to walk out. With reasonable luck, he could make it to Haradh before the bad heat of the next day, and there he could get a camel or horse to ride back to camp. There was very little moonlight, but the stars offered good course markers.

Looking back at the wedged wheel again, JJ studied to find some way of freeing it. He realized that the only equipment he had was a totally inadequate tire tool and a jack that he couldn't find a way to place in position to use. The boulders which the car was trapped on were actually part of one huge, mostly buried, limestone block, weighing several tons. A thorough search of the entire area within sight of the partially hidden car had failed to yield anything except more rocks and sand. Not even an old fence-post like he had relied on one time in a similar situation while doing surface work in west Texas.

Finally, JJ decided his best bet was to get under the car, dig out a place to put the jack, and then raise the car at the upraised rear wheel, and scoop dirt and rocks under the wheel. Then he could lower the rear end and hope to have sufficient traction from both rear wheels to free the mechanical beast. Of course, he would have to first somehow jack the wedged wheel up even if the front of the car was to stay resting on the jack as he tried to back off.

With some effort, JJ struggled under the car and started removing rocks along with a little digging with his hand to create a place to put the jack under the car in a viable position to jack it up in the right place.

Suddenly he became aware of a scurrying fuzzy shape and in about one-tenth of a second comprehended that he had stirred up a sun spider that was as startled as he was. Though the spider had a jump on him, within that same one-tenth of a second he flinched away from the big scary spider.

The arachnid was fully as frightened as JJ and both were trying to put distance between each other as fast as possible. After rapidly flinching and squirming backward away from the spider, he banged into a large rock with his right elbow. In natural reaction to get away from this new assailant, he reached out with his left hand toward a small clump of desert shrub under the car.

His senses somewhat dulled by these rapid fire events, JJ failed to react fast enough to the slight brushing sound issuing from the base of the bush. As the blur of the wide open sand viper head flared toward JJ's hand, he whirled over to his right, banging his head and shoulder against the car in the process. But he did not move with sufficient speed. He felt a flash of severe pain as the snake struck home and discharged his venom. Almost instantly, JJ seemed to sense without really comprehending that his snakebite kit was in the car, even as the fangs found their mark.

Before the snake could fall back from his successful strike near the base of JJ's left hand thumb, instinct caused him to jerk away in order to prevent the snake's recoiling for another strike. With his injured left hand, now numbing, he whipped a cloud of sand toward the snake as he quickly squirmed backward and to the right.

By this time, the snake, also called a horned viper for the raised scales above its eyes, was quite anxious to quit the scene. The viper was interrupted from its daytime rest by this unknown attacker and only wanted to get away so he could continue to rest for his normal nocturnal hunting. JJ watched the viper sidewinding away across the sand, but he had other things to be concerned about.

Realizing the need for maintaining slow blood circulation and minimum nerve reaction, JJ rolled away from the rear of the car, got to his feet and stumbled around the car to the left. The medical box was always just behind the driver's side of the front seat.

The numbing now began to develop into a throbbing, searing pain. JJ struggled emotionally to keep his control and try to avoid fear that would increase movements of body fluids. He forced himself to think that he had just cut his hand, it needed medication, and he had to get ready for that party tonite with a fantasized beautiful Saudi girl he had just met. All was good. He was happy. Just a little cut to fix.

Still he had to remember some fundamentals of snakebite care. As he stumbled, he started fashioning a tourniquet about his forearm with his handkerchief. Holding one end of the handkerchief in his teeth and the other in his right hand, JJ completed the task, and then repeated the process with his belt in order to place a second tourniquet about his upper arm.

As soon as he finished the second tourniquet, JJ opened the door and slowly got in the back seat and sat down. Reaching down, he raised the lid on the medical box and pulled out the little black plastic box he had carried so long without ever using.

Inside he found the disinfectant, suction cup and plunger, salve and blade. Noticing that swelling had progressed about two inches up his left arm, he made several incisions up the arm from the actual fang marks as well as at the marks in order to better remove the poison.

For the next half hour in the blazing midday heat, JJ carefully made small incisions and applied suction until no further progression of the swelling was evident. Other than occasional waves of nausea or faintness, JJ now felt little pain from the bite. The cuts he had made hurt some, but the stinging iodine masked most other pain. But he knew any further strong physical exertion was out. Therefore, he would have to wait for help or wait and rest for the remainder of the day and night hoping that his body would dissipate the poison he had failed to get from cutting and sucking.

He refused to believe that he would get so sick he couldn't

work on the car tomorrow. He was healthy and knew that if any man was in proper physical condition to stand a snakebite, he should be. He still had an ample supply of water which he drank freely as a poor substitute for food.

Even so, he kept up with the fantasizing of good and happy things in order to reduce body activity, doing his best to stay relaxed and calm.

As time wore on, JJ began to notice more severe waves of nausea accompanied by cramping and pain throughout his entire left arm. He had carefully loosened the upper tourniquet every twenty or twenty-five minutes, then tightened it again after a few minutes. He supposed some poison probably got through each time the tourniquet was loosened, but he didn't really know for sure. He felt sick and hoped he could hang on, thinking that with time, maybe he would feel better.

Glancing at his watch, JJ saw that it was 3:15 P.M. Still have a long wait, he thought. Looking up to the northern horizon, he was suddenly informed by Mother Nature of a change in the weather.

Rolling toward him from the north, hugging the ground, came the debris. This conglomeration, with the appearance of a giant brown amoeba lumbering over the desert, consisted of dust, sand, small pebbles, desert shrubs, twigs, and sticks, all forming a dirty, stifling, penetrating mass. A typical Arabian dust storm. The type that usually pushed ahead of a weather front.

Since he knew that this thing would strike within a few minutes, JJ struggled out of the seat to prepare as rapidly as he could. Sick as he felt, he had no choice but to prepare. He first put his shirt on, buttoned it up tight, pulled his hat down tight on his head, then struggled to get the canvas top up on the car and fastened. The maps and survey gear were already in the equipment box in the rear seat or on the floor.

Lovely dirt - here it is. As he stuck his nose in the front of his shirt for better breathing, JJ felt fairly secure from the howling wind and debris. He knew that this sort of storm was usually short lived, and was followed by hail or rain. If it rained, he hoped it might aid in freeing the car, and make him feel better. God, he felt terrible.

The canvas top flapped, pebbles bounced off the car with flat metallic sounds - occasionally highlighted by a ringing slap as the bumper was hit, and flying sand and dust flurries left his mouth feeling gritty, his eyes caked, and a general feeling of dirtiness all over. Then he noticed a few splatters of dust laden water on the windshield.

In a matter of two minutes, these few drops of water became a veritable downpour, with the rain falling in great wind blown-sheets. JJ tried to keep dry by huddling back in the car. The effort was not totally successful. Then quite suddenly, the rain became what appeared to be a solid wall of water in all directions as far as the eye could see. Which was about eight feet. It seemed to JJ that he could faintly discern a roaring sound above the din of the downpour. Listening carefully, he decided that he could distinctly hear this sound. At least this storm was taking his mind off pain and discomfort for a little while.

As suddenly as it had commenced, the rain ceased. Then the roar that JJ heard became very evident. Realizing by now that the noise he heard was water bearing down on him in the sharply inclined wadi, JJ hurriedly abandoned the car for higher ground. He scrambled up on the natural levee and looked back to the northeast up the wash gradient, and there it came. Rushing, gurgling, tossing weeds, sticks, and rocks up to the size of his head, came this rarely witnessed sight of a small-scale flood gone wild. JJ estimated the main wadi to be about four feet deep and thirty feet wide - strewn with cobbles and boulders. The water front was washing over the banks, adding a few more stones to the natural levee.

Boy, that Ford is about to get a thorough washing, thought JJ. I hope the water doesn't completely soak it. Well, anyway it won't be any worse off if it does. Contact!

The debris laden forefront of the water slashed into the car with a resounding roar, rocking it well over to one side, then allowing it to slowly settle back with an uneven rocking motion. Water continued to rush under, around, and through the car, causing it to jerkily bob about. JJ began to realize that after the vehicle had dried out, he might be perfectly free to drive away--because the roaring water furnished impact leverage he had been unable to apply. Possibly this would free the stuck wheel.

As would be expected from a limited torrent of rain, the flooded wash subsided in less than half an hour from a roaring river to a mild stream about a foot and a half deep. JJ slowly got up from his perch and made his way to the car. He was soaked to the bone, but somehow felt better...maybe it was because he was now a bit chilled.

The wedged wheel was free. It was obvious before he got within ten steps of the boulder. Now the car was resting on all four wheels evenly, with the troublesome fractured boulder situated just to the front of the left front wheel - offering a challenge to any vehicle to try passing over it again. The trap set by Lady Fate had been sprung by the same vicarious Lady.

After a half hour or so, during which time he wiped sparkplugs and engine wiring, with an increasingly swollen and painful left arm, JJ had the engine dry enough to start, he hoped. Fighting back a wave of nausea, he climbed in the soaked car and, with deep concern, attempted to start it.

It took exactly seventeen minutes of cranking, carefully pumping gas with fear of flooding the engine, painfully climbing in and out of the car, and drying plugs and block to get the thing started. But it did start - and in very short order, a weak and pale JJ was driving over the trackless wasteland toward the trail he had left behind the afternoon before.

Several times during the next three hours of driving, first cross-country, then the more established trails, and finally the main camel road north of Haradh, JJ had to stop and rest. He was beginning to feel very weak and nervous -- this being aggravated by spells of sickness, and pain-racking cramps. But little by little, step by step, mile by mile he was getting closer to camp, a distraught partner, and medical help.

He felt sure that Huey was considerably upset by this unexpected 24-hour delay. Also, he knew Huey had sent help out looking for him -- in the wrong place.

There was the jabal that marked his Haradh camp. Around the jabal, up the slight rise to the rock-sheltered camp. I'm tired, sick, just bone weary, thought JJ, and damn near ready to check it in. Controlling his emotions had been a big and maybe helpful effort, but that too had drained him.

An exhausted JJ got carefully out of the car and started toward their sleeping tent, stumbling a time or two over small rocks. The camp site was faintly lighted by the last rays of sunlight. As he approached the tent, out came Huey who cheerfully greeted him.

"Hey, JJ, what the hell took you so long? All you had to do was go over to Harmaliyah and get a little water...and...my God, JJ," noticing JJ's slight stagger and pale look, "What...are you OK?"

"Sand viper didn't like my disturbing his sleep, and there's a bit more, but...for now, maybe a hand would help." Huey rushed over, grabbed JJ and said, "Hang in there, old buddy, ain't nothing that a little good food and charmin' company won't cure. Yahiya and Ajab will have a lot to say and do, and what a fine case history you'll make!"

- - - - - - -

JJ was transported to Jubail where he could get more complete medical observation and treatment in a regular bed at the field headquarters. The headquarters buildings complex now consisted of several small, low, single-story structures. As it turned out, he never had any serious new symptoms or complications. He was mainly weak and felt tired for a few days.

By the middle of the following week, he was ready to get back and help Huey close down Camp Yabrin.

One of the pickups was loaned to JJ to drive back to Camp Yabrin so that it could be used for the move of camp supplies and equipment back to Jubail for the end of the field mapping season. This time JJ took no short cuts, followed the regular camel roads, and took a full day to drive the approximate 430 kilometers back to Yabrin.

Huey walked out of the tent, "Well, buddy, it's good to see you back in one piece," he said as JJ got out of the pickup.

"It's good to be back and feeling good, although I'm not really all that thrilled to be back to this God-forsaken desolation," answered JJ. "I realize it could be a helluva lot worse, but sometimes at this time of year I have difficulty figurin' out how!"

Huey: "The good thing is that we are about to go back to the luxury of Jubail."

"Yeah, now that's real luxury, with temperatures 110 degrees in the shade, and no shade except inside a building, and the high humidity just makes it really wonderful. If you think that's luxury, let me tell you about East Texas under a pecan tree in April, sipping a cold beer. Seems to me I do remember what a cold beer tasted like...maybe we'll find out again someday."

"Probably," said Huey, "But not very soon. We got another year on our assignment before we find out what anything with alcohol tastes like again. But you gotta admit, where in the U.S.of A. could you have the reasonable chance to find an oil field that could really impact CASOC?"

"I guess it's not very likely we could find a multi-billion-barrel field over there, but we might find something over a hundred million barrels. However, you're right about finding something really big. This is our best chance to be associated with such a discovery. But for now, what do we have to do here before leaving?"

"A little summation sketching, and it would be nice to measure that Al Khunn section and shoot it in before we leave. Other'n that, just load and leave!"

The following day, the geologists went south of camp to some prominent *jibehl*, and got underway describing a rock outcrop and measuring the thickness of the successive lithologies, then they traced a bed to another outcrop so as to describe and measure another bed or series of beds above or below the traced bed.

By continuing this procedure for most of the day over several outcrops on a number of the hills, they succeeded in getting a cumulative section of about 94 feet. It consisted of two thin beds of conglomerate, several shales and sandstones, some calcareous, and a rather distinctive chalky limestone containing oyster-like echinoid fossils near the base of the section. This echinoid bed was a good marker bed for more regional mapping. They judged this to be a Miocene section.

Over the next three days, they measured the position and elevation of the Al Khunn section from their Yabrin base station, completed their notes of the section, sketched in a number of outcrops, dips, and elevations they had studied and accumulated, then got ready to leave.

Early Saturday morning, June 29, 1935, Burke and Larsh pulled out of Camp Yabrin with both the pickup and the car loaded to the hilt.

Huey drove the pickup with JJ as passenger; Abdul Jamban drove the car with Ajab Ben Thanian as his passenger. They drove through Harad village, the city of Hofuf, then Abqaiq village on the way. All included drab, grey-brown, low mudbrick buildings. The roads were the typical trails across the sandy, rocky, sparsely vegetated, countryside. They arrived at Jubail shortly after sundown, tired, dusty, thirsty, and very happy to be at their destination.

After a shower, a good night's sleep, a fine breakfast, and some good-natured exchanges with other personnel now in from the field, JJ and Huey undertook their unloading and organizing. Their principal function over the next few weeks was to assemble and coordinate their work with data similarly prepared by the other field geologists. The first day, Huey and JJ found no time for anything except unloading and storing or placing their gear. Then for the next few days they did nothing but assemble their many notes and sketches into meaningful reports and maps, from which their data was transferred to the regional maps kept in headquarters.

By mid-July, all of the geological field crews had organized and assembled their data into regionally usable form. In the process, they all learned that the many sections could for the most part be tied together and correlated in a reasonably sensible fashion. Of course, some of the sections might as well have been from Alaska for all the sense they made.

The assembled dips, structural elevations, and other structural information such as indicated inliers, outliers, and older or younger beds at certain elevations, began to suggest the possibility of "highs" or anticlinal structures in several areas, perhaps most notably in the Harad-Al Udayliyah region. Another season's mapping might add a great deal more.

Another big item during this headquarters visitation was mail. There were letters to read, and letters to write. Writing was a bore, but reading was a thrill. A young geologist in a faraway land can be awfully lonely at times, and a little mail from home can go a long way toward coping with the isolation. JJ learned that Ruthanne Cook was home from the University of Texas for the summer before her senior year, sister Mary Jane was about to get married, and that business in general was barely scraping along. His dad, Homer, was managing to get by on the operation of his Nacogdoches general store, and the cash from that plus their garden and farm animals provided a good living.

His mother described the continuing Depression, the homeless, the beggars, the failed businesses, and all the other evidences of hard times.

As bad as it was, the families in East Texas with land enough to have a garden could get by on very little cash. Such families without telephone or utilities needed only $10.00 to $15.00 per month to buy enough kerosene, brown flour in 100-pound bags, coffee, sugar and salt to get by in pretty good shape. Most farm, and many small town, homes used wells or rainwater cisterns for water and had no electricity. For times like these, no utility costs represented real savings. The real suffering was in the cities where little or nothing could be grown and some utility costs were a necessity. A $2.00 water bill looked big when wages were $1.00 per workday when work could be found.

The approximate $240.00 per month pay earned by Larsh and Burke were really fine salaries. And they were very glad to have such high-paying jobs. In the States, with about twenty percent unemployment, $100.00 a month was a good salary, and the majority of those employed did not make that much. So, even with the dust, sand, heat and humidity associated with field mapping in Saudi Arabia, the geologists were quite happy with their jobs.

On top of having jobs, they knew they were the forerunners of a great adventure and each had a chance to be the initial and key link in a chain resulting in a truly magnificent discovery. Such a discovery might be worth more than even the recently discovered East Texas Field, maybe the largest in the United States, with possibly 4.5 billion barrels of oil. Such heady adventure would breed excitement in anyone.

(As would be later learned, East Texas Field, with nearly 6 billion barrels of oil, would indeed be the largest U. S. field until Alaska's Prudhoe Bay Field was discovered some 35 years later.)

~ ~ ~ ~ ~ ~ ~ ~ ~ ~ ~ ~ ~ ~

CHAPTER 8

Cairo

Vacation time! It was now Friday, July 12, 1935 and JJ's six weeks vacation started tomorrow. He had learned that the large airplane they occasionally saw in the air above Jubail was an Imperial Airways flight between Bahrain and Baghdad, Iraq. Several weeks earlier, he checked his money and decided the experience was worth the cost to try this new travel mode rather than the conventional ship, rail, and car transportation. Such travel was furnished by CASOC for the field geologists to and from a summer "headquarters" in the Metropole Hotel in Beirut, Lebanon. But after much consideration, JJ had decided to try the air travel and Cairo, at his own expense, and obtained permission from the District Geologist, Bert Miller, to do so.

Huey had decided he didn't want to spend the extra money to take the air travel, so he arranged his summer vacation in Beirut, but a bit later than the first group of geologists because of his planned visit to Palestine and Jerusalem first.

Burke was to travel in the normal manner by company launch from Jubail to Bahrain. Then, he had arranged passage on that recently inaugurated flight from Bahrain to Baghdad where he could travel by train and auto to Cairo. Then he planned to arrange passage on a vessel up the Nile to visit the Egyptian ruins above Aswan, then return by way of Beirut to Jubail. It was an ambitious plan, but he wanted to take advantage of any free time in this part of the world to see sights that he might never have the opportunity to see again.

JJ left Jubail early Saturday morning on the company boat to Bahrain, and boarded the Imperial Airways plane the next morning for Baghdad. The plane was a large airship with two wings, an unusual tail, and a fuselage he judged to be about fifty feet long and about seven feet across. The lower wing came into the fuselage about midway from fuselage top to bottom, and the much larger upper wing was well above the fuselage. The wings were tied together with struts and bracing and two large engines with four-blade propellers were mounted at the center of the upper wing. The tail was composed of three vertical stabilizer-rudders and two horizontal stabilizer-elevators.

He hoped it would fly!

With a mighty roar of engines, the airplane gained speed down the runway and finally became airborne, not too gracefully, but nonetheless airborne. JJ was on his way.

Within the last year, air travel had become the desired way to travel in the Mideast. Flights could now be made connecting Bahrain, Baghdad, Damascus, Cairo, and to western Europe. In this area the main two airlines were Imperial Airways and Air France. There were still many limitations wrought by weather, aircraft availability, personnel, and most of all, maintenance. In the desert areas, blowing sand was a significant source of engine problems, and good mechanics were not always available where needed. Still, air travel was clearly the coming way to travel in this region of poor or no roads and limited railways.

Most of the field geologists went to Beirut, Lebanon, for the summer vacation and limited work periods aimed at assimilation of their field notes and sketches into more meaningful maps and reports. Soak Hoover, Krug Henry, and Hugh Burchfiel left on Saturday, June 30, 1935, traveling the conventional company arranged way. Their route had been from Jubail to Bahrain by launch, then aboard the S. S. Baroda from Bahrain harbor to Magil, Iraq to board a train to Baghdad.

The S. S. Baroda made several port calls on the way and took five days of rather informal travel before sailing through Shatt Al Arab, formed by the confluence of the Tigris and Euphrates rivers just north of Kuwait. Then on the morning of the sixth day, Soak, Krug and Hugh settled in at the rest house of Iraq Railways at Magil. Here, after their long months away from a modern world, they enjoyed the view of nice homes, acacia trees, and good food offered at Magil. Early the next morning, they boarded a train to Baghdad, where they stayed in the Maude Hotel. Here they were exposed to a truly international atmosphere. They saw French, British, Japanese, and German visitors, most on business of several varieties. Although not fully modern by European standards, Baghdad was an international center, with all the food, comfort, and entertainment facilities associated with great cities.

The Beirut group took nearly 24 hours to travel by auto from

Baghdad almost due west across the desert to Damascus, Syria. Not bad, considering the mainly sand and gravel trails and roads and 460 miles, or 765 km distance. They checked in at the Orient Palace Hotel, and then after a shower to remove the desert dust, and lunch, they motored on to Beirut. From Damascus, it took slightly over an hour to travel the approximate fifty miles, or about 83 km, mostly through rather mountainous terrain, to the Metropole Hotel in Beirut.

Soak, Krug Henry, Krug's wife Annette, the former Mlle. Rabin from France who Krug had met and married the previous summer in Beirut, spent the next six weeks in the Beirut area. Then, they went separate ways sight-seeing until the return of the geologists to Jubail in mid-September.

(CASOC geologist J. W. (Soak) Hoover actually made this Jubail to Beirut trip in July, 1935)

- - - - - - -

Meanwhile, Burke arrived in one piece in Baghdad, where after an overnite stay he boarded an Air France flight to Cairo. He had booked a room in the Victoria Hotel. Since these were his first flights, JJ was thrilled by the sights of the Gulf, the rivers, roads, and countryside from the air. He spent all his time aboard the aircraft trying to keep oriented for location, and did rather well until about an hour out of Baghdad where he lost all sense of location.

Of significant interest, he could see so well the evidences of past civilizations. Most outstanding were the different soil colors outlining numerous ancient irrigation fields. Also, vague patterns portrayed homes, villages, even cities, long since forgotten. When viewing these signs of high culture as much as six thousand years earlier, JJ felt quite humble, and also imbued with a new sense of respect for the people of the region, some of whom must be descendants of these early innovators and inventors. It took him two days to cover the same distance requiring nearly two weeks by surface travel.

He arrived in Cairo in mid-afternoon, and was met by a bus from the Victoria Hotel that took him straight to the hotel. There was so much to do, and so little time to do it! However, he was grateful that he had two months, instead of a normal stateside two weeks, vacation.

As he showered and dressed he began to think about his plans. It was about an hour by auto to the Suez Canal which he wanted to inspect, and about two hours north to Alexandria on the Mediterranean. Also, there was a Ford Agency in Cairo and he wanted to see the latest model as well as what cars were shipped overseas at what cost.

The next few hours were spent exploring the hotel and its vicinity. Nothing particularly unexpected, but all quite different than Houston! The evening meal was good, and since everything looked so elegant, he felt safe drinking water in the hotel dining room; hopefully he would be correct. In many places, it was much better to drink wine, coffee, or tea so as to avoid the "trots."

Cairo, Egypt, on the River Nile, is credited with having been founded in 969 A.D. by the conquering Tunisian General Jauhar. Actually, it was only 14 miles north of the ruins of Memphis. Earlier villages in the area had been occupied so far into antiquity that no record exists as to the real founding of a first "city."

The city of Memphis is reported to have been established as capital of Egypt by its first king, King Menes, about 3100 B.C., and shortly became a major center with huge granite temples, large stone buildings, and a well-developed culture.

The city had its origins much earlier and grew around the point from which to the north the river had developed many courses over the past several million years as the river built the Nile Delta out into the Mediterranean. This was the point at which the vessels from the sea would reach the Nile, regardless of the course used. It was a natural place for a large city to develop. For millennia, it was the point through which all river traffic passed between the sea and points upriver past Thebes, near present Qena, all the way to Khartoum, some 1,500 miles inland at the confluence of the Blue and White Niles, and even beyond.

Only after Alexander the Great of Macedonia founded Alexandria on the sea in the fourth century B.C. did Memphis lose a large part of its seaport setting. By that time it was not only a port, but was a crossroads of the Arab world. Memphis was destroyed by

Arabs in the seventh century A.D., and was not commonly known to have existed at the time Cairo was founded some three centuries later.

The first order of business for JJ was to make a trip to a dentist of all things. During the last few months he had developed several cavities, when he had hardly been so troubled in the past. After examination, and learning where JJ had been, the dentist informed him that he probably had developed incipient cavities over the last several years. But a good part of the reason for the cavities showing up at this time had been a recent lack of calcium in his diet. That made sense. JJ normally drank milk, and ate calcium-high fruits, but in Saudi Arabia, milk to which he was accustomed, cow's milk, was not to be had, and he had not learned to like camel and goat milk. As for fruits, only canned peaches and pears were readily available, along with dates now and then. He determined to correct this diet factor in the future, one way or another.

With new teeth fillings, JJ arranged for a trip to Suez on the canal the next day. Bright and early, off he went. He was impressed with the canal system, but surprised that such a famous waterway was only about 14 feet deep, not nearly deep enough for really large ships. It was about 95 miles long from Port Said on the Mediterranean to Suez on the Gulf of Suez that emptied into the Red Sea to the south. Thinking of that, JJ wondered at the fact that while the Nile River was only a little over 200 miles from the Red Sea not far north of Khartoum, it chose to flow northerly to the Mediterranean Sea over a thousand miles away. The "Suez" canal was considered by Alexander, and possibly by others before that, and it was feasible at that time since it was dug largely into sand. But nothing happened until European capital became available in the nineteenth century.

Although Burke was interested in and wanted to see all he could of ancient Egypt, he also had more mundane desires that could not be furnished in the Saudi desert: New cars! So, the following morning, he determined where the Ford Agency was located and took a long leisurely sight-seeing walk to it.

He walked up to the agency, housed in a brick and plaster building with rather modest windows through which passersby could not easily see the treasures within. JJ entered, looked around, and a two-door roadster caught his eye. He had seen Fords similar to this in Houston, but this one was more streamlined, and had long vented hood panels with the narrow vents slanted to the rear top to bottom. It gave the vehicle a racy look. The hood on the left side was raised and doubled over to permit a view of the engine. Ford had come out with the first V-8 engine only a year or two earlier, and by now had a powerful and reliable prime mover.

As JJ walked over, a well-dressed Arab stepped up, "Hello *Sayyid*, you are British?"

"No, American," answered JJ, "and I think you have a real beauty here."

"We think so. We also think many others like it, but unfortunately there are many more who like it than can buy it! It is interesting that an American would come to our showroom the same day our American agent is here. Perhaps you would like to meet her?"

"Her? You mean you have a woman agent this far from home?"

"Oh, yes *Sayyid*, and also one who is both...what you say...knows the business, and catches the eye as well. To an Arab, this is very unusual, but if Ford wants to send a woman, we are grateful it is this one."

At times, it was a little difficult for JJ to understand what the man was saying because of the rather heavy accent, but the message came through.

JJ asked, "Where is this lady?"

"Ah," replied the salesman, "there she is now, over near that small truck."

Looking in the direction the salesman waved, JJ saw a woman in a business suit, with short dark hair, leaning away from him and looking into the cab of the pickup. He thought, could it be? No, it couldn't be. Not this far from New York. But it looks like her...I'll walk a little closer..."Thank you," he said to the salesman, "I believe I will say hello to my fellow American."

"It is most unusual the way American men go up to a strange woman. It could never happen with an Arab girl," murmured the Arab.

"I know, I know," said JJ. "It is just a difference in our customs. I guess either of us could learn the other's ways if we had to. Anyway, thanks for showing me this lovely car. Maybe someday I will buy one!"

JJ walked toward the young woman, being careful to walk in a direction such that if she turned, she would not easily see him. As he walked closer, he knew...yes, 'tis she. Without a doubt, that's the hair, the neckline, the shoulders. He was so confident, he walked up, tapped her on the shoulder, and said, "been to Penn Station lately?"

"What, Penn..." as she turned, "JJ, oh, JJ, oh how marvelous, JJ, it is wonderful...you, here, of all people..."

"I know, you too are an absolutely incredible sight for these surprised eyes...I could not believe it was you, Suzy, but I decided I had to check, and as I walked closer, I knew only you could have that trim dark bobbed hair atop such an attractive carriage!"

"JJ, I have never been so delighted with anything in my life. To think that I would find a friend in this far corner of the world, and a special friend at that...how...I knew you were in Saudi Arabia, but you never mentioned coming here in your letters. It never occurred to me that you would stray this far from your work area."

"Well, on the other side of the coin, I think if you had mentioned your travels to this part of the world in your letters, I would have made a point of meeting you."

"Regardless, my big green eyes, here we are! Both in the same place, thank God! The reason I didn't mention my coming here, is because I had no idea I was coming until two weeks ago. Our regular agent for Cairo was on vacation, and a shipment of several vehicles was damaged while being moved from the ship to this dealer, and my boss decided he'd take a chance with this little gal going to get the story. That pickup is one of the vehicles damaged...see the dent in the door and fender?"

"Yep," answered JJ, "and regardless of circumstance, I, like you, have never been more delighted to see anyone. When will you be free to leave here? Could you have lunch with me?"

"Sure can," said Suzanne Stuart, export agent from New York, "In fact, let me make a few notes on a bill of lading and we'll leave right away! What a great surprise!"

So, a little later, they left in search of an interesting place to have lunch. They found such a place in a restaurant with a courtyard-like area overlooking the Nile, where they could watch the river traffic as they had lunch.

"I don't think I was ever so shocked as when I heard this familiar sounding voice say '...Penn Station,' and just as I was turning, I had an instantaneous thought...'Penn Station...JJ'...and then, there you were," spoke Suzanne in a quiet but happy voice.

JJ: "Isn't is great? Now, the next thought that occurs to me is what are your plans for the next few days, few weeks?"

"I had already been thinking about that," answered Suzanne with a little building excitement as she talked, "And hoped you might bring it up. You see, I knew that since my trip over here was as a replacement, I could not count on doing it again anytime soon, so I arranged to take my vacation while I was over here!"

"Marvelous! Would you be interested in a trip up the Nile to see a bit of Egypt past?"

"I had already planned on it!"

"Well then, the only thing left to do is arrange a trip."

With a faked haughtiness, Suzanne: "Mr. Burke, what kind of girl do you think I am? Do you think I would come all the way over here without getting information together regarding a boat trip?"

JJ: "I did!"

"Yes, but men tend to blunder about a little while we efficient gals plan ahead."

"Alright, smarty, tell me about it."

And she did. Suzanne was booked in another hotel a few blocks from JJ, and after their lunch, they returned there briefly so that she could hand JJ her notes and pamphlets on Nile River travel. Then she returned to work for the afternoon while JJ studied the river trip.

It seemed that there would be a few days delay before a particular eight-day river cruise was available. This cruise visited many of the ruins, including one ancient village that had been restored to show things pretty well as they were in the second millennia B.C. Also, Suzanne's work required that she spend the rest of this week cataloging vehicle damage and ascertaining details of the accident, corroborated by local police.

Her work would be finished by Saturday, and her extended two weeks vacation was to start Monday. Her schedule required that she board the S. S. Excalibur at Alexandria on Thursday, August 8, 1935, for France, wherefrom she would return to New York. So, their planning had to work within that schedule and it was now Thursday, July 18th. The cruise they planned was to start July 29 and end August 6th.

For the next two days JJ and Suzanne had most meals

together, but with her job requirements, there was little time for anything more. He continued sight-seeing and made an extended museum visit to see the relics of ancient Egypt and learn more about it. While at the museum, by reading and visiting with an Egyptian curator, he learned substantially more than he knew about the up-river Egyptian history.

The following Monday was the first day of their joint vacation time together. They spent one full day traveling out to, studying, and returning from, the pyramids west of the river valley in the desert. That evening, they returned exhausted, and went to their respective rooms without even dinner together. But the next day they made up for lost time!

They met for a late breakfast, visited the museum together, lunched, rested in the afternoon in their hotels, then met for dinner at their now favorite restaurant with the open courtyard overlooking the Nile. They had a lovely meal together, took a horse and coach ride in the late evening through the streets of this crossroads of the ancient and present world, then on to her hotel for a nightcap and goodnight.

They sat together in the hotel bar sipping cognac and liqueur and discussing their times together, beginning with the train en route to New York. Shortly after midnight, JJ took Suzanne by the hand, said "Well, all good days have to end sometime, and I guess we're gettin' pretty close to the end of this one."

"Such a good one should never end," murmured Suzanne, "but I suppose the reality is that it is about to end; in fact, we're already underway on the next good day!"

Together they strolled over to the wide, carpeted staircase, then slowly up the stairs to the second floor and down the hall to her room. At the door, JJ tenderly pulled Suzanne close, held her in his arms for a few moments while he drank in the beauty of this lovely female whose beauty and softness were enhanced by the low hall lights. Then he slowly kissed her full on the lips, lightly, followed by several more light kisses, and then they passionately embraced and kissed for the next several moments. Finally, JJ gently pushed Suzanne back, said "Honey, I simply can't take any more of this without a great deal more happening," and started to walk away.

Suzanne grasped his arm: "I understand what you say, what you mean, and have a great deal of respect for what you do."

And with that, they parted for the night, to undertake new adventure the next day!

The next day over lunch, Suzanne described some of the other Ford Agencies in the Mideast, and in particular the one in Jiddah, Saudi Arabia. This agency was founded by John B. Philby in 1930. The same Philby who was one of the early explorers of Saudi Arabia, who wrote about it, who was converted to Islam in 1930, and who was a good friend and trusted advisor to King Ibn Sa'ud. She described what she knew of Philby, and JJ did the same. Together they pieced together a fairly good biography of this rather remarkable man without whom SOCAL would have had considerably more trouble making their deal to explore Saudi Arabia for petroleum. Philby's extensive knowledge of Saudi Arabia and the politics of both Saudi Arabia and Great Britain made him a unique arbiter for any Saudi-Western relationships.

As soon as Suzanne mentioned Philby, JJ interrupted, "I know of Philby," and went on to describe Philby's Saudi exploration, writings and position with the King. They discussed their jobs, the objectives, difficulties, and so on, and finally got around to a discussion of their river voyage the next week.

The next three days went by like a breeze as they explored the Great Pyramid of Giza, along with the other pyramids, then the ancient Sphinx, and the museum again to learn more about what they had seen.

Of unusual interest was the Sphinx. Although the date of construction was unknown, it was accepted by most archeologists to date to the third millennium B.C. However, during their tour, JJ noted some erosion patterns in the bedrock that formed its base that seemed inconsistent with that age, at least as far as the base was concerned. He pointed these out to Suzanne and commented, "I'd guess the base of this magnificent structure was initially carved several thousand years before 2500 B.C. But then, what do I know?" And so ended this possible conflict of geology and archeology.

It was a glorious whirl of events, of laughter, awe, wonder, and a great deal of affection. They visited more of Cairo, went to Suez and the canal again, ate often, and especially enjoyed the evening carriage rides together. And, they found it easier and easier to lovingly caress, "accidently" bump, and have passionate goodnights, and harder and harder to not simply use one room at night.

They also found time to study Egyptian history and the river lands they were about to see.

They had arranged passage on a sizeable riverboat that transported goods as well as tourists, but that was mainly designed for tourists with perhaps two dozen staterooms, a pleasant but rather small dining room, two coffee/tea bars, and limited deck seating areas covered with white canvas for shade from the penetrating sun.

Going upriver to the south was slow, with an average trip speed of less than ten miles per hour against the current. Coming back, with the river current, much better time would be made.

This particular trip was scheduled to go to the town of Aswan and dock for two full days. During that time, guests could investigate the ancient ruins at Aswan, or take a smaller vessel about three and a half miles upriver to the recently modified dam across the Nile. Then another small boat could be taken in the lake behindthe dam upriver a mile and a half to explore the First Cataract. The Aswan Dam had been constructed over thirty years earlier, and modified and enlarged since then, the last work being done in 1934.

From the Second Cataract, tourists who wished to go still farther could take another small vessel and travel some 175 miles upriver from Aswan, to a terminal point at Abu Simbel.

To Aswan, the voyage covered over 450 miles by river, and took nearly three full days. A remaining trip upriver to Abu Simbel took at least two full days, and it was a litle close geting back to Aswan in time to board the main vessel for return to Cairo, arriving there around noon of the eighth day after departure.

The trip upriver was a voyage back in time. At ancient Egypt's maximum, the New Kingdom in the eleventh century B.C., occupied the region from the Red Sea to a western boundary about 100 miles west of and approximately paralleling the Nile. This New Kingdom had a southern boundary just south of the great bend in the river near Napata, an Egyptian customs post established in the fifteenth century B.C. within the ancient Kingdom of Kush. Napata is about 125 miles north-northwest as a crow could fly from Khartoum. Over a distance of about 175 miles, the Nile flows southwesterly through the area of Napata.

In the eighth century B.C., the black Kushites drove northward into the declining Egyptian empire and for a few decades occupied all of the ancient Egyptian kingdom. During and after that period, the Kushites, who had already largely adopted Egyptian culture, preserved and created new manifestations of that culture in their southern empire. The Kushites were driven out of Egypt by Assyrians in the seventh century, and then the Assyrians were removed and the Kushites driven farther south by Egyptians in the fifth century B.C.

At Giza, just west of Cairo, the greatest of all pyramids was built for Cheops, greatest of the Egyptian Pharaohs in the third millennium B.C. Thus the area of Cairo was the heartland of earliest Egypt, continuously occupied by humans for at least 10,000 years, and probably far longer.

Both JJ and Suzanne were extremely impressed with the antiquity of the Egyptian culture and how it was developed perhaps simultaneously with Mesopotamia of the Tigris-Euphrates river valleys. Both areas had developed to the stage of irrigated farming perhaps eight thousand years before JJ and Suzanne appeared on the scene.

It was in this aura of wonder at ancient culture that they boarded their riverboat on a typical hot and rather muggy Monday morning, July 29th. They were underway very shortly, and they spent the next few hours unpacking in their respective cabins, and exploring the available facilities of the boat. Then, they sat together in the shade on deck and watched the passing scenery for awhile, went back to their cabins to get ready for dinner, then dinner and to bed for the end to a full day.

The next day they settled into a routine of breakfast, visiting together, reading, and a lot of sight-seeing, with ever-recurring ancient ruins and several towns along the way to intrigue and hold their interest. They spent most of the afternoon and early evening of the second day at the ruins of Thebes and partly overlying Karnak, near the modern city of Qena. The big event of the third day would be the splendor and wonder of the ruins of Luxor.

After dinner that evening, they strolled arm in arm up on deck to observe the clear night sky and compare their knowledge of constellations. JJ had the upper hand: He had obtained an astronomy merit badge as a Boy Scout!

Both were dressed casually but neat. JJ wore a loose white shirt and dark blue trousers. Suzanne wore a loose white blouse with yellow and light blue flowers, puffed sleeves, high but open collar, and a little lace on the front. Her skirt was full and fluffy, white with dark blue trim, and struck her just below the knees. JJ thought she was extremely feminine and could hardly wait for the goodnight kiss.

It was nearly eleven PM when they slowly arose and walked back inside, then down the hallway to Suzanne's room. "Here we are again, and 'tis time for goodnight," said JJ. And with that he started to pull Suzanne close for a kiss when another couple came down the hall. They spoke to the other couple who soon disappeared into their room.

"This is no place for a goodnight," muttered JJ, "Let's get out of the traffic." With that he took Suzanne's arm, opened her cabin door, and they both entered. "This is more like it," he said as he again took her in his arms, kissed her lightly on the lips, and then lost control of his hands which suddenly developed a mind of their own.

Both hands dropped down to Suzanne's hips, then loosened her blouse, and slid inside on her soft, smooth and warm skin, then in one continuing movement, up to her bosom where each hand found a full and soft breast to gently grasp. But the brassiere was in the way.

His hands slowly slid around her feminine chest inside her blouse to the clasp at the rear which, after a few moments fumbling, he opened and pulled the brassiere loose. Then back to the front with both hands to the warm, full, and most exciting breasts for one overfilled handful each.

All the while, they had been passionately kissing, and Suzanne had not interrupted JJ's exploration. But now she gently pulled back and whispered, "JJ, not now...I can't."

Feeling like he had been hit in the face with a bucket of water, JJ asked the perennial male question, "Why? Have I been too aggressive, too rough, or is there something else?"

Softly, Suzanne replied, "It is not you, JJ, it is me. There are times when a girl has no choice but to limit her desires."

"Oh...is it the wrong time of the month?"

"Yes," she answered in a small voice.

So ended the second day of the cruise.

The next day, the ruins of Luxor held their attention, but the previous night kept recurring to both. It somehow seemed unusually romantic to have such intimacy in this world of old, to be surrounded by majesty of the past while feeling drives more ancient than even these incredible monuments to talents and abilities that had been lost for so long after Egypt declined.

That evening after dinner and their evening on the cool deck which they looked forward to each day, and knew they would never forget, they again returned to Suzanne's cabin for goodnight.

After a long and passionate kiss, Suzanne slowly pulled back and whispered, ever so softly, "The bad time has gone..."

With that, JJ said, "I believe I understand..." and then passion and the natural drives of a man and woman at their sexual prime came upon the scene and conquered all else....

- - - - - - -

The remainder of their trip took on a new central theme, but at the same time became a most memorable romance among the many symbols of ancient greatness. They needed only one cabin for the last five nights. At the same time, they were filled with joy and warmth wrought by their new-found love, the scenes of the past, the starlit nights, the rocking movement of the boats, and being together.

All too soon, they were moving rapidly back downriver toward the end of this voyage into paradise, and the beginning of a new reality.

They disembarked as planned on Tuesday, August 6th, returned to their hotels, and had two more days filled with joy, love, and, at times, passion, before the sad parting that had to come.
Thursday morning, August 8th, JJ and Suzanne boarded the bus to Alexandria. It took most of the day to get there, find and get to the dock area and hand Suzanne's luggage to ship personnel.

They found a horse-drawn carriage rental agency near her ship's dock, and decided they had just enough time for one good carriage ride scheduled for a little over two hours. The driver helped them get seated with two other ship's passengers in the long, softly sprung carraige, then with a light clicking of his tongue to the large mare hitched to the carriage's single tree, they moved out. To explore this monument to Alexander the Great. All too soon came the late-afternoon when Suzanne had to board the S. S. Excalibur. Long before either of them had time to see more than a smattering of this busy and ancient city. JJ was allowed to come aboard to help her get settled. Then in her cabin, they had one last longing kiss of parting. They slowly returned to the deck, held hands to the last moment at which JJ had to disembark, then he broke loose and walked down the gangplank with an overwhelming sense of loneliness.

As the ship slowly moved away from the dock, they both put on smiles that belied their inner feeling, and waved until Suzanne had slowly disappeared into the distance as the ship moved out into the Mediterranean....

- - - - - - -

For the next few days, JJ had a tremendous sense of loneliness and longing, and it was extremely difficult to plan the next few weeks before the return to Jubail and the reality of his world of geology.

Of course, Suzanne was undergoing the same emotions, and having an even more trying time because the work she returned to was much more mundane than the exciting exploration for treasures in Saudi Arabia.

Even so, they both did manage to continue their existence, and slowly returned to reality. Suzanne spent her recovery period traveling by ship, train, and ship again to New York. Meanwhile, JJ traveled by train, bus, and auto from Cairo to Beirut and the Palace Hotel. Here, JJ met several of the other geologists, and mainly, old big red-headed Huey Larsh, who he was quite happy to see.

JJ, sometimes alone, sometimes with one of the other geologists, but most often with Huey, explored the beautiful ancient city of Beirut overlooking the Mediterranean and backed up by mountains to the south and east. Lebanon was a French Mandate and had been so since the end of the World War. But, since 1926, it was a republic with considerable self-government.

This general area, between the sea and Damascus, which lay barely fifty miles east-southeast, was indeed one of, if not the, most beautiful areas of the Mideast. What with the cool mountains, limited forests, more abundant vegetation, ancient ruins, and the beautiful sea, against the background of modern buildings, hotels, and city life, this region of two great cities provided an atmosphere of beauty and comfort not to be found elsewhere in the Arabian peninsula. That was why it had been picked as the main summering place for the field geologists.

Sunday, September 1, 1935. JJ and Huey left Beirut for the Orient Palace Hotel in Damascus. They spent most of the week in this lovely old city known for its high-quality steel, then on Thursday, began the trip back to Jubail. First, by auto to Baghdad, then train to Basra, then ship to Bahrain and finally, company launch to docks near Dhahran and the old familiar Ford touring car to the company quarters at Jubail.

The summer vacation was over.

~ ~ ~ ~ ~ ~ ~ ~ ~ ~ ~ ~ ~ ~

CHAPTER 9

Harmaliyah

Tuesday, October 8, 1935. A blustery wind out of the north brought loads of sand and dust through the partly sheltered tents, and the main occupation of all was to try to breathe and protect everything. Maps, instruments, beds, clothing, and most of all, lungs. Human lungs. The camels had their own protection, developed over the eons. Visibility ranged from almost nothing up to a few hundred feet between sheets of sand. The sand got into everything that wasn't canned or sealed. Canvas and cloth covers partially protected some of the data and gear; neckerchiefs did a pretty good job of cleaning the air breathed.

Larsh and Burke had moved into Camp Harmaliyah two weeks earlier from Jubail, at a location about 30 kilometers northeast of Harad, and very close to one occupied by Soak Hoover and Krug Henry in May and June. There were numerous *jibehl* in the area with a lot of opportunity for sectioning and some structural work. They had the earlier work by Soak and Krug, and the idea was to expand it.

While subsisting during the sandstorm, JJ and Huey occupied themselves reading various reports, including reports on Dammam #1. In the five months since the well spudded, it had made it to a depth of nearly 2000". This was getting pretty close to the limit of the cable tool rig and, if it was to be taken much deeper, it would be necessary to move in a rotary rig. Knowing that additional wells would be drilled, it was understood that such a rig was forthcoming. In drilling #1, it had been necessary to use casing in part of the hole while drilling in order to protect against caving from part of the shale that had been penetrated. The casing was suspended from the calf wheel on a steel cable.

During the summer, the air photos had been processed to form a few rough mosaics that served quite well as detail maps as far as roads, trails, other cultural, and topographic features were concerned. Such mosaics did not establish elevations, rock dips, or rock age, but did show some useful geologic features. In particular, the mosaics showed lineaments that were often invisible from the ground, but after seeing it on the air photo, was often identifiable on the ground as a fault or fracture. Also, when drainage patterns were compared to rock outcrops, gentle dips could sometimes be indicated that were not readily apparent on the ground.

For example, if on an air photo a rock outcrop could be seen to gradually disappear into the sandy surface in a certain direction, and a nearby wadi was aligned in the same direction and draining into a larger wadi, then most likely that rock bed was dipping in that same direction. These clues, along with lineaments, outcrops, jebehl, and other features allowed the surface geology to be mapped much more rapidly than in days before such photos. Often, possible dips were marked on the photos, and then confirmed on the ground.

Another technique that was discerned early on, was the effect of three dimensional relief that could be created by stereo observation of overlapping pairs of air photos taken from different aircraft positions. Some of the geologists found the ability to hold up two such photos in front of their eyes while looking at a point beyond the photos and suddenly see the topography leap out in three dimensions. Such procedures were not universally usable, but it showed the desirability of stereo lenses for such viewing, and such lenses were forthcoming.

Both JJ and Huey were aware of the old stereo holders that had been sold in the States for decades to view interesting pictures. JJ had used such stereo holders and photos to see many World War battle scenes. He had such a holder sent to him from home, then he and Huey got extra copies of the overlapping air photos, cut them to fit the holders, then clearly saw the topography in three dimensions. This proved quite helpful in identifying probable dips, faults, and other geologic parameters.

Late one dusty afternoon while returning to camp, Huey spotted an outcrop at the bottom of a wadi he was crossing. He got out, chipped off a piece of the rock, touched it with a drop of 15% HCl acid he had in a small bottle and saw it fizz slowly. Clearly carbonate, but probably dolomitic. Then with his hand lens, he found fossil shell outlines in the somewhat chalky limestone. This rock was unlike the other limestones they had measured in the Harmaliyah area, and he thought it might be an inlier of older rock. Such a feature would be quite significant. He hurried to camp to get JJ and a plane table.

"Burke, we may have something about four miles north of here," spoke Huey as he got out of the car. "Let's take the alidade back out there and see if we can get a three-point for dip, if you agree with me that it is probably an inlier."

"I've been waitin' for something worthwhile," replied JJ, "and just maybe you've stumbled onto it!"

"Hell, I didn't stumble one bit. I got out of the car, and with my trusty hammer busted a piece off and professionally studied it! I'm a geologist, hombre, a professional. How dare you imply I stumble?!"

"Ain't that difficult, you just say 'you've stumbled,' and git on with it! Anyway, stumble or no, we go!"

About an hour later, after both of them had looked at fragments from the outcrop Huey had found, JJ said, "I think you're right, Huey, these look like Nummulites shell fragments, and the limestone seems dolomitic. The mollusks look kinda like those we saw last spring out of Udayliyah. May be Eocene, sure not the Miocene rocks we've been working."

"Yeah," returned Huey, "and did you notice there seems to be a little gravel up the slope above this bed?"

"I hadn't noticed, but I see now what you mean up there. One thing for sure: It's an inlier. Eocene or not, it's older, and we're standing on some kind of uplift because we're in older rock but we're not any higher than that Miocene stuff we've been working over yonder," said JJ as he pointed back to the southwest.

Over the next hour or so, they traced the rock through five small outcrops in two wadis about a kilometer apart. They set the plane table and alidade up on a slight rise and JJ took off with the rod while Huey ran the "gun." JJ set the rod on the five outcrops, one after another, while Huey shot them in, then clambered across the rocky terrain back to Huey.

"What's it look like?"

Larsh: "That third outcrop surely isn't the same bed; it's too high. It has to be another bed. But the other four shots are pretty flat, but distinctly dipping westerly. Looks like we got something."

As in the past, they had found an anomaly, but could not be sure if it would turn out to be an anticlinal fold. For the next few weeks, they searched the area for outcrops, measured some sections, and took a few more plane table dips as well as rough dips with the

Brunton compass. All they could be sure of was that there was an uplift of some sort. They could not determine the amount of closure or the shape. Detailing the structure would have to await core drilling, gravity, or seismic.

The work continued as winter started and wore on. Occasionally a rain shower broke the monotony of winds and dust. The nights were downright cold and they lowered the tent flaps and tied them down against the wind. During the days, temperatures commonly climbed into the sixties, and sometimes the eighties.

At night, it occasionally dropped down near freezing, but most often was in the forties.

One of their jobs was to shoot in Polaris in the different localities so as to establish their latitude, which could be done rather precisely, knowing the time and the fixed position of Polaris at any given latitude for a given time. It was simply a matter of measuring the elevation of Polaris and consulting tables for that elevation at that time. Longitude was an entirely different matter, and was much more difficult for them to establish with accuracy. But again, measuring the elevations of certain stars of the Zodiac, then entering those elevations and the time into tables gave a fair approximation for the established latitude.

At the same time of shooting Polaris, they could measure its deviation from magnetic north by transit compass and thus establish local magnetic declination from true north. A grid of such measurements would serve to define a true declination for future use, and with such measurements over a period of years, establish annual magnetic drift as well.

For occasional breaks, the geologists went into a *soukh*, or bazaar, in Hofuf to shop, and sometimes to visit with local Bedouins over coffee. Such visits were not frequent, but were always interesting, and often educational as the Americans soaked up more and more of the Saudi culture. In addition to some food items, always dates, and occasional clothing articles, the geologists acquired local hand-made boots that were durable as well as comfortable.

In mid-December, Burke and Larsh learned that the well-respected surface geologist, Max Steineke, was mapping with Tom Koch in the Hofuf and Harad areas. In their En Nala area they had mapped an anticlinal axis trending slightly east of due north and felt sure that they were onto something big. This axis, or crest of up-folded rocks, was just east of the area in which Larsh and Burke had earlier found anomalous west dips near a possible inlier they had mapped out of the Udayliyah camp. Steineke put together the work he and Koch had done with earlier work by the various teams to make a firm declaration of such an axis.

In November, 1935, J. W. "Soak" Hoover and T. F. Harriss saw evidence that may have been associated with the En Nala trend.

> (To quote Soak Hoover: "Harriss and I took a trip over to Jebel Dam, Tuesday, November 26, 1935, climbed to its summit and looked until our eyes hurt. The Khashm at Dam seems to form a structural nose, plunging slightly to the N.E. The plateau behind the Jebel is capped by...gravels.")

At this time all the geologists felt they were onto something big because of the numerous anomalous dips, and some possibly older rocks outcropping in some areas. But it was still not clear whether they were dealing with a large anticline that could trap oil, or if it was simply a structural ridge without specific trapping closure for oil. At least the anticlinal axis had a name: "En Nala."

One day, Larsh and Burke drove out of their camp and headed for the Uthmaniyah area some twenty miles northwest. As they approached the area, JJ commented: "Huey, why do you suppose that plateau up there manages to survive when all of the same rock all around has been eroded away?"

"Beats me. Maybe it's got some chert in it, or something like that. Wanta go look?"

"You bet. Let's do it."

Actually, the plateau was relatively low as plateaus go, not more than a few dozen feet high in much of the area. However, it was prominent and was surely there for some reason. They stopped the car, climbed out and climbed up the slope to the rock outcropping at the top. Clambering along, they took repeated samples with their hammers, testing with acid and looking with their hand lenses.

"Just looks like more Miocene limestone to me," said Huey.

"Yeah, but did you notice how most of it almost explodes

when the acid hits it? Seems mighty pure carbonate, not much else in it."

Larsh: "Well, I don't see any siliceous evidence, no metal left after scratching with my knife, and looks like a good limestone. Maybe it's here because of carbonate enrichment?"

Burke: "I suppose that's as good a guess as any. But how is another question. Do you suppose it overlies a large high, and was so during deposition of the bed with the water depth such that more shellfish lived in this area than in the deeper waters to each side?"

"Sounds like a good theory to me. Let's assume it's true until something else comes by, to see if we can find geology that agrees."

"Okay. We'll do that."

(And such was to prove to be the case: This dissected resistant limestone plateau overlies a part of the giant Ghawar structure)

The geologists walked and drove around the area for the next few hours, taking notes, dips, and sketching the plateau shape. It was cut by wadis and fractures, creating an overall appearance of a plateau from which slices had been removed, then roughed up by later wind, sand, and rain.

They noted that although the area was not covered with sand, the current wind and dust made it clear that a lot of sand moved through the air. The resistant plateau limestone was not much affected by the winds and sand, but the rounded surfaces here and there indicated there had been some erosion.

Most of the erosion of this bed in the surrounding areas and the dissections had probably occurred during the heavier rainfall periods starting some few thousand years earlier and recurring intermittently for the previous few million years.It surely had not been effectively eroded during the thousands of years of human habitation in the area.

Geologists noted that this general area was similar to most of the other areas they had worked; generally rocky, some sand in leeward wind traps, no clear erosional patterns, vegetation consisting largely of small, wind-resistant shrubs, and no water at all anywhere, except...straight down, in several aquifers.

The normal drainage patterns of tributaries draining into creeks, into rivers, and so on, were absent. So little water fell that it sank into the porous rocks, then into fractures, on downward to aquifers, or evaporated. It usually travelled short distances on the surface, though sometimes in a brief torrent down a local wadi.

During the late fall and early winter, one of JJ's continuing interests, rarely completely off his mind, was Suzanne. Though they kept the mails alive with their letters, there was no way to talk, and writing often produced a little melancholy, though Huey rarely let JJ stay melancholy about anything very long.

He had learned about the summer romance and how serious it had become, but he tried to lay the humor on thick when JJ got down. JJ regularly wrote letters on a weekly or bi-weekly basis to his family and to Ruthanne, but now he wrote two or three letters each week, although sometimes he was delayed in posting them to the point that often there were a half dozen or more letters to send with the recurring supply or other trips to Jubail. Of course, he got letters in batches also.

~ ~ ~ ~ ~ ~ ~ ~ ~ ~ ~ ~ ~ ~

CHAPTER 10

Haradh II to Udayliyah II

Work was completed in the Harmaliyah area by early December, 1935, and Burke and Larsh had moved their camp twice since then. Their work was much the same in all of the areas; sectioning, describing, sampling, and structural mapping from the mostly small outcrops. Little by little, ghostly structures began to take shape, but always with limited actual measured data. This resulted in a lot of interpretations from limited data, but one large structure seemed to be relatively sure in the Abqaiq area.

It was now mid-April, 1936, and the news from Dammam #1 was pretty old, but interesting. Mainly, it had proved that oil did exist in possible large quantities, but probably deeper or on a larger structure. The well was spudded 4/30/35, reached 2271' on 11/27/35, and a cement plug was set at a total depth of 2372' 1/4/36. This was about the limit of the cable tool rig that had averaged less than 15 feet of hole a day below 500' depth. It created a great deal of excitement when numerous oil flows occurred in limestones below 1700'depth, but none proved to be commercial at this remote location. Such wells would have been quite profitable in the States.

A rotary rig was moved in on #1 a few weeks earlier, and was now about 3200' deep, below the good pay zones in the producing Bahrain field. No apparent commercial pays had yet been encountered in #1. Regardless, several more wells were planned, and the old cable tool rig had been used to spud Dammam #2 in February, 1936. The rotary rig would be moved to #2 as soon as it was released from #1.

(Dammam #2 reached 2135 on 5/11/36, and at that depth, tested 335 BOPD on June 20, and after acid treatment, tested at nearly 4000 BOPD. Again the production decreased rapidly. Finally, Dammam #7, spudded 12/7/36, after many drilling problems, established large and sustainable production at rates approaching 4000 BOPD in March, 1938, from the Arab D limestone at 4727' total depth. This Dammam Field was to prove quite modest compared to later finds.)

In April, 1936, CASOC management spirits were beginning to be dampened by the lack of success in #1, but the geologists were encouraged: There were lots of oil signs. The geologists were by no means downhearted and were quite excited to follow up on additional work in the Harad-Udayliyah trend behind the important and clearly identified Eocene inlier recently found by Max Steineke and Tom Koch. By this time the work by those geologists, along with that of other CASOC geologists, had established the anticlinal axis dubbed *En Nala*. The chase was now on to better define this En Nala anticlinal axis, mapping in the surface Miocene and Pliocene rocks.

The geologists had been cautioned about the very confidential nature of their work. It was recognized that they might find something that could be worth a major fortune, or it was also possible that their efforts would prove completely fruitless. But because of the possibly profound result of their work, they had little to say about it. They talked freely among themselves, but spoke only in broad generalities to outsiders. Even in their correspondence with family and friends, notes, diaries, they said little about what they were finding.

The area around and north of Haradh was becoming more and more interesting to the field geologists. Steineke and Koch had camped near Haradh, not too far from an earlier camp by Huey and JJ. Still, it was desired to try to gather more data from the area, so Huey and JJ had been assigned to again set up camp there, and then move some 100 kilometers north to their old Udayliyah camp for more work in that area.

Huey and JJ moved in and called Haradh II home now. It was their second camp in this general area, and it was just as hot, dusty, rocky, and barren as it was the first time.

They missed trees. There were no trees except in the areas of oases and springs, and many of these were only the small acacias or palms. Except in the oases there was no natural shade except that created by the topography, and during most of the day, when the sun was high in the sky, even that shade was lost.

Much of the area looked strikingly similar to deserts of the American Southwest, except that there was generally less vegetation and no cacti. In all their mapping, neither JJ nor Huey could remember seeing any cactus or prickly pear such as that common in Texas west of the Pecos River. What they did see was a rather repetitive variety of small shrubs and isolated grass plants, usually widely scattered. However, it was almost amazing how fast a flat wadi or sabkha would become verdant after a rain shower. Seed that had been dormant for perhaps years would quickly sprout, and grasses and flowers would develop within days. Of course, this was the basic reason for the nomadic nature of the Bedouins who searched for these food sources for their animals during the winter "rainy season."

Now, in April, the frequent high winds of the late winter and spring had subsided somewhat, and the dust was not a constant irritant. Still, one could count on at least some dust problems every day. But there were pleasant times also, and even though treeless, the desert environment could be strikingly beautiful at times. In the quiet of early morning or late evening, long shadows were cast by the bluffs, sand dunes, the *nigga* (huge sand dunes often hundreds of feet high), buttes, mesas, and *jibehl* of every size and shape.

These shadows, along with the many-hued rocks, and the frequently and dramatically painted sky, created memorable scenes of somewhat stark beauty that could exist only in a desert. So, even though heat and dust were constant irritants, one could protect against these, and there was beauty there for those who observed it.

But, beauty or no, there was work to do. Using the air photos, previous sketches, and observed topographic changes, JJ and Huey searched for ever smaller and more hidden outcrops in the right places to help them better define structural characteristics of this vague En Nala ridge. Even though it was difficult to convey to CASOC management that they were onto something, the geologists knew better. Even though there were sometimes only hints, there were many of them, and all the signs pointed toward some huge northward trending anticlinal ridge on which several oil fields might be found.

Out of their Harmaliyah camp JJ and Huey had found many of the signs of En Nala, such as the inlier, counter-regional dips of the rocks, the dissected plateau, and divergent drainage. The plateau and drainage features indicated an uplift, but not necessarily an anticlinal structure where the inverted bowl shape of the rock layers would form traps for oil resting on water in porous and permeable layers sandwiched between shale or other impermeable layers. The inliers of older rocks also told a geologic story of uplift, but again, not necessarily an anticlinal structure. But the counter-regional dips did indeed indicate anticlinal conditions, and when fitted into the overall picture of uplift and folding, formed an indisputably large elongate high.

Huey rolled off his cot, "Hey, loggerhead, you wanta sleep all your life? We gotta get out and find that En Nala ghost," he said as he looked over at JJ sound asleep. Between themselves, Huey and JJ referred to the vague En Nala structure as "the En Nala ghost," or sometimes, just "the ghost."

Aroused by this raucous sound, JJ turned over, "You need not speak so loudly to such tender ears in the middle of the night."

"Hell, man, we're burnin' daylight, and I'm sorta interested in checking that area in those *jibehl* just north of camp...maybe we can find another exposure or two in the right place."

"Okay," mumbled JJ, "if we must, I guess we must, but food and other things come first."

With that, they both slipped on their khaki trousers, walked out to water the neglected local shrubs, then came back in, washed up with their one bar of soap and pan of water, then went over to the mess tent for breakfast.

After a solid breakfast of eggs, dates, canned ham, bread and lots of coffee, they returned to their tent, put on their bedouin robes and American felt hats, climbed into their Ford touring car and took off across the rocks and sandy trail leading to the north.

This day proved rewarding. They found not one or two, but actually six different outcrop exposures scattered over an area of several miles. Two of the exposures indicated relatively flat-lying beds, but the other four measured west dips ranging from one to three degrees. This was another bit of data to add to En Nala ghost's shape.

When they found an outcrop, it was usually another Miocene-Pliocene sandy marl or sandy limestone, apparently of continental, not marine, depositional origin. This added a major complication to the structural mapping.

Sediments laid down in water tend to lie in sheets, especially if the water is agitated, such as by wave action. If the water is a sea or ocean, such deposits are referred to as "marine." If the water is a lake, the deposits are "lacustrine." Deposits within or by rivers or streams are referred to as "continental" if they are deposited on a land area, but marine or lacustrine if dumped by the river or stream into a large body of water. There are numerous other classifications of sediments and sedimentation, but these are the three broad categories commonly used.

While marine sediments are often of rather uniform thickness over a distance of several hundred feet or more, the beds or layers of continental deposits may be highly variable in thickness, over distances of as little as a few feet. Thus some of the dips observed in continental deposits are depositional and not structural. Most dips measured in marine beds are structural, that is, the underlying beds, on average, dip in the same direction as the observed bed. If several rock exposures are available, a geologist can use multiple, carefully selected surface dip measurements in continental rock layers to ascertain a reliable indication of the dip of deeper layers in the subsurface. It is easier in marine beds. Geologists use the terms "beds," "layers," "strata" interchangeably.

Another aspect of geology important to JJ and Huey was the matter of correlation; the ability to identify that a layer or stratum observed in one place is part of the same stratum as observed in another place. When correlations are good, a series of layers or strata, for example, a limestone with shells overlain by a layer of shale, overlain by a sandstone layer, overlain by a blue marl, would occur in separate outcrops in the same sequence and with the same thicknesses. Continental beds are much more difficult to correlate than marine beds. Herein lay a key problem for the field geologists in eastern Saudi Arabia. Correlations were commonly quite difficult.

A fundamental reason for all the rock section measuring done by the geologists was to search for correlations of rocks found in the scattered and often restricted outcrop exposures. For example, the above mentioned blue marl might also have a particular fossil shell in it, making it highly distinctive. Perhaps at place "A" the elevation of that marl was measured to be fifty feet higher than at place "B," and the correlation was made with a high degree of certainty because there had been no other such marl measured in any rock section tabulated. This would mean that layer dipped fifty feet from place "A" to place "B."

After hundreds of such measurements, along with isolated single dip measurements, observations of topography and drainage patterns, the geologists could piece together the structural picture of the rocks at and near the surface. Unless it is known that deeper unconformities exist, it is reasonable to believe that the surface structure is fairly indicative of the structure several thousand feet into the earth.

An unconformity is a horizon or plane that represents a gap in deposition; that is, a time when no sedimentation occurred, and instead, erosion may have taken place. Thus, at times, beds below the unconformity plane (in outcrops appearing to be a rough line) might dip in one direction, even vertical, while beds above it dip in another direction, perhaps near flat. This would indicate that a series of layers, perhaps several thousand feet thick, had been laid down, then uplifted and folded, then eroded off down to a fairly flat surface, then again covered with layers of sediments.

In early May, JJ and Huey moved their camp north to Udayliyah and dubbed it Udayliyah II since it was the same site they had occupied over a year earlier when they had made friends with the family of Zaki Ahmed Khaled and learned to hunt with falcons.

The field work continued through April and May and into early June, 1936. Then over a period of a few weeks, all the field geologists reported to the Jubail office to compare notes, aggregate their observations, and prepare for the summer vacation. When all the field data collected was compared and correlated, En Nala ghost began to take even more shape.

JJ was to leave for the United States in September after the summer vacation and work session in the cool mountainous Beirut, Lebanon area. But by this time he was enthralled with En Nala ghost and wanted very much to get an overall picture from all the field work before leaving this difficult but intriguing land.

JJ and Huey arrived in Jubail in mid-June, 1936. They spent several days organizing their field work, writing reports and letters, taking regular baths, Insha Allah!, and packing for their coming trips. They also cleaned, re-calibrated, and packed the geologic gear for the next field session's crew that would take their place.

"Huey, look at this," exclaimed JJ. "What do you see?"

It was early one hot July morning in Jubail, a few days before they were to leave for Lebanon, and several days after all the geologists had submitted their work and some had already departed for Beirut.

"Well, a ridge for sure, 'tho the dip boundaries aren't at all clear," replied Huey.

They were poring over a very broad sketch map at a scale of 1:250,000 (about 1" = 4 miles, or 1 cm = 2.5 kilometers) on which they had plotted many of the dips which had at most measured about two to three degrees. Then in the places where there were crop shots (where plane table elevations were taken on the same bed in more than one outcrop), JJ sketched in contours. Then, with notes about the inliers, the topographic plateau and disorganized drainages, he had sketched in rough contours over a very broad area at least ten miles (16.7 km) wide and over a hundred miles long. Although it was crude, with irregular highs, and the contours being phantom contours (variable spacing values), an anticlinal ridge was evident.

"I know," said JJ, "But, there's something more that I think I see. Step back about five feet, just glance at it and tell me the first thing that comes to mind."

"Okay," spoke Huey as he turned his head away from the map, then abruptly turned his head back, took a glance at the map, then, "A wet rag."

"Exactly," returned JJ, "a wet rag draped over an irregular pile of sand and rocks."

"Oh, you think the ridge we see in the surface rocks may represent a broad depositional high over an old uplift, as opposed to the surface rocks being deposited and then uplifted?"

"That's what strikes me," said JJ. "I know it's pure fantasy as far as science is concerned, but that's what it might be. And if so, think of the consequences."

Huey: "I'm already there; it would mean that our En Nala ghost is truly a ghost, much older than the surface rocks and consequently more likely to have occurred at a time after oil migration began, but before it ended."

"You bet," replied JJ. "We had worried about the fact that

even if the surface rocks showed a structure, it might have occurred too late to trap the migrating oil. But with this being a reflection of a ghost, it could be a beautiful trap...present at all times of migration, and a better chance to be full!"

They decided to show this to District Geologist Bert Miller and see if he wanted them to make a more correctly plotted and contoured such map before they left Beirut for the States. He did. And they did, later that summer that ended this field mapping tour for James J. Burke and Huey Larsh.

After nearly two years at this new and unusual work, JJ and Huey prepared to leave with distinctly mixed emotions. They were very excited about returning to the States, their families and their loves, but it was with some sadness and a feeling of emptiness that they prepared to leave this, perhaps the most unusual chapter in their lives...or so they thought.

But leave it they did, on a hot July morning. They went to Bahrain, then to Baghdad, Damascus, and Beirut, where they settled in for two months of vacation and work before beginning the trek back to New York and then to their new SOCAL assignments.

~ ~ ~ ~ ~ ~ ~ ~ ~ ~ ~ ~ ~ ~

CHAPTER 11

Love Lost and Won

The roar of the engines lulled JJ into a dream fantasy-land where he drowsily thought about what lay behind, and ahead, mixing real with fantasy, intermixed with half dream, half awake, fantasies and thoughts about and with Suzanne Stuart, the jobs ahead, and this mighty aircraft.

He had left Jubail, Huey, and the others with a good deal of sadness mixed in with his joy of going home. He knew that this was ending a chapter in his experience that would never be repeated nor lost to his mind, that it was an unusual experience, and that he had made a number of firm friends for life. But all things must end sometime, and he was certainly excited about what lay ahead. And first of all, in New York: Suzanne!

In Dhahran he had boarded this same large Imperial Airways biplane that he first flew on the previous summer to Cairo, and it managed to lumber into the air for the long flight to Paris via Baghdad to Cairo for a plane change on to Paris. He understood that there would be another stop or two along the way. Shortly after takeoff, the passengers had received a snack and cup of coffee, then JJ settled back for the long flight ahead.

Midday Wednesday, July 15, 1936; Paris, France. JJ debarked from the airplane for his two day layover in Paris. He took the special automobile for downtown and his hotel, and he planned to catch up on a lot of big city shopping and Paris sight-seeing for his two days. And that is exactly what he did. As two years earlier, he found this city to be as beautiful and exciting as any city he could imagine. It was certainly larger and more cosmopolitan than the largest city he was really familiar with, Houston.

As scheduled, after two days of shopping for several clothing items, some reading material and camera equipment, plus much sightseeing and museum visiting, JJ started the next phase of the trip home. First, there was the night train to Boulogne on the English Channel, then the ship to New York, and after a week or so there, the train to Houston, and finally the bus to Nacogdoches.

It was all an enjoyable repeat of the trip some twenty-two months earlier. First the colorful and interesting French countryside, then the boarding of the ship and the welcome aboard party, and the next morning they sailed on the tide. As before, ship life was enjoyable as long as the weather was cooperative, and most of the passengers had interesting, even fascinating, occupations, lives, or both. Except for one afternoon and night of rough weather and fairly high seas, the Atlantic crossing was an unbroken string of pleasurable days and nights that ended all too soon, seven days later.

JJ disembarked in late afternoon and took a bus into New York, found his hotel, settled into his room and picked up the telephone. He dialed a well-memorized number and waited excitedly for the expected feminine voice: "Hello?"

"Hiyah, Babe...got anything planned for tonite?"

"JJ! How wonderful...how was..."

JJ, interrupting, "As I wrote, here I am, all in one piece, after flying, riding, sailing, and walking, to get here."

"I'm delighted!" responded Suzanne, "I was expecting you, but didn't know what day you'd arrive. Anyway, it'll take me about an hour to get to your hotel. May I be so bold as to suppose that you might stand for dinner?"

"You can bet on it. Just get your pretty self down here as soon as possible and we will find a place to eat!"

And so they did. Again and again over the next several days. They picked up where they left off in Cairo, visiting all the sights and sounds of New York and thereabout, and by the third night, they had also returned to the affectionate closeness they felt aboard the ship on the River Nile, and in Cairo thereafter.

It was a mild Tuesday night, July 21, as Suzanne and JJ returned to the bus stop where Suzanne caught her bus back to her apartment. They had a long evening of dining followed by a rendition of a Lullaby of Broadway show with many beautiful and leggy ladies that sort of aroused this old East Texas country boy. After the show, they had walked arm in arm down the sidewalk, then through a part of Central Park, and back out and to the bus stop. Rather abruptly, JJ ventured, "How would you like to stop by my hotel for a nightcap before the run home?"

"Well, it would be fine except tomorrow is a work day and it's already near midnight."

"I know, but Suzanne, look at it this way...we're only young once, and it might be another long wait 'til we meet again, time's a'wasting, and all that sort..."

Laughing, Suzanne said, "OK, you've made your point! But we must remember that this girl still needs her sleep, so we'll have to keep it kinda short."

"You've got a deal. Let's go!"

They walked to JJ's hotel, went into the bar, and ordered cognacs. After two cognacs, JJ held forth again: "Suzanne, it's after twelve, and you'll take an hour to get home, and I have a better idea...why don't you just spend the night here. We could buy the few things you'd need in the hotel shops, and you'd end up getting a couple of hours extra sleep! Now, isn't that a helluva idea?"

"Mr. Burke, I know perfectly well what you have on your mind, and even though the idea of the extra sleep appeals to me, it just doesn't seem right for a girl to willingly go into the hotel bedroom of a virile young man."

"I know, it is a bit suggestive," returned JJ, "but you can rely on me. I'll be the perfect gentleman! You can take the bed and I'll sleep on the sofa."

Suzanne spoke with a soft and lilting voice: "OK, based on that, and being as how I'm kinda tired anyway, and it is a long bus ride home, I suppose it will be alright."

So, off they went to JJ's room. They each took a turn getting ready for bed, JJ found an extra blanket, they murmured their goodnights, kissed, and each took to their respective resting place.

It took JJ about five minutes to decide that this sofa wasn't very comfortable after all, and besides, he hadn't really kissed Suzanne goodnight, and she probably thought he didn't care all that much about her unless he at least properly kissed her goodnight: "Suzanne?"

"Yes?"

"Suzanne, I just realized I didn't kiss you the way I feel, and wonder if you would..." And by this time he had crept off the sofa and across the floor to the side of her bed.

Suzanne answered sleepily, "I think it would be alright..."

JJ knelt down beside Suzanne, took her delicate head in his large hands, then gently kissed her...followed by a rather passionate large hands, then gently kissed her...followed by a rather passionate kiss, then, whispering, "Suzanne, that sofa is might hard, and this bed would be a lot more comfortable...do you suppose...?"

She responded very softly, "It will be alright, but you must remember, I have half the bed and you have half, and the twain shall not meet. OK?"

"Yes, I understand, the twain shall never meet..." And with that, JJ moved around to the other side of the bed and crept in. Suzanne was lying on her side, facing away from JJ. A few moments passed, JJ rolled over on his right side, facing Suzanne. As he rolled, his hand brushed her shoulder..."I'm sorry, Suzanne, it was an accident, I didn't realize you were so close when I rolled over..."

"Remember, JJ, never shall the twain, etc."

"Yes, I remember." A few moments later, JJ could stand it no longer, so he reached out with his hand and brushed Suzanne's thigh. No response. Well, thought JJ, nothing ventured, nothing gained...so he moved a bit closer, then reached over and gently grasped her left breast in his left hand while his legs brushed against hers.

"Suzanne, about this twain thing..."

She murmured, "What twain thing?" Dead silence followed for perhaps ten seconds, then JJ moved up firmly against Suzanne who had now rolled toward JJ. And nature followed its course again, just as it had aboard the Nile River craft.

It was again as it was in Cairo. Suzanne worked and JJ saw the sights during the days, and they were together every night and for all meals. This continued until Friday when Suzanne took a day's vacation. They then spent the next three days doing all the things that vibrant young lovers do...the visiting, shopping, riding on buses, trains, ferries, ships, the museums, all the wonderful opportunities offered by this great city, but most of all...being together, touching one another, and...sleeping together...just as in Cairo, it was an idyllic, joyful, exploring togetherness.

They discussed their work. JJ explained that he would be returning to Texas for an assignment in Houston to do subsurface geology in the Texas Gulf Coast, and might return to Saudi Arabia within a few years for another tour there.

Suzanne explained her work: "JJ, we are at the beginning of the greatest expansion ever witnessed on this planet. Vacation travel in its infancy and will explode in growth; we are exporting more and more automobiles, trucks, many consumer goods, and agricultural products. The only thing that stands in the way of bounding foreign exchange is the possibility of war."

"And war is a very real possibility," replied JJ, "but all the signs are that Mr. Hitler is not inclined to try his luck against the Maginot line. The French would probably chew him up there. So maybe war won't be a major factor overall."

"I hope so," said Suzanne. "Since I returned from Cairo, I have been given a large account area of my own. You remember, I was just filling in for someone else when I came to Cairo."

"Yes..."

"Well, now I have the western British Isles for my own account. I make trips over there every two or three months, and handle a number of coordinating chores here in New York. My automotive exporting business is doubling every few years, and my responsibility, and remuneration!, grows with it. I believe I have a good career and want to see what I can do!"

As she talked, JJ thought, it seems like there may be a problem developing in our romance. We can't both be full career types and think much about a life together...

Slowly, thoughtfully, JJ spoke: "It seems like our directions may be a bit troublesome to align."

Silence for a bit. Suzanne: "It is true that we may have some difficulties for a while in getting together, but when I think of you, of your nearness, my love for you, it may come to pass that all else has to take second place."

"Anyway," replied JJ, "be it as it may, we've got today! And we shan't borrow trouble; let's take it while we have it and make the best of it...whatever "it" is!"

"Agreed!" Suzanne almost shouted as she reached to hug her man.

The day of parting arrived much sooner than either of them would have liked. But JJ had to get back to Texas in time for a couple of weeks in Nacogdoches before he reported to work in Houston. The family was counting on it and everybody had made plans for several parties and get-togethers.

The bus roared northward on Highway 35 out of Houston

through the stifling and humid heat of the Big Thicket forests of Liberty to Polk counties, Texas. It was dead summer. As miserable in this country as it gets. July was ending and the dog days of August were about to start. Traveling on a bus in this country this time of year was a constant dilemma: either remain fairly cool with a window down and wind blowing in with whatever it brought, smoke, dust, odors; or, stay clean and unblown in the heat. Most of the passengers did a little of both. Some of the ladies used their small paper cardboard fans.

Within a few miles out of Houston, the pine forests became a solid mat of trees, saplings, vines, and much undergrowth, all of which composed a scene of beauty in March, with the new flowers, the scattered dogwood with its white shower of blossoms, occasionally intermingled with redbud and its pink shower; but summer...ah, it was another story.

In August, it was quite normal for a person to sit perfectly motionless within the stillness of the Thicket and sweat. No movement or exercise, but the sweat would slowly collect and trickle downward over the warm skin, picking up more moisture on the way. As a result, people wore as little as was decent. And, within one's own home, it was common to wear only underwear, and sometimes, nothing. The main blessing was the fan. Prior to the current generation, fans were hand-held and moved slowly back and forth to create a small breeze around the face. But, gratefully, electricity had changed the fan in the home to a real assist to comfort. The electric fan could be picked up and taken to rooms as needed, and with its wind on the sweaty skin, life became pleasant again.

But, JJ was heading north, and after passing through the small town of Goodrich, just north of the Trinity River in Polk County, the low-lying flatlands gave way to rolling hill country with more variety of forest and flower, and more common dogwood and redbud, as well as hardwood. He noted that the highway was now paved throughout his trip whereas part of it was still gravel when he left in 1934. At least the window could be left down without fogs of dust!

He had taken over two days by train getting to Houston from New York, but now he was on the last leg of the journey that began nearly a month ago at 'Jubail on sea' in Saudi Arabia. He left Houston shortly after eight in the morning, and now, just after a lunch stop in Lufkin, the bus approached the old, scenic area of Nacogdoches, home of Stephen F. Austin State Teachers College.

He stepped off the bus at its station, and there was not only mother Alma, but also sister Elizabeth, and...totally unexpected, but ever so delighting...Ruthanne! "Well, I never expected such a charming reception!"

Elizabeth, totally uninhibited ran up and jumped into JJ's arms: "We thought you were going to take forever, my long-lost and only brother! What kept you soooo long?"

"Time and distance, my baby sister, just time and distance. Coming up from Houston, there was a little delay near Diboll because of road work, but other'n that, no real delay. Looks like little sister has filled out a bit...maybe eatin' too much?" He observed as he quickly dodged over to his mother and with deep warmth, caught her and hugged her tightly, "Mother Alma, my Lady of the South, your blue eyes never lose their startling character in such a lovely face...."

"JJ, I do believe you are learning the graces of a gentleman after all! There were times when I doubted your ever making it!" Alma turned toward Ruthanne and said, "And look who I talked into being part of the reception committee!"

Elizabeth had a thing to say, "Now listen, brother dear, I may've added a pound or two at my 21st birthday party last month, but I'm still skinny enough to not have to wait in line for boys!"

As he looked her over a bit, "I can see that the extra pound or two appear to be in the right places, younger sister." JJ now directed all his attention to this smiling vision in the corner of his eye...as he turned, he was taken aback much like he had two years earlier; this was no longer a little girl. Her alert green eyes smilingly followed him as he walked over for greeting.

Rather playfully, he picked Ruthanne up and swung her around, "I can tell that *you* haven't put on a bunch of extra pounds; you're still light as a feather!"

"Mr. Burke, you lie, but you lie well. I'm no feather, but I suppose I'm not a rock either..."

"You better believe there isn't the slightest similarity between you and a rock," said JJ as he drank in the beauty of this 5' 6", well-shaped, confident woman with long dark, auburn hair that fell about her most feminine shoulders. She wore a fluffy light blue cotton blouse against which her dark hair contrasted strikingly, with a full, white cotton skirt with faint vertical light and dark blue stripes.

They all walked into the station, picked up JJ's travel bag, and went out to Alma's 1935 Chevrolet sedan for the ride home, talking all the time about JJ's trunk to come by train in a day or two, their joy on this hot East Texas day, and the many subjects of lives in East Texas and Arabia the last two years. Each had so much to say and ask that the conversation jumped sporadically between highly divergent subjects. At this time of happiness, any talk of unpleasant subjects was avoided. The women were delighted to have this tall, strong man back in their midst, and he was equally delighted to be in the presence of these particular three women.

JJ had difficulty taking his eyes off Ruthanne, even to the extent that his uninhibited sister said, "JJ, I do believe that if momma ran this car into a tree, you'd know nothing about it...you haven't taken your eyes off Ruthanne since we got in the car!"

"That's not so," said JJ, "I distinctly remember looking up to see the ice house when we passed it. But, then, I admit that I have more than casual interest in the blouse she is wearing, and perhaps from time to time I might have looked at her hair or something...."

"You bet, something!" retorted Elizabeth. "Anyway, I guess there are worse ways for you to use you eyes...."

Now Ruthanne spoke, "I can think of a lot of things to talk about that are more interesting than my blouse! For example, JJ could tell us about his Saudi Arabia adventure...."

The chatter continued back and forth as they drove along, JJ being ever aware of this soft, warm female sitting next to him in the rear seat. They arrived at the Burke home, unloaded, had an ice tea break, then JJ went for a walk with Ruthanne.

He learned that she had graduated from the University of Texas shortly after her 21st birthday in May, with a Bachelor of Arts Degree in Education with English and Music minors. Her plan was to start out teaching junior high school English and work up to high school English, and also work with the bands.

She had a great interest in helping young people achieve and decided that teaching was the best way for her to earn a living and at the same time try to do something worthwhile for society. She also felt that the major source of problems between people was communication and she aspired, even yearned, to do her bit to allay that source, through better understanding and use of our language.

Also a part of her decision for education was the need to plan a course of study that a young woman could fit into without controversy. Teaching and the arts were a natural for women, along with a number of non-professional endeavors but, otherwise, the professional hill was rather steep. It was not easy for a woman to become an engineer, or lawyer, or accountant, but teaching and the arts offered many opportunities, and Ruthanne was quite happy to follow that route. Even though a tiny wedge of resentment crept in now and then when she had lots of time to think.

Ruthanne Cook was a rather serious minded young woman, who enjoyed music and the arts, could play piano rather well, and could do water colors that were not too shabby. She was quite intelligent though not an outstanding student, making mostly B's in school. She also enjoyed the challenge and fun of games and sports, and could hold her own quite well when it came to repartee.

And she had good control of herself. A few years earlier, in the fall of her senior year, 1931-1932, while coming home from a football game, she was tested.

She and her date, Johnny Boggs, were traveling north on Highway 35, a gravel road, after a rainy mud-slinging game at Livingston, about 45 miles south of Lufkin on the same highway. They had won the game, barely, on a drop-kicked field goal! They left Livingston about eleven PM and had just cleared Lufkin. It was fifteen minutes after midnite. There was almost no traffic. Practically none going south. Perhaps twenty or thirty cars were strung out heading home to Nacogdoches from the game.

Johnny had gotten permission from his dad to take the family Plymouth sedan for the trip; his parents knew Johnny was careful, and further, they knew he would be especially so if Ruthanne was along! Because if nothing else, Ruthanne would make him! They admonished him to be particularly careful on any of the hills where gravel had worn away exposing slippery clay. It had been a rather wet fall and there was plenty of water.

Both kids were sleepy. Ruthanne kept nodding off, even though she tried to keep a conversation going in order to keep Johhny awake. Going through Lufkin had aroused them to a fairly good state of alertness. But some ten minutes out of town, they were both losing that alertness. Ruthanne had simply dozed off. Johnny was singing and chewing gum furiously to keep awake.

Then, he nodded briefly, his eyes closing. Just as they were approaching the Neches River bridge. A slight swerve jerked him fully awake, but it was too late. The car skidded to the right on loose gravel, and went on into the bar ditch, which was quite deep along here on the approach to the bridge. It slammed onto its right side, then momentum kept it sliding on the rain slick clay. Right toward the rain swollen river.

The car finally slid to slow motion at the river bank, with the front wheels and part of the motor in river water. It was slowly sliding, sinking, into the river. Johnny had banged his head against the steering wheel or door facing and was stunned, sluggishly rubbing his head. Ruthanne had been shaken awake, braced herself with her hands and arms, and was now fully alert. Normally, the river at this location would not be over eight to twelve feet deep, but because of the recent rains, it was running nearer eighteen feet deep in the central channel.

Ruthanne could not open her door because the car was resting on it. And Johnny was laying across the gear shift, partly on her, partly on the steering wheel. She pushed and shook him, "Johnny, Johnny, wake up! Wake up! We're sliding into the river!"

Johnny kept rubbing his head, as he slowly reached out with his left hand to the left door knob. "Mmmmm...wha' happen'."

The car was now fully in the water, with the left door partly covered. Obviously something had to be done now, or the car would slip on into the main channel.

Ruthanne awkwardly climbed over Johnny, finally got to the door handle and opened it. Water rushed in. She could not push the door up and keep it up. It fell back, but water kept pouring in through cracks. The window. That's the way. She grabbed the window knob and rapidly turned it, bringing the window down. Or in this case, sideways. Now water really poured in.

She climbed out through the window and onto the side of the car. Meanwhile, the cold water had jolted Johnny fully alert. He now understood the problem fully, but the water was pouring in so fast he was partially blinded, and could not work against it. Ruthanne reached in and yelled, "grab my hand Johnny! Grab my hand!"

He caught hold of her hand, they both grabbed hard, and Ruthanne pulled with all her strength. The water was now about a foot above the side of the car she was kneeling on.

She helped him until he got his hand on the window facing, then with a mighty heave, he chinned himself out of the car. They both crawled along the car toward its rear, then jumped off into the muck at river edge. They then crawled and stumbled out to dry ground, collapsed, and gasped for air.

"Ruthanne," gasped Johnny, "you may have just saved my life!"

"Oh, I don't think so, Johnny. Just helped a little!" she gasped in return.

Meanwhile, one of the game cars had stopped, then waved down another. The wet and very muddy kids, wrapped in blankets, knocked on the Cook's door in Nacogdoches at 2:37 AM, to be greeted by very startled parents! By now, the kids were nervously joking about it and hoping Johnny wouldn't be punished too severely for destroying the Plymouth.

In days and weeks to come, as Ruthanne's coolness in the face of disaster became known, she was something of a heroine. This little 105-pound girl had pulled a 162-pound boy out of a wrecked car under water! Upward!

- - - - - - -

JJ had to report to Houston for his new job assignment on Monday, August 17, so he had a good two weeks left for fun times. He read, dated Ruthanne, fished, dated Ruthanne, wrote letters to Suzanne (and read hers), studied the regional geology of the Gulf Coast, and dated Ruthanne. He became confused about his loves.

He had a very special feeling for Suzanne and read her letters with pleasure and anticipation; but had an underlying feeling that it would be exceedingly difficult to maintain a relationship with her considering the distance between them and her professional independence. On the other hand, it was quite nice to have Ruthanne handy to assuage his mild anguish over Suzanne's absence. In fact, as the days wore on, he hardly noticed that anguish, and instead found himself replacing it with an ever-increasing desire to be in the presence of Ruthanne at all times. However, his mind was on another subject also: A car.

He had planned and saved to buy a new car after getting settled, and to that end had briefly visited a car dealer in Houston on his way home. He found that he could buy the car he wanted, a Pontiac Coupe, for about $780.00 in Houston, and would check that price out in Nacogdoches. He already knew pretty well what he wanted, so went to the Nacogdoches Chevrolet-Pontiac dealer, and negotiated for his car. He bought a Pontiac Coupe, one with a radio and heater, and had a small rubber fan mounted on the steering column. The total cost was $804.00.

After a few days, JJ managed to not only have his evening meal with Ruthanne, he found ways to have breakfast, lunch, and most of the hours in between. The only problem in their summer romance was her need to meet her job interviews. Shortly before JJ was to leave for Houston, she learned that she had a job in the Lufkin School District, teaching 7th grade English and band.

She returned from Lufkin on Thursday before JJ had to leave on Sunday the 16th. That afternoon they set out in JJ's new Pontiac for an evening picnic out on a hill near the Cook family farm southeast of Nacogdoches, near the village of Oak Ridge. They spread their picnic blanket at a location well known to the Cook family, where several pecan and hardwood trees grew near the hilltop located several hundred yards from the old Cook family homestead. It was here under the shade of an old oak stalwart overlooking cotton fields in full cotton, where gentle breezes tickled one's senses while keeping the flying pests at bay, that JJ realized that Ruthanne was the one.

To stir the emotions and whet one's interest still more at this location was the legend that this same hill was a resting place for travelers on that part of *El Camino Real*, The King's Highway, that connected Nacogdoches and Natchitoches, about a hundred miles to the east in what was to become the state of Louisiana, in the seventeenth century. While picnicking here near sundown, in the quiet of memorable moments, JJ and Ruthanne could almost hear the ghosts of laughter and shouts past, of straining mule teams and the sounds of slapping harness leather and the wagon wheels' iron tires grinding on road gravel and rocks. It was difficult to avoid dreaming together of times past on this old hill from which so much of this verdant countryside could be seen.

The picnic was past and they were sitting arm in arm leaning back against the massive oak. JJ pulled Ruthanne close, leaned over, and kissed her gently on the cheek, then again at the corner of her soft warm lips, then again full on her lips. She responded ardently. JJ's hand slipped down toward her bosom, whereupon Ruthanne gently pushed back.

She whispered softly, "My dear JJ, this girl has some things that are precious to her, and her body is near the head of the list. Though I might want to be more amorous with the man who has become so important to me, I simply cannot actually do more...except with the man I marry."

"Well," JJ responded softly, "there is a way to fix that...and it has been more and more on my mind. If I were to ask you if you would marry me, would you say 'yes'?"

"Now that's a rather presumptuous question for a girl. Are you actually unsure, and want to have an option...to exercise or not at your whim? But I might. Maybe."

Whereupon, JJ was unsure no longer. He jumped up, knelt before her, took her hand in his, and stated: "My Lady Love, since I have an overwhelming desire, nay, need, to be with you forever, to feel the gentleness of your love, to sense the passion of your heart, and I fear death only will suffice otherwise, Will You Marry Me?"

"Ah, my love, you said that so well I almost feel that you rehearsed it."

"I didn't, but I find it on my mind continuously of late."

"Then, with affection, with wonder, my answer is..." and she hesitated for several seconds, "Yes!"

And so the young man from Arabia, the Burke heir, the Texas Aggie geologist, hopefully the oil finder, became engaged. The only problem was, "My beloved lady, my precious female, I have overlooked planning and must report I have no ring. But, that will be remedied tomorrow!"

The only thing left to do was set the date. They both realized that it was desirable to get organized in their new jobs, and she wanted to fulfill her obligation and finish at least half a year before going to join JJ in Houston. So, as the evening closed in and the stars began to shine, they decided on the following spring to legally bind their marriage. But...their marriage was emotionally and physically bound under the old oak tree, witnessed by the heavens alight.

The next day, Friday, JJ followed through as promised, and after getting her approval, bought a ring set. That evening, before dinner with her family, he lovingly placed the engagement ring on her finger and secured the wedding ring for the later date. Both families were very pleased and happy with the occasion, and all started planning for the actual event.

Sunday afternoon, JJ parted with his family, loaded his new Pontiac, went over for goodbye to Ruthanne, and set out for Houston. He left with a sense of sadness, of loneliness, but also happiness for his life ahead with this lovely girl who had consented to share his life and for which he was so grateful. He also drove along with the knowledge that only five days lay between successive visits with her over the next few months. He would burn up old Highway 35 every weekend in his great new car.

~~~~~~~~~~~~~~~

CHAPTER 12

Houston

At last, in Houston the weather was beginning to cool a bit in late September, 1936. Most days were still fairly hot and always humid, but under a fan at night, it was quite comfortable now. JJ had rented a furnished apartment in a large old frame house out near San Jacinto High School, about two and a half miles south of downtown Houston. The house had been designed for the prevailing southeasterly breezes so that most rooms had windows that provided cross ventilation. That, along with its ten-foot ceilings and large ceiling-mounted fans in most rooms, provided reasonable relief from heat.

His apartment consisted of a bedroom, living room, kitchen and bath on the second floor. The kitchen was large and also served as a dining room. If needed for special company, the living room could serve as a dining room. He was neat and well organized in the care of his apartment, being careful to avoid creating messes that required cleaning. He was quite frugal in the use of cooking ware, dishes, and silverware, to the end that he created about one sink full of dishes to wash per week.

To minimize cooking, he bought numerous pre-prepared canned foods, and cooked large portions of meat or other basics. By careful test, he found that cooked ground beef would keep adequately for about seven days in his ice-box, but it did start changing color after about five days. He bought a 50 pound block of ice every other day from the ice truck, and found this to keep things adequately cool except on the hottest of days if he opened the door very often. The ice-box came with the apartment, and he was not about to buy one of those expensive electric refrigerators until he got married.

JJ had put a lot of miles on his '37 Pontiac going to Lufkin or Nacogdoches every weekend that work permitted. One occupation he had not planned for was "well sitting," a job somewhat like baby-sitting, except the "baby" was a well being drilled for oil. This took up some weekends because the wells operated 24 hours every day and the geologist had to be available when the well reached any critical point.

He was assigned to the Middle Texas Gulf Coast Cenozoic. This encompassed the Tertiary and younger beds from the surface down to a depth of about 10,000', between the vicinity of Houston and the vicinity of Victoria, Texas. Other geologists were assigned to the other areas covered by the Houston Division office. Some of them worked in Cretaceous beds in East Texas and in the San Marcos-Luling trend. But most of the effort of this Division office was directed at the newly developing deep-seated salt dome fields.

In most of the Gulf Coast region from Texas to Alabama, as well as part of East Texas, and including southern Mississippi, there are many salt domes. These are domes of mostly NaCl salt with some other salts and numerous impurities, that rise up from mother salt beds of mostly Jurassic age buried mostly below depths of 30,000' in these regions.

Within JJ's work area, the sediments at the surface vary from recent to Miocene in age. Successively beneath these beds lie Oligocene and Eocene sands, clays, and shales of Tertiary age, and then come Cretaceous limestones, sandstones, and shales followed by Jurassic beds that are mostly carbonates and evaporites. Evaporites are those beds left behind when sea water is evaporated by heat, and consist largely of salts, and the salts are mostly regular table salt, NaCl. The Cretaceous and Jurassic are Periods of the Mesozoic Era; the age of the dinosaurs.

After the Mesozoic salts were buried to great depths by later deposition, two factors became paramount: The salt was lighter than all but the shallowest of the overlying beds, that is it was and is less dense; and, it will flow by crystalline action. The nature of salt to flow is enhanced by the great pressures and temperatures created by deep burial. In combination, these two forces will cause the salt to flow upward in a fashion not unlike a giant piston moving upward through the sediments, uplifting and piercing them.

In some areas, such as coastal Louisiana, piercement salt domes have reached the surface and upraised the terrain into localized areas of hills and valleys over an area of a few thousand acres. Such areas furnished salt to Indians before European settlement, and all occupants since. The domes that pierce the beds to relatively shallow depths, say 4000', are called "piercement salt domes," or piercements for brevity. Deeper domes whose crests lie at greater depths are generally called "deep seated salt domes," or deep seated domes for short.

After Spindletop Field was discovered in 1901 near Beaumont, Texas, oilmen have searched high and low for similar structures. This magnificent, but very polluting, discovery was something the world had never witnessed. Major quantities of oil were found in the earth beneath this low hill called Spindletop, with such pressure that it would blow out and stream up into the air well over 100 feet like a giant black geyser. Up to this time, never had oil been found in such overwhelming quantities where thousands of barrels could be filled in a single day from a single well. These were the first "gushers."

Spindletop is a piercement salt dome with the top of the salt only a few hundred feet below the surface. Oil was trapped above it, in its caprock, and on its flanks, where the oil had moved upward by gravity flow through water in the porous rocks until it encountered an impermeable bed that acted as a seal to further movement.

Piercements have numerous surface expression, including mounds, hilly areas, stream diversions, breaks in the sediments (faults), and paraffin dirt. One of the "sure" signs of oil to the early explorers, 1900 to 1920, was paraffin dirt, the material left behind when oil that had seeped into the soil had evaporated and left behind the heavy base petroleum material. After Spindletop, many such fields were found in the Texas and Louisiana coastal areas, until by World War I, such search was winding down with few new finds. Domes with obvious surface expressions were all found.

In the early twenties, a geophysical instrument known as the torsion balance, was used to find more salt domes. This instrument measured the effects of earth gravity, and since salt was less dense than the surrounding sediments, a gravity minimum indicated the possibility of a salt dome. Then came the gravimeter, a more sensitive gravity measuring instrument, and then in the late twenties, refraction seismograph was developed.

The gravity devices were best suited to find shallow piercements, deep enough that there was little surface expression, but not too deep for the gravitational effect to be significantly distorted by other factors. Refraction seismic could explore deeper and functioned by using explosive charges to generate energy that traveled down and through the earth to distant receivers or geophones. If the energy passed (refracted) through a mass of salt, it traveled slower through the salt and got to the distant receiver slower than if there were no such mass. Thus by measuring the travel time in fractions of a second on many lines between explosive and receiver, it was possible to isolate salt masses whose crests were as deep as perhaps 6000', deeper under some conditions.

By the time JJ arrived in Houston, the industry was searching for salt domes where the salt top might be 10,000 or more feet deep. The device in use was the reflection seismograph. In this case, the explosive charge caused energy to go down into the earth, and reflect off the various layers back to an array of receivers at the surface at variable distances from the explosive. This was the method that led to the great Dulce (pronounced dulsay, meaning sweet in Spanish) discovery.

"Hey JJ, I've been working on these records for three days now and I can't figure out what's goin' on." This was David Hatcher, geophysicist, age 29, with a degree in math with physics minor, who was an excellent seismologist, that is one who worked with the still rapidly developing science of seismology...the study of earthquakes and the results thereof.

In the petroleum industry, the "earthquakes" were the explosive charges detonated to generate energy waves that traveled into the ground, and the resulting energy reflections were recorded as inked lines on long strips of paper measured in seconds, or seismograms, commonly called records. The explosives were normally placed in holes about 25-feet to 50-feet deep, called shotholes, about a half a mile apart, with recording instruments, or geophones, commonly called "jugs" because they looked like jugs, strung out on either side of the shotholes.

The wiggly or wavey lines, called traces, moved to the right every time the geophone, was shaken...ever so slightly...by energy returning from a reflection off a subsurface interface between layers of different densities. The trace moved farther to the right with increasing amount, or amplitude, of reflected energy.

The deeper in the ground the reflection, the farther down the strip of paper came the movement of the inked trace. Several traces, usually about 16, were inked on a single strip of paper, one for each geophone measuring the reflected energy from a single explosion.

Each curve, similar to a half loop, formed by the ink trace, indicated the return of reflected energy. Such individual looped curves were called wavelets. Wavelets on several traces at about the same time position on the record formed a mappable reflection. These reflections could then be correlated to similar reflections on other records, and thus indicate the direction the subsurface layer that caused the reflections was dipping.

Geophysicists and geologists commonly worked together, the geologist inputting what earth forms might be present to cause the wavelet changes interpreted by the geophysicist-seismologist.

Together, the geologist and geophysicist could make a much better interpretation of what was actually present thousands of feet down into the subsurface, than either alone.

"Tell me what you see," asked JJ.

"Well, you know we have been shooting (discharging explosives in shotholes over variable distances, with geophones in between the shotholes) an area just north of Little Hill Dome, and we can see the dips off the dome just fine, then about a mile out, all reflections below about a second go to hell, just hash."

"Continuing out from the dome, how far before the deep reflections come back in?"

"About three to four miles," answered David. "It's pretty obvious that there's some kind of change down there."

The two studied the records together, each putting in his expertise. They found that an east-west line that crossed the north-south line had some fairly decent deep reflections where the other line was hash. After several days of trying various things, consulting with some of the older geologists and geophysicists, and making numerous sketch cross-sections and maps, Hatcher and Burke developed a theory: There was a large, older, buried part of the Little Hill piercement salt dome that created a domal anticline covering several thousand acres.

This would have tremendous potential if true, so they tried to find a way to test their idea before recommending an expensive test well.

They started with the record for the east-west line that had better reflections, then comparing a reflection wavelet on it at the same time position as on the north-south record, developed a vague short reflection on the north-south record at that same time position. Then working with similar vague reflections on two or three traces above and below that time position which they computed to be about 8500' to 9000' deep, they developed a "ghost" reflection, that is, one being a combination of numerous vague reflections at similar time positions on just a few traces. Using this ghost, they interpreted a vague up-bowing of the beds on this line that occurred around 8500' to 9000'. They had a similar up-bowing on the east-west line.

With these vague indications of a large domal (rounded) anticline, they approached the District Geophysicist and recommended the shooting of additional lines in that area, at angles to the known piercement dome, so as to avoid the many strong reflections coming off the steeply dipping beds on the flank of the dome.

The new shooting was approved, and the field work was done a few weeks later. By November, the geo-scientists had the records in hand and excitedly undertook interpretation. JJ asked David several times when he would be through with his interpretation of the reflections.

"Burke, just settle down, I'm hurryin' as fast as I can!"

Late one Thursday, Hatcher said, "OK, JJ, I'm ready to talk."

"What's it look like"

"What we thought, but kinda rough..."

"Does it look like 4-way dip?" asked Burke.

"Without a doubt, we have those dips, but the crest is not real clear, and I don't understand the slight east-west elongation. Do we have reservoir sands at this depth?"

"In this area, wells on the dome indicate that we are dealing with a lower Yegua, or maybe Cook Mountain, section in the range of 8000' to 9000' depth. And if so, there should be a number of good sands. Two wells on the east flank of the dome found good sands in this section."

"Then," said Hatcher, "let's start building sections and maps!"

"OK, I'm ready."

It took another three weeks to make their sections and maps, and to get them drafted for printing. Then, another week to write their report and recommendation. Finally, in early December, they made their joint recommendation to acquire leases over about 3200 acres and drill an 8700' test well at a specific location on the leased acreage.

"Burke, get on your horse." It was District Geologist Al Clark.

"What's the depth?" returned JJ.

"They're at 8400', making a trip for bit, and should make the rest of the hole with the new bit...barring problems."

JJ thought for a few moments, then, "Seems like they oughta be at TD sometime tomorrow night, and ready to log the next day."

"Yep," replied Clark. "That'll give you a full day to log the samples before logging."

The plan was for the geologist to go to the wellsite a day or so before the well was to reach TD, or total depth, and work the samples from drilling. While drilling, the derrick man had an extra job of collecting samples off the shale shaker where the drilling mud from the hole flowed through a screen into the mud pit. The derrick man's normal job was to rack pipe in and out of the hole from his small platform about 85 feet above the derrick floor. During drilling, he had more free time than the other roughnecks so it was his job to collect samples as instructed by the geologist.

Since there were three derrick men during a 24-hour period, the geologist tried to talk to each of them, but often relied on their passing his instructions from one to the other. In this case JJ had gone out to the well when it was drilling out of surface casing at 2200' depth. The main purpose of his trip was to tell the day-tour derrick man and day driller exactly what they wanted.

He instructed them to catch 10' circulation samples at each significant drilling break below 7500', and, in addition, to catch a representative sample every joint, or 30' length of drill pipe. This meant that each time the bit moved deeper more rapidly, drilling a foot in two minutes for example instead of the normal eight minutes, the driller was to drill ten feet, then circulate the mud for about twenty minutes without drilling. This would somewhat isolate that 10' batch of cuttings as they came up and out of the hole and across the shale shaker. The derrick man was told the circulating time for cuttings to reach the surface from TD, allowed for that time, and then caught cuttings over a period of about 15 minutes around that specific circulating time. He then put these cuttings in a cloth bag, labeled the depth, and thus collected a sample of the drilling break.

In addition, this man similarly prepared samples for each joint of pipe drilled. Geologists referred to the samples as "break samples" and "30-ft samples."

It had taken nearly seven months from the time Burke and Hatcher recommended the well to get approval, buy the leases...a most time-consuming and difficult negotiating task..., develop a drilling program, contract a rig, prepare the location, and get the rig on site. And this was record time! It normally might have taken some two years or more to accomplish the same jobs. However, this prospect caught the fancy of everyone who saw it, management, landmen, and engineers. It was a large structure with the possibility of finding large reserves, so the more the prospect was discussed and reviewed, the more excited the explorationists became.

JJ was carefully negotiating his company Chevrolet sedan through the mud holes on the County dirt road off the paved highway from Houston to San Antonio. After some eleven miles on the County Road, he turned off on a dirt ranch road that would have been little more than a quagmire except for one thing: Board road. The spring rains had made the roads and location quite soft, and incapable of supporting heavy traffic without substantial effort.

To correct this problem, the drilling engineers had employed local road and location contractors to strengthen the two small wooden bridges on the County Road, gravel several low places, then build a board road off the County Road the last mile-and-a-quarter to the location. At the location, the rig site and an area around it was similarly boarded. This all resulted in a major cost before the rig had even moved in.

He drove up on the turnaround and found a place to park next to a small trailer house used by the drilling contractor as a rigsite operations center. JJ went in the trailer. It was 10:30 AM, Thursday, May 13, 1937.

"Glad to see that you fellows are still taking nourishment," said JJ as he walked in on the toolpusher and day driller eating donuts with their coffee. They shook hands. "Anything unusual?"

The pusher, Dewell Davis, spoke, "Well, as you know from the drilling reports, we've been getting a number of drilling breaks from 7900' down, and there's been gas with some of them."

Dewell Davis, the man in charge of the rig and to whom all three tours reported, was an oil business history in himself. He had started to work as a roustabout, or day laborer, in Beaumont during the Spindletop boom that started in 1901. For years he had tried to make a living for his family on a small farm, and it was such a struggle that he figured this new oil business might be a way out. By 1905, with all the activity there, he had worked up to driller, at the age of 33. He had worked in a number of oil fields, and in the twenties was a pusher on a rig drilling wells in Saratoga Field in Hardin County, northwest of Beaumont.

One day, the drilling pipe got stuck and the driller couldn't work it loose. Dewell went up on the drilling floor at the base of the derrick and told everybody to get off the floor. He then started applying unusual power on the cables to the draw works that lifted the drill string. He exceeded the normal limits and pulled the rig in. The collapsing rig fell on and around him, broke his back and several other bones, and put him in a hospital for eleven months. But, with a false arm and two steel plates, he survived. He was well known as an unusually courageous and very knowledgeable man, and his rig was busy when others were stacked (not working and stored).

JJ responded, "Yeah, I noticed that you'd reported several gas shows with the breaks. That's a good sign usually, but the problem is, you don't know whether its one inch or 100 feet of oil sand, or maybe gas sand which would be worth nothing."

"I know," replied Davis, "but the gas would increase again when we drilled into another sand, and as you know, we had a sheen on the mud pit from two of the gas shows. And that sheen didn't come from our waste oil."

"Let's hope these aren't just teasers," said JJ. "What's our TD?"

"8578' about ten minutes ago," the driller stated. "It's been drilling fast because of a lot of sands from 7900 down. If it keeps drilling like it has since midnight, we'll have TD sometime tonight."

JJ: "I'll go get my mike and light and look at some samples." He was beginning to feel twinges of excitement. Things were so close; just don't let it fall apart now.

"You can set up on that desk if you like," offered the driller.

JJ got his microscope and mike light, plus his fluorescent light, set them up on the desk, and plugged them in at an electrical outlet.

He picked up the first drilling break sample and poured out part of the pound or so of cuttings from the cloth bag onto a small metal tray that he placed on the microscope base. He looked through the mike lenses and immediately saw what he thought was a little oil stain on the fragments of rather loose sand, hardly a sandstone, that composed the cuttings from the bit. With some excitement, he quickly took the tray from the mike and placed it under the fluoroscope. The sand fragments glowed yellow. "Well, we got some oil. I don't know whether it's a puddle, pond, or lake, but it's some!"

JJ continued to study the break samples, then some of the 30' samples. He worked on, took a lunch break, and late that afternoon, he concluded, "If I had to guess, I'd say we have a well. It's clear that the sands are porous and permeable enough to be a productive reservoir, and I keep finding oil stains in both the break and 30' samples of the upper sands. It looks like there are several pay sands."

"I hope you got it right, Mr. Burke," said Davis, "'cause if Calco makes money, I make money. That is, if you let me drill more wells."

"You can bet you'll get a good share of the drilling if this pans out," said Burke. "The next step in this puzzle is the electric log. I do believe though, we have a producer."

JJ put his gear back in his car and left the rig to go to the nearby small town of Campo Dulce (Spanish for sweet camp; perhaps associated with the honey bee hives that thrived in a grove of several old oak trees at the east edge of town). He had to call in a report of his findings. He did. Clark was very pleased with the report and asked for a call as soon as JJ had the first information on the electric log.

Burke stopped at a combination bus-stop/cafe, bought and wolfed down a t-bone steak followed with lemon pie, then returned to the rig for the night.

He awakened to gentle shaking, "Hey, geolopher, we're ready to log and Schlumberger is here. Want anything?"

Sleepily, "Reckon I oughta go talk to the logger about scales, elevation, and so forth...."

Wearily, he pulled himself out of bed and glanced at his wrist watch in the soft light of the single low-wattage ceiling light: 3:20 AM. He rolled over and out of the bunk bed, slipped on his khaki pants and boots and started out without tying his boot laces, but he did slip on a shirt as he went. He spent a few minutes with the logging engineer, told him the well elevation and location and asked that the logger put that on the log heading. At that time, most operators put little such information on the actual logs, making it more difficult for others to get that key data; as a result, it made working electric logs more difficult for all geologists. He then reviewed the scales to be used on the two log curves, excused himself, and returned to the sack. But not to sleep, as it turned out.

JJ turned and tossed, thinking of the well, the possible discovery, Ruthanne, the well, Suzanne, his job, the well, astronomy, and on and on. Finally he fell asleep again. A few moments later he was being shaken again: "Mr. Burke, we have a log."

It was the logging engineer. He was aware that day had come, but no sun yet. He again glanced at his watch. Now it was 7:25 AM. He did sleep again after all; maybe only a couple of hours, but plenty for now.

After dressing and grabbing a cup of coffee, he followed the engineer out to the logging truck where the engineer's assistant was developing the film of the log. This log was produced by lowering instruments into the hole to measure electrical self-potential, somewhat like voltage; and resistivity. The overall unit, a *sonde*, was lowered down the hole, then pulled back out making the two electrical measurements.

The two electrical curves were measured by making thin exposures on a long roll of film about 8 1/2" wide, with depths shown every 100 feet, and each 100' further divided into 2'. Thus the long roll represented the 8722' deep hole, and the electrical characteristics could be read over the entire hole. A sand layer would usually stand out with a high self-potential relative to the overlying and underlying shale layers. The resistivity curve indicated the fluid in a sand; in this area, the waters yielded very low resistivities of about one ohm on the log, oils produced 5 to 10 ohms, and gas usually over 10 ohms.

The engineer pulled the wet film out, handed it to JJ and commented: "Looks like you got a winner!"

It took only a glance for Burke to surmise the same. It was not a matter of whether there was oil, and probably gas, here; it was only a matter of how much. The two curves blossomed out in opposite directions at nearly each and every one of the nine sand zones between 7921' and 8722' TD. There were two thin sands in one overall zone with good self potential, but no resistivity: Water sands. Then, near the bottom of the log, two more sands, one pretty thick, had good SP and very high, off-scale resistivities: Probably gas or very gassy oil sands.

"How long before you can make me a print," asked Burke.

The engineer replied, "Probably take about an hour to get dry enough to try."

"Okay, then, do you have a roll of the paper handy?"

"Yep...here 'tis."

JJ took the roll of paper, held the film up to the window of the truck, with the paper roll hanging down from his hand holding the film. "Would you hold this, please..."

The engineer grasped what Burke was doing and cooperated. JJ traced off the two curves over the critical intervals, let the log film and paper drop down and traced some more until, in about five minutes, he had a rough tracing of the electrical curves for all of the key sands, as well as depth markers.

"So long for now, be back in a while," JJ said to the Schlumberger men as he quickly picked up and threw a few things in his briefcase. He grabbed the damp film, the log heading that the assistant had just finished typing out, ran out, jumped in his Chevy, and spun a little gravel taking off for the telephone. He waved his arm out the window as he saw Davis walking up, "I'll be back in a little while."

The damp film was now in folds about eighteen inches long. JJ tucked the film and heading into an unoccupied section of his leather briefcase.

Burke glanced at his watch: 7:55 AM. Boy, one helluva lot has happened in the last 30 minutes. JJ's mind was racing....

Everything is quiet and beautiful in the countryside...wonder how long it'll take for the land owners to realize what they have? The seismic picture indicates a broad flat anticline with at least 150' minimum closure on the pay section, and two of these sands are nearly 100 feet thick overall, and resistive to their base. That means the productive area probably extends down to near the base of closure, meaning probably at least 3000 acres productive. He continued to fantasize as he raced for Campo Dulce and the phone....

Let's see, there appears to be at least eight sands with oil, overall maybe 350' of pay. Assuming 200' over 3000 acres at 400 barrels of oil per acre-feet would be...is that right?...Yep, it is! 240

million barrels of oil! Man, if that's anywhere near right, it'll be one of the biggest oil fields in the Texas Gulf Coast...not many, maybe a dozen larger...

He stopped at the bus stop, got out and walked quickly to the door. It was best to not appear overly concerned about anything. He went in and found several patrons having breakfast, probably some of them waiting for the bus. He asked for the telephone and asked if he could make a collect call and got approval.

"Hello?" It was Al Clark.

"Morning, Boss. I wondered if you were at the office yet."

"What do you mean, if? I'm always here by eight...maybe some of you playboys don't make it, but somebody has to answer the phone. Got anything yet?"

"Well, I have a log." Everything in the cafe quieted down. Several of the people knew about the well, and that this man had come from the well. Everybody was pretending to not listen, but listen they were, with all their powers of listening...a bit of key news here could make somebody rich!

"Are you alone?"

"Kinda like there at the office."

"You mean there are several nearby?"

"You can bet on that, Al"

"Well, let's go to our code." They had developed a code in case it was necessary to speak in another's presence. On wildcat wells, it was common for the wellsite geologist and the District Geologist to pre-prepare some way of communicating in the presence of others who should have no knowledge yet of what had occurred. In their case, Clark was to say when he was ready, then Burke was to start reading nine-digit numbers: The first number was a random number, meaning nothing. The next four digits were the depth to top of sand, followed by three digits for the thickness of the sand, then last, a number identifying fluid content: water, oil, gas, or oil on water.

"Have you talked to Sarah yet?" Asked JJ. Any mention of Sarah was a signal that it was too complex to do completely by code.

"Okay," said Clark, "just give me the top three sands."

"All right, Boss, please say again, was that serial number 879210472?" This said that a 47' oil sand was topped at 7921' depth.

"Woweee," shouted Clark off to the side so it wouldn't be

picked up in the phone. "I'm happy if that's all the oil, but give me the next two sands anyway!"

"Just a minute, Al, let me write down those other two part numbers, then I'll pass it along to the pusher. Yeah, okay, I'm ready. I copy 479931422 and 682080882. Is that right?"

"Burke, I'm speechless. Just head for home right now. I know you have nothing more than a wet film now. Just bring it in right now. I'll tell Davis what's happened and what to do, and release Schlumberger when he makes his regular 8:30 morning report. We'll get the log printed and headed later."

Clark knew that the last two numbers meant 142' of oil pay at 7993' and 88' of oil pay at 8208' depth. Any one of these alone would be a significant discovery; together, they would be a major, once-in-a-lifetime discovery. He also knew that he had nothing on the remaining 450' of hole where there might be something more. Finally, he was well aware that this was only a beginning, that although everything *looked* good at this time, it could all turn to crap. It would take several weeks before the well could be cased, prepared and tested thoroughly. But it was damned exciting now!

Filled with more excitement than he had ever known, JJ sat down to get some toast and eggs, and coffee, to hold him for the drive back to Houston.

Twenty-two minutes later on this Friday, May 14, 1937, Burke was on his way to Houston, still fantasizing.

In Lufkin, Ruthanne was winding up her first year of teaching 7th Grade English. It had been a real education to her in that the kids were not what she expected...some much better, some much worse than her expectations. Regardless of what she did, it seemed that some of them simply had no interest in learning and were only interested in somehow getting by until they could quit this nonsense! Gratefully, this was offset to some degree by the ones who had very strong drives to learn, to accomplish, and stand out above the rest; sometimes plain old competition.

These were the children of merchants, storekeepers, and all the other expected occupations, but also loggers, sawmill workers, and other timber workers. One of her most unusual students was the daughter of a common logger with grade school education.

This young lady, 12 years old, seemed to memorize pages at

incredible speed. She could recall a certain word's position on the front or back of a page, and usually the page number. Expectedly, she rarely made less than perfect on tests of anything written, English, History, Reading, and so on. She also was straight A in all other subjects. Ruthanne just hoped that such an outstanding person would have the opportunity to get a college education and get into research where she should excel. Such children made it all worthwhile.

But now, wherever she went, whatever she did, this upcoming major event preyed on her mind. She always felt a chill when it came to mind; sometimes she caught herself with a slight tremble. This was big stuff, this marrying. It always came to mind when her senses became logged, as at some of the redundant teachers' meetings. Still, bit by bit, the affair was taking form and she found a tremendous amount of work was required.

What with bridesmaids, dresses, invitations, reception, and the hundred other things, Ruthanne felt completely swamped at times. Inexorably, Sunday, June 27th crept closer. Maybe she couldn't get it all done in time? No, with mama's help, along with JJ's family, we'll survive! Millions of other have, so...so can I.

"You know, Burke, you and Hatcher are now absolute heroes!" expounded Al Clarke. "Two hours after our report on the bottom sand testing at 840 barrels of oil a day, San Francisco was on the line. They wanted to know who generated the prospect and all kinds of stuff. I wouldn't be surprised if they make me give you guys a raise!"

"Well, Al, you know how it is, heroes one day, goats the next...but a little raise for a man about to get married wouldn't be exactly unwelcome!"

"Seriously, JJ, you and David did a fine piece of integrating the sciences to produce this discovery. You deserve recognition."

It was a good time. Everybody was all smiles at the office, with JJ and David Hatcher constantly receiving some kind of commendation. Everybody knew that a good deal of plain old luck was involved, but the secret of success is the recognition of luck. In the case of Dulce, everything followed the luck of the young men spotting an area of no seismic data off the north flank of Little Hill Dome, and recognizing that something anomalous caused it. The anomaly could be good or bad; but possibly good. From that point on, it was a step by step procedure to the big event: Flowing oil!

It was now mid-June and the location for two more wells at Dulce were already spotted, that is located on a map, then surveyed on the ground. The plan was to drill one of them, and if it was successful, drill the second with the same rig. If both wells proved out, the plan was to contract two, then three to four rigs to undertake drilling possibly as many as 75 or more wells on 40-acre spacing.

The land department had hired several contract brokers and an outside law firm to conduct title examination on all of the leased acreage, and to secure leases on a few infill tracts as well as possibly productive fringe acreage. It was a very busy office. For a limited time, the focus of most of the geologists, geophysicists, landmen, and engineers, as well as some administrative and management personnel worked on Dulce.

Amidst all this happy furor, JJ was planning a vacation. He had to report to Nacogdoches on Friday, the 25th for rehearsal for the big event two days later. Then, he had arranged to take his vacation during the next two weeks. Actually, it worked out okay; he and Hatcher had done about all they could with the mapping until another well was drilled. The second well was planned to spud in mid-July. Then, things might really move into high gear for a year or so.

The old man walked in the gate, then up the two steps onto the unpainted wooden floor of the open porch. He walked over to a white-haired lady doing needlework. "My Lady, I think we are a part of something unusual."

Lady looked up as she laid down her needlework. "Well, don't keep me in suspense!"

The old man, Henry Khulen, answered, "You know that drilling rig that was working on our north pasture?"

"Yes, go on," said Flora Khulen.

"As you know, it moved out, and we thought maybe it was just a dry hole, but I just found out that those trucks in here the last two weeks were testing the well and hauling out oil! Can you believe that?"

"Whoopee!," exclaimed Flora as she quickly rose out of her chair, "Maybe we're gonna get a little of that oil money after all!"

"Let's hope it's not a fluke. I hear in Campo Dulce that the county courthouse is alive with people from the oil company. Seems that they think they have something big enough to wanta be sure they have what they think they have."

As she walked away, Flora commented, "This is big enough news that you can't expect me to keep it to myself. We gotta have a little special supper for all the family we can get together."

This was to start the major wealth of the Khulen family. To this time, they had farmed mostly rice, ran a few cattle, and managed to make a fairly good living from the 4400-acre farm and ranch that had been initially put together by their respective families. Over the years, they had combinedtheir adjacent tracts and added to it a little from other family members and other owners. Twenty-four hundred acres were leased to the discoverer.

~ ~ ~ ~ ~ ~ ~ ~ ~ ~ ~ ~ ~ ~ ~

CHAPTER 13

Lufkin to San Francisco

All too quick as far as preparations were concerned, rehearsal date, Friday, June 25, 1937 arrived. Because of need to fit work schedules of the many people involved in the wedding of Ruthanne Cook and James Jonathon Burke, it was necessary to set the wedding on a Saturday, and the rehearsal and rehearsal dinner the day before. This created a profoundly hectic operation for the Cook family, but to JJ, it was rather easy. All he had to do was show up with the right clothes ready late Friday afternoon, and then do what he was told to do for the next 30 hours. After that, he had plans of his own. Which he had reviewed only briefly with Ruthanne.

The only thing that interfered with the weather was the weather. Although the mornings were fairly pleasant, by late afternoon, temperatures of over 95 degrees and humidities with numbers to match, created environments where the best thing to do was sit quietly in the shade, or under a fan on a porch, and sip ice tea. Preferably with a little lemon in it. And that's just what JJ did after getting home in Nacogdoches that Friday afternoon. His boss, Al Clark, had let him leave at lunch that day and JJ was on the porch sipping tea by 5 PM.

The rehearsal was to start at 6 PM, followed by the dinner just thereafter. All the windows and doors of the large Methodist Church building were open to allow the occasional breeze to drift through and pick up some of the collected heat. Ceiling fans helped a little. And this was June. Just think what it might become in August when things really heated up!

The heat failed to dampen spirits. Everybody knew quite well how to dress for hot weather, and rarely let it interfere with any desired activity. Especially *this* activity. With much joking, laughter, and a party atmosphere, the rehearsal was conducted, then off to the dinner. And, even though it was a little illegal in this dry county (no sale of alcoholic beverages), someone brought a few bottles of champagne. Thus, with natural good humor, good food, and good alcohol, a real party developed. After the dinner, JJ got his younger sister, Elizabeth to drive them home. He was a bit wobbly.

Saturday morning dawned bright and clear and JJ had one job to do before the heat set in, so he was up and out in the yard by 6:30 AM. He felt a little headache, but really not much...rather surprising considering his taste for champagne the night before. His job was to get the yard mowed and raked for the reception planned for that evening. Over the years, the Burkes had developed a beautiful and very large back yard, where they often spent most of the late afternoons.

On the back of the house was a roomy screened porch which often served as a bedroom during the hot months. Homer Burke had set up a ceiling fan on the porch, and with this and the portable cots and mattresses, even the hottest nights could be handled with no duress. Along with the night sounds, the birds, and the stars visible through the trees, summer nights could be downright pleasant on this porch. And JJ had spent many nights there.

Three wooden steps set on a brick foundation led from the porch to a graveled walkway in which several flat red-black ironstones had been set as stepping stones. The ironstones had come from an informal quarry deep in the hills southeast of Nacogdoches, where it was easy to pick up rather flat slabs a few inches thick. The walkway wound past a clothesline hung from neat white cross posts, through flowerbeds and several large oak and pine trees to a low smokehouse and storehouse located about 200 feet from the house. The house faced south, so the large backyard lay partly in the shade of the house. The only thing wrong was the grass. It had to be mowed. Over half an acre of it all told.

The Burkes had a Negro yard man who also operated a painting business. He was an interesting man in himself, well read, a good country fiddler, and well liked by everyone. His name was Spartan James. It seemed that his folks had read about the Greeks and the Spartans, and liking what they read about the courage and braveness of the Spartans, decided that was just like their son should be. And so it was. Spartan normally did the mowing as part of his yard deal, and the Burkes paid him $4.00 per month to take care of their mowing, flowerbeds, and shrubs. Since he had about fifteen yards he handled, Spartan made nearly as much per month doing yards as he could make with a job in the sawmill, or lumbering, and he had his paint business besides.

All in all, Spartan and his family fared quite well for Negro families in East Texas at this time. He knew it, and was proud of it. And so were his many clients and friends. But, he had gone over into Louisiana, near Many, to visit some of his family this particular week and couldn't do the yard. JJ was thinking about all this as he took Spartan's place and found out just how big nearly 6/10 of an acre was when it was mowed with a reel hand mower only 18 inches wide.

About 7:30, his mother Alma called out, "James Jonathon, I have some scrambled eggs and ham that's just dyin' to be eaten, and if you don't try, it'll get cold...even hot as it is."

"Yes, ma'am," hollered JJ as he stopped in mid-stride, abandoned the mower and literally ran to the house. By this time he had worked up quite an appetite and was anxious to rid himself of it!

He partook of his delicious breakfast and coffee, then returned to the mowing job. He had cooled down while eating, and it was now very nice under the large trees, with a little breeze blowing the grass cuttings away from him when he could manage it. All in all, even if he was warm, the scent of new-mown grass mixed with the sweet odors from the flowers, along with the tree shade and the sight of giant trees and all the stories they must have locked in their fibers, created a pleasant fantasyland. Stir in the fact that today was the beginning of another major and exciting highway of life, and feeling good anyway, and it was a pretty good stew, thought JJ. He figured this back yard would be a fine setting for the reception after Ruthanne and he had tied the knot.

He finished the mowing, put the mower up and started for the house. As he started up the stairs, he called out, "Mom, how about a giant glass of ice tea?"

She answered, "I had already prepared for your thirst. I have a little surprise for you."

JJ walked in, saw a huge glass mug of what looked like tea, with large chunks of floating ice. "Looks like tea, did you do something to it...maybe added lemon?

"Not exactly. It *is* tea...but not lemon."

JJ picked it up and in one continuing motion, grabbed the mug with both hands and gulped down a couple of swallows. "Wow, this sure ain't tea...regular tea, that is...it's sassafras!"

"Indeed it is," answered Alma. "Last week Spartan brought in a bunch of roots he had cut down on his old family place near the Neches River, and thought it made such good tea that he brought some back for several people. Just like root beer, isn't it?"

"Yeah, except no carbonated water, and a little sharper, fresher taste. This is about as good as anything I ever drank for a thirst quencher. I remember it well from a lot of years ago."

JJ continued to sip on the sassafras tea as he cooled down, and read the wedding invitation and schedule for the day's events. He knew he would remember this day as long as he had memory, and was looking forward to it. The wedding was scheduled for seven that evening, with the reception in the Burke backyard at eight.

As the afternoon wore on, clouds formed and, as if on cue, produced a cooling light shower about 4 PM that filled the air with the clean odors of flowers, of fresh plants and all else. This must be a good omen, thought JJ; maybe even the Almighty decided to make things a bit better.

The wedding was performed in a comfortable environment, with the ceiling fans and open windows creating a pleasantly cool atmosphere, augmented by the all-encompassing faint odors of the multitude of roses, carnations, even magnolias, and many other flowers. Added to the beauty of the bride in her pearl-laden white gown, and her four maids of honor in their pale blue and white gowns, the wedding was a creation out of fantasyland. It was a wedding that would not easily be forgotten.

To JJ and Ruthanne, it was all they could ever have dreamed of. Ruthanne was nearly overcome with tears as it came to the final "I do's"; she was filled with happiness and joy, all mixed with contentment, that this important event was story-book perfect.

Following the wedding was a gathering for photographs, then the company followed the leaders over to the Burke backyard for the reception. The most popular foods were the appetizers, hors d'oeuvres, of East Texas foods such as ham and sausage bits, shrimp, catfish, and numerous vegetables, salads, fruits, as well as the large tiered cake and bowls of champagne punch. Ruthanne and JJ attended briefly, cut the cake and served it, then disappeared.

It was JJ's intention that their wedding night would be spent in the Adolphus Hotel in Dallas, and to that end he had reserved for a late arrival.

They did make it to the Adolphus. They did consummate their wedding vows and bound the knot tightly.

The newly marrieds had a loose schedule for the next two weeks, to drive into northern New Mexico and on into Colorado, then back to Houston.

They found the mountains cool as anticipated, beautiful, striking, and exciting. They thoroughly enjoyed this wedding trip. They also found much of each other. And finally, they felt they had bound a tight knot that would not likely come unbound.

On their drive back to Houston, they saw much of the Depression of 1937. It was in the newspapers, even with riots in some places; people in desperation, needing food for their dependents, clothing, medicines. But mainly, just something to eat. The newlyweds felt guilty with their happiness, JJ's job, their car, and all they had. But they also knew they alone could not make much impact. They could only help this person or that one, and hope that others would do the same. The roads were filled with hitchhikers trying to find a source of work. Families in old cars, with large bundles tied on tops or rears.

On their return to Texas, the greatest number of destitute travelers were found on the main east-west routes between Sante Fe and Amarillo. There was no steady stream; just one, then another, then two or three together, then perhaps a quarter hour with none. They worked their way from Amarillo to Abilene, then Brownwood, to Austin, and to Houston. After Amarillo, the signs of Depression were not nearly so evident as in East Texas where many travelers were reduced to begging for food.

Even in East Texas, food was plentiful compared to the northern cities. This Depression of 1937 was worse for some than 1933. The Stock Market had fallen back to Depression lows of 1933, Germany was making war sounds, and little money was available to do any construction or building. It was indeed a time when Americans learned that the mundane was paramount. A job, any job, was a prize. There were few organized programs of welfare; many starved, or froze during the winter. Children in ragged clothes, barefoot, malnourished, ill, were common sights. In every town, on every major highway, beggars, tramps, hobos, were frequent reminders of the one major problem: Jobs.

This was a time to do all possible to work long and work well. Many stood in line for every job of every kind; talented people, educated people. It was a great delight to have a paid vacation. For this, JJ was most grateful and intended to never forget this California Company that provided his very life during such soul-wrenching times.

Back in Houston, they settled in. Ruthanne had started her efforts at getting a job in the Houston School District the previous spring, but had nothing firm to this point. She was to interview for a particular position in an elementary school off Harrisburg Boulevard. It was just off a bus line, but an old school and one not so inspiring as her school in Lufkin. But any teaching job was far better than none, and she knew that it was difficult getting in the Houston District; many others wanted in also. She hoped to work into a high school teaching job someday, but knew that was impossible without several years' experience.

They were able to get another apartment in the same old converted house that contained JJ's small apartment. Their "new" apartment consisted of a combination kitchen-breakfast area, two small bedrooms, a small living room, and a bathroom. It had all been created out of two large downstairs rooms in the old original house. It was conveniently located just two blocks from a bus stop.

Riding the bus back and forth to work was as cheap or cheaper than driving, and JJ had often ridden the bus, and left his Pontiac parked. Ruthanne was prepared to do the same. If she got the Harrisburg area job, she would have to take a bus downtown, and transfer to the Harrisburg bus, taking nearly an hour to get to work, but that was OK. The job was first; everything else was behind that. They needed to have two pocketbooks for the next few years while they saved money for the children they hoped to have later on.

The rest of the summer flew by and, in August, Ruthanne learned that she could have a substitute teaching job at the Harrisburg school, on call as needed. This was disappointing, but far better than nothing, and she made the most of it.

Both she and JJ had a rather happy outlook on everything; nothing kept them down long before he was chasing, pinching, patting, and doing all the wonderful things with this beauty that he never thought possible. To him, she was a never-ending joy, the personification of happiness and warm companionship along with her positive attitude and creative manner. To Ruthanne, JJ was much the same, with a little more emphasis perhaps on strength and security. Together, they felt they could handle anything.

Summer turned to fall, then winter, as the two adjusted to their jobs and lives together. Ruthanne was working about half the time, sometimes, like in December, nearly three-quarters, and they saved every penny she made. With 3-1/2% interest added on, the kitty would grow over the years.

Toward year end, JJ learned that a seismic crew under Dick Kerr had moved into Saudi Arabia over a year earlier. He suspected that this crew would learn a lot. Especially if they could find some way to improve the reportedly poor records. Of more interest to JJ, he heard that the first core or sampling rig had moved in some months earlier with Krug Henry in charge. With that, how could they miss? Might not find oil, but they would surely find structures. As soon as he heard of that core rig, he immediately thought of the vague anticlinal signs at En Nala and wished he could be a part of core drilling there.

The geologists commonly called the small rigs capable of drilling perhaps a thousand feet, core rigs, and the holes they drilled, core holes. This was so even if the rigs produced only the regular cuttings that were bagged by depth, then described and logged by the geologist.

But these rigs were also capable of taking cores, cutting usually 5-to 10-foot cylinders of the rock being drilled so that the rock and the fossils therein could be more closely examined. Sometimes these cores were put in cans and sealed as soon as they were recovered at the surface so that they could be sent to a laboratory for measurement of characteristics that had not been altered significantly from the way the sediments existed in the earth.

Such canning preserved some of the fluid that existed in the rock when it was in the ground in place. The lab could measure that fluid and identify its type and content. Thus, for example, fresh water aquifers could be defined. Depending on circumstances, the geologist decided whether to drill ahead or core. Usually, for structural data, that is, the tops of formations, regular drill cuttings were used.

Because of their frequent use for getting formation structure tops, perhaps only 30 or 40 feet deep, some people, usually not geologists, referred to the rigs as structure rigs, and the holes as structure holes.

He also learned that the first well at Dammam, #1, was a poor oil well and had finally been shut in as a probable gas well, something of almost no value at that time and place. Dammam #2 was drilled and completed in 1936 as a good oil well, especially after acid treatment, but not a great well for such a remote location. Based on these good signs, San Francisco approved more drilling, even before Jubail recommended it, and undertook a major buildup of the entire program. Several wells were set to be drilled, even up to Dammam #7, a projected deep well to test the pre-Tertiary beds of Cretaceous and maybe Jurassic age. This last well really excited JJ...now that was getting on with it! Also, a test well on a new structure, Al Alat #1 was approved. He just hoped the #2 held up, and that was yet to be proved.

Then, unexpectedly, the Burke plans changed. In February 1938, JJ was transferred to San Francisco. As it turned out, it occurred as the result of an innocent conversation with Al Clark just before Thanksgiving, 1937. Al had asked him how he liked his work, and what his ambitions were during one of their occasional after-work beers. Burke thought nothing of it, just two friends talking. But JJ had mentioned that he thought that great things were possible in Saudi Arabia, and he hoped to get back into that part of the company sometime. Clark relayed this to San Francisco when they had asked him about JJ in January.

So, he was to be transferred to San Francisco, and perhaps later, back to Saudi Arabia. But his job was to be Saudi Arabia geologic coordinator for the time being; a management staff position, and a good job, though not such as a District Geologist. At this time, he did not know that a major buildup in the Saudi operation was underway as the result of a recent major event.

"Well, look who the dogs drug in!" Burke turned and looked down the hall toward the voice, and there was the tall redhead from the desert, Huey Larsh.

"Huey! I had no idea you would be here. What are you doin'."

"What you are gonna do is coordinate, you're replacing me."

"Look, Larsh, I don't want to beat you out of a job and I know there must be a lot more to this and I wanta hear it in detail. But now

I'm supposed to attend a meeting about my work, so could we delay this to a beer after work?"

Larsh grinned, "Same old A, B, C, Burke...sure, how about meeting me out front about 5:30?"

"Done," said JJ as he started walking away. "Huey, it's mighty dam' good to see you!"

"Same for me, buddy."

Burke had just arrived at the Socal offices and was walking down a hall to his briefing meeting where he expected to be brought up to date on the Saudi activities and learn his new responsibilities as well. He and Ruthanne had wound up their jobs in Houston, and arranged for shipment of their few furnishings and personal items that wouldn't fit in the Pontiac. They had then taken a long weekend to visit with family in Nacogdoches, and set out for California from Nacogdoches. Traveling in late February was pretty good until they ran into a blizzard in the mountains just east of Sante Fe.

That proved to be rather harrowing for a few hours, driving through snow so blinding that the hood ornament was invisible. They couldn't stop for fear of becoming snowbound, but couldn't see where they were going at all. They settled on looking out both sides of the car for the road as they crept slowly along. Fortunately, the blizzard dissipated within about 30 minutes to the point they could see ahead fairly well, but now the snow drifts were interfering with movement. Finally, in the grey gloom ahead they saw a drift as high as the car. They had no choice but to stop. Now they could go in neither direction. There was nothing to do but sit and wait and hope that a snow plow would come along. And it did, about two hours later.

Nothing was ever more welcome to the couple than the sight of the big plow breaking through the light snow into the big drift ahead. JJ jumped out, got his shovel he always carried in the trunk, and threw the snow drifts around the back of the Pontiac toward the bar ditch. He then got back in and backed up a little to allow the plow room to get by. It did, and they worked their way past it and were back underway. They drove slowly through the snow, passing several cars behind the plow, and got into Sante Fe by dark.

The rest of their trip to San Francisco was uneventful, and they had already arranged for temporary housing there through company help. They got set up in their small apartment and each went their way the next morning, JJ to the office, and Ruthanne to search for permanent quarters.

That afternoon, JJ checked with Ruthanne by phone, told her about his meeting with Larsh, and arranged for dinner out with her about eight that evening. Then, a little after five, he started looking for Huey. And found him. Over three beers and two hours, Huey brought Burke up to date.

"JJ, you remember when we left Jubail in early summer, 1936, we had heard about a core drill being brought in? And you and I talked about Dick Kerr's work with the seismic crew even before we left."

"Yep. And in view of the poor seismic records indicated on the first few lines, we thought that core drilling was the only sure way to get the near surface structure, which along with seismic and gravity could be used to get the deep structure."

"Well, they did bring in all that and wait 'til you hear what happened!" And Huey summarized the story of Casoc in Saudi Arabia from 1936 to the current February, 1939.

In late 1935, a seismic crew was brought in and Dick Kerr was put in charge of it. They proceeded to shoot numerous lines, but early on they discovered that the records were frequently useless below the Miocene, just a jumbled mess of energy recordings. It was interpreted that the main cause of the poor records was probably cavernous porosities in several Tertiary (Miocene and Eocene) limestones. Similar problems had been encountered in West Texas in some areas, so it was not totally unexpected. In doing this kind of seismic work, a hole was drilled about 30 or 40 feet deep, an explosive was placed in the bottom of the hole and discharged. Energy from the explosive traveled down, some reflecting off layers of rocks, but if an energy shock wave entered a water-filled cavern, it simply reverberated therein instead of reflecting back toward the surface. This reverberation also destroyed other energy that had reflected off deeper layers and tried to pass through the cave on its way back to the surface. The net result was poor to useless deep seismic records in many areas of Saudi Arabia.

During 1936, seismic was being conducted in several areas, as well as a continuation of the surface geologic work. At the same time, numerous other activities were being conducted. Dammam #2, on the Dammam dome, obvious from surface geology, was spudded 2/8/36. It was completed for 3000 to 4000 barrels of oil per day in late spring, a rate 20 to 40 times greater than most oil wells completed in the United States.

This created euphoria at all levels and a great expansion of effort took place: More drilling was authorized; Dammam #3, #4, #5, #6, and #7 plus a test at the Al Alat structure about 20 miles north of Dammam. The pier at Al Khobar, some 50 miles south of Jubail and just across a narrow neck of the Arabian Gulf from the island of Bahrain was enlarged. Water surveys to find deeper channels for larger ships were conducted.

Dammam camp had replaced Jubail as headquarters, though Jubail was maintained for some geological work. Personnel increased several fold, with Fred Davies replacing Bert Miller and taking over as general manager, and Max Steineke became Chief Geologist. Core rig work was started; gravimeter work started; vehicles were improved. Major fresh water supply wells were found and dug, both for the Casoc operation and the Saudis. Also, the faithful Fairchild aircraft, which had served so well earlier, was dismantled and stored. And all these events occurred between late 1935 and the end of 1936. This was a time of major expansion.

By summer 1936, Dammam was making mostly water, with only 100 to 200 barrels of oil per day; hardly exciting for this remote locality. By the end of 1936, Dammam #3 was completed as a marginal oil well, #4 was a plain dry hole, #5 was drilling, and #6 was ready to spud with derrick built. All wells after #1 had been drilled with rotary, not cable tool, rigs; and these were steel, not wood derricks. Even #1 deepening was by rotary. Significantly, #7 was planned to penetrate the Eocene that was highly productive at Bahrain, and test the deeper Jurassic Arab zone that had oil, but mostly gas, shows at a Bahrain well. At this time, Bahrain Field on Bahrain Island was a major oil field and a large refinery had been constructed there to process the crude oil.

Of considerable significance, the core drilling was started in November 1936, and conducted by one of the original ten geologists, Krug Henry. And also of much significance was the arrival of paleontologist R. A. Bramkamp who set up a lab to study micro fossils called foraminifera that were imperative in establishing the age of some rocks.

By the end of 1936, all of the exploration work had identified the obvious Dammam dome, plus surface indications of anticlines at Abqaiq, Qatif, and An Nala.

At the same time, gloom was settling on San Francisco and many of the personnel in Saudi Arabia. At that time there was no commercial production from the four wells completed and one drilling. And all of these had been located on a definite large closing structure, similar to Bahrain, and the Bahrain major pay zones had been tested by all the Dammam wells. The major oil flows from #2 created the major buildup in effort; its rapid decline carried emotions with it.

On December 7, 1936, Dammam #7 was spudded, then drilled down and set 16" casing at 1741'. This well was designed to test the Arab Formation at a total depth of about 4600'. The Bahrain Field pays were found in limestone rock around 2300' in the earlier Dammam wells. This well was started before #6 because now it was "do or die" time and, since it was to test deeper objectives, it was most important.

The year 1937 was mainly a time of continued exploration and setting up for a long program expected to last for decades. During this year it came to be expected that if #7 failed, there would probably be severe curtailments, but operations had to be planned for possible expanded operations as well. In the spring, the first two wives arrived and occupied two of the six air-conditioned cottages then in place.

In planning for permanency, quarters for families had to be constructed. Pre-fabricated air-conditioned cottages were designed and delivered in early 1937. The pre-fabricated bunkhouses were also air-conditioned about the same time. Into this community at Dammam came Annette Henry and Nellie Carpenter, the first American ladies in this area. Actually, Annette Henry was French, the beautiful woman won in a whirlwind romance by Krug Henry in Lebanon in 1934. These ladies were very special to all the men, and were treated as queens or movie stars might be.

The female population rose in the fall with the arrival of four other wives and three children, including Max Steineke's wife, Florence, and their two children. After much discussion on culture adaptation, these ladies decided to not wear veils as required by Islamic law, but they did avoid slacks, shorts, and other wear that exposed much skin. Naturally, the women and children were all celebrities, and were recipients of great respect and attention.

Although at first the women stayed strictly in the camps, so as to avoid Islamic law confrontations, by the end of 1937, they had been taken on excursions all over the area of eastern Saudi Arabia then active to Casoc.

In January, 1937, the Saudi police operations came to a head. These policemen, assigned to each camp area, were heavy-handed and did not hesitate to use force or violence, while demanding respect and obedience all the while. This attitude was especially profound with non-American employees, but Americans also observed plain arrogance and violence. Floyd Ohliger, the manager, complained to the Saudi government and obtained a new police chief. After that, relations with the police improved markedly.

In April, the well at Al Alat found major Miocene fresh water aquifers, and these proved to be of more significance at that time to the local Saudis than anything else. Such supply was quite critical to the Casoc operations, as well as a boon to Saudi agricultural needs.

A major geologic event of 1937 was the spring traverse of Saudi Arabia by Max Steineke and four other geologists. This was the first such traverse since the one by Bert Miller in 1934. Since most of the trip was across open country with no roads, it proved to be a difficult and time-consuming excursion, but scientifically quite rewarding. They started at Dammam, went to Jiddah on the west coast, and returned after a considerable delay in the mountainous area of central and west Saudi Arabia.

It was at this time that the basic framework of Saudi Arabian geology was set. It was later to be better defined by the work of R. A. Bramkamp and others, but this was the reconnaissance trip that yielded the basic data establishing the sequence and regional structure of all the sedimentary rocks lying above the Pre-Cambrian (Pre-Paleozoic) igneous rocks of western Saudi Arabia. They observed anticlines, synclines, faulting that formed downfallen blocks called *grabens*; the Paleozoic-igneous contact, the relatively thin Paleozoic section and the overlying Mesozoic section in the Tuwaiq Mountains (*Jibehl Tuwaiq*) near Riyadh in central Saudi Arabia, and recognized the Jurassic beds of the Mesozoic at al Kharj about 60 miles southeast of Riyadh. These Mesozoic outcrops in the Tuwaiq Mountains are the source of much fresh water in these beds to the east where they are deeply buried.

Interestingly, on this trip, one of the major problems was water. Sometimes in the form of flash floods in the wadis, sometimes as a wadi with several feet of flowing or standing water, sometimes cloudbursts. All this in the desert world of Saudi Arabia. Such water is the basic source of all the springs to the east, after sinking into porous layers and moving easterly downdip in such layers, called aquifers, to fault interruptions, then up along the fault fractures to the surface, or near the surface.

Elements of geology on this trip proved useful in interpreting the structure of folds over a hundred miles to the east. This was understandable when it was considered that at the outcrop, it was possible to see and date the rocks by fossils and rock type, but to the east where the drilling was being done, no wells had penetrated below Eocene limestones, sands, and shales. And the boundaries were vague or unknown as to the Miocene/Eocene and Eocene/Cretaceous. At this time, there was deep well information from Bahrain Field, and now, this new information from the outcrops.

On the last day of 1937, Dammam #7 blew in at 4535' depth after topping the Arab formation at 4500'. To this point, the well had been nothing but one problem after another, and had taken nearly 13 months with a rotary rig to get to this depth. Such a depth in the United States would have been attained normally in two or three months, even with similar rock types such as in East Texas. But #7 was drilling in completely unknown rocks, and had penetrated the entire Tertiary and Cretaceous by this time. After getting control and testing, this blowout proved to be gas, at about 30 million cubic feet a day. No oil. And gas here at this time had less value than dates.

Consequently, 1938 opened on gloom. All the wells to date were bad. Expensive. Non-commercial. San Francisco issued orders: No more wells until #7 is done; limit all expenditures as much as reasonably possible. Chief Geologist Max Steineke went to San Francisco to update top management on the overall operation, his interpretations, and his recommendations. He recommended drilling #7 deeper because it had not penetrated the full Arab formation. They approved; but with a "better work, or else..." attitude.

And work it did. As drilling progressed slowly, more gas was found, then gas and some oil. 8-5/8" casing had been set at 4480', so the plan was drill, then test any shows as encountered. First had come the upper Arab gas test, then drill a little and run another test: gas. Then drill and test, drill and test. At 4692' depth another test was run. The well flowed oil, at the rate of 5832 barrels a day, with considerable gas. Total depth was 4727'. It was all anyone could do to contain themselves.

Euphoria reigned again.

And this time, it was for good. On various production tests over the next few days, the well flowed at rates from 1500 to 3700 barrels of oil per day. This got the attention not only of all Casoc and Socal people, but the Saudi government, their royalty, the British, Mussolini of Italy, and many others. Over the next few months, Dammam #2 and #4 were deepened to the Arab zone D, and also made excellent oil wells.

But, just to be sure, production from the wells was maintained for several months before, October 16, 1938, Bill Lenahan, General Manager for Saudi operations, notified King Ibn Sa'ud that commercial oil production had been established.

By summer, 1938, the boom was on. Central air-conditioning for the bunkhouses, new trucks and equipment ordered, new tires designed, more building, more wells planned, more exploration, a new pier designed, refinery considered, and on and on.

By this time, Huey was getting hoarse from talking, and besides, three beers on an empty stomach were coming on a little strong.

"JJ, as of this time, there are numerous wells among the *jibehl* at Dammam, they're building a major port facility at the sand spit about 40 miles north, Ras Tanura, I believe they call it, and I think there is a refinery planned at Ras Tanura also. And I'm dam' near talked out."

"Larsh, you have told me one of the most, no, the most, interesting story I've ever heard. I think that's terrific in every way!"

"Well, you gotta remember, your're a little drunk, and besides, you're quite prejudiced."

"Maybe so, well... yes, that's true, but still I can hardly wait for more to happen. Most everybody is now at Dammam?"

"Yes, but, wait, I forgot, they renamed the camp, it's now

Dhahran. And I think that covers the area around Dammam, including the al Khobar pier."

"How do you spell that, d-a-h-a-h-r-a-n?"

"Yep, except drop that first 'a'."

"Oh, there's one more thing. Burke, you remember how we learned to break dates open before we ate them?"

"Indeed I do, still do now, even when I get a pack at the grocery."

"Well, just the other day, somebody told me that a visiting management type was eating dates and nobody told him anything and he was just washing them and eating them whole."

Laughing, JJ responded, "How long did that go on?"

"Until he asked somebody else why they broke them open and looked at the seed first."

Both men laughed uproariously, being a little drunk anyway. But also because they both knew of the little date worms that buried in near the seed and ate away at the date.

"One last thing, Huey, and it's a big thing: What are you gonna do if I'm taking your place?"

"I have a new assignment, preparatory to returning to Saudi Arabia next spring. While you are to be the geoscience coordinator, I'm to be the exploration equipment coordinator, taking the place of Tom Henderson who recently resigned to work in South America with Esso."

"OK, I got it. We're both coordinators and will be working together some. Sounds like a helluva deal to me."

"You know, JJ, I think we're part of something that will never happen again anywhere to anybody...."

"Maybe so. It'll be fun to see."

Over the next few months, the Larshes helped the Burkes get settled and introduced them to San Francisco and its many sights. The two families blended well and they all looked forward to the "good times." It made them all feel a little guilty to have such a good life.

However, times were getting better in the United States. The 1937 return to depression in the economy was being reversed in 1938 and here, toward the end of the year, the economy was in better shape overall and unemployment was not the specter it had been.

One of the causes for the upturn was the gradual movement

by the government toward better national defense. This meant more planes and other military equipment were being manufactured, which created more jobs. At the same time, the military was being beefed up, not dramatically, but steadily, and this provided home and work to many young men. There was a decided concern for the intentions of Nazi Germany after its conquest of Austria without a shot being fired in anger. Now it was Czechoslovakia.

In September, 1938, the British, French, and Germany agreed in the Munich treaty to avoid war for now, "in our time" some said, by ceding part of Czechoslovakia to Germany because "historically it is Germany" said the Nazis.

Little wonder that any Western country with any sense was beginning to gear up for a possible fight. However, in the United States it was a relatively modest effort. Not so in France and England, where major military buildups were underway, in anticipation of possible conflagration.

Ruthanne found a band teaching job at a local elementary school and enjoyed her work most of the time. As always, in teaching, there are ups and downs, but when most of the students are eager to learn, the experience can be exhilarating. And she had good students here, so it was a good job. She and JJ constantly felt that their cup had indeed "runneth over."

June, 1939. The nights were quite cool, and the days were pleasant here in San Francisco. Sure different from East Texas this time of year. JJ thought that this was about as pretty a city as he had ever seen and he and Ruthanne were enjoying the stay immensely. During the last sixteen months he had been kept very busy trying to keep track of all that went on with exploration in Saudi Arabia and communicate some management needs to the Dhahran office.

"JJ, we have passed a milestone," said Huey Larsh as they crowded together on the cable car headed for work.

"Yeah, that's without much doubt...the gamble paid off," replied Burke, "and the only way now is up!"

They were speaking of the celebration some six weeks earlier, on May 1, for the loading of the first tanker of oil at the brand new Ras Tanura terminal just north of Dhahran, where final touches were still being applied. King Sa'ud himself opened the valve for the first load."Huey, I heard that Krug Henry had left Saudi Arabia for Egypt.

Did you hear that?"

"Yep, sure did," said Larsh, "I understand he left right after the Ras Tanura celebration. Regardless of what he does for the rest of his life, he'll never be a part of anything as big and dramatic as this. He was the last of the original 10-man exploration crew."

"You know, Huey, this is one complex operation. The more I act as a go-between, the more I find how complex it really is. Did you know that at the same time there are several major operations going on simultaneously? There's the constant negotiation, administration, and remunerations to and with Saudi Arabia that takes several people full time. And all that has to be coordinated with the exploration, development, and now the shipping of oil. And each one of those has several offshoots and a bunch of coordinating. Then on top of all that, we have just negotiated a huge increase in the Saudi concession. At a price, I might add!"

"And, JJ, did you know that now we are conducting gravity and seismic?"

"Yes, that's been part of my job, tryin' to keep track of all the things that are going on at the same time. It got started back in March, under Dick Kerr."

Huey sat back, "Well, there is no doubt that this is one hell of an operation, and who knows, we may not yet see what it might come to be. We know there's a large structure at Dammam, there's evidence there may be one at Qatif, Abqaiq, and En Nala; and there's a good chance at least one of those will work out for a discovery. Now I hear evidence is shaping up for one up near Kuwait."

"And any one of those might be as big as East Texas Field!"

The two geologists had by this time arrived at their office building and were walking in. "Hey, you guys, have you heard that another core drill has been approved for SA?" said Margaret Janak, their secretary, and all- around assistant. By this time, amongst some of the people working on the Saudi Arabian program abbreviated it all by use of "SA."

"Well, it might be more structure, than core, drilling," returned Burke, "but no, I hadn't heard...your're one up on me!"

"That's not so unusual, Mr. Burke, sometimes I think I *stay* one up on both of you!"

"And, maybe you do," said Larsh, "but we're *smarter* than you!"

"Says who?" she came back, "if you're so smart, why aren't you rich?"

"She's got a point, Larsh; she does have a point," laughed Burke as they all turned from the hall into their small office complex.

The next item on the Burke agenda would be to decide if they wanted a core drill assignment now, considering the world upheaval that seemed to be building. He knew if he went, he'd have a lot of precedent in operations. Krug Henry had developed this over the past two-plus years since he started the first core drilling in 1936.

But, the next item on Casoc's mind was Dammam #12. On July 8, while starting in the hole with a perforating gun to add perforations in the Arab Formation below those already testing oil, the gun discharged prematurely. Later, it was determined that the gun probably fired because it was stopped and then blown by pressure, or pulled back up so that the firing pin on the gun slammed against the top of the lubricator causing it to go off.

The lubricator is a device designed for rotary drilling that aids in the control of possible blowouts especially when the drill or work string is out of the hole. It is placed just above the casing head and is often used as a means to go in a cased hole that is under some pressure from a formation that is open to flow into the hole. A tool, such as a perforating gun, can be inserted in this lubricator, then lowered on a wire-line into the hole. The lubricator usually consists of one or two lengths of casing to which are connected several pipe and valve assemblies that permit the pumping in, or flowing out, of mud or other fluids from or into the hole. Pressure gauges are mounted in one or two places on the assembly. After it is closed and the tool is on its way down the hole, with the wireline sliding through a pressure seal, the lubricator provides a means to pump heavy mud into the hole to counterbalance high pressures building up in the hole.

The only problem at Dammam #12 was that the gun fired within the oil and gas filled lubricator. The gun discharge triggered an immediate and profound explosion which destroyed the lubricator and thus eliminated any easy way to kill the well. So, the explosion was followed by a massive oil fire that soon produced a huge plume of black smoke that was visible to any Casoc people in that part of Saudi Arabia. The fire and smoke belched upward in a many-colored boiling mass of yellow, orange, and black, with the colors diminishing to black alone near the top of the 135-foot steel derrick. Strong winds carried the smoke to the south, where within a few days, it seemed that all of the Gulf inhabitants would became aware of a disaster.

Ten days later, using a great deal of ingenuity and inventiveness, and very little proper equipment, the Casoc men extinguished the fire. They stopped the flow, killed the well, with heavy mud. Their problem was particularly severe because there was no blowout preventer or wellhead to close off the unrestrained stream of oil that fed the fire. Perhaps as much as 10,000 barrels per day. These engineers and production men were not professional fire-fighters, but they proved that determination, creativeness, pure strength, and work beyond human capacity could overcome unexpected disaster. There was a brutal price. Two men died.

Then, on September 1, 1939, that which was anticipated to occur, did occur; it was not a matter of "if," only "when." Germany invaded Poland and the British and French ultimatums to Germany to disengage or suffer declaration of war, was ignored. Europe was at war again.

Even so, after much discussion, with deep emotion, JJ and Ruthanne decided to proceed with plan CD, their code for the core drilling operation in Saudi Arabia. They felt that JJ's tour would not extend over two years at most, and at this time, it seemed that there was a good chance that the European war could be kept there. They also felt that there was no reasonable chance that the Germans would purposely attack neutral Americans.

The principal reason for their decision to go was JJ's career and their joint excitement at the opportunity to live and be a part of a possibly mammoth operation in a strange land with a mysterious culture to learn. If JJ was to strive for professional acceptance and corporate achievement, among other things, he needed widespread experience, including foreign service.

Still another persuading factor was the recent transfer of the Larshes to Dhahran, where Huey was to act for at least some period as a development geologist at Dammam. JJ and Huey planned to work together, hopefully each with his own rig crew, at core drilling the next year. Provided JJ and Ruthanne decided to come. Now that they had, a letter to Huey would be underway shortly.

And, so it came to pass, that on a moonlit night in October,

1939, the Burkes decided to accept the Saudi Arabian adventure. They capped the decision with emotion in a way achievable only by a man and woman in love. In a bed. Not sleeping.

~~~~~~~~~~~~~~~~

CHAPTER 14

Back to the Kingdom

Their apartment was part of a complex of two-and three-unit buildings, mostly two-or two-and-a-half stories high, set into the southerly side of a steep hill overlooking the Golden Gate and the city of San Francisco across the bay. The builder was well aware of the scenery available and had constructed his building for both apartment units with a large picture window on the southerly side with its grand view. In the evenings, Ruthanne and JJ enjoyed having a drink before dinner, sitting together, drinking the view as well as their drink, as they discussed the events of the day, and events to come.

Such sittings sometimes led to a little snuggling during the perennially cool late afternoons and evenings. This then sometimes led to a little more expression of affection; to still more; until not infrequently, they found themselves closing the window drapes and following the course of soaring passion. Each new experience was as if none prior existed; each was a fountain of glory reaching to new heights.

One of these adventures in exhilaration took. They didn't know it at the time, but it occurred the previous July. By late August, 1939, Ruthanne was well aware that something was haywire in her body, like nothing she had previously experienced. She suspected what it was, and by early September, confirmed it. She was to be a mother.

And so, during the winter and early spring, they both watched and felt her body's manifestation of growing new life. The culmination of this great event was the following spring.

On Sunday, April 28, 1940, Mary Ellen Burke greeted the world with bright inquiring eyes, as if to say, "What in the world is going on, this is not at all normal...it's supposed to be dark, warm, and cozy all the time, and here I am in this cold, blinding place with no one to cuddle me."

Of course within seconds she was cuddled, swathed, and would never thereafter want for love. Now there were three. And number three quickly took over as number one. And she did so with the complete heart and soul of Ruthanne and JJ. They had known abounding excitement and affection before, but now this was joined by a new stimulation of togetherness, extension of themselves, an affection they neither had felt before.

This was a real "sweetness of life" period for this small family. This period in early 1940 was also a period of world unrest and Saudi Arabian petroleum expansion. The German Army had invaded Poland the previous September and, in spite of immediate declaration of war against Germany by Great Britain and France, swept across Poland within weeks, obliterating even the slightest resistance.

All during this period of increasing military activity on the Western Front between Germany and the Allies, JJ was busily assembling equipment and contractors for the new additional core-drilling project to be undertaken as soon as possible in Saudi Arabia. It was his job to do most of the detail work, under management direction, in getting all the necessary equipment together and on its way to Dhahran by June. These two rigs were to join others already active in the Kingdom.

The main equipment was the actual core-drill units. These consisted of a truck-mounted rig similar to the rigs commonly used for drilling shotholes for seismic work. However, there were two main differences. These rigs were capable of drilling deeper, perhaps to as much as 600 to 800 feet, or occasionally even more, while normal shothole rigs were usually limited to depths of about 200 to 300 feet. The second difference was that the core drill carried core barrels and coring heads, or bits, that could be assembled and screwed on the bottom of drillpipe so that, as the pipe rotated, a cylinder of the rock being drilled pushed up into the core barrel. Then, when the pipe was pulled out of the hole, prongs at the bottom of the core barrel sprung out from the inner wall of the barrel, penetrating a part of the core, perhaps on a fracture or relatively soft rock, to form a trap for the core above. These prongs, of different shape, size, and strength, depending on the type of sediment being cored, are called core catchers.

Modification of one or more of the shothole rigs already in Saudi Arabia to core drills was considered, but since those rigs were needed for the ongoing seismic work, additional rigs strictly for core drilling seemed necessary. In addition to the actual coredrill rig, each complete drilling team required at least two additional trucks: A water truck, and an equipment/personnel truck. Then, there were portable mud pits, drill pipe, an assortment of core barrels, bits, dry sacked drilling mud, and a number of extra tires, slips, and a host of other parts of the rig and auxiliary equipment.

The rigs and equipment were delivered to New York for loading aboard a seagoing vessel, and were underway by ship in early summer. JJ was to leave via air travel so as to arrive in Dhahran around the end of August to meet the arriving core drills.

Burke's core drilling, or structure drilling, operations would not be the first done by Casoc in Saudi Arabia. Actually, Krug Henry had been in charge of such drilling in the Dammam area starting in November 1936, and within a year had accumulated considerable data at Al Alat, Qatif, as well as Dammam. In fact, by this time, such drilling had been successfully used in the Abqaiq area to help define that ghostly anticline on which Burke and Larsh had worked in 1935. And in March, 1940, Casoc completed a test well in the Abqaiq area, and planned another test immediately. The first test found oil at 10,115', but more testing was needed to determine profitability.

It had been decided to expand this core drill work since it would provide a means to define near surface structure in a number of promising areas where, to date, the seismic and gravity data lacked clear definition.

The gravity data distinctly indicated a north-south trending ridge out from the En Nala anticlinal prospect evident from surface geology. The gravity showed a maximum trend, indicating uplifted basement rocks...perhaps granites or other high-density igneous or metamorphic rocks. These basement rocks underlay all of the Paleozoic, Mesozoic, and Cenozoic sedimentary rocks that offered possible oil reservoirs in the region. Since a few rock dips and outcrops of older sediments had been found in the Harad area of this vague structure called En Nala, it was obvious that there was some expression of the basement uplift in the surface rocks. The gravity showed there was a basement uplift. The surface geology showed that the uplift extended to the surface. Now a great deal of core or structure drilling was needed to define the near surface, that is, within a few hundred feet of the surface, structure. The rigs to be used by Burke and Larsh were to help in this definition.

By early summer, 1940, a well-equipped camp had been constructed at Dhahran for full families. An air-conditioned cottage had been set aside for the Burke family, who were to join the Larshes who were already there, and a large contingent that together formed a rather nice-sized city. At this time, there were some forty wives and nearly half that many children of American employees, a total of nearly 400 American employees, and well over 3000 Saudi Arabian, Bahraini, Indian, and other employees in this boom town.

After the successful completion of the major discovery, Dammam #7, and the following development wells still being drilled at Dammam, there was no longer any question of the viability of commercial oil production in Saudi Arabia. The only question was how much and when. The blowout and fire at Dammam #12 the previous July had caused considerable consternation, but all in all it helped bring the Casoc team together even more, by showing that such a major potential disaster could be handled by these transported oilmen at this remote location, even without the multiplicity of tools and equipment available in the States.

It was a cool mid-summer night in the Burke apartment. JJ came back into their bedroom after checking Mary Ellen, and headed to the bathroom to brush his teeth before going to bed. There stood Ruthanne brushing her teeth, in panties. Period.

Their bathroom was somewhat narrow, such that one person walking past another at the wash basin would tend to brush against the basin user. Well, in this case, Ruthanne was the basin user, and as JJ walked past, his hand rubbed across her scantily clad seat. Then, he said, "Oops, forgot..." and turned around and walked back past Ruthanne, and again rubbed across her seat with his hand, pressing against her as if it was a very tight squeeze. He turned back around, and started back in, "guess I don't need it after all..." and this time he pressed his body against her seat as he squeezed by.

"JJ!"

"Yes, sugar?"

"Cut it out!"

"What?"

"You know very well what!"

"Oh, the squeezing by you? You know what a tight squeeze it is in here."

"I certainly do, and it isn't *that* tight!"

He eased up against her, reaching around with both hands for her breasts, and found them..."Well, I'm not made of iron you know, and when I live with a sexpot, it's hard to think of much else when I'm close to her..."

"Ummff..."

"I think we oughta go lie down and think about all this for a while," all the while he was gently caressing her.

"Well...maybe we should...," she murmured as she allowed herself to be lovingly picked up and carried to the bed.

And another "sweetness of life" day drew to a close.

The next morning while sipping coffee after breakfast, JJ said, "Honey, I'm scheduled to leave for the Gulf next week."

Ruthanne replied, "So soon? I thought you wouldn't have to go for another month."

"No, the rigs and stuff are on their way, shipped out last week. And I've gotta be there a few days before they get there, so there's not much room for waiting. Besides, our place is to be ready right away, and you and Mary will be right behind. Maybe two or three weeks."

"What about this war? What with the Germans all over France, and the British seemingly helpless, do you think it's safe?"

JJ thought a little and answered, "I think things will get a lot worse down the road a way, even to the extent that we'll have to come home before our assignment is up. But as for now, I do believe there is no danger for us as long as we're on civilian aircraft out of the war zone. And our scheduled flights, even though partly British, should be in no danger."

"What do you mean, partly British," she asked.

JJ responded, "As I understand it, each of us on our separate trips, will fly the new Pan American Dixie Clipper from New York to London, then British Overseas Air from London, via Cairo to Bahrain. I don't know for sure, but I think the BOAC plane may fly south from London to some point in Spain or Tunisia for fuel before going on to Cairo."

"Well, it doesn't sound like the safest thing in the world to me," said Ruthanne. "But it's not quite scary enough to keep Mary and I from going with you!"

"You know, my sweetheart, this may have a little uncertainty to it, but then, we're young and can take a lot. If it turns into an adventure, we can handle it, and maybe profit from it."

"Whither thou goiest, etc, etc.," whispered the auburn-haired 25-year-old East Texas piney woods beauty.

JJ arrived in Bahrain in late August, just ahead of the two rigs, which were on a Spanish ship. He had a joyous meeting with Huey Larsh on his arrival at the dock and, together, they directed the unloading and temporary storage of the rigs. Burke and Larsh then laid out their schedule for reloading on a barge for delivery to Dhahran. All proceeded about as planned, except for slight damage to one of the derricks during the final unloading at Dhahran.

For the next few days, Burke and his old buddy Huey Larsh were quite busy getting their rig crews organized, finding the Burke family cottage, and overseeing the unloading and placement of Ruthanne's and JJ's things that arrived in three large trunks via ship. JJ had hardly two weeks until Ruthanne's scheduled arrival in mid-September.

He was to have one geological crew, and Larsh had a second. Each such crew consisted of three geologists, and they were assigned plane tables, alidades, altimeters, Brunton Compasses, a Ford pickup, water cans, canteens, tools and sundry other equipment. Burke and Larsh got together with their crews at one time and explained their plans.

The other four geologists were all single except one of Burke's men who had a wife in Oklahoma, planning to come over within a year if the war allowed. Each man had some kind of field experience, and one on each crew had worked briefly on core drills in West Texas.

Each core drill crew was to handle one rig that would operate normally on a 24-hour schedule. JJ and Huey were grateful that it was not necessary to do permitting like in the States. A good deal of such a crew's time in the States was spent finding roads and ingress to locations, then getting permission from landowners to come on their property and drill their shallow holes. Here, roads and permits took no time; there were no roads, and all was owned by the State.

A large number of locations had already been set up by existing sketched structural maps and notes derived from earlier geologic work, augmented by seismic and gravity data. The plan was to develop additional locations based on map upgrading from the new structural information generated by the core drills. The three geologists worked together on each crew so that any night work was rotated to allow for adequate rest for the night worker.

Ruthanne arrived in mid-September, and got settled in during the last few days JJ was receiving his instruction from the District Geologist, doing the setup work, and planning the first holes.

"Mr. Burke, I must say, you have picked one desolate place to bring your wife and child. The least you could have done is set us up in an oasis. They do have oases here somewhere don't they?"

"Sugar, they do indeed have oases, but there are none near where we have to locate for expediency of shipping, etc., and besides, once you get used to it, things aren't so bad. Remember, the Saudis live here all the time!"

"And they have never known any better," Ruthanne replied. "But forlorn or not, we'll make do with what we have, and enjoy the difference! And if the Saudis can do it, by golly, so can I."

"We're coming into a pleasant time of year in another month or so," said JJ, "and I think you'll truly enjoy the nights, with the heavens like some gigantic picture, set against the waters of the Gulf."

She responded, "My husband, if joy is to be, it is up to me; if I find nor make none, then it is me, not thee, not this."

Ruthanne and Mary became part of the community right away. The ladies already there welcomed newcomers and introduced them to their bridge, tea, and other entertainment functions, as well as schooling, medical and other needs that were established in this location so different and so far from home. Meanwhile, JJ got on with the core drilling.

Rather than take regular weekends off, each drilling party typically stayed in the field for about two weeks, with continuous 24-hour operations, then operations would be shut down for a few days for repairs, maintenance, resupply, and recreation. This was to continue throughout the winter and the following spring. There was no exact schedule; an off-period was often triggered by failure of some part that could not be repaired or replaced during operations, or by supply breakdown. A rig simply could not operate in parts of this area without some drilling mud, as opposed to little need for it in many other areas with sediments composed largely of shale or clays. But, when the section was strictly sands, conglomerates, and limestones, a little mud was a necessity for good operations.

Another critical item was water. If the water truck broke down, operations stopped. If water could not be found close by, drilling delays occurred. However, these rigs were nothing like regular oil drilling rigs. It was possible to makeshift temporarily with even sea water; with no drilling mud; and without a full crew. They did all these things at one time or another.

The geologists performed several operations. First, they selected the exact locations to be drilled; dictated first by the need for structural or rock control, and second by terrain. There was constant modest modifications of the desired location because such a location was on the crest of a large sand dune, or on the edge of a bluff, or in the middle of a wadi during rainy season.

Their second function was to get the location correctly spotted on their maps. Usually this was done with the plane table and alidade, though sometimes it was done by transit using triangulation or other means to measure distances. Precise drill hole elevations were necessary, and were usually determined with the alidade or a transit. Without precision in the elevations, at least relative to other rock elevations from holes or outcrops used on a particular map, the mapped structure was meaningless. So the geologists were very careful with elevations. They were very aware of a phony structure being created by a bad elevation.

The third major function of the geologists was to log the hole. This required catching drilling samples, washing them, then describing and marking their descriptions by symbols and words on a long strip of heavy paper. This strip of paper then constituted a log of that hole, and the description, location, and elevation of the hole was placed at the heading of the log. Since many of the rocks were very similar, and exact dating and/or correlation required fossil or other characteristics determinable only from a whole rock instead of tiny drill fragments, cores were taken. A typical operation was for the geologist to pick a coring point at a certain depth at a given location. Then, a geologist had to be at the drill site several hours before the core was pulled in order to log the samples before getting the core, then the core.

Occasionally, the geologists canned cores. This was done to preserve fluid content in the core for lab analysis. At the same time, it provided a good sample for porosity and permeability measurements. For example, if it was desired to know what kind of water, salty or fresh, that might occur in a given formation at a given location, a core would be broken into fragments and canned in regular tin cans with the same kind of hand-operated canning machine that Aunt Susie used to can her garden vegetables. This preserved the core in a state not totally different from the way it was in the ground before being cut. If there were any hydrocarbons, they were thus preserved. If the water contained sulphur, it was identifiable. If the salt were potassium instead of sodium chloride, it was measurable. This procedure was about the same as was done on regular oil drilling rigs, for the same reasons. These rock and fluid characteristics not only identified what the conditions were at this location but, when correlated with the same data from other holes, could be used to project estimated reservoir conditions at oil-bearing depths downdip.

In any case, whether by samples or cores, and whether the cores were simply described on location and destroyed, or carefully preserved and stored, the basic object of core drilling was to determine the elevation of specific rock layers at specific locations. For example, if the elevation of a particular hole at the surface was +300 feet, and the Jumble limestone was found at a depth of 60 feet in that hole, then the elevation of the Jumble would be +240 feet there. The + sign designating above sea level. Using similar tops of the Jumble limestone in a number of other holes, plus elevations from a few outcrops, a map could be made on this layer, similar to a topographic map. The "hills" were anticlines, and the "valleys" were synclines.

Another common technique was to use the top of another rock type, called perhaps Marker X, that had been found and measured in surface sections or some other core hole to be, say, 32 to 36 feet above the Jumble limestone. Thus, if the Jumble could not be reached in a typically 50 to 200' hole, or found in an outcrop in the area, then Marker X could be used, if found, to indicate the Jumble occurred at an elevation about 34' below Marker X at that location. Similarly, with other markers, over perhaps several hundred feet above and below the Jumble, elevations of the Jumble could be approximated, if not measured, at almost *any* location.

Finally, the extensive En Nala core drilling operation that most of the geologists had wanted to conduct for several years got underway in late 1940 near Harad. But, prior to that, another event occurred that changed family plans for all the employees. On October 19, 1940, Dhahran and Bahrain were subjected to something that London had been undergoing for several months: Air Raid!

In the early morning hours an air strike was carried off by Italian planes from out of nowhere and which, after dropping their deadly cargo, disappeared into the night to the west, apparently to an African base. The damage from the raid was slight and had no effect on operations at Dhahran camp, or the Bahrain refinery target. But it did have a substantial effect on the Casoc employees.

It was decided that all women and children should return to the States for the duration, but the work would continue, even if somewhat reduced. The first wives and children left within two weeks, and all were gone by May, 1941. And by that time, a significant number of the men had returned to stateside jobs also, leaving a distinctly reduced staff. However, the core drilling operations continued.

The ghostly anticlinal structure indicated by scattered surface geologic data in the Harad and Hofuf areas, referred to as En Nala, where Burke and Larsh had worked several years earlier, was their target for the core drills. Finally the geologists had a tool that would create a geologic section of near-surface rocks at or very near the exact locations where such data was needed to make a reliable structure map of this apparent En Nala anticline. The main problem was that they had been unable to define the exact location of the crest of this fold in the rocks, and they were unable to find the ends. The south end was probably somewhere in the Harad area, but the northerly end was completely unknown.

The earlier core drilling under Krug Henry, started in late 1936, but fully active in 1937, had finally defined the Miocene stratigraphy, that is, the description, thicknesses, and sequence of the Miocene-age near-surface rocks. Though the stratigraphy was by no means perfect, and it would surely change from area to area, it was sufficiently defined by now that Burke and Larsh had a good takeoff base for their operations.

And, much more meaningful, Abqaiq #1 was completed as a Jurassic Arab Formation oil well in November, just as Burke and Larsh were preparing to move their crews to the field. This well, along with the earlier Abu Hadriya #1, defined an apparent major discovery if the two wells were connected as was thought probable. At this time the evidence was that this, to be called Abqaiq Field, was something many times the size of the currently productive significant Dammam Field. The geology and intuition of the earlier surface workers, especially Max Steineke, based on sparse outcrops and topographic features, led to seismic and gravity, then core drilling, to finally shape this very large anticline. The initial drilling was undertaken in the face of reservoir uncertainty, and geologic timeliness questions, but proved once and for all the major significance of oil in Saudi Arabia.

One of the worrisome questions that ate at the exploration geologists was the age of trap formation versus age of oil migration, that is geologic timeliness. When structure is found in Miocene rocks at the surface, it is clear that at least some of the structure present in older rocks was formed after Miocene time...or quite recently. Since some, perhaps all, of any oil to be found in the objective Jurassic beds had probably migrated well before Miocene time, perhaps even before the end of the Mesozoic Cretaceous, maybe it went right on through any Jurassic reservoir at that time because no structure trap was then present. Or maybe the migrating oil was trapped in some structure that was then present, and the current structure is a combination of the structure that was present at that time, plus the more recent structure that is evident in the surface rocks. Thus, to the geologists, not only was it important to have a structure to form a trap, but at least part of that structure had to have been formed in time to catch the oil that migrated sometime after the reservoir was formed.

The requirements for a commercial oil accumulation are 1) reservoir, 2) seal, 3) timely trap, and 4) available source. All these things worried the Casoc geologists in this new frontier but, being the perennial optimists that they were, they used science to the fullest extent possible, then relied on Lady Luck to provide the rest. And each and every one of them were fully aware of one fact: With a test well there is some chance of success; without it there is no chance.

By Christmas, Burke and Larsh were underway with their crews and drills, and they added useful information that helped shape En Nala with each new hole. Early in their operation, Burke decided to try a new procedure to speed their work. He worked and fumbled with it for several holes until, by February, 1941, he had it down. In order to be sure that their key formation tops were picked accurately, it was better to use a core rather than drill-cuttings samples alone. The samples consisted of tiny pieces of the rocks penetrated, and try as they might, using microscopes and great care, there were times that the formation tops were not clear when picked from the samples.

For example, their main markers were the Hofuf, Dam and Hadrukh Miocene Formations. The Hadrukh was mainly sandstones, the Dam mainly marls (limey shale or clay) and limestones, and the Hofuf was sandstone, marl, limestone, and conglomerates (a hodgepodge of broken limestone fragments, pieces of sandstone, and gravels). Thus, Hofuf could be confused with the other formations unless the sequence, thicknesses, and fossils (in the limestones) were right. However, going from one location to another, and knowing what the sequence was in the prior hole, it was possible to reasonably predict what might be first drilled in the new hole.

But, stopping drilling to come out and change to a core barrel, then core, then pull the core out every ten feet or so was a slow operation. It would be so much faster if the coring could be reduced to just remote new holes. Even though their holes were often miles apart, using various geologic clues they could often tell that a particular marker rock or formation top would likely occur within a given interval of say, 100 feet (30.77 meters).

Each different rock type drilled differently. A loose sandstone would drill fast, a dense limestone slow. A gravel conglomerate would cause the drill string to chatter, a marl would drill smoothly. JJ thought that if he and the driller on a rig could work closely, they could log the layers with accuracy while drilling, without having to stop and core to be sure. So gradually, JJ worked out this new logging technique. He worked with a tall buck-toothed driller from California by the name of Sam Swartz. Together, they made it work.

The system they developed worked like this: JJ would stand beside Sam at the back end of the drilling truck, with a clip board laying on the iron work shelf between the drilling kelly and the controls handled by Sam. The kelly is a drill pipe that is square-sided so that as it drops through the rotating rotary table the rotation is imparted to the kelly which is screwed into the round drill pipe that extends into the hole. Thus as the rotary table turns, so turns the bit or core head at the bottom of the pipe that makes up the drill string. These rigs worked basically the same as the big oil rotary rigs, just scaled down.

As the drilling fluid circulated back up and out of the hole, it ran into a metal trough about eight inches wide and five or six inches deep, then on into the portable mud pit, a metal container about eight to ten feet long, up to three feet wide and about a foot and a half deep. The drilling mud flowed into the mud pit, dropping its cuttings, then on to an outlet at the rear and into a flexible pipe that ran from that point to a pump which pumped the fluid back down the inside of the drillpipe into the hole to and through the bit and back up the hole on the outside of the drillpipe to the surface. As long as circulation was not lost in some cavernous or highly porous rock, the system worked well.

As the fluid came out of the hole, JJ would lean down, scoop up a handful of cuttings in the trough, look at them with the hand lens hanging from his neck, then reach over to the work table for a bottle of acid to test for calcareous content of the rock, and thus describe the cuttings as they came out of the hole. Each time the drill pipe changed sound or speed of penetration, Sam would say, "JJ, we're into another kind of rock." Typically, JJ would return, "OK, take a sample."

Then Sam would stop drilling at all for about a minute, then drill as hard and fast as he could to penetrate about a foot, then, stop drilling again, and circulate strong for about a minute. The whole sample taking procedure lasted for about three minutes. The result was a steady stream of cuttings coming out the hole, followed by a stream of mud with little cuttings, then a flood of cuttings, followed by a paucity of cuttings. The flood of cuttings was from the new layer of rock that made the different drilling sound.

After so logging the hole, they ran a simple electric log tool on a wireline in the hole to take measurements of electric resistivity and self potential (natural microvoltage). This log was excellent for defining the boundaries between rock layers, and even had certain electric characteristics that could be recognized for some rock layers in different holes. This provided some correlations from hole to hole, then when combined with the lithologic (samples/cuttings) logs, provided usually excellent correlations between holes if the same rock layers were penetrated in the compared holes.

JJ's new lithology logging method resulted in his locating

boundaries between rock layers at the same exact depth as the electric log. Prior to that, regular sample logs produced from bagged samples caught every two or five feet, often logged such boundaries up to ten feet different than the electric log, or missed minor boundaries completely. And, most of all, this procedure provided a good log of a hole in one or two days on a typical 100' hole, instead of two to five days when done with the conventional coring procedure. Of course, some cores still had to be cut, and were, but many of the holes were logged with similar accuracy to coring, and in half the time or less.

There was one drawback to this fast, good log procedure: A geologist had to be at the well continuously during the drilling, whereas with the bagged sample routine, he would be there for perhaps one-third of that time. This resulted in a tougher schedule for the geologists, but increased their output of holes considerably. Also, with about half the total time being taken up with rigging down, moving, and rigging up, there were rarely more than thirty or forty hours of continuous drilling. And if there were such long periods, it was because of lost circulation, drilling problems, repairs, or hard rocks, during which times the geologist often had two or three hours for napping or handling other errands. And with three of them, they rotated the logging work while the other two were sleeping or finding and surveying the next location.

It was long and hard work while the rigs were in the field, but interspersed with periods of a few days rest along with properly labeling logs, and bringing maps and notes up to date. Then, for various reasons, the rigs did not always operate on 24-hour schedules. Sometimes they worked only two shifts; sometimes only one. But, when it was one shift, it was from near daylight to near dark; none of this eight-hour business.

"JJ, I am damn near worn out," said Elmer Roach, one of the two younger geologist on Burke's crew, "and we've got another four or five months before we get a real break!"

"Yeah, I know," replied Burke, "but you're just worn out now because of that two days without getting into a proper bed. In another few days, you'll be able to do another two-day stint!"

"I suppose so, at least right now I can't think of anything I'd like better than a twelve-hour stretch in a regular bed in a room with a big, lazy revolving ceiling fan! Not a cot, mind you, nor in a tent; a regular bed in a gentle breeze. It's not that I want cool air so much, it's not that bad now as far as temperature is concerned. Just clean, not dust-laden, not sand-filled, air."

JJ returned, "Elmer, you wouldn't know what to do if you had those conditions all the time. Just think, five more days on this run, and we can all sack out for a while. In clean air, with clean sheets."

"I'm looking forward to it. Well, anyhow, back to that hole I just got off of: I'm beginning to think there is no north end to this structure. I'm not even sure it's a viable prospective structure; it's more like a ridge, sorta like the Nemaha Ridge in Kansas."

"That is peculiar, but it seems there may be individual closures on the ridge."

"I noticed," said Roach, "and at least the main En Nala area near Harad may have as much as a hundred feet closure. Do you suppose it's possible that any dip closure on the whole blamed ridge could be productive?"

Burke replied, "If everything is right, it could be. Or if only one of the individual closures was like Abqaiq, it could be really big."

"I'm getting less worn out by the minute. You keep talking like that and I'll be so adrenaline laden that I'll just have to go charging back out right now!"

"I got a giant picture of that!" laughed Burke.

While this discussion took place, Roger Evans, Burke's other geologist team member, was off scouting the next location for their rig. Evans returned shortly, and Burke joined him for a surveying run with the plane table and alidade to the next location. This had to be done immediately, because the rig was preparing to rig down and would be leaving for the next location within hours. So, while Roach rested, Evans and Burke started the several hours of survey work ahead. Evans would catch the next logging run while Burke rested and did office (actually tent!) work, and Roach scouted for the next location.

Day after day it went, in dust storms, occasional blinding showers, through flooded wadis, over rock-strewn sabkha. The loose sand of the *uruq* (sand ridge), that was sometimes piled up over a hundred feet high. All interspersed with beautiful Saudi mornings, evenings, nights. They pushed on until physically stopped by nature, terrain, or equipment failure.

Any rain shower was a blessing. Not only did it bring grass for the sheep and other animals of the Bedouins, it provided clean fresh water, a rare commodity in this environment. At these times, all skins, canteens, water cans, anything that would hold water, were filled. Most of such water was saved for drinking and food preparation, but sometimes splurged for taking baths or some other such luxury.

The weeks wore on, then the months, with a few breaks for trips to Riyadh, Bahrain, or even the barren mountains to the west where springs and water were more readily available. The drilling and mapping continued on to the north. By July, they had worked their way from Harad up past Burke and Larsh's Harmaliyah camp, nearly to their Udayliyah camps, and still no end to the ridge. By now, Burke, Roach, and Evans were satisfied that the best they could hope for were a few oil fields along this ridge in the areas where they mapped the few closures, or local anticlines. But, the ridge might prove to be a good regional feature where oil would migrate in the reservoirs up on this ridge and fill even the smallest closure. That kept their interest up. Since Abqaiq, they felt pretty sure that any anticlinal closure in this region would have at least some oil.

At the same time Burke was progressing with his drilling, Larsh was doing the same. And, Larsh thought Burke's fast log method was good enough that he copied it for many of his holes. Both Larsh and Burke reported to a Structure Drilling Supervisor, who oversaw and coordinated their work with other such work simultaneously underway.

Neither Burke nor Larsh reported their fast log method because they were afraid it wouldn't be allowed because of possible extra personal risk for the geologists. But that didn't keep them from somehow producing a lot of unusually well-matched lithologic and electric logs, with over fifty percent more holes than some other crews.

(NOTE: It is unknown if any of the Saudi core/structure drill work was done using the fast good logging method, but it was indeed used as described above for carefully controlled lithologic work in the Delaware Basin of West Texas and New Mexico.)

Before the temporary discontinuation of the field drilling for repairs, maintenance, resupply, tons of office work, and reasonable work hours during the blast furnace days of July to early September, additional drilling crews were assigned to the En Nala ridge program.

By now, it was general knowledge that this ridge was an excellent place to find anticlinal closures because there was a high likelihood of oil occurring in such places. It was, therefore, desirable to define this ridge as best possible in the shortest time possible because the world news pointed more and more toward the United States becoming involved in the European war. Already American shipping was fair game for German submarines.

Little thought was given, except perhaps in the wild dreams of some deranged geologist, that the entire ridge might be productive. Even so, it was an exciting chase. Probably several fields would be found on this ridge; after Abqaiq, there was no obvious reason why an anticline would not prove productive. At last there was now a good reliable tool, the core drill, to map the shallow structure and, when added to all the existing and newly added geophysical and surface geologic data, evermore clearly defined this profound, possibly grand, structural ridge.

During the summer respite, JJ had a little time to read, to think, and to reflect on the course of his life. First and foremost, Ruthanne and Mary Ellen were constantly on his mind. While in the field, his loves were recurringly on his mind, but he had little time to fret or beset himself over their absence. Now, however, with fairly regular work hours, he found more distress, loneliness, even torment over that absence. Yet, he had a job to do, and planned to make do as best he could during this period of personal trial.

He used several ways to avoid his loneliness for his two girls. One was to keep busy. Another was to plan and consider his obligations ahead. Still another was to take advantage of his Arabian visit to learn more about this ancient country.

Perhaps most of all was the receipt of batches of letters from Ruthanne, written almost daily, but received in Dhahran in sporadic bundles. Each bundle was like a cherished book, and he read them several times. Then, he would read them again. And then again. Also, he received mail from his parents and sister, and occasionally from personal and business friends. His mail was his Godsend. It was his home tie. And he had a lot to say about much of it, so he spent a fair amount of time writing, answering and asking questions, describing, discussing plans, and on and on.

The keeping busy part was easy. There were at least ten jobs waiting to be done at any time. Mapping, writing reports, making sketches, preparing sections through the earth using their core hole data, finishing off logs, organizing the mounting load of scientific and other data, and pursuing so many other parts to this gigantic Arabian puzzle.

As for learning more about Saudi Arabia, he visited some of the old Portuguese forts, Roman ruins, Bahrain, Hofuf, the oil seep bitumens up the coast. He watched the Saudis at work and play, to better learn their culture. And he read. He read the same books and articles again that he had read in 1934 by Charles Doughty and H. StJ. B. Philby, then *Seven Pillars of Wisdom* by T. E. Lawrence (Lawrence of Arabia) that was published in 1935. He also read parts of the Koran (or Quran) description publication in 1934 by A. Y. Ali so as to understand a bit more about this somewhat mysterious, yet powerful religion of Islam.

But perhaps his most cogent, most striking personal thinking was about the war. With sea warfare against American ships, ongoing and bristling talks with the Japanese, and German successes in North Africa, there was almost no way for the United States to avoid this conflict indefinitely. And, from his letters from home, he knew that the U.S. was almost on a war footing at this time. This had a particular impact on him, because even though he had not maintained his Artillery Reserve commission all these years; having had one, he was almost certain to be called up, regardless of personal factors, if a shooting war got underway.

It was with all these activities, thoughts, work, and planning that James Jonathon Burke spent the hot summer of 1941.

In mid-September, it was back to the boondocks. A full effort was underway to complete the En Nala ridge core drilling program as soon as possible. There was full anticipation that the war might at any time cause a reduction if not complete shutdown of the program. But, at least at this time, it was full steam ahead!

Burke and Larsh managed to have little get-togethers occasionally, and they both had regular sessions with their partners, in order to avoid error by non-communication.

Alcohol in general, beer in particular was sorely missed by the

Americans. Not only was alcohol strictly forbidden by the Saudis, possession alone was grounds for being fired by Aramco. For that reason, none was to be had. Except when the enterprising Burke and Larsh found a way to make a rather sorry drink that was a weak and poor excuse for beer. One windy day when it seemed that northern Saudi Arabia was busily transporting itself to south Saudi Arabia, and field work was shut down, the core drill geologists got together in a tent in the lee of a bluff, and the conversation turned to alcohol.

"You know, this is a time when a few cold beers would make life a helluva lot more fun," said Elmer Roach.

"Got any under your bunk?", spoke Larsh.

"You know I haven't, but there might be a way to get something a little like beer without the alcohol violation."

Burke spoke up: "Whata ya mean, beer without violation. Beer's, beer. It has alcohol, and alcohol is verboten."

"Not exactly," replied Roach, "Our cough medicine, our disinfectants, have alcohol. So, some alcohol is possible; anyway, what I was thinking about would have so little alcohol in it that it probably couldn't be measured."

"Okay, lay it on us," said Burke.

"The way I figure it, we have sugar, so if we could get some grain someway, we might be able to germinate the grain, get a little malt, then use the sugar and make a little home brew."

"I don't know about this," said Bob Killgore, a geologist on Larsh's crew, "I helped make some home brew back at college, and as I remember, it was pretty involved. Maybe we can find a way to get something that tastes like beer, but isn't beer?"

"Well," said Burke, "there's always sassafras brew."

"You mean root beer, like the soft drink?", asked Roach.

"Yep, but with actual sassafras root bark, you can boil it, then flavor it all sorts of ways, like with cinnamon and sugar, to get a drink that's got a little bite to it, but no alcohol."

And, so it came to pass that they all decided to see what could be done with sassafras. Now, the only problem was getting it. JJ wrote to Ruthanne who made a deal with their black friend, Spartan James, who seemed to know everything about the woods near Nacogdoches, for a delivery. Thus, shortly before Thanksgiving that fall of 1941, the first shipment arrived.

This was a big event. By now, everybody knew the sassafras story, and were waiting with great anticipation to see what Burke could cook up. Burke took the dried bark, boiled a batch of it, tasted it, added a bit of cinnamon, tasted, then sugar, then a little strong regular tea, a touch of salt, and kept experimenting until he got a very slightly sweet drink that did indeed have a sharp taste that lingered. He tried it hot and cold, and decided it was best when cold. When finished he had nearly two gallons of cold "beer" for the first evaluation meeting.

"Burke, this is about as much like beer as mud!" said Larsh. "But tasty!"

"You'd better say that, you red-headed refugee from an eleemosynary institution," returned Burke. "I worked hard to get this."

"Well," said Killgore, "it really does have a slight beer whang to it, and the taste stays...and stays...and stays...and stays!"

Thus was developed the "beer" for the core drill crews of Larsh and Burke. They eventually experimented with other spices and roots, but did develop a drink that was a bit like beer, and all quite legal. When back at headquarters and refrigerators, the drink was really quite refreshing.

The two old friends were sipping their "beer" just before the big Thanksgiving dinner the cooks had prepared for a mid-afternoon feast.

"You know, Burke, this war is goin' to get a helluva lot worse before it gets any better," spoke Huey Larsh.

"It seems that way, doesn't it," replied JJ Burke. "It's just a matter of time 'til we get in it. And then it might be fun getting home if we're still here."

"I've thought about that," said Larsh, "I suppose we'd have to try to find some neutral ship, maybe to some place in South America, or something like that."

JJ spoke seriously, "our first problem might be getting across Saudi Arabia. But, to hell with that problem for now. I've been meaning to ask you a question about an entirely different subject. You remember when we found those anomalous dips in the Abqaiq area, that partly resulted in the core drilling and the discovery?"

"You bet I do. What about it?"

"Well, now that we know there is a pretty thick oil pay there, how much oil do you think is there?"

"I don't know how thick the Arab pay is there, maybe 200'?"

"Maybe; let's assume that."

Huey Larsh did a little figuring. "With 200' of pay on that structure that looks like it should be over twenty miles long by some two miles wide, it's a bunch, probably over a billion barrels, maybe ten times that."

"I was thinking in the multiple billion range," said Burke. "Maybe another East Texas Field here in Saudi Arabia. Kinda exciting when you think we were in on the beginning."

"Yeah, and think about En Nala. We don't know how big that structure is yet. Of course, it may be a ridge like the Nemaha in Kansas, with oil here and there, but nothing really big. But you know, JJ, that ridge is already indicated to be over a hundred miles long and maybe two townships wide. It could be bigger than anything ever."

Speaking quietly, Burke said, "no question about it; all this Saudi Arabia stuff is potentially big, and En Nala could be the giant of giants. I just hope we can get our work done before our war starts. But I'm afraid we won't...before the U. S. of A. gets in. And then, who knows, we might not be the ones who finish it."

With that, the two men headed for the dining hall and the feast that lay waiting.

~ ~ ~ ~ ~ ~ ~ ~ ~ ~ ~ ~ ~ ~ ~

CHAPTER 15

War and To Home

Sunday, December 7, 1941. It had been another long day monitoring the core drill, laying out new locations, driving into Dhahran and, now, mapping. So often, each new structural elevation point obtained from the core drilling resulted in considerable alteration of the contoured map that JJ constructed from all data available.

The purpose of this important map was to produce a structure map of a key stratum (layer of rock) at or near the surface, called the Top of the Hofuf Formation, or Top Hofuf, or even shorter, TH. These sedimentary rocks were laid down in broad sheets, one atop the other, until the overall appearance was a gigantic layered cake. Each layer was somewhat different than the ones below or above, depending on the source of the sediments and the environment of deposition.

To do this, JJ used elevations they had measured with surveying instruments of the key stratum in the very few places where it could be seen in a surface outcrop. To this, he added the new elevations determined by drilling with the core or structure drills to the depth of its occurrence below the surface. Then, by subtracting the depth to the key stratum from the surface of the hole where the elevation had been surveyed in, he got the actual elevation of the stratum at that location. The intervals between strata (plural of stratum) in the core drill holes, as well as in the few measured sections where a section of strata outcropped, provided thickness of and between strata. By using these known thicknesses and an outcrop or drilled depth of some stratum other than the key stratum, he could get the elevation of the key stratum even when it was not present in an outcrop or in a drilled hole.

Then, by using the directions and angles of the slope of strata, called dips, they had measured at outcrops of other strata, he got rates of change in elevation of the strata in a number of places. Also, drainage patterns from aerial photos or sketch maps, aided in interpretation of directions of dips of the layers when there was no other data.

The key stratum was less formally called, "marker bed," as well as a specific name such as Hofuf, or perhaps Dam, formations. Names are usually assigned according to the locale of the best or first finding of that stratum or strata, called a "Type Locality." Thus a particular rather widespread surface formation in the En Nala region was the Hofuf Formation, and its top constituted a natural marker bed. Thus, the term between the geologists for this mapping horizon came to be simply "TH."

By this time, it was clear that the En Nala structure was no simple anticline. It was a structural ridge. Somewhat like the backbone of a horse. Very long in relation to its width. The crest was poorly defined in most areas, but when all data was incorporated, the crest could be fairly well interpreted if not fixed by actual measurement.

What was startling about En Nala was its length. It was now apparent that it was at least 100 miles (166 km) long, and maybe 150 miles (250 km) wide. The largest field in the United States was East Texas Field, about 42 miles long and seven miles wide. This En Nala ridge appeared to be over ten miles wide and over 100 miles long.

En Nala was so extensive that most of the geologists felt it could not possibly become one gigantic field, but that it might be reasonably possible that several individual large fields might occur on the ridge. Perhaps even an East Texas-size field.

The door opened and in walked Huey Larsh. "JJ, when are you goin' to wrap that TH map up? You know we'll never find the north end of this thing. Maybe it's clear up in Baghdad!"

"Where the hell did you come from?" exclaimed Burke.

"Well, I figured that since you had come in to clean up and eat good, I oughta be able to do the same," replied Larsh. "I got as much right as you do to play! But, back to my question, does En Nala go to Baghdad?"

"Who knows," said Burke. "Maybe it goes to Beirut!"

"Kidding aside, James Jonathon, any signs of north dip?"

"Just small suggestions here and there, nothing clear. I just hope this surface structure indicates the deep structure. If it does, and a thousand other things are right, this could be fantastic!"

"Changing the subject, what do you think will happen next in North Africa?"

JJ returned, "Looks to me like the tide has turned again. I

hope this is the last turn. Let's see, last fall some 80,000 Italians attacked a reported 30-or 40-thousand British, and all ended up dead or as prisoners, with the British occupying Bardia, and all of Cyrenaica in northern Libya by last February. Then in March the Germans attacked, Rommel was past Tobruk by June, and who know how close he got to Cairo in November...some say less than a hundred miles."

"Yeah, but he never took Tobruk!"

"That's true I guess, at least that's what we heard. In any case, the Brits did a helluva job at Tobruk."

"JJ, do you think Rommel will turn it around and chase the Brits to Cairo? It seems to me this might do it."

JJ laid his pencil down, slowly rose from his drafting table, and said, "Mebbe so, we better hope so! But right now my big red-headed buddy, I got a different, and I think, super, idea: Let's eat!"

"Great idea, Burke...sometimes you astound me with your wisdom."

After supper, they visited with some of the other geologists and production men, mostly about the war, played a rousing game of penny-ante poker, and went to their respective cottages. Burke and Larsh were well aware that all too soon they'd have to get up and beat it back to the sand dunes and tent life. But for this one night, Burke intended to rest well and enjoy the comforts of the cottage. He was intensly interested in the war in North Africa. Not only because of the interest that war generates in a man with his Texas A&M military training, but because if the Germans did turn around and succeed in taking Cairo, Aramco might have to completely close down for the duration. But at least for now, the British 8th Army under General Auchinleck seemed to have Libya under control. This was good news; if the Brits could keep the Germans at bay, the Aramco oil search could continue, even though rather restricted. One problem was, if the Germans ever took Cairo, it might be difficult to get them out because there was a great deal of Egyptian sympathy for the Germans.

It was nearly eleven p.m. on this Sunday, December 7, as JJ rolled over to go to sleep...just as the bombs began falling half a world away.

"JJ, wake up! Wake up!" said Larsh as he gently shook JJ by the shoulders. As was his manner, Burke went from solid sleep to full awake in about three seconds; he was up sitting on the bed immediately. He saw Larsh in pants with no shirt on, and two other men, including their seismic plotter and radio/instrument specialist, Charlie Dye.

Burke looked at his wrist watch lying on the small bedside table: nearly 2 a.m. "I know you all didn't come charging in here to wish me good night, so which rig twisted off or got stuck?" He had been awakened like this many times when something went wrong. His instant thought was how the hell can we get replacement equipment for whatever broke or went to hell?

Larsh spoke quietly: "JJ, we are at war. The Japs bombed Pearl Harbor. Charlie picked it up on London shortwave just a few minutes ago."

"That's our big Hawaiian naval base, isn't it?" asked JJ.

"So the radio said," replied Charlie. "We have nothing yet about how big, or how the Japs did it, but according to the radio, it is 'massive,' and the planes must have come from carriers."

"I'll be damned," said JJ. "I really don't know what to say or think right now. It's obvious our lives are turned around now, and God only knows what will happen next."

Larsh murmured, "We might as well try to get some sleep...if we can. I got a feelin' that tomorrow we'll be tryin' to figure out how to get home."

There was little sleep for anyone the rest of that night. JJ spent most of the time lying back with his head resting on his hands, looking in the darkness at the ghostly shapes of the furnishings lit by pale star and moon light. He would doze off, wake up, doze off again, and this continued until about 5 a.m. when he dropped off into a sound sleep. A little over an hour later, he was awakened by the many noises of a camp aroused from sleep by the tragic news.

JJ knew that he had no choice but to try to get home. He was in the Inactive Reserve, and had been kept there so long as he was employed in a critical industry overseas. But under these circumstances, he knew that he would be getting a call shortly, and he had to try to answer it.

By 7 a.m., the camp was in the mess hall for breakfast. Talk was rather limited, and quiet. Most of the men were lost in their own thoughts about what they had to do individually. At about 7:45, there was an announcement in the mess hall that there would be a top management statement later in the morning.

The management statement addressed the seriousness of the situation, the unbelievable treachery of the Japanese, and the effort to help all who wanted to get home as soon as possible. Actually, there were only a few Americans still in Dhahran who intended to ride the war out. So the management offer to help applied to only a few. Obviously, the time to leave, for those who were to leave, was *now*. There was little doubt that the Germans would side with the Japanese, with the result of a true World War.

At this time, there were only two women left in the Dhahran camp, both nurses. And one of them was scheduled to leave the next week. That would leave one American woman for the remaining 120 or so American men in camp who would probably come to adore, if not worship, her! As to the men who were to leave, it became a crash effort to plan the trip home and start it.

It would have been nice to take the BOA plane from Bahrain to Cairo, then on to London and the Pan Am Dixie Clipper to New York, and the train to Houston, but that was not now possible. The only practical choice was to get to Beirut, then someway by ship to a neutral country of Central or South America, then by some means to Texas. After a great deal of discussion, four of the core drilling geologists elected to try to get home: JJ, Huey, Elmer Roach, and Roger Evans. The company agreed to furnish a driver and car to travel up the coastal "roads," actually poorly marked trails for the most part, to Basrah, Iraq, where train and bus travel was still available to Beirut.

Thus it came to pass on a blustery, sandy, dusty Monday, December 15, 1941, the traveling geologists loaded the car and commenced the long and uncertain journey. They took all the canned food, bread, crackers, and water they felt necessary for the 540 km, or 320 miles, trip to Basrah which they planned would take two days or, with trouble, longer. But, since they were all seasoned desert cross-country travelers by car or truck by now, they were ready for most problems. They had bed rolls, extra springs, frontend rods, bolts, nuts, tools, tires, and two rifles if needed for protection, or just in case some foolish gazelle wandered too close! As was usual for cross-country travel, they had two extra cans of fuel and four extra cans of oil.

One special item was Oreo cookies. Somehow, a very large

shipment of these goodies came in with the last ship a few weeks earlier, and it was probably more than would be eaten before they got stale, so the cook was pushing Oreo cookies. So, Huey agreed to take a case of them in the car, so that each man could have some sweets for the trip. They even had both chocolate and vanilla.

They all agreed this trip had a lot of uncertainties in it and that it would probably take several weeks. They had to travel light and take a minimum of space with luggage. Each man would be allowed only one large bag that he could carry for a good distance if needed, which limited its weight to some thirty or forty pounds. This meant that very few books, paper, or extra clothes could be taken, and each man had to decide for himself whether it was more important to have an extra pair of boots, or more pants, or a camera, or whatever. They finally got underway a little after nine a.m. after unexpected delays in loading, and one false start. The car was fully loaded, with hardly sufficient space for the five men to sit amongst the bedrolls, luggage, and boxes. But with part of the luggage tied on back, it was not uncomfortable; just close.

They had just cleared the camp area driving north about forty miles per hour on a lightly graveled sabkha, when Roger Evans leaned over from his tight rear seat position toward the front seat and spoke loudly against the wind noise, "Elmer, did you put the extra parts in the trunk?"

Elmer Roach leaned back and replied, "Yep, but I didn't see the tools there. I suppose they are under the rear seat."

They drove on for a few minutes, and Roger spoke out loudly so all could hear, "Maybe we oughta check?"

Huey asked the driver, "Hasman, did you check the tools?"

"No," he answered, "it was not my job."

"Please stop," said JJ. Hasman stopped, they all got out, unloaded piled up luggage, two of the fuel cans, and food boxes, raised the rear seat, and found no tools. Each man thought the others had taken care of it.

They turned around, went back to camp, found tools, unloaded, then re-loaded, and finally got underway.

They drove through one hard, dry, flat, gravel-laden coastal sabkha after another, usually separated by stretches of sand that was fairly firm, but which occasionally was loose and wind-blown, even into dunes. Most of the dunes were only a few feet high, but some were small hills and very loose. All of the dunes required some planning to avoid getting stuck, and the large ones were especially troublesome. By this time, all the desert vehicles had large balloon tires designed to travel over most loose sand, but with their heavy load, they still could safely negotiate only so much dune sand, and had to travel some very circuitous routes to avoid bottoming-out or sticking.

All went well with only a thirty-minute lunch stop and two pee-stops, and they were averaging over twenty, maybe nearly twenty-five miles per hour in northerly travel. They planned to make it into Kuwait by sundown, and were pretty much on schedule. Since they had nothing better to do, and there was a bright sky, they continued on, a bit slower, after dark, hoping to make it to Burgan Field before stopping for the night. By nine p.m., they were traveling on the better-established roads through the southern part of Burgan Field in Kuwait, looking for a Kuwait Oil Company (KOC) field office of some kind.

KOC was owned 50-50 by Anglo-Persian Oil Co. and Eastern Gulf Oil Co., and was formed in 1934 to explore their Kuwait concession. Their first well was a 7950-ft dry hole on an anticline they called Bahrah, where oil was found later. Then in October, 1937, they selected a second location close to a sidr tree, near some bitumen deposits thought to be a seep from an underlying oil accumulation. The well location was also based on a magnetic anomaly that indicated a basement high, plus rather poor but distinctive seismic data that indicated a large northerly trending anticline. Rumor had it that this location also was influenced by a dream by the local British KOC chief, which led to a conversation with an old woman who lived in the desert in this part of Kuwait. This lady interpreted his dream that he should seek oil by a sidr tree. (Scott, 1991).

Burgan Field had been discovered in March, 1938, with excellent oil production from about 3900' depth. It was by no means fully developed and, like Casoc operations to the south in Saudi Arabia, drilling had been curtailed. But it was common knowledge that it was a large field and would be very important to the Kuwait Shaikhdom after the war.

Larsh spoke: "OK, Hasman, stop at that shed." It was now nearly ten p.m.

They pulled up to a large tool shed beside the road-trail, where

KOC had stored several pieces of drilling equipment, including some core barrels, drill bits, wellheads, valves, and other common oil field tools. No one was present. The large drive-in doors were unlocked, as was common in this Moslem world where theft was extremely rare.

Supper consisted of canned meat, beans, and peaches, with bread and water, on the unloading porch of the tool shed.

Since the night was so beautiful, no one felt it necessary to sleep inside, even though the temperature was now below fifty degrees F, and still falling. Instead, the men bedded down with their bed rolls on the loose sand in the lee of the building. It wasn't very comfortable, but at this time and as tired as they were, there was no problem finding sleep.

The travelers were up, fed, washed with a little water they found in a barrel in the shed, and on their way by the time the sun fully cleared the eastern horizon.

They arrived in Basrah in mid-day, found a hotel for overnight, and the timing of the train for Baghdad the next morning. After a bath, a good night's sleep, and a hearty Arab breakfast, the geologists bid goodby to Hasman who left to return to Dhahran. Then, the trek to the train station, boarding, and wait for the train to finally move out for Baghdad. Each man was careful to get his share of the Oreo cookies and find a way to carry the eleven boxes each.

The 275 miles to Baghdad were slow. The train was a local that stopped at every village to let someone off or to take a new passenger aboard. But, it did make it, and all were bedded down in a nice inn close to their bus departure location by ten that evening.

The next two days were spent in small busses with narrow, hard seats on which two of the geologists could barely manage to sit side by side. As the day wore on windows were opened to provide some cooling. And dust. At times, lots of dust. It was a matter of taking dust or heat. Dust won out. Gratefully, from late afternoon to the next late morning, the window could be kept closed. Except for some passengers who just had to have outside air. But with only two or three windows open, the dust was acceptable.

The first day on the busses ended at a small, dusty, uninviting inn on the road to Damascus. The second day saw the end of the 480-mile trip to Damascus, then by nightfall, they had covered the additional fifty miles into Beirut, their first big objective of the trip.

It was now Saturday, December 20, with Christmas the next Thursday. But, this was a time that Christmas would be just another day; the trip home was all-controlling, and every day conditions of travel worsened. The big objective for the four geologists now was to find a neutral-country ship out of Beirut for the Western Hemisphere, preferably Cuba. With the help of a travel agency operated by a displaced Frenchman and his wife, Charles and Lynette Fortier, passage was found.

The geologists divided up chores. JJ Burke and Elmer Roach were to work with travel agencies, hotels, or any normally knowledgeable sources of trip planning data; while Huey Larsh and Roger Evans were to work the dock areas searching for unconventional passage information. On the second day, Burke found the Fortier's agency, which had a deal with a Spanish shipping firm to find passengers for the limited space available on their freighters. Such ships commonly had space for a few passengers who were willing to travel under rather spartan conditions, taking the same food as the ship's officers, and required to stay out of the way of the crewmen as they performed their work.

The Fortiers fully understood the plight of the Americans and their need to find a neutral ship for passage. In addition, they knew of all the non-military ships that came in and out of Beirut and Alexandria, Egypt. A basic problem with Beirut's port was its limited facilities, and the fact that most shipping was rather small vessels with ports of call limited to the Mediterranean, and mostly to the eastern Mediterranean at that. The Fortiers advised the Americans to take a small Arab vessel to Alexandria and board a Spanish freighter there. And so it was agreed.

It was easy to find a dhow or other small vessel to Alexandria, and the Fortiers arranged for passage to Cuba on a Spanish ship that was due to leave Alexandria Wednesday, December 31st, the last day of 1941.

With the war, the Fortiers cautioned the geologists to plan for delays, try to learn a little Spanish, and dress and act like Spaniards once they boarded the Spanish freighter.

The first small vessel available to Alexandria was a Syrian motorship of perhaps 1500 tons displacement, with a cargo of dates, olives, and olive oil. The Americans departed Beirut on Christmas Day.

"A rather unusual Christmas, wouldn't you say?" observed Huey as they settled into their small cabin on the main deck of the vessel.

The first to respond was Elmer, "Let's just hope that this is an auspicious beginning. Since Christmas is marked and served by only things that are all good, maybe, just maybe, it so marks this occasion."

"Wow! What wonderful philosophy. You're almost poetic, Roach!" Larsh remarked flippantly.

The passage took two days and most of a third, after a brief call at Port Said to pick up a small cargo left there by a Suez Canal lighter. But the Americans still had three days 'til departure, so there was no panic rush.

Their Atlantic passage was aboard *El Caballo* (The Horse), so named by its owner who loved his horses, and so named this, his own first ship. The ship was out of Cadiz, the ancient port city on the Spanish Iberian Peninsula, about 50 miles west of the Strait of Gibraltar. The owner came from an old trading family who had owned ships since the days of Napoleon, and who also raised horses at their country place between Cadiz and Seville.

It was late in arriving because of trying to stay away from German warplanes and British warships, but came into the port of Alexandria the day it was supposed to leave. That delayed departure of the Americans until Saturday, January 3, 1942.

They met the ship's captain, Captain Del Roca, whose family name came from a rocky coastal area of northern Spain, thats claim to fame was that Hannibal had camped here with his elephants and army in the second century B.C., on his way to attack Rome through the Alps during the second Punic War. The Captain advised the Americans that Spain was not at war, that he wanted nothing to do with the Germans or Allies, but saw nothing wrong with transporting some apparent Arabs to Cuba. But he also pointed out to the geologists that both Germans and British warships sometimes stopped them to check on their cargo and passengers. So, from that point forward, the Americans became Arabs. They just had to do a little skin and hair fixing, as well as adapt their clothing to better suit Arab dress.

The geologists planned their appearance and cover. It was decided that they should appear to be Arabs from eastern Saudi Arabia, traveling to Cuba as business emissaries to try to establish a Saudi source for sugar that was now more difficult to get. In exchange the Cubans had some interest in dates, olives, wool, and camel hair. So, there were grounds for such emissaries.

The four well-tanned geologists could easily pass for Arabs as far as skin color was concerned, and since they each had wanted their families to see how they dressed on occasion in Saudi Arabia, each had a headdress in his bag. Since Arabs now often wore pants and shoes under their Arab dress, their clothing could be made to fit in quite adequately. So long as their hair was the right color. Larsh's red hair and Burke's reddish brown hair would simply have to be colored. Roach had black hair, and Evans' was brown. So, they decided to use black shoe polish on the hair of all but Roach, if and when it seemed that it would be necessary. They were not concerned about their eyes, because some Arabs had very light brown, even green, eyes. Evans and Roach had dark brown eyes, Larsh and Burke had green eyes. Still, they planned to not expose themselves, especially their eyes, any more than might be forced, if indeed the ship were to be boarded.

As far as body hair was concerned, they would simply keep it covered, and either color or shave off any on the wrists, ankles or elsewhere that might show. The next key item to consider was language. Since they all now spoke a little of the Arab tongue, they felt they could carry this off pretty well; at least sufficiently so unless, by some unusual chance, an investigator from a warship spoke Arabic fluently. To cover this small chance, they planned to talk very little, but at least a little, in the presence of any such investigators, using a few simple words like, "get the food," or "did you read the papers?" Not enough talk that their ignorance or accents would show, but enough to appear authentic. Evans was the best in Arabic, and would be their spokesman insofar as possible, if the situation arose.

Finally, they needed some kind of papers to prove their mission and Alexandria was an excellent place to get them. They needed a letter of introduction written in Arabic and Spanish, with a proper appearing Saudi business letterhead. They worked out just what they thought was needed that was expressed as an Arab might express it, even with the fictitious letterhead, Khamis Ben Thanian,

Haradh, Saudi Arabia. Now they needed to get the words into good Arabic writing, a Spanish version, and a printing shop.

The Spanish version was relatively easy. At their initial meeting, Captain Del Roca introduced them to their cabin boy, Jaimito Azul (Jimmy Blue), a university student on academic leave, who was very interested in the Americans and their geology. Jaimito spoke a little English, and JJ could handle a little Spanish, and between them, they could communicate fairly well. JJ had studied Spanish in high school and could speak it fairly well, and read it very well, at the end of the second year. But now, he was pretty rusty. For Jaimito, he had studied English for a year in a similar manner, and now had the chance to use it.

Between JJ and Jaimito, they got the Spanish version of the letter done satisfactorily. JJ knew he could get the Arab version done at the print shop by the Arab-speaking proprietor.

Alexandria, Egypt. Founded and named by Alexander The Great of Greece (Macedonia) 332 B.C., after conquering and destroying the ancient, but then rebellious, city of Thebes, over 300 miles south up the Nile, in 336 B.C. It was here that Alexander lived for several years, but it was not his final selection. He reserved that for Babylon, about 50 miles south of present Baghdad, where he died at age 32. But the Egyptians revered him and named him Pharaoh. Alexandria lay about 100 miles northerly from Cairo, or, at his time, Memphis (which lay just south of Cairo), on the western side of the main tributaries of the mighty Nile River. Not only did he found a major city and become Pharaoh, he undertook to change the very character of the Egyptians by intermarriage with his Greeks. And to some degree he succeeded.

The geologists learned these details about the beginning of this great city while visiting with the tradesmen and reading museum booklets, but now that they had the preliminaries out of the way and had made their plans and decided on their cover and disguise, they were ready for a little sight-seeing.

The very first thing that came to their attention was the life and style of this old city during a time when devastating war was being conducted as little as 100 miles to the west. The geologists were amazed at the apparent lack of concern by the populace. Good food, even steak, was readily available; as well as wine and beer. Work and play went on as if there was just a business boom, plenty of money for all, and no cares at all. Indeed there *was* plenty of money, plenty of work; everybody was busy, ships, trucks, and trains came and went; night clubs and bars were booming, and there were girls galore! However, the geologists had to handle business before play.

Burke found a print shop with a cooperative Arab proprietor, and together they constructed the Arab letter of introduction for these Arab businessmen from Haradh, Saudi Arabia. Using the letterhead they designed together, they typed the letter on an Arabic typewriter, then the Spanish on an English one. The Spanish letters required a few hand entries because some symbols could not be made on the English typewriter. But then, that should be as one would expect; after all, a businessman in Haradh would have a tough enough time finding an English typewriter, much less a Spanish one. Just as here in Alexandria.

Then for the next two nights, these young Americans saw the town. They enjoyed the food and wine, the strikingly provocative Egyptian dancers, the music, and the diversity of humanity. There were black, white, brown, yellow, and various in-between humans. Fashionably dressed, in rags, costumes, uniforms, pantaloons, turbans, headdresses, hat, caps, and all kinds of combinations. There were Egyptians, Arabs of several varieties, British, Turks, Greeks, French, American, even some Italians and Germans. Perhaps that Egyptian bellydancer, or that taxi driver, or tourist guide were spies. For the Germans, for the British, maybe for others. And they heard that all this was even more so in Cairo!

And all the while, brutal killing was going on as close as a hundred miles to the west. Men in tanks, planes, trucks, and afoot, doing their best to kill as many of the enemy as possible, and at the same time destroy their weapons and their resolve. Neither side had succeeded. God only knew the destruction to come before this war of all wars was to end.

The Americans were like everybody else: uncertainty lay ahead, so it was live fast while living was available. However, they studiously avoided womanizing, except to watch. They could see nothing but problems resulting from sexual activity, profoundly difficult though it may have been hard to restrain!

El Caballo set sail for its next port of call at Tobruk, Libya, three days behind schedule on January 3rd. In case of interception, the ship's Captain made certain that the cargo for Tobruk was indeed medical supplies as listed on the manifest. The British were short of many supplies at their fortified position at Tobruk, which had been under siege by the Germans. Del Roca would not have considered taking *any* cargo into Tobruk except for the fact that the cargo consisted only of eight crates of American goods, furnished by the United States, and weighing a few hundred pounds each. And, the Americans were willing to pay well to get a neutral ship to deliver the supplies.

The Captain was not concerned about their main cargo: Egyptian cotton bound for Cuba. As was common for freighters from this part of the world, there was wool, camel hair, olives, and dates in the cargo.

Starting the previous March, Rommel and his Panzer units moved out of Tunisia and attacked the out-gunned British, pushing them out of Libya by mid-April, and had some units move as far east as central Egypt by June, perhaps as close as 75 miles west of Alexandria, after several brutal battles. In November, the British attacked the Germans with strong reinforcements and pushed them back out of Cyrenaica into central Libya, again, after fierce battles. From early April to November, the Germans had besieged Tobruk after several major attacks failed. German warplanes were active in the area, and had been since the previous March.

German warplanes were particularly interested in minimizing British supply to Tobruk, both during the siege of 1941, and also at the present time. News reports made it clear that Rommel was only waiting for the right opportunity, at which time he fully intended to drive the British out of Egypt, taking both Cairo and Alexandria, and controlling the Suez Canal. Of course the British had completely different ideas, and were trying to hold Rommel at bay until they were sufficiently reinforced to drive him out of North Africa.

This was the state of affairs when *El Caballo* prepared to enter the port of Tobruk shortly after dark, with the plan of quickly unloading its small cargo and be well out to sea by daylight. All went well until about thirty minutes after they cleared the dock, moving out to sea. Then all hell broke loose.

German planners knew that they could not completely control

supply to Tobruk by sea, but they knew that continuing, but irregularly timed, attacks would cause all but the most determined shippers to steer clear of the port. And they were right. Only speed and money had enticed Captain Del Roca.

The warplanes consisted of a squadron of Stuka dive bombers, one of the most terrifying weapons the world had ever seen. As these planes made their dive, they lowered flaps that had holes positioned within. The result was a long, terrifying scream from the diving airplane that preceded the falling and bursting bombs. The first knowledge the Americans had of trouble was this unsettling scream. The scream was combined with the roar of aircraft engines, and followed by short whistling sounds of falling bombs, then explosions.

Fortunately for *El Caballo*, the warplanes had targeted another, somewhat larger, ship that was still at the docks. And they hit it. On the after decks. There were some eight or ten distinctive explosions, with most of the bombs hitting the water or the dock, but from the geologist's point of view out a porthole in their small cabin, at least one bomb hit the ship. Within minutes, there were visible flames from the stricken ship.

Burke said, "We better get ready, they aren't gonna let us leave whole."

"Let's pile up what we can and get in it," yelled Larsh as he grabbed the bedding from one bed and draped it over the single table in the room. Within seconds, all four mattresses were draped over the table, and the double bunks were pushed next to the table. Then all four crawled under the table. Just as they began to hear clanging, popping, and ricochets of bullets hitting their ship. They were being strafed. All four men tensed, as probably others were doing all over the ship, waiting for the bombs to hit. None did.

The Germans had used all their bombs on the larger ship, and only made strafing runs on *El Caballo*. It was all over in less than five minutes. Then all was deadly quiet except the dull drumming of the ship's engines.

After a few minutes, the Americans left their cabin and went out on the deck. They saw nothing in the darkness, except for two barely visible men carrying another on a stretcher. The distant ship continued to burn, but the flames seemed to be under control. *El Caballo* had escaped relatively unscathed. Except for Jaimito's friend

Carlos. Carlos had taken a ricochet that tore a fist-sized hole in his chest where it came out. Jaimito saw him gasp during the rain of machine-gun fire, and fall backward, rolling over as he fell, and hit on his face. As he fell, Carlos looked at Jaimito with a questioning look, but said nothing. When Jaimito reached him, Carlos was perfectly limp, with blood pouring out of his chest, and eyes open but unseeing. He had died almost instantly; alive and vibrant one second, gone from this world the next. Jaimito was not hit.

The ship suffered little damage. The Stukas had aimed for the forward end of the small cabin area, evidently trying to destroy controls. They failed. But the warplanes did break windows, smash a barometer/temperature instrument, and damage several tables, chairs, cabinets, and various utensils. The decks and hull were only scratched or dented. El Caballo could maintain full speed. And it did. For its Spanish port of call at Cadiz on the Spanish south coast, where the earthly remains of young Carlos would be left for a despondent family to collect.

As it turned out, only one other sailor was hit, and his hit was in his left hip from flying splinters, that were very painful, but not serious so long as infection was avoided.

"Welcome to war," said Huey Larsh. It was now daylight, and they were gathered around a mess table drinking coffee.

Elmer Roach replied, "I guess we were lucky, but it all seems completely senseless...to kill a young Spanish boy who had and would have nothing to do with the urge of the Huns to conquer."

"The fact is, it's only beginning for us," said Huey, "when it's all over, I just hope we are able to have coffee together again."

Burke spoke up, "How many of us are reservists? I am, and expect a call to be waiting when I get home."

Larsh answered, "I'm not sure what my status is, but I expect to get in some part of it."

"I am in the inactive reserves," said Roach, "and there isn't any doubt that I'll be in the Army within a few months. That is, if we get home whole!"

"Well, I'm not in anything," said Roger Evans, "but I plan to join the Marines, like my friend Mike Dixon, who was in Hawaii when the Japs hit."

The geologists were to spend many more talk sessions on

their plans and probable actions, but first, they had to get to Cuba.

The next thirteen days went as planned. First, *El Caballo* made a planned call at its home port of Cadiz. Then they stopped at Funchal, Madeira Islands, about 300 miles north of the Canary Islands, where cargo was exchanged.

The only thing of real importance during the first few days was that Burke found he wanted no part of a hammock. The first day after passing the watchful eyes of the British at Gibraltar, the geologists decided to try hammocks as several of the crewmen did. Jaimito helped them, and four hammocks were strung in their cabin. Now they could all be gently rocked to and fro with the motion of the ship and undoubtedly find even more refreshing slumber.

Wrong. It took Burke about twenty minutes to discover this would never work. Within two hours, they were all out of the hammocks and trying to bed down any way they could for the rest of that night. Hammocks failed to live up to what they were cracked up to be. Instead, the constant motion, back and forth, up and down, back and forth, was enough to turn any but the most powerful stomachs! So ended the hammock caper.

The next item of interest was the cookie cure. JJ first discovered it. Then the other three men found it successful. Each man had several boxes of the Oreo cookies still in their possession. About the second day at sea in the Mediterranean, the weather got a bit rough, and *El Caballo* began to act like her namesake, tossing and bucking, pitching and rolling. One after another, the men got queasy stomachs; just short of throwing up, but sickly miserable. JJ thought he'd try one of the Oreos; the worst it could do would be to make him throw up and get rid of all that unnecessary stomach filling. It didn't. He started feeling better almost immediately after eating the Oreo.

This became the universal cure for seasickness the rest of the trip for all four men. When the going got rough, they ate cookies. Slowly, one after another. Their only concern was if the cookies would hold out. Evans swore that the chocolate ones did the job best, but the others could tell no difference. By eating them slowly, only when there was a lot of ship motion, all of the geologists except Huey Larsh held out and still had Oreos for the last rough weather two days before landing at Havana in Cuba. And they shared a few with Larsh.

Shortly after dark on Monday, January 19th, their fourteenth day out of Tobruk, and the second night before they were to make Havana, the geologists were sitting on deck outside their cabin, when they heard a cry from the lookout. Then Jaimito came running up, speaking excitedly in a combination of English and Spanish of which JJ could immediately decipher enough to make him jump from his deck chair and run for the cabin.

As he ran, he hollered, "Periscope, probably German sub! Hurry!"

No other invitations were required, all four men burst into the cabin and grabbed for their makeup. All but Roach had to put shoe polish on their hair, yet keep it off their hands. They had already set a procedure: use the polish dispenser, hair brush and a comb. Their first need was to get the polish on so that it could dry while they completed their disguise.

All but Roach went to work with the shoe polish and worked it into their hair. Then they put the polish and dispenser back in their shoe kits where it belonged.

They each had a *kafiya* and *aghal* (headdress and holding cords), but Roach had no *abayah* (overall dress-like garment) like the other three men. Roach quickly slipped on his head gear and went outside to serve as a sentinel. Burke, Larsh, and Evans finished with their hair, then slipped on their *abayah* over their pants and shirts. They all had and wore the typical blousy white shirts worn by Arab men, along with ordinary dark-colored slacks. They had several of the shirts they had bought in Saudi Arabia or Bahrain.

The shoe polish was dry within a few minutes, and Burke, Larsh, and Evans could readily pass for black-haired, even if partly green-eyed, Arabs! The three with colored hair then affixed their head gear and looked like they just stepped out of a Hofuf *soukh*.

Roach stuck his head in the doorway. "The Germans have called for a boat to come aboard."

"You mean a skiff or something like that?" said Larsh.

"I don't know what they said. They called out something, then after a few words response that I couldn't understand, Captain Del Roca ordered a boat lowered."

The other three men now came out, and they all four walked over to the portside rail to watch what was going on. They felt it best to be obvious so as to deter German suspicion.

The whole world was well aware by this time that German submarines were very active in the Atlantic, and particularly so in waters off the United States east and southeast coasts. So this intercept came as no surprise, and the Captain had already planned to cooperate as requested by any German, British, or American war vessel. He had nothing to hide and was not at war with anyone.

The Spanish skiff was lowered into the water, then the crewmen rowed over to the sub. Two German officers and two sub crewmen boarded the skiff and the Spanish crewmen rowed back to El Caballo. All climbed up a lowered staircase into a below-decks passageway. In a few moments, the Germans appeared on the main deck where they approached Captain Del Roca.

One of the Spanish crewmen, a Second Mate named Arrizo, could speak a little German. Arrizo had served in Franco's army during the Spanish Civil War of the 1930's and worked with German soldiers then assigned to Franco forces by Hitler's commanders. His German was poor, but he greeted the Germans:

"I speak little German and will help."

Surprisingly, a German crewman answered briskly in Spanish: "It is not needed, I speak Spanish. My officer wants to know your cargo and destination."

Del Roca replied, "Mostly foodstuffs for delivery to Havana. Would you like to inspect our holds?"

"Yes, if you please," the German answered politely, but rather curtly.

For the next hour or so, everybody aboard El Caballo practically held their breath as the Germans inspected everything. They were experts, knew all the hiding places, and checked each hold and compartment. Occasionally, they would even look in a locker or trunk, somewhat spot checking for anything they felt could be of value to the British and American Allies in the war. Perhaps a special rifle, or arms, sound or other eaves-dropping gear, radios, code equipment, anything that would label this as a ship of value to the Allies. Finally, they all came back on the main deck to face Del Roca.

One of the German officers spoke in German to their crewman, then, "We notice you have passengers?" the German crewman said questioningly.

Del Roca spoke, "We have four Arab passengers from Saudi Arabia with business in Cuba."

The Arab-geologists were only a dozen steps from the little group of Germans and Spanish, and Burke could hear and understand enough of the Spanish conversation to know what was going on. He turned and spoke in Arabic to the others,

"The Germans wonder about us."

It was their plan to purposefully talk among themselves very briefly in Arabic so as to hopefully satisfy the suspicions of the Germans. So they talked back and forth in their limited Arabic, with simple observations regarding the German underwater ship, the Germans, and this unusual event. It didn't work completely.

One of the German officers came over and asked in crude Arabic, "From where you come? What you do?"

The Americans had considered the possibility that a German might speak Arabic, and hoped that he would not be fluent. Obviously, he was not, so if their Arabic "expert" Evans could do the talking, things might be okay.

Evans replied in typical Arabic firmness: "We are from Hofuf, Saudi Arabia. We seek business with Cuba to trade agricultural goods."

"Ah, Hofuf," spoke the German, who was well-read on Roman and Greek conquests, and knew that Hofuf contained Roman ruins. "I understand Greek ruins there."

"We have Roman ruins. None Greek. Greeks were in Egypt," said Evans matter of factly.

"Ah yes," returned the German with a slight smile, "now I remember, it Roman." Though he was a little concerned about the two Arabs with green eyes, this validation of Hofuf knowledge by Evans satisfied him. He also knew from his readings that Arabs with green or blue eyes, while uncommon, were not at all rare. He turned to his superior and said in German, "They seem authentic Arabs. Should we search their quarters?"

"No," his companion replied quickly, "let us leave immediately. Our ship has been exposed too long already. We are in dangerous waters as you well know."

And with that, the Germans abruptly saluted Captain Del Roca, turned, opened and stepped through the passageway door leading to the stairway to the deck with access to the skiff. Within thirty minutes, they had returned to the sub, boarded it, closed hatches and submerged. This latest crisis was over.

The German intercept turned out to be just north of Caicos Islands, SE of Bahamas, at 22 degrees, 30 minutes North Latitude, and 71 degrees, 30 minutes West Longitude. And 2 days out of Havana, their next port of call.

Two days later, the Americans hired a taxi in Havana to take them across Cuba to Guantanamo Naval Base where they hoped to find transportation to Florida.

They made the trip safely and spent the next night as unofficial guests of the United States Marines in a marine barrack, actually officers quarters. These American geologists from Saudi Arabia, in their Arab garb were the toast and delight of the naval and marine personnel at Guantanamo. And all the military men were quite interested in their story. Also, there was no trouble arranging transportation to Miami aboard a shuttle vessel that made the trip daily. Which, after another night as guest of the Marines, they boarded to embark on their last leg of this voyage to home soil.

And so, on Saturday, January 24, 1942, four American geologist employees of Standard Oil Company of California stepped off the Guantanamo naval shuttle onto American soil in Miami, Florida.

Their first order of business was telephone calls home. More joyous calls and arrangements could hardly be imagined. Much happiness and merry anticipation filled the hearts and souls of these wayward geologists and their families.

The second order of business was to check in with San Francisco for permission to take a vacation before reporting back for duty. They were all advised that they should check in with their draft boards or reserve units first, because military enrollment might be required. They knew of this and planned to follow up.

But now, Home Time! They all immediately arranged bus and train passage home, then gathered together for one last dinner together at a nondescript, but highly recommended seafood restaurant overlooking Miami beach.

The next morning they came to a parting of company, not knowing when, or even if, they would ever meet again.

Larsh turned to Burke, "Well James Jonathon, see ya' in the next boom. And, don't forget the tiddy caper."

"Who, but Huey Lyman Larsh would remember a single night in Hofuf in, let's see, December, wasn't it? Yes, 1934! Anyway, old buddy, let's hope we work together again some day...."

And, with final goodbyes, the geologists embarked on their uncertain, uncharted, and unpredictable paths down different forks of the trails of life that lay ahead.

~ ~ ~ ~ ~ ~ ~ ~ ~ ~ ~ ~ ~ ~

CHAPTER 16

Home and to War

All was well in the Burke household in Nacogdoches, Texas on this fine Sunday, February 1, 1942. Ruthanne had been living at home with her parents during this period of JJ's absence. Now, they both moved in with his parents, Homer and Alma, while they decided what to do regarding a permanent residence. For the first few days, they gave no thought to such things as what lay ahead, or where they would be. Instead, they lived for the moments they had, knowing the uncertainties ahead.

It was a welcome relief to be concerned about such things as tree-trimming and fence repairs for a while. At least until the second Monday in March, the ninth, JJ was to catch up on family matters and family fun. There were feasts at the Burke home and the Cook home. And parties, receptions, picnics. And a little help with Homer Burke's store inventory and accounting. This was family time!

Being with Ruthanne was more dear than anything JJ could imagine, and it was obvious that she, too, was a little happy that her JJ was finally home. It was a time to catch up on all the tender moments lost, to just enjoy each other and their little daughter, Mary Ellen, to face the uncertainties ahead and talk of how to cope with them. They made no long-term plans. This was a time for precious Mary Ellen who, at age two, kept them well informed of her thoughts and needs, and was fully responsive to love, fun, and games.

It was a time for love, togetherness, visits to the Cook family farm near Oak Ridge, southeast of Nacogdoches; and enjoying the idyllic life they had at this time. They particularly enjoyed the farm visits where they walked on the trails and in the woods, and along the little unnamed streams that finally drained into creeks that added to the flow of the Angelina River.

As the weeks wore on, the call of duty loomed ever closer. When JJ arrived, he found a letter from the Army informing him that all inactive Reservists were being activated, except for unusual family circumstances, or a sensitive national defense occupation. JJ felt there was a good chance that he could get a military exemption because of his job to develop oil reserves available to the U. S. military machine, but he also felt a sense of duty to use his military training and participate directly in the war effort. He had old fashioned ideas of duty and country, and other such ideas of honor that were considered blase' if not downright doltish by many.

His first order of business after he arrived in Nacogdoches and found the Army letter was to call San Francisco and discuss his position. Socal was very considerate of his Army call, advised him that they would work for an exemption if he wished, or support him if he decided on military service. When he told them of his wish to answer the Army call, the company approved his decision, wished him every success, advised him of considerations available to employees going into the military, and finally that his job was waiting when he came back.

He advised the Army that he could respond to the call, explained his inability to reply earlier as officially required, and was told to report to Fort Sam Houston in San Antonio for induction and assignment. In a chat with Captain Getzinger, Induction Officer at Fort Sam, he was informed that in all probability he would be sent to Fort Benning, Georgia for a four-month training period, and would then be assigned as an artillery First Lieutenant in either the 36th or 45th Divisions. Both these divisions were expected to see action before the year was out.

"Sugar, do you think we might work out a way you can go with me to Georgia?" JJ asked softly one night as they lay in bed awaiting sleep.

"You couldn't keep me away with a team of horses," said Ruthanne as she rolled over on his arm and threw her soft loving arm across his chest.

"I know it'll be tough getting a good place to stay, and at this time I don't know how much time we'll have together, but in any case, it'll be more time than if you stay here."

"I agree completely, my darling. Any time together will be infinitely more than none at all...."

JJ turned toward Ruthanne, "Honey, how about Mary Ellen. Do you think that with the uncertain living conditions, it might be better that she stay with Mom and Dad, at least 'til we get established conditions?"

"I was thinking about that already, and as much as I'd miss her, I think it would be healthier for her to stay here for the time being...assuming Mother Burke agrees!"

They discussed their plans further and settled on the plan that JJ would get his assignment at Fort Sam Houston, then together or separately, as the Army dictated, proceed to Fort Benning or wherever JJ was assigned. Then they settled back, with their plans set, and in the quiet and chilly, but not cold, night with only the sounds of gentle breezes rustling the great pine outside their partially open window, at the Burke homestead in Nacogdoches, Texas, sleep entered upon the scene....

"Well, what did you find?"

JJ ran up to meet Ruthanne as she stepped off the military shuttle bus near the main gate into Fort Benning, Georgia.

She replied excitedly, "Ah, Lieutenant Burke, how striking you are in your uniform. I hadn't thought I'd be hugging an officer in the United States Army!"

"Oh yes you are," he replied, "a full blown officer! One of several hundred thousand, I expect! But, our abode? A tent? A cabin? Maybe just a sleeping bag?"

"'Tisn't big, but it's no tent or woodland cabin. Just a small place in an old house. But it's neat. And the bed is sound and the tiny kitchen is quite satisfactory."

"I know married officers move through here like through a revolving door," said JJ, "and it seemed likely that some apartment should have just become, or was about to be, available."

"Actually, in these last two days, I found six that were empty or about to be vacated, and the one I took was the best of the lot," said Ruthanne. "Now all we need is for *you* to be able to use it."

JJ described his understanding: "Well, the best dope I get is that I can stay off post on weekends after the first three weeks, then all the time after about ten weeks."

His wife laughed, "that's not perfect, but it's one hell of a lot better than it could be!"

"You better believe it," said JJ as he picked her up and whirled her around in an enthusiastic hug.

He had reported to Fort Sam Houston, and as a result of his time as a Reserve Officer, was inducted as a First Lieutenant, and assigned to Fort Benning, Georgia. He had come by train, while Ruthanne, leaving little Mary behind, came by bus a few days behind JJ, as they had arranged by telephone.

She spent the first two nights in the apartment of Joanne Johnston, wife of Lieutenant Dick Johnston, a fellow Texas A&M graduate JJ met his first day at Fort Benning. As planned, as soon as JJ got the lay of the land, he called Ruthanne and told her how to contact Joanne with whom she would stay until she could find their own apartment. The Johnstons were in Fort Benning for the same reasons as the Burkes, but six weeks ahead.

Time passed quickly as JJ got updated on the latest howitzers and guns, and was considering the possibility of anti-aircraft artillery, perhaps the new 90-millimeter guns or the half-track mounted quad-fifties that mostly supported infantry units against low-flying aircraft.

He studied maps and mapping, computation of trajectories and range for the different artillery pieces, deployment, transport, and other work associated with tactics, strategy, and use of the weaponry.

Also, he was qualified in carbine, pistol, and sub-machine gun. Then, he studied leadership, conduct, responsibility, accountability, administration, and other facets of the job of a battery commander.

The Burkes and Johnstons struck it off well, and found out that they had a number of things in common. One of the main common traits for the women was music. Both had studied music, Ruthanne basically as a teacher, and Joanne as an artist. While both could play the piano skillfully, Joanne was outstanding.

They all learned to love just sitting around, sipping beer or wine, while Joanne worked her way through such pieces as DeBussy's *Clair De Lune*, Beethoven's *Fur Elise* followed by all three movements of *Sonata Fantasia*, the *Moonlight Sonata*. This woman was good.

None of the other three had ever heard anyone play so well except on a concert stage. With someone like Joanne, who could skillfully play everything from Boogie to Beethoven, with Glenn Miller and Chopin in between, what more did they need. Along with a glass of wine and good company!

Each of the four had something to offer that was of interest to the others. Ruthanne, the teacher. JJ the geologist. Dick Johnston, the mechanical engineer. And Joanne, the artist!

It was a good life, exciting, changing, and so typical of that for most young men and women of this booming, war-driven time when the warriors and warriors-to-be took their entertainment when and as they could, and let the future be damned.

The training at Fort Benning stretched out a little when JJ elected mobile anti-aircraft as his first choice. At this time, the Army was in need of trained officers in practically all areas, but none worse than mobile anti-aircraft.

So his four-month tour stretched to five months, and then he was to be transferred to Fort Hood, Texas to join a newly formed mobile anti-aircraft battalion with three batteries of four half-tracks each.

The Johnstons left in early July for a delay en route furlough to Fort Meade, Maryland from where Dick would leave for destination unknown in the European Theater of Operations. And thus ended one of the brief but intense friendships of wartime America. Sure, the Burkes and Johnstons would write, would keep in touch, but never again would they know this unique wartime closeness of their days together at Fort Benning.

In late July, Ruthanne and JJ boarded a Greyhound bus in Fort Benning, bound for Shreveport, Louisiana, where Homer Burke would meet them for the two-hour drive home in Nacogdoches. Homer had saved an extra gasoline coupon from his Class C permit in order to have the approximate fifteen extra gallons of gas needed for this trip.

The wartime rationing was not completely restrictive as to the use of gasoline, but it did force everybody to plan their driving carefully. There was none available for pure fun. At least not officially....

Homer picked up the couple, returned through Logansport to Tenaha, Texas where he picked up U. S. Highway 59 on into Nacogdoches.

JJ had only two days before he was to report to Fort Hood,

and he used them to the fullest extent. Little sleep, lots of talk, lots of love and play with a darling Mary Ellen, some visiting, and then...on the road again. Now without his love....

He reported to Fort Hood, found his battalion and, even though still a First Lieutenant, was assigned as Commander of C Battery, 3909th Anti-Aircraft Automatic Weapons, Self Propelled, Artillery Battalion. This unit was to be assigned to the 36th (Texas) Division, as infantry support, after training was completed.

On Thursday, October 1, 1942, the Battalion was ordered to Fort Meade, Maryland for shipment to destination unknown in the European Theater. The vehicles and equipment were loaded aboard train on Saturday, and the train pulled out on Sunday, bound for Dallas, then Kansas City and points east.

Two of the Battalion's officers and ten enlisted men, including two master sergeants, went with the train. All other personnel were given a ten-day delay en route furlough to report to Fort Meade.

(A real AA AW SP Battalion did join the 36th Division in North Africa after American Forces landed there November 8, 1942. A real 390th AA AW SP Battalion saw combat in Europe in 1942-45.)

To maximize time together, Ruthanne had scraped together enough gas coupons to drive their '37 Pontiac the 180 miles to Temple, where she would meet JJ who was to catch a ride into Temple with another soldier out of Fort Hood.

She and JJ would then return to Nacogdoches, where they would have almost a week before JJ had to board a bus to Dallas, then train via Kansas City to the east coast.

It was Saturday afternoon, October third. JJ was waiting at a Humble station on U.S. 81 just north of downtown Temple where Ruthanne was to report. He peered northward. No '37 Pontiac coupe. She was supposed to arrive shortly after lunch and it was now nearly 3 PM. He kept peering, and worrying, until by four o'clock he had a headache. Still nothing. He knew nothing to do but wait here. The plan was that if she had car trouble, she was to call the state police and ask them to find him at the designated Humble station. Finally, a thought occurred to him.

He addressed the station manager: "Is there another Humble station up the road a ways?"

"Sure is," the manager replied, "about a mile up ahead over that hill."

JJ explained his worry and plan with Ruthanne, then, "could you take me to that station. I'll be glad to pay regular cab fare."

"Don't be silly," said the manager, "the least I can do for a soldier is take him a mile up the road!"

They walked over to the station man's pickup. JJ tossed his B-4 bag in the back and climbed in. He observed that the truck was not dirty and greasy as he would have guesed. It was a '36 Chevy, and though a little banged up and obviously well worn, it was clean. JJ offered, "seems you take a little pride in your truck. Maybe that's an indication of how you handle your tools and people's cars."

"Well," replied the man, "all I got to offer is service. And it'd better be pretty good or there won't be any to do."

They backed out, drove up the road the mile, and just after they topped the hill, JJ had his answer.

There was the '37 Pontiac. Neatly parked at the side of the station. With a frustrated and worried Ruthanne standing beside it. JJ thanked the man for his courtesy and got a smile and "No trouble, soldier" in reply. He jumped out of the pickup, grabbed his bag from the back, and turned toward his special lady.

They ran to each other, Ruthanne with tears running down her face, murmuring, "My darling man, I was so, so worried. What happened. Are you hurt? Is something wrong?"

As they hugged tightly, "No, my beloved mate, nothin' wrong except that there are two Humble stations on this highway just north of Temple. Finally, I got a brain storm and asked. So, here we are, my precious lady. But I do have one question."

"Yes?"

"Do you have any aspirin?"

"It just so happens that I do. Almost always. In my purse side pocket."

She handed him the box. He took two, went over to the water fountain and gulped them down with water chaser. He walked back over, grabbed her in a hug and, "Now, kitten, let's move out for Nacogdoches!"

Late Thursday afternoon, October eighth. JJ and Ruthanne had driven out to what they called their mating tree overlooking the hill, just off the pathway from the Cook farm house that they had for the night. And just off the legendary passageway of the Old Spanish Trail, El Camino Real.

Here, beneath the large pecan which was one of several pecans and hardwood trees on this hill of legends, this young couple, this soldier and his wife, picnicked and drank a bottle of white wine. They were all alone.

Not even a squirrel came to investigate. Perhaps a bird or two knew this was a special time.

Here they had become engaged. Now, here, on their last night together for an unknown length of time, with a future that may not exist...this man and this woman in the spring of life, with complete love and desire, with passion and fullness, mated.

In God's way, on this day, a new life was begun.

And so ends The Early Years.

~ ~ ~ ~ ~ ~ ~ ~ ~ ~ ~ ~ ~ ~

End Book One

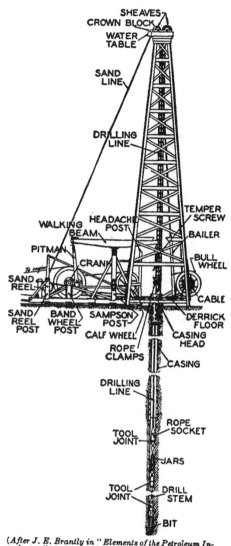

(After J. E. Brantly in "Elements of the Petroleum Industry," courtesy of Am. Inst. Mining Met. Eng.)

Fig. 1 — Cable Tool drilling rig

Fig. 2 — Saudi Field Geologist's dress, Saudi Arabia 1934
J. W. "Soak" Hoover

Fig. 3 — Camel supply train coming into camp: 1934-5

Fig. 4 — Field Camp scene, 1934

Fig. 5 — Airliner, 1935

Fig. 6 — Fairchild field observation aircraft,1935

Fig. 7 — Rotary driling rig, 1937 vintage

Fig. 8 — Rotary drilling rig, 1990's vintage

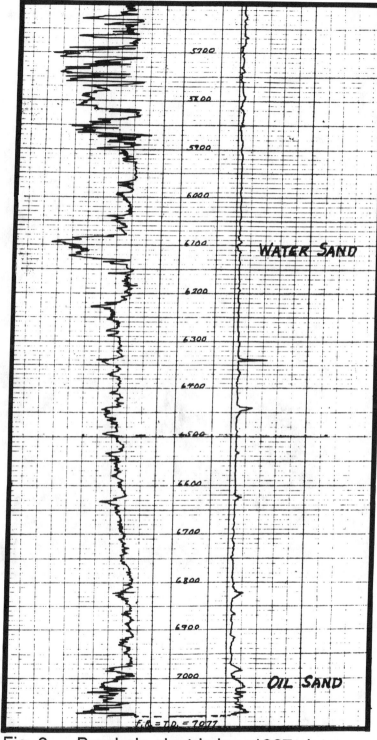

Fig. 9 — Borehole electric log, 1937 vintage,
Chambers County Texas

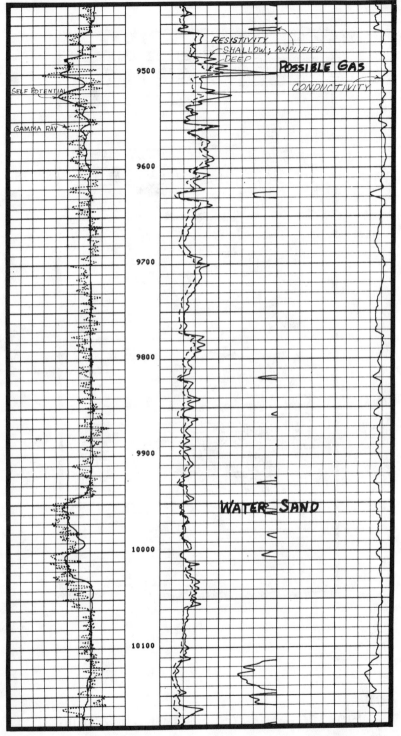

Fig. 10 — Basic borehole electric log, 1990's vintage

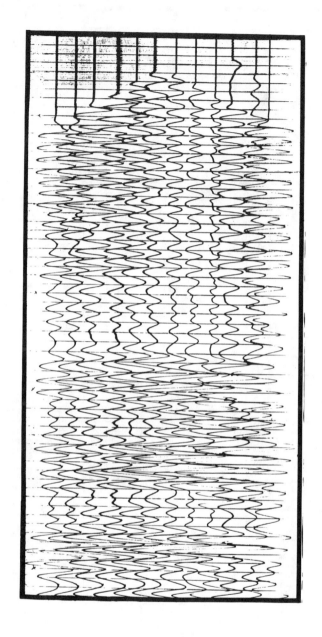

Fig. 11 — Seismic Record, 1937 vintage

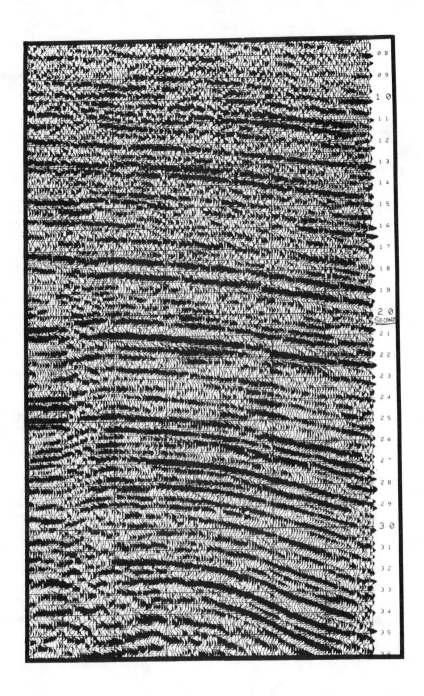

Fig. 12 — Seismic Record, (section), 1990's vintage

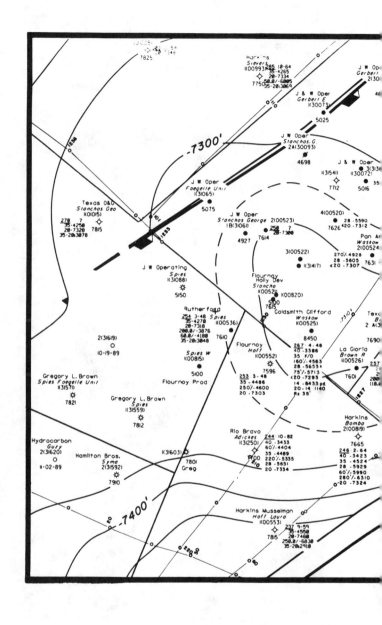

Fig. 13 — Structure Contour Map with Fault

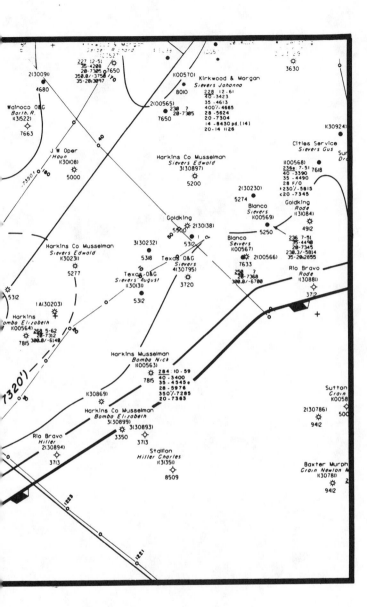

BOOK TWO

The Nineties

CHAPTER 1

The First Signs

The horse reared up as Rashid Ben Rimthan tried to quiet him. Holding the reins firmly, the Saudi gradually quieted Wundeen enough to start walking him out of the *wadi*, or normally dry creek, up toward the trail back to the old road. Both were still quite nervous, and walking seemed the best thing to do right now.

It had been a normal mid-November visit home up to this time, but no longer. Rashid wondered, what in the world is going on?

Slowly, they worked their way over the rocky trail around this particular *jabal*, or hill, to the road. Actually, to a casual and uninformed observer, there was no road; just a strip where there were fewer rocks than on either side, and where tracks could be seen here and there in patches of sand. Rashid swung up into the saddle, with Wundeen unnaturally skittish about the whole thing...but he did let Rashid mount. The Saudi then broke Wundeen into a jog as they made their way to the paved highway three miles east, which wound its way south toward Riyadh. This highway passed just east of his old home village that was pretty well isolated at a location about one hundred kilometers west of Riyadh.

As they rode along, Rashid tried to evaluate what he had just experienced. He knew it was an earthquake, and that it was a pretty strong one, but that was about all. Where was its center? What caused it? Maybe his friend, Achmed Asker, the seismologist in Dhahran, would have some answers.

Now he was riding along the shoulder of the highway and could see his home village in the distance. This village had its origin in water. Here a well had been dug near a spring in ages past, and the village developed around the well. The Rimthan family originally had a home tent and animal corral site at the edge of the village, and most of its inhabitants were part of the overall family group. They had been there for many generations and had followed the custom of following the rains with their herds of mostly sheep and horses, returning each year in the spring to their home.

Shortly after World War II, Rashid's father, Yahiya Ibn Rimthan, had built a permanent home and corrals to replace the tents and rock and rope corrals used during generations of the annual migrations to and from grazing.

The "corral" was actually a closed-in field that served both as a grazing area and a place for holding animals. It had originally been created in a small box-like canyon formed by a wadi dropping over a thick limestone outcrop. The "canyon" was only a few feet high at the lowest walls, but as much as 100 feet of sheer cliff in other places. It varied in width from a few dozen feet, to over half a mile at the widest. In generations past, digging and rock wall work had been done on the few places where the walls sloped, so as to form essentially vertical walls the height of a tall man, with steep slopes beyond.

The walls were not vertical in all areas, but if not vertical rock outcrops, there were very steep slopes of broken rock and limestone beds. Thus, a natural corral with rock walls was formed. Then, it was only necessary to run ropes across a narrowing between the wadi walls to form a natural corral, inclosing several hundred acres. And so it had been used for several hundred years, modified now and then, reworked occasionally, but always serving the same practical purposes. As one of the modifications, a rock wall fence had been constructed across the opening originally closed by ropes. This fence was old when Yahiya was a boy. At the time of the Rimthan construction in 1951, a rope gate across the rock fence gap was still used. With the easier post-war availability of lumber and other materials at this inland location, it became practical to build more variable and permanent facilities, and Yahiya had done so.

As Rashid rode up to the corral, he opened and entered through a metal gate, and looked at the current state of the family operations.

The farm, perhaps some would call it a ranch, was now a secondary business, and they raised horses only, no sheep. Their effort was directed at breeding top quality riding horses and they had a fairly well established market for their animals. Occasionally, a racer was born, and in recent years, a little more breeding effort had been given to these beautiful, sleek creatures. The natural corral was still used, but there were cross fences, a barn, stalls, and outside feeding areas. Now, feed was brought in to supplement modest grazing within a few miles of the home place.

The business had changed to meet current factors. Rashid made most of his money working elsewhere. There were no annual grazing migrations. The horses were limited in number; it was a quality, not quantity, breeding operation. There was no need for more than a few work animals, no need for meat for sale.

Their village home was a typical 1950 Saudi country home. It was made in the traditional manner, low, thick mud brick walls with plaster covering, and tile roof. It had a central courtyard with several surrounding rooms that, over the years, had been tastefully furnished and decorated by various members of the immediate family.

Yahiya had become a guide for Saudi geologists in the thirties, and had worked for several years with JJ Burke and Huey Larsh. During that period, his wife Fuana and his family remained at the family place and it was here that Rashid spent all his years from his 1943 birth until he left for college in 1961. His two older sisters and younger brother also had grown up there. All had their elementary schooling in nearby small schools. With his earnings and Aramco help, Yahiya was able to send his children to boarding schools for secondary and pre-university schooling.

After continuing work during and after World War II with Aramco, finally as a field production superintendent, Yahiya retired in 1969 to his home to raise horses. He died in 1986 after a very full and successful life, and left two endowments for his progeny: Education and Family. Plus, a fair cash inheritance as well as the country home and farm. Fuana, being nearly ten years younger than Yahiya, had continued living and still lived in the ancestral home, though she had lived off and on for many years with her husband in apartments near his work. In her later years she had spent long periods with her children, and had traveled to the States twice, and to Great Britain or other European countries several times.

Fuana was a strong adherent of the principles, if not all the detail practices, of Islam and carefully followed all Muslim guides in public. At home, or with her children, she was much more open, but still gentle and considerate by nature. Though a real gentlewoman, she did not hesitate to firmly direct the two men who, on a part-time basis, cared for her place, or to speak her mind with her children. With the help of her children, she continued the horse business, and enjoyed the work. With four children, and their children, the country home, with its attractions, rarely went more than a few weeks without visitors.

At Aramco, Yahiya had seen what education could do for a person, and particularly what the opportunities were for a well-educated Saudi. The children grew up expecting to get full educations, with university training for the boys, and also for the girls if they wished it so. He suggested that his boys prepare for and finally attend Texas A&M where they could study geology or engineering as did his friend, JJ Burke. He felt they could get training for a career with Aramco at Texas A&M as well as several other U. S. schools, and he liked the ideas of discipline and tradition that seemed so strong at A&M.

And, so it came to pass that after a year in a preparatory school, Rashid attended Texas A&M, with an Aramco scholarship to help pay the way. He got his degree in petroleum engineering with extra courses in field geology and statistics.

He was now employed as a reservoir engineering supervisor for Aramco in Dhahran. His section specialized in computerized probability projections of reservoir fluid movements resulting from variable production rates, and possible reservoir water encroachment into zones drained of producible oil. It sounded a lot fancier than it actually was. It was somewhat like, "where will the oil and water go if we get some of the oil out?"

Rashid quickly removed saddle and bridle from Wundeen, then walked rapidly toward and entered the house. "Yasmeen, Yasmeen, where are you?"

"Here, beloved," she spoke as she walked in the doorway to the courtyard, "I have been preparing your green beans for a vegetable feast!"

"Did you feel the earthquake?"

"There was no way to overlook it. Several cans in the pantry fell off the shelves. One of the olive bottles fell, but fortunately, did not break."

"Well, my wife, Wundeen and I were quite disturbed. He perhaps, more than I. At least I knew what it was. He did not. Now I would like to learn more about it."

She replied, "You might try Achmed."

"Just who I had in mind. I know little about these things, but it seems to me that this is unusual. I never heard of a real earthquake in this part of Arabia. They are common in Iraq and Iran, but here? Seems peculiar."

Yasmeen said, "This is the first earthquake that really got my attention, but it is not the first that I have felt. In Jiddah, we sometimes felt small shakes, but nothing like this. I was told that the quakes we felt there were probably caused by volcanos or something like that."

They had spoken in both English and Arabic, as they often did. Without further delay, Rashid called Achmed. He was not home, but would be back shortly.

Rashid had met Yasmeen the second summer after he had begun employment with Aramco, in 1967, while on temporary training assignment in Bahrain. She was a nurse in the hospital where Rashid went to get a bad cut stitched up. He had gone in the emergency room, and made a joke of his slip with a wrench while working on a car fender. An edge of the fender metal made him pay for the slip by slitting his skin for about an inch and a half. In came this nurse who immediately got Rashid's full attention. She looked at his cut, teased him about his carelessness, and prepared it for the doctor to stitch. While waiting for the doctor, Rashid quizzed this dark-eyed beauty to find out if she might just possibly be available. It seemed that just by accident, and a recently broken romance, she was. Insha Allah!

By the time his arm was repaired, Rashid had arranged for a dinner with this flower, and had learned from whence her name had come. When she was born, she was so perfect in the eyes of her father that the first thing that came to his mind was the beauty and delightful smell of Jasmine blooms he had once experienced while on an excursion out from New Orleans while there on a business trip. After a brief review of it all with her mother, it was agreed that this little flower would be known as "Yasmeen," and to them, "The Beautiful."

It took Rashid only three months to convince this lady that her future lay with him. They were married in 1968, and had hardly gotten settled before they were transferred to New York for a staff assignment. Then later, it was Houston. Altogether, they spent nearly half of the next twenty years in the States. English, with a Texas twist, became their second language, with which they felt almost as much at home as Arabic.

They had good foundations by studying English in schools, as did many Saudis of this time. Often, in their own home, they would slip into English instead of Arabic if something triggered it; perhaps an English word that offered better expression, then back to Arabic when an Arabic word seemed best. They were truly bi-lingual. They wore Western clothes most of the time, except Yasmeen was careful to follow Muslim custom when circumstances so indicated. Neither of them had strong religious drives but, also, neither had any desire to change the world. They had other drives that to them were more important.

The telephone rang. Rashid picked it up, "Hello?"

"Hello, yourself, you Anglicized Arab," said Achmed Asker with a lilt to his voice. He responded in English after Rashid's form of greeting.

They switched back to Arabic, but then back and forth with English as they talked.

"Achmed, I suppose you are aware of the 'quake I felt out here today? It seemed a little strong to me, and rare?"

"You are right. It *was* a little strong, and it was indeed rather rare. Using our measurement plus others in the World-Wide Network, we measured it at Richter 6.1, with an epicenter about 250 km west, and slightly south of Riyadh. Although there is some faulting in that area, I can't remember a 'quake there. There are occasional temblors in the west, near the Red Sea, but not this far east. Some of those have been associated with volcanics as well as fault movements, and would be expected in that area where the Arabian and African Plates join."

Rashid spoke, "I thought I remembered there were 'quakes in the Red Sea area, and I know they occur pretty regular in western Iran and Iraq."

"That's right. I believe the area within about a hundred kilometers of the eastern and northern shores of the Persian Gulf average over ten shakes per year. And some of them are very bad. There were some 25,000 deaths in Iran as a result of the September '78 'quake, near 8.0 Richter as I remember. And they have problems of some kind in Iraq almost every year from shakes."

"Tell me something, Achmed, how bad can temblors get?"

"Who knows? Since the academics started keeping systematic

quantitative measurements a little over a hundred years ago, I believe the record is about 8.6 Richter, in China and South America. Any 'quake over 8.0 has always been very devastating, especially in the poorer areas where homes and buildings have little tensile strength in the walls, with little or no structure, just bricks or rocks stacked up. But 'quake strength is not necessarily the key parameter."

"How's that?"

"Mainly culture. An 8.0 'quake in the middle of the Sahara Desert will have only a small fraction of the damage of a 6.0 in London. Then, another factor is the degree of earth movement. If one block of earth moves laterally along a fault plane..."

Rashid interrupted, "You mean a strike-slip fault, as opposed to a normal or reverse fault?"

"Yes. When the earth blocks move sideways, even if only a few inches, that plays hell with everything from buildings to oil well casing; roads, power lines, bridges, pipelines, you name it. If the blocks move vertically, up and down relative to each other a few inches, it just makes a bump in the road, or pipeline, or other elongate structure. Of course, those movements do a good job of causing major damage to buildings and foundations, but usually not so much as sideways movements. But most of the damage is usually caused by earth waves, not earth block slippage."

"Yeah," said Rashid, "I've heard about those 'P' and 'S' waves."

"Don't worry about names. Just think of what happens when you drop a pebble in a tank of water. The waves move outward in concentric circles. Seismic waves, also called *tsunamis*, or tidal waves, especially in oceans or large bodies of water, are similar, but move much faster, up to 1000 km/hr. But, you know Rashid, we better quit this telephone talk or you will have to use next month's salary to pay this bill!"

"As usual, Achmed, you are right. But I want to talk more about this when we can get together."

And with that, the two friends ended their telephone talk. Rashid had a lot better feeling for what had happened, but still didn't know how or why.

Rashid walked into the kitchen where Yasmeen was preparing their "evening feast." With rare exception, Yasmeen took time each day to prepare one good meal, usually in the evening, but sometimes around midday. When money had been short in their early marriage, they learned to concentrate on one good meal a day, and in humor, they called it their "feast." The name and custom stuck.

"It is a wonderful thing to have knowledgeable friends," said Rashid.

Yasmeen replied, "Who are kind enough to share their knowledge."

Rashid described to Yasmeen most of what Achmed had said. Then she observed, "Perhaps you should call or write Jon?"

"James Jonathon Burke, Jr. You are right. He will be most interested in this unusual animal. But I'll write instead of calling, so he can see and study the words for better understanding. Besides, it is cheaper! However, there is one serious thing of most significant importance."

"What is that?" asked Yasmeen.

Rashid laughed, "When do we eat?," as he dodged her playful slap.

This earthquake was puzzling. In time, the puzzle would make more sense.

~ ~ ~ ~ ~ ~ ~ ~ ~ ~ ~ ~ ~ ~

CHAPTER 2

The Burkes

The old man walked briskly up the slight rise, "Come here, you wild dog...before you become mince meat!"

Thunder, the big, black Labrador Retriever, trotted back across the road and dutifully fell in step beside the man. He didn't exactly heel, but he stuck pretty close when told to do so.

It was a typical late November day in East Texas; slightly overcast, cool, and a little sun every now and then. The hardwoods were almost bare of leaves, but the pines stayed ever green and colorful. Sometimes the leaves would not fall by this time of year, but this year saw an icy Thanksgiving after unseasonably cool weather in late October and early November; thus the now near barren trees.

As he walked along, the man remembered when this was a gravel road so many years ago. Now it was paved with an asphalt compound, with deep bar ditches to remove the occasional heavy rainwater. Boy, was it dusty then. If I had any choice, I wouldn't be walking here in the thirties when there was much traffic. But on this Sunday, traffic was light, and the road *was* paved and not dusty at all.

Just three cars and two pickups in the last half hour. All quiet and serene. The road is paved, and has a nice shoulder to walk on. A great day to make my three-mile walk with my buddy. He liked the walk too. Even if he was five years old, Thunder acted like a puppy when the old man asked him if he wanted to take a walk.

The man and dog came to an intersection, crossed the road, and turned left on the cross road. Three blocks later, just as he was about to walk in the broad pea-graveled driveway, a lady's voice rang out:

"JJ, get yourself in here. I've had the fried potatoes ready for the last fifteen minutes. What in the world have you been doing all this time?" Ruthanne spoke loudly to be sure JJ heard her, but with good humor in her voice as she addressed this man who had shared her life for nearly six decades.

"Honey, it goes like this: Thunder thought he saw a covey of quail back there on the old Henson place, you know, that grazing pasture where they used to grow cotton. He stalked out there about a hundred yards, and I stalked with him. And it was beautiful! Musta been at least ten of them in the covey. Probably a family. Sounded like a plane taking off. Then we worked our way back out of the pasture, but that did take a little extra time. The last mile, I've been more and more aware of brunch time. Did you make biscuits?"

"Does Thunder have fleas?" she replied.

"Maybe every now and then, but not if he gets his regular bath!"

"Well, come on in. It's gettin' cold."

This was a weekend tradition for JJ and Ruthanne. Had been for many years. Occasionally, JJ's three weekly walks of two or three miles fell on a weekend, as it did this Sunday. On most walking days, Ruthanne accompanied JJ, but not when it fell on a weekend. She couldn't fit the walks in on those days. But, walk or no, they followed their weekend routine: They started with juice and coffee while looking over the morning paper. Then, about ten a.m., Ruthanne would start their brunch, for eating around eleven. Most of the time, they had biscuits with fake butter and no-sugar preserves, or with flour gravy made using vegetable or olive oil, and fried potatoes and onions. Sometimes they had rolls instead of biscuits. Or pancakes, or waffles. But almost always, fried potatoes and onions. A down-east-Texas breakfast!

JJ was getting on in years. He was in his mid-eighties, and Ruthanne was not much younger. But they enjoyed their retirement, and reveled in their children and grandchildren. The years had been eventful, productive, and rewarding. While they had not become rich, they were quite comfortable financially.

After returning from the war, JJ had rejoined Aramco, where he worked, either in New York, Dhahran or Houston, until his retirement. Part of the time on assignment to Exxon production research where he participated in Saudi Arabian reservoir development studies. He served as an exploration geologist, then got into exploitation geology, went back to exploration as a project supervisor, and finally retired as a manager of exploration.

Their first born, Mary Ellen, was born in May of 1940, and was with the family in Saudi Arabia for a brief period in 1941. James Jonathon, Jr., their second and last child, was born July 14, 1943, with the family in Saudi Arabia for a brief period in 1941. James Jonathon, Jr., their second and last child, was born July 14, 1943, while JJ was in North Africa fighting Germans.

These days, this old geologist took care of his investments, worked a little with his few cows and two horses, and tried to keep up with the radically changed oil and gas business. While their investments were not major, they were substantial, and involved over thirty different stocks, bonds, and an interest in two small businesses. Along with a good deal of reading...newspapers, magazines, and a book now and then, JJ kept rather busy in his retirement.

But, compared to Ruthanne, he was loafing! She not only ran the home, cooked every day, entertained her grandchildren, and seemed to drive somewhere every day as part of her commitment to her children, she taught. She was still a part-time high school music and English teacher, filling in when one of the two regular teachers for those class combinations were out for some reason. She enjoyed working with this blooming generation, and felt she might have a little impact now and then. Students accepted this grandmotherly lady in a rather special way: more respectful, more gentle and considerate than these active teenagers usually endorsed teachers. At the same time, they found her knowledge seemingly boundless!

Ruthanne maintained a lifelong characteristic: patience, and the ability to employ her strong will without offending others; even JJ! She rarely displayed anger, because she rarely felt anger. And she didn't bottle up anger; it just wasn't there. But lack of anger did not mean she was docile. Far from it. She always spoke her mind, had strong opinions, and the will to carry them out. She had an unusual mix of patience, understanding, and a strong will to do what she thought was best after listening to what others had to say. Her relationship with JJ was very solid, but he sometimes called her "old velvet ironpants!"

It was not quite the same with JJ. Although he had mellowed as to his strong, even sometimes arrogant, opinions, he still got mad at lots of things. Much of his anger was directed at what he called the idiocy of society: government intervention in every breath of life, absurd liability laws, unbelievable disparity of salaries and wages for reasons totally unrelated to any real creativity or innovation...the only things that made much difference in life, and crime. Ever-increasing crime in the face of an ever-more ridiculous judiciary. But he managed to keep most of his anger under control, never forgetting his mother's "keep your temper, JJ, no one else wants it." He was fortunate to have a wife who thoroughly understood him, and still loved him dearly. She knew he was an unusually bright and creative man who seemed knowledgeable about almost anything!

Both parents of JJ and Ruthanne had gone to join their parents. JJ's dad, Homer, in 1970 at age 87, and his mother Alma at 89 in 1976. In settling the substantial, but not major, estate of their parents, JJ and his sisters' families divided it in such a manner as to keep properties whole. Elizabeth Ann and her family ended up with the store and everything associated with it, Mary Jane's surviving child and grandchildren received most of the liquid assets, and JJ took over the family home, which he and Ruthanne decided to remodel for their final retirement home.

When JJ's father, Homer, bought this land and built this home in 1911, it was a six-acre tract some six miles northeasterly of downtown Nacogdoches. By the time JJ was in high school, the city had grown a little, and most of this area consisted of homes built on three- to six-acre tracts; not a real residential development, just a comfortable living area. Several of the families had gardens or a few farm animals, some had barns or stables. But all earned their living elsewhere. Most were merchants or professional people, but one of the most beautiful homes belonged to a carpenter who spent a great deal of his own time building it just as he and his family thought it should look.

Now, in the nineties, some of the homes were run down, but most had been kept up, remodeled or even rebuilt. The city had never grown much beyond this country home settlement; a few service stations and stores, even one very nice apartment complex less than a half mile distant, toward town. But there was still plenty of open country to admire and explore. The grassy and forested rolling terrain was much as it had been a hundred years ago, and kept the beauty that attracted the Burkes to build here so long ago.

The city of Nacogdoches occupies the site of an encampment area used by the Nacogdoches Indians for centuries before the first Spaniards established a mission there in 1716 on El Camino Real. This was little more than a village for nearly a hundred years, but in the early eighteen hundreds was, along with Galveston on the coast, the two main gateways to Texas for the Anglos streaming in from mostly Tenneessee, Kentucky, Alabama, Georgia and Florida.

Some of the Burke family left Florida for Alabama in 1808, about the time the turmoil began to build up to the War of 1812. That war resulted in the annexation of West Florida into three different states, newly acquired Louisiana, Mississippi and Alabama. The Burkes left Alabama in 1810 to settle in Texas. They got settled near Nacogdoches just in time for JJ's great-great grandfather to be recruited, trained a little, then marched to New Orleans to fight in the Battle of New Orleans. The most important battle in the War of 1812. Fortunately, he survived unscathed, as did almost all of the American soldiers in that battle, and got back to his family and Texas homestead about seven months after he left.

Nacogdoches became a lumbering and agricultural center just before the Texas-Mexico War of 1836, and by the time JJ was born in 1910, it was a college town as well. Now, in JJ's late years, it was a rather typical university town with many quiet streets shaded by elderly, full-canopied hardwoods, old homes, and a rather ordinary but perhaps above-1961 average educated, population of some 30,000 souls. It was a good place to be. At least that was the thinking of the retired Burke family.

Of real importance to this couple was the Cook family farm where they visited during their courting days so many years before, and which was still as beautiful as ever. The old pecan grove beside State Highway 21 was still extant and much the same as it had been over a half century earlier when they sealed their marriage vows under spreading limbs. This current paved highway followed the route of El Camino Real, sometimes called The Old Spanish Trail locally. El Camino Real, The Royal Road, was blazed in 1691 by hard-working men under the Spaniard, de los Rios. Although the road, or trail, had been in continual use since its origin, it consisted of little more than a trail of wagon ruts through the wilderness until the late eighteen hundreds when it was improved, at least in this area.

Ruthanne became the heir to this rural property, situated to the southeast of Nacogdoches, not far from the village of Oak Ridge. JJ delighted in this farm, and it was magnificent for many reasons. Not only was it relaxing and, at times, striking, in its beauty, but it had a special serenity that inspired planning and creativity. Maybe it had something to do with the proximity to ancient Indian and Spanish presence, perhaps their prescience.

This country place was mainly a retreat, still well off the beaten path, with the old, but remodeled and comfortable farm home sitting on a ridge in the midst of a pine and hardwood forest, overlooking a small pond trapped along a spring creek at the base of the ridge. JJ now maintained a few purebred cattle on the 36-acre place, more as a hobby than a business. Over the past 30 years, along with Ruthanne and JJ, their family had grown to love this woodland place, and someone was there often enough that Ruthanne had to keep reservations!

JJ's younger sister, Elizabeth Ann, married a civil engineer who ended up wealthy in real estate, and was doing fine in retirement. They still traveled, making at least one big trip each year.

In 1957, JJ's older sister, Mary Jane, became the only tragedy in the family. She was killed in a car wreck, along with her married daughter, when a drunk went to sleep, swerved across an open highway and collided with their car, head-on. The drunk and his equally drunk companion, survived. The drunk's driving license was suspended for six months. JJ considered going after him with a shotgun, but Ruthanne managed to convince him that any satisfaction gained would not balance his sure prison sentence. And besides, this was crazy thinking! She said. He wasn't completely convinced of that.

JJ's mapping partner from the thirties, Huey Larsh, retired in Oklahoma, was still alive and well, though he had trouble with his knees, first one, then the other. He too, exercised regularly, using various exercise machines for about three hours weekly. He had to give up walking several years earlier. The Burkes and Larshes had a traditional get-together each spring, usually in April, at some mutually selected travel point, along with one to three other couples who were old friends.

Daughter Mary Ellen, now approaching fifty, married a handsome young man who decided to become a mechanic, studied at Texas State Technological Institute for two years in Automotive Technology, then went to work as a mechanic. He now owned and operated five Firestone/Bridgestone Service Centers. Mary taught music in high school, and still did so as a substitute; not because she had to, but because she enjoyed it.

Son James Jonathon, Jr., went to Texas A&M the fall after high school graduation to take petroleum engineering. His first year was general engineering, like all other engineering students. Then he started both geology and petroleum studies the next year. By his junior year he realized he liked geology better than pure petroleum engineering and switched to that major, with a minor in petroleum engineering. He graduated from Texas A&M in 1965 with a B.S. in Geology, a Petroleum Engineering minor, and a Reserve Officer's commission as a second lieutenant. His college experience had been nearly a carbon copy of his father's. Partly intentional, but also partly unintentional.

During his years of growing up, he was called 3J, J3, and Jon by his family and friends. Finally, Jon stuck as his main moniker, but old friends still sometimes called him J3. He had an inquisitive manner and in his early years was berated now and then by some people for asking so many questions, a good part of which had no exact answers.

He went through the model airplane building stage, at the same time he was building up merit badges in the Boy Scouts. He never got further than seven merit badges because two of them led him into lifelong pursuits: Geology and Astronomy. By the time he finished high school with almost an "A" average, he knew the solar system, how the planets and moon orbited, all of the first magnitude plus some other stars, some thirty or forty constellations, and several deep-sky bodies and phenomena.

At the same time, he had already read books on physical geology, land forms, aquifers, and one, that he really didn't understand too well, on geologic structure. It was quite natural that he would pursue earth science in college.

The summer after graduation from Texas A&M, following in his father's path, he interviewed and accepted a position as trainee with Aramco. He was to receive training in both geology and engineering. He worked for a few months in New York, then was transferred to the Dhahran office for further training in engineering and exploitation geology. Most of this stint was occupied with field work. Largely with drilling wells and doing all the work associated with the location, undertaking and completion of such operations.

Aramco transferred Jon Burke back to New York in December of 1967, then on to an assignment with Exxon in Houston just after Christmas. It was in Houston in January of 1968 that Jon came to an important fork in the road of his life.

As a result of his reserve commission which he had maintained, Jon was called up in 1969 for service in Viet Nam. Even though he was married by then, his training and commission were in a needed specialty, mobile artillery, and the Army called. He took a military leave from Aramco and his Exxon assignment in Houston, spent about seven months in training, then flew to his assignment in Viet Nam.

Four months after arrival, while in a fortified hill outpost, his unit came under heavy rocket and artillery fire. A mortar shell explosion in their dugout took the lives of two friends and ended Jon's service. He caught shrapnel in five wounds on one side, including one that lacerated an ear and scalp, plus another that entered the stomach cavity and penetrated a kidney.

He was flown out by helicopter for immediate surgery, then spent the next five months in various hospitals and rehabilitation centers. He overcame the injuries, though his kidney continued to give him some trouble for years, and required secondary surgery some two years after the initial surgery.

Jon returned to Aramco after a little over a year's military absence. He ended up as a reservoir engineering supervisor at Aramco, and was replaced by his good friend, Rashid Ben Rimthan, with whom he had resolved many reservoir problems.

After 23 years of geology and reservoir engineering with Aramco, he left in 1988 when offered a consulting job with the U. S. State Department. As a consultant, he expanded on his knowledge and training and became an expert in Saudi Arabian reservoir mechanics. In order to become expert in the mechanics of fluid movements in subsurface reservoirs, a person needed to integrate geology and engineering. Either alone was insufficient. Jon happened to have that background and adapted well to this technically demanding specialty.

He had occasional visits with his old friends at Aramco and enjoyed keeping up with their work and careers. He now spent most of his time on consulting work with Aramco, the State Department, or other oil firms in the Mid-East.

Astronomy remained a strong hobby with Jon, along with photography, oil painting, hunting and fishing.

Although he enjoyed the results of his oil paintings, for which he had fair artistic and good mechanical abilities, he found the actual painting rather laborious. Accordingly, he painted only when he got some particular urge to create a particular scene that could not be shown by photographs. Often he would see something that was truly beautiful, but power lines and poles, plus some junky house blotted the scene. The only way to capture the original scene was to paint it. He worked from sketches and photographs, using his mechanical drawing training to lay out the painting, then sketch, draw, and paint it. He bought a few books on methods, color combinations, types of media, and preservation.

He was always ready to hunt or fish when he had time and place. Especially with old friends. It was during these outings that he did some of his best photography, and a few paintings. But dropping a big buck at two hundred yards with one shot through the heart produced more instant excitement than anything else he did.

Jon believed that kills had to be eaten or it was a violation of nature. As a result of this concept, there was always a little inconvenience associated with a kill. Not only did it have to be dressed and taken in, he had to find a home for what he didn't want. This was fairly easy most of the time: their part-time maid and her family, some of the rural sharecroppers who eked out a living from small farms near the old Cook place, the Woodland. All these people who could rarely hunt large game such as deer, appreciated sharing Jon's kills.

But perhaps the best part of both hunting and fishing was the chance to share experiences, yarns, and politics with old friends. He was a rather strange mix: a man who enjoyed creativity, innovation, mental stimulation, acts of charity, and killing. Killing for food, that is.

Jon was now in his fifties, successful but not overly wealthy, with an endearing and very capable life mate, Lee-Anne, and two daughters.

The country place, the old Cook Farm, which they all now called Woodland, played an important role in a family trial that developed in the early sixties.

One morning in mid-April 1962, JJ awakened, feeling a little rotten, but not so much as to prevent going to work. So, he got out of bed and went into the bathroom for his morning relief, shave and shower. As he stepped up to get his shaving cream, he glanced at the mirror and immediately took a closer look. His hand automatically came up to his throat as he moved closer to the mirror. Yep, it's some kinda swelling. On the left side. Wonder what it is...couldn't be the mumps; I've already had them...long, long ago. Or could it? As he shaved, he thought more and more about this abrupt swelling. It couldn't be cancer because it happened overnite and cancer grows gradually. He noticed that the swelling was overall firm, but seemed to have a small area that was rather hard. Ruthanne came in.

"Hello, my sleepyhead. I guess that's part of the secret to your everlasting beauty."

"Mmmff," replied Ruthanne.

"Honey, I have a little swelling on my neck that came up overnite, and I can't figure out what it is. I've had the mumps, when I was a kid. To come up so fast, it must be an infection of some kind, but what?"

"My lover, it is just a bit early for me to take on such a heavy topic. Let's wait 'til coffee!" Actually, she was well aware of what he said, and was already thinking about it, but wanted a little time to come up with an idea without alarm. She, too, knew that unexplained swellings sometimes marked malignant tumors, but also knew instantly that these lesions didn't develop overnite.

She went on into the kitchen of their Memorial-area home in Houston while JJ finished his cleanup and dressing for work. They both kept thinking about this thing on JJ's neck, but also thought about other current activities, of which there always seemed to be too many. And this was with no kids at home! However, a lot of activities revolved about their son Jon, who was now a freshman at Texas A&M, with a very full calendar.

JJ walked in, "You know, even though I feel a little lousy, I'm still hungry. I've decided that most likely this thing on my neck is a glandular infection. That seems to fit everything, including my feeling a bit rough. I don't have any fever; I checked it while I was dressing."

"You mean in the lymph or other glands, sort of like mumps?"

"Yeah. I don't know why some infection other than mumps couldn't happen."

"Well, it does make sense. But the thing to do is find out. And get some antibiotic to fight it."

"I'll call Dr. James and let him look at it."

JJ went on to work, and in mid-morning called the doctor and arranged for this old friend to work him in for a quick check on his way home. He would take off a little early so as to get there just after the doctor's office hours. During the day, JJ continued to feel poorly, but not really bad, and continued with his work as an engineering section head.

"James J., I haven't any better idea than yours about what this is. It definitely is an infection of some kind, so we'll start antibiotics, and have a blood sample tested for a few things." The doctor knew that this infection could be the result of lymphatic resistance to malignant cells from some other source, but it could also be a half-dozen other things. A blood test might find antibodies indicating something.

With aspirin and the drug, JJ seemed to get better within a day or so, and two days later, felt fine. But the swelling was still there. About two weeks later, he felt poorly again, went back to Dr. James, got another prescription, and this time was recommended to a head and neck specialist who might have a better answer for this puzzling swelling. By this time, JJ was more than casually concerned that this was no longer a simple swelling because it stayed the same. It never was really painful, just a little sore part of the time.

During the next two months, he visited the specialist three times, had a needle biopsy, took antibiotics and, as recommended, applied damp heat to the swelling. It never left. JJ never got really sick, just felt bad for brief periods between the antibiotic courses. The needle biopsy revealed dead bacteria, a little pus, and no malignant cells. The specialist kept him on heat treatment.

As time wore on, JJ decided to take things into his own hands. The specialist was going too slow to suit him. He asked for neck surgery to make a better effort to find out what he had. The specialist demurred; just keep up the heat treatment. So, JJ went to a second specialist who agreed immediately that it would be desirable to do a proper biopsy and tissue study. By this time, the whole Burke family was concerned about JJ's neck swelling, and hoped a firm answer could be determined. And so it was.

JJ checked into Memorial Hospital late one afternoon in June, and was awakened quite early after a good night's sleep. He was prepared for surgery, wheeled into the operating room, and was put to sleep by the anesthesiologist. A little while later, he awakened groggily to make out a smiling Ruthanne looking down at him.

"Well, how did it go? What's the story?"

Ruthanne's smile became a little wan, but she replied in a cheerful voice, "All is OK. Just a little infection that will take a while to heal. The doctor is coming in within the next few minutes to explain all about it."

JJ knew something was wrong. He hadn't lived with this woman for 26 years without learning when she was holding back. But he didn't press it. He'd learn the results in good time, and no need to make her feel worse.

"Mr. Burke, there is good news and bad news....The bad news is you have cancer. The good news is that this kind of cancer has an eighty percent cure rate." The doctor speaking was an associate of the specialist who actually did the biopsy. "We delayed taking you out of surgery until we had a preliminary pathology report. We didn't want to remove all the lymph glands and affected tissue unless it was malignant. We waited for the report, and after getting it, we removed all tissue that might be malignant. We are confident that we got all of it."

JJ asked, "what is it?"

"Squamous cell carcinoma. The neck infection was caused by lymph nodes acting as a filter to malignant cells that were traveling through the lymph system. These cells break off a primary tumor, travel through the lymph system, and if you are lucky, as you were, the body traps and fights the bad cells like hell. Thus the infection, discomfort, and perhaps low-grade fever. The lymph nodes catch the cells, hold them, and the blood brings all its troops to fight. That battle is what alerts you something is wrong. By making you feel bad."

"You mean I have a tumor somewhere else."

"Yes. Probably above the neck, and probably small."

"What do we do next?"

"At this point, we'd recommend you report to the Head and

Neck Clinic at M.D. Anderson Hospital in the Medical Center. They will follow through as needed to find the primary tumor and treat it."

And that is what happened. About two weeks later, JJ checked in at M.D. Anderson. By the time he got to see a doctor, he was almost ready to go somewhere else. Ruthanne kept him company the whole time. JJ complained, "These people are like the army, hurry up and wait, hurry to the next place and wait. On and on!"

"Honey, it's pretty trying, but remember why we are here."

"Yeah, I know, I know. This is where they have seen and treated every kind of cancer known to man. Or woman. Or child. Or horse. And if they don't know how to do it, who does?"

"Exactly. So we keep going."

Finally, they got in to see the doctor in the H&N Clinic. He had JJ open his mouth, then he sprayed some concoction down JJ's throat that he felt had to be Mace. It was designed to numb the throat. It certainly did. Then the doctor had JJ open his mouth again, and asked him to breath normally, but gently. And he stuck a little mirror on a rod down JJ's throat. "There it is."

JJ pulled back. "There what is?"

"The tumor, I think," said the doctor. "But we'll have to biopsy to be sure."

Two nights later, JJ checked into M.D. Anderson. With Ruthanne by his side all the time. But she went home for the night. Early the next morning, with Ruthanne back again, along with Mary Ellen and Jon, JJ was wheeled to surgery. He was back in his room in about two hours, and the doctor came in shortly.

"Looks like this is the one. We'll know more in an hour or so. I'll be back then. But all looks pretty positive at this time."

Early in the afternoon, the doctor came in and explained that the pathology report confirmed his interpretation. JJ had a tumor about the size of a nickel, and not too much thicker, in his naso-pharynx back behind his nose. The cells were the same as found in his neck lymph nodes. The doctor had removed the small tumor, and JJ was to report back two days later to Radiology. The doctor explained that JJ would undergo some more testing and then a seven-week radiation program.

JJ underwent additional blood testing, x-rays, and brain scan. No additional tumors were indicated. Then the radiation treatment was set up. The radiologist marked off areas of his face and throat with colored marker, and was advised that he could not wash his face until the treatment was completed over six weeks later. He could shave with an electric shaver if he wished, but was told to not disturb the markings because these were what the radiology technicians used to align his head properly for the radiation.

Radiation was done five days per week. Within two days, JJ was sick. Not bad sick, just nauseated. He felt really lousy by Friday night when the first week was over. Then by Sunday afternoon he felt pretty good. Until Tuesday. And by Thursday, he was sickish again. This routine continued for six weeks. With a dirty face, that got dirtier and dirtier. Or so thought JJ. Finally, it was over. He had no taste; couldn't tell the difference between sugar and salt, steak tasted like cardboard, and the only difference between fluids was viscosity, whether oil, milk, or water. And his mouth was powder dry.

He was told he would recover his taste in about six months, and would gradually get most of his saliva back within a year or so. Just a year "or so." Meanwhile, keep a little water jug handy all the time.

The doctor decided it was not necessary to do chemotherapy. That pleased JJ very much. He wasn't sure he would have done it then anyhow, because he felt so lousy.

And that is where Woodland came in. For the next several months, JJ alternately felt very bad, bad, and rotten, then very bad again. His resistance was down. So was his weight. He caught flu and thought he wouldn't make it. But he did. After about two months, he wanted a change someway. So he and Ruthanne got permission to keep Woodland for two weeks and drove up there. The quiet and serene Woodland acted as a balm to JJ's bruised body. He felt better there than anywhere else.

This started a routine that continued for the next four months. Every other weekend, spend a long weekend at Woodland. Finally, about seven months after the radiation, JJ realized something.

"My sweet mate, I feel good again! I simply feel good!"

"Oh, JJ, that's marvelous! It's been a long fight, but so good to hear you say that."

And, so it came to pass that Woodland was the needed therapy for a harshly treated man who felt they had hopefully killed the cancer, but apparently designed the treatment to stop just short of killing the patient! Without Woodland, JJ would have survived, but that Woodland retreat with its natural beauty, its serene change of pace, made it much more pleasant.

Over the next two years, JJ learned the results of four other of the eight or ten patients who had undergone the same treatment for the same cancer at the same time as JJ. They were from Washington State, Georgia, Hong Kong, and Panama. All were dead. He never learned the status of the others. He was lucky. The main difference was timing. He had caught his before it had successfully spread.

- - - - - - -

While JJ was undergoing his treatment and recovery, their son Jon was learning to be an engineer. Preparatory to the great adventure ahead in which he would play a part.

~ ~ ~ ~ ~ ~ ~ ~ ~ ~ ~ ~ ~ ~

CHAPTER 3

Lee-Anne

Tuesday, January 30, 1968. Jon had been back from Saudi Arabia about three weeks, and was settling down to his new extended assignment in production research at Exxon in Houston. This assignment was similar to one his dad had several years earlier. Although he had progressed past the beginning training stages, he was still in training, but also doing necessary work. Specifically, his assignment was to work on the detail reservoir geology of Ghawar and Abqaiq fields, updating some maps that showed the shape of the rock layers that contained oil, called structure maps, and the maps that showed the fluid content of these oil-containing layers or strata. These fluid maps showed the position and net thickness of oil and gas in the reservoirs, and from these maps, net oil volumes could be measured. When these volumes were combined with rock porosity, permeability, pressures, and laboratory tests showing recovery factors, total recoverable reserves could be computed.

Some of the work he did was partly duplicative of work in New York or Dhahran, but other interpretations and even artificial differences were created in order to study such possible effects on future development and production. At this time, Exxon, an Aramco partner in Saudi Arabia, did much of such research for the joint venture.

The ARAMCO office in Houston was not to open until 1974, when the first office was opened at 1100 Milam Building after moving from New York City.

When all the reservoir volume and reserves data were combined with permeability measurements that were oriented as to direction, and combined with well flow data, water production, and salinity of waters, then the necessity for new wells, well workovers, or conversion of a well from oil producer to water injection could be assessed. Jon would be working on this project for months, perhaps much longer.

One of his co-workers, a geologist by the name of Virgil Kapsinger who had been assigned to the same section some six months earlier, showed Jon the ropes around the office. Virgil was a tall, muscular, good-looking man about four months older than Jon, who had graduated in geological engineering at Colorado School of Mines. He was good humored, easy going, and bright.

Over the next two weeks, he and Jon got to know each other pretty well, worked together, and found a few of the entertainment places and beer halls in Houston. Especially the beer halls. The ones with the good-looking women!

Jon was working with well logs one day in early February when Virg came up, "Hey, buddy...been down to the log library lately?"

"Not in person...but I've been gettin' logs and well files delivered to me."

"Did you notice anything about the people you talked to down there?"

"Well, I've only talked to women, one or two sound young. As a matter of fact, one of them sounds British, and the other young-sounding one has a rather perky way of talking."

"I think you should go check out "perky." That's a real cutie!"

"Okay," replied Jon, "I just realized I was a little short of the logs I need, so I'll just go down there and see if they've got those latest logs on the north end of Ghawar. And, maybe do a little checkin' in the process...See ya' later."

Jon was getting up as he talked, and made his last statement over his shoulder as he walked out of their dual office, heading for the elevator. If there were female candidates around, one didn't waste time finding out more!

He got off the elevator, walked down the hall to the library, entered, and headed for the log section, keeping eyes alert all the time...and there she was. There wasn't any doubt. That was "perky." He walked up, "Hi, could I get a few Ghawar logs?"

She replied in her normal quick and bright manner, "We got racks and racks of Ghawar files. You say what, and we will find. Gotta help the geologists and engineers get things right. You are one of those, I guess?"

As she talked, Jon took her in. Her red lips were sensitive and expressive as she talked, and were exactly half way between her perky, slightly uptilted nose and the base of her gently rounded chin. Her deep-brown hair was parted in the middle, fluffed up on top of her head, then fell in large curls about her sholders. She wore a puff-sleeved pale blue blouse and straight navy skirt with a wide, blue belt. She presented a fetching picture.

Jon replied, "yep. James Jonathon Burke, III, ma'am. And the Jonathon is spelled without an 'h,' and without a second 'a.' Seems somebody back down the line couldn't spell very good and I got tagged with a name not spelled like some Johnathans. Have you been working here long?"

"Just a couple of months."

"Where you from?"

"Abilene."

"Texas or Kansas?"

"Texas!"

"So you are a West Texas gal?"

"Straight down the line!"

"Like this job?"

"Well, it's not the most exciting work I ever did, but it is interesting to learn what the files represent and how important it is to keep them organized so you guys can do your job."

"You know, it...I need to know at least who you are..."

"Lee-Anne Gardiner, the Lee and Anne hyphenated, and an 'i' in the 'Gardiner'."

"Pretty. Family name?"

"Yes, my grandmother's."

"Where was she from?"

"Alabama. She came to Texas as an infant in the twenties. Her husband was a railroader. Got a job with Texas and Pacific in Sweetwater, and ended up working most of his career in Colorado City, Odessa, and El Paso. You may not remember the old T&P company."

"As a matter of fact, I do. Not because I knew them, but because my daddy worked out there in the thirties, and rode on their trains a number of times...and told us kids about how it was! Where did you grow up?"

"Well, my grandmother's son, my daddy, also was a railroader.

Also worked for T&P for a while, then as trucks began to take over a lot of the shipping in the fifties, he got into trucking, finally with his own trucks. I was born in Abilene, lived in several other places in Texas, but ended up back in Abilene just before starting high school."

"So you are a real, true-blue West Texas lass. Did you know all your grandparents?" By now, Jon was trying to learn something about this pretty girl's background, but didn't want to be too obvious, he hoped.

"Sure. They all lived close enough that I got to know them all. In fact, only my mother's daddy is not now alive. He succumbed to stomach problems, something he caught on a trip to Guatemala."

"That's terrible, to be killed by a trip. But still, all in all, that's pretty good," replied Jon. "It's nice to grow up knowing a lot of family. I had the same good luck. You look a little like a German girl I knew. Are you German?"

"As a matter of fact, most of my folks were of British origin. But for as far back as I know, they all lived in the United States." You mentioned that your grandfolks were still alive, except for the one sad happening...seems that you've been pretty lucky though anyhow, to have never had much contact with some debilitating disease like cancer."

"My mother and my namesake grandmother have always said that we're all healthy as oxen!"

What was unknown to Lee-Anne was that Jon was looking for a wife. He had the specific goal to find one now as soon as possible. He had finished his formal education, got a good job, and was now ready to settle down with some good solid girl. He'd dated several off and on over the last three years, but had gotten serious about the "right girl" business only in the last year or so.

There had not been all that much opportunity in Saudi Arabia, but he came pretty close on one Pennsylvania girl working in Dhahran. And, he would have gotten pretty close to one Saudi girl except for one thing: Moslem law. He knew this daughter of a Saudi engineer, saw her at the engineer's home several times, but realized that even though she was a real beauty, and very personable to go along with it, it could never work. So Jon didn't pursue it.

Then, there was a girl in New York, and another in Houston that attracted Jon, but neither seemed to be what he wanted. He wanted a good-looking Texas girl, healthy, without religious extremes, and hopefully with long-lived family members. She also had to have an upbeat and pleasant manner, and would hopefully be mentally quick.

Jon had seen numerous separations and divorces that happened because the couples had not considered their basics before getting married. He wanted female companionship in the worst way. But at this point in his life and career he didn't want to waste a lot of time finding out the "basics." Thus, the rather pointed questioning of this girl and it took him less than ten seconds to know that she met the beauty and personality requirements!

Jon continued. "Well, Lee-Anne Gardiner, are you a church girl?"

"Yes. Baptist."

Jon thought, boy, all's well so far. Now, wonder if this she is available. And if available, is she available for this old rough country boy? "I would be most appreciative if you would have dinner with me tonight."

"Boy! You work fast!"

"Don't take long when you see the right girl! Think you might break bread with me? You do have to eat, don't you? Or do pretty girls like you just sniff flowers?"

"Mr. Burke, I have plans for tonight. But I wouldn't mind a raincheck."

By this time, Lee-Anne was beginning to wonder what in the world was going on. This man was subjecting her to a real third-degree, and she had never laid eyes on him before! But, he was a tall, fine looking, man, seemingly strong and confident. He would be worth spending at least a little time with to learn more...

"Okay, how about tomorrow night?"

"Sorry, same song, second verse."

"How about Friday night?"

"I can't make Friday, but I would be available Saturday."

"That's it!" said Jon. "We'll make it dinner and a movie?"

"Fine."

They arranged the time and place, and thus began an unusual affair. The next few days seemed to move along slower than normal for Jon. Hell, he had a pretty girl to chase. She wasn't on his mind all the time, but she was there more than anything else!

Saturday evening about six-thirty, Jon drove over to Lee-Anne's place, knocked on the door and was immediately greeted by a vision that almost left him speechless. "Good evening, Mr. Burke," the Vision said.

"Good evening to you, ma'am," replied Jon. "That's a mighty pretty dress you're wearing."

"Well thank you, Mr. Burke. That's mighty kind of you!" Lee-Anne spoke with an obviously phoney Southern drawl.

Actually, Jon felt a great deal more than any normal courtesy would allow him to say. This lady made him want to grab her and see if anything so pretty was real...all soft and pretty as she was. But he restrained himself, and they got in his car and drove away, with her perfume, or was it cologne?, making Jon's driving a bit risky!

They had an enjoyable dinner of red snapper at The Country Playhouse. They decided that instead of a movie, it would be more fun to go to one of the dinner theaters and watch a play. It was a delightful evening for both, except for one thing. The weather.

It rained before they went. It rained all the time they were there. And it rained when they left. Jon took Lee-Anne home in the rain. To the door of the apartment she shared with another single girl, in the rain. And the blasted rain kept him from even trying to get a kiss for the evening! It wasn't a hard rain. Just a cold drizzle. Enough to cool budding ardor. For now. Only for now, thought Jon. Lee-Anne was just glad to get inside where it was dry and warm. Jon went back to his car and drove away with a light heart and hopes high, heading for his small apartment that, fortunately, was only a little over a mile away.

That evening, Jon learned much more about this pretty West Texas girl. She was born July 12, 1948, in Avoca, Texas, a small farming community near Abilene. Jon quickly noted to her that her birthday was only two days before his, and that must mean something, according to Astrology! He also learned that she played on her high school basketball team and ran track, so he better not think he could outrun her!

After high school, Lee-Anne attended Abilene Christian College in Abilene for one year, then shifted to a business college to learn more secretarial skills. By that time she felt her best objective was to get a job as soon as possible so as to carry her own load. Her parents, while not poor, had enough problems paying all their bills without trying to pay for more formal education for a daughter. At least that is what Lee-Anne thought. Actually, her parents would have starved if that were necessary to provide education for their daughter. But Lee-Anne would have none of that. She had to make her own way!

She had no grand plan for acquiring a husband, but it did occur to her that if she could get a job with a big company, there might be that sort of opportunity available, as well as a few candidates to squire her around. She wasn't opposed to just plain having a little fun, and learning a skill was a good way to start on her plan. After some seven months in the business college, she went to Houston, where a cousin lived and worked for Shell Oil Company as a secretary. Lee-Anne stayed with her cousin, Suzan Farley, while she searched for work.

Then, Aramco stepped into the scene. The powers that be decided that Jon and Virg should rotate to Saudi Arabia for the drilling of two investigative wells on the southerly end of Ghawar Field. It was observed that some of the water production from a few wells on that end of the field were beginning to make some low-salinity water with oil, instead of the originally observed high salinity-water. This suggested the possibility that the water trapped with the oil and the water surrounding the massive reservoir were not the same. Two well-located test wells with full hole cores and careful fluid collections should significantly help answer the question.

But, it did interfere with Jon's new-found love life. Just when it was getting started. So, without remembering to say anything to Lee-Anne, Jon climbed aboard the plane the following Tuesday, and was off to Saudi Arabia for a quick core and log. He thought he would be gone only a week. Until the well developed drilling problems and the hole had to be partly redrilled. Each day, he thought he would be leaving within a day or two. It drug on for a month. Finally, the work was done, the cores and water samples in the lab in Dhahran, and the logs in hand.

Jon flew back to Houston, and was replaced a few days later for the second hole by Virg Kapsinger. After work on the first day back, in early March, Jon went to Romano's cafeteria where he usually ate. He had white fish and vegetables, topped with a cut of lemon pie, a meal that he had frequently here because it was tasty as well as filling. As he was checking out, he glanced across the large room, and there sat...was it?...looks like...can't be sure because her back's to me...Lee-Anne? Had to find out. He quickly walked around where he could see her face clearly, and sure thing. It *was* Lee-Anne. She was in jeans, wearing a white blouse, and had her hair in curlers. And just as pretty as a piece of poetry.

Jon walked up to her back, and tapped her on her shoulder. "Say lady, don't you know you can't come in a classy restaurant like this in jeans and curlers?"

Startled, Lee-Anne quickly looked around and up. "What do...Jon! How nice to see you."

Jon returned, "I was on my way out and thought I saw you, and sure enough it *was* you."

She looked at him just a bit coyly, "I wondered what happened to you."

"Well, I went to Saudi Arabia for a few days, and it ended up taking a month...me thinking each day I'd be leaving in a day or so."

Actually, Lee-Anne knew full well what had happened. She had discretely inquired as to his whereabouts when he failed to call, but would by no means let him know she knew!

"Oh. Well, it's nice you have returned." She was not about to let him know that she had any interest other than pragmatic.

"May I pick you up tomorrow night for dinner?"

"Both tomorrow and the next day, I'm occupied, but I could make it Friday evening."

"Okay," replied Jon, and as he started walking away, "but I'll be down to see you tomorrow at lunch." Lee-Anne had no chance to say no.

The next day they lunched together. When outdoors, Jon noticed that Lee-Anne's hair had a slight reddish tint in sunlight. Perhaps indicating hidden fire!

The next day they lunched together again. Then Friday, dinner. And for the next eleven days, it was lunch *and* dinner together. Then after one day of missing an evening together because of a prior date Lee-Anne had made, they not only had lunch and dinner together, Jon came over for breakfast as well.

Around day fourteen, Lee-Anne told Jon about a date she had made with an out-of-town male friend over a month earlier, for the following Saturday night. She felt she should keep it because the man was very nice and was driving about 400 miles to keep the date. Jon agreed. So, Lee-Anne kept the date; Jon moped around for the evening; and checked in at her apartment around eleven p.m., and visited with her roommate, Liz Simpson, until Lee-Anne came in a little after twelve midnight. She later playfully chided Jon for being alone with her pretty roommate for so long, but was not really worried.

One day in late May, after supper with Lee-Anne and Liz in their apartment, Liz left on a date, leaving Jon alone with Lee-Anne. Later on, they were sitting watching a television show, she on a couch, and Jon in a rocking chair. A commercial came on, Jon turned the sound off, and spoke softly to Lee-Anne.

"You know, I find I want to be with you absolutely all of the time. When we are together, even if we are reading, I feel comfortable and content. I'm not sure exactly what 'love' is, since I've never had bells ring or an alarm go off because of affection, but I am satisfied that you are the woman I would like to share the rest of my life with. If that's love, then I have it, head over heels. I hope you feel the same. If I asked you to marry me, would you say 'yes'?"

In a small voice, without even thinking about the way the question was put, she replied, "Yes...I would."

Jon hit the arm of the chair with his fist. "Then, by George, let's do it! I'm ready!"

And, as it came to pass, on that evening, they found something more dramatic than a television show, left the television, and sealed their vows in the way man and woman have been sealing affection for thousands of years.

They announced their engagement three days later on Monday, June 3, 1968, and were married at Lee-Anne's church in Abilene on Saturday, August 31st. Lee-Anne had celebrated her twentieth birthday some six weeks earlier on July 12.

- - - - - -

In late June, she had gone home to Abilene to have her tonsils removed, a date that had been set the previous January. Except for that eight-day absence, Lee-Anne and Jon were together every day from their sealing of vows, and had almost all meals together. They never lived together at night; she stayed with her roommate, Liz. Until Sunday night, September 7, after a week's honeymoon trip to the Big Bend country of West Texas. Then she moved in with Jon in his apartment. For good.

Over the years, Lee-Anne and Jon grew closer if anything. They had arguments, and occasionally, downright fights. But, even so, they always found ways to get over their problems, their sulking after fights, their sharpness and sarcasm. And there were plenty of reasons for differences, considering the moving, going back and forth to Saudi Arabia, their finances and, finally, their children.

Lee-Anne was very practical, as well as intelligent and attractive. But she was not particularly good with numbers and abstract reasoning. She could remember telephone numbers and hundreds of things about people that Jon promptly forgot, and this was a continuing source of amusement between them. As time wore on, Jon became more and more knowledgeable about his profession, science in general, math, and business. As a result, on things having to do with business, professions, and the world in general, he had become, as Lee-Anne stated it, "a walking encyclopedia."

To which Jon responded, "you bet...of worthless information."

Their first child, Elizabeth Anne, named after Jon's close sister, was born June 16, 1972. Then, on September 12, 1975, another child, Nicole Brittany, was born. Elizabeth came to be known as Lisa very early, so the family had no confusion between her and her aunt: It was Aunt Elizabeth, and Lisa the younger.

Lisa got a degree in Business-Accounting from the family alma mater, Texas A&M University, August, 1995, after an extra summer of graduate courses aimed at her CPA exams.

Lisa and Brit, as she became known casually with her family and friends, had one full year overlap at Texas A&M. Brit studied Computer Science and boys.

Lisa developed as the stable, thoughtful, very intelligent sort, clearly destined for a professional career. She was an attractive, though not beautiful, woman with light-brown hair, keen perceptions, and good humor. When you talked, her green eyes seemed to penetrate your mind to grasp not only your words but the inferences and introspection that went with them. She was the sort of woman who grew on a person with time.

Brit was entirely different. She was a beautiful redhead, with blue-green eyes, and while reasonably intelligent, was not an outstanding student. She barely made it into A&M. But wherever she went, she was a center of attraction, especially with young males. She had learned to be studiously conservative in her dress to reduce problems. Though a little flighty, she had solid principles of responsibility ingrained as she grew up.

But Brittany could not stay away from her main life guide: Have fun and smell the roses as I go my way, because I travel this trail but once. She had captured this saying from her grandfather JJ and then, later, read other versions of the same thought.

To Lee-Anne and Jon, these two girls were the lights of their eyes, their joys. Even with the many clashes that went with high spirits and strong individuality.

~ ~ ~ ~ ~ ~ ~ ~ ~ ~ ~ ~ ~ ~

CHAPTER 4

The Driving Force

Jon slowly closed his book and laid it on his chair-side table. It was after midnight and he was more than ready to join Lee-Anne in their king-size bed, one luxury they had splurged on years ago. But the book had been so interesting it was hard to quit. He sat for a few minutes recapping the story told. It was about the comeback of Kuwait after the Iraqi destruction of 1991.

When defeat was inevitable, the Iraqi dictator, Saddam Hussein, ordered the Kuwaiti oil fields destroyed. His troops set out to destroy the fields and found that they could not really destroy the fields. But they could, they hoped, destroy the capacity of Kuwait to produce and refine oil, and perhaps seriously damage the field in the process. So they set explosives around the wellhead of each and every significant oil well, and strategically placed explosives on all key surface processing and refining facilities, and set them off. Leaving a "burned earth" behind as they departed. This action alone cost Iraq the lives of hundreds of soldiers who had no choice but to obey or die, and the Allies saw to it that many of these men did die, and dispersed heavy destruction in their homeland as an additional price.

Saddam had no concern for the environment. If it destroyed half the world, it was not as important as his scorched earth policy. After the well heads were exploded, oil flowed freely from all the wells that could flow without pumping, and this included literally all of the several hundred major wells. Ruptured flow lines and storage tanks drained rapidly, adding massive oil quantities to the burning streams from the wells. Black, sooty smoke covered thousands of square miles, oil slicks covered the western part of the Persian, or Arabian, Gulf for hundreds of miles. The damage measured in the tens of billions of dollars. But it was finally controlled. Mainly by the heroic effort of well-paid oil well fighters. The wells were all capped, and all facilities cleared in little more than a year. But that was only part of the problem.

There was massive effort at costs in the billions of dollars, to put the fires out, get the wells under control, rebuild facilities, flow lines, pipelines, tanks, and all the hardware necessary to produce several million barrels of oil per day. Meanwhile, massive well repairs and workovers were required, and some of this took longer. Especially since some of the holes were seriously damaged by the uncontrolled uprushing oil from pressured reservoirs.

The massive Burgan Field, one of the top fields in the world, was damaged. Other fields were damaged. The uncontrolled flow of oil caused some channeling of water through and around oil in the subsurface reservoirs, and once water has channeled past oil, it is very difficult to recover such isolated oil. Some oil leaked from ruptured casing into shallower rocks, probably lost forever.

Still the Kuwaitis persevered. They did whatever was needed. They redrilled some wells, and added new wells. And within about three years, they had their production back to a level not much lower than projected for that time had no destruction ever occurred.

But many millions of barrels of oil were burned, lost, or left unretrievable in the subsurface. Lost reserves were suggested by well performances in the first year after the re-start, but the rather large quantity of the losses was not clearly established until several years later.

Jon rose from his chair, and thought about such needless

destruction, not only to man, but to the environment, to future generations. And all for what? To nurture the ego of a single man. Absolutely nothing else.

Jon could see one bright side to the Kuwaiti losses that resulted from oil being bypassed and left in the reservoirs: most of it could ultimately be recovered down the road when the price is right. All this thinking caused Jon to have a little trouble going to sleep that night, but not too much!

The last few years, Jon had gotten more and more involved in analyzing fluid movements in large reservoirs, such as the Mideast fields. He had developed considerable experience in this area, and was recognized by various United States agencies as well as some companies operating in the Mideast. Most of his experience was in the Saudi Arabian fields, but he had worked some in various Kuwaiti, Iraqi, and Iranian fields. He was called upon to interpret water encroachment into hydrocarbon reservoirs, the variable flows of fluids through permeable rocks that were originally wet with some other kind of fluid.

Petroleum geologists knew that a sandstone or grainy carbonate rock might have originally been deposited in the Persian Gulf with only the original connate water in between the grains, and wetting the grains. Then, later on, oil or gas might migrate through this reservoir and finally get trapped at the top of an anticlinal fold, or against a break in the rocks, or fault, where an impermeable rock had been shifted up along the fault plane, into juxtaposition against the permeable reservoir rock. Thus the migrating oil stopped at this barrier and piled up behind it until a considerable quantity might be trapped.

The reservoir rocks are normally wet with connate water, and if the permeability of the rock is low, it might require some force to push oil into the reservoir water. Sometimes the available force is not enough, and the oil gets trapped somewhere else along its tortuous migratory path. There is an entire area of study in geology and engineering devoted to

40

the business of how and what will flow through what under a given set of circumstances. Even another kind of water, perhaps fresh water, could migrate into a reservoir and replace part of most of the original salt water, setting up another completely different ballgame. And this has happened in Saudi Arabia. And would play a part in future events.

Rain or snow falls and splashes on the surface as meteoric water. Then, part of it soaks into the ground, and part of that gets into fractures or faults that provide a passage for gravity drainage of the water, now called vadose water, down in the earth to some porous and permeable layer. Then part of that water might move through the reservoir if the pressure behind, from say, a column of water to the surface, is greater than the pressure ahead. When oil is produced from a reservoir, it leaves space for something to move into. Ultimately, vadose water might be this something.

The more Jon learned about this business of fluid movements, the more complex he realized it was. But he felt that if it was to be understood, he would give it a whirl, and he did. Now, he was rather widely sought as a consultant to help solve unusual observations in productive reservoirs. He was now in his early fifties, and his consulting kept him busy most of the time. Most of his two years in operations research and many of his 23 years with Aramco were spent in reservoir work where he employed both his geologic and engineering training.

A significant part of that experience had been in eastern Saudi Arabia, a great deal in the Ghawar-Abqaiq area.

- - - - - - -

Immediately after World War II, Aramco came back with heavy exploration and development work in eastern Saudi Arabia. Abqaiq had already been discovered, and now they could pursue the En Nala structure that so excited JJ Burke and Huey Larsh in 1935. By now it was clearly a long anticlinal ridge, quite possibly a place for several oil fields.

After conducting additional structural and core drilling, along with gravity and magnetic mapping, they started drilling a well in early 1948 on an anticlinal fold that is part of the overall En Nala anticlinal ridge as then mapped and called. This well was in the northern part of the ridge, the 'Ain Dar area, about twenty miles southwest of the known and productive Abqaiq structure.

JJ, back in Dhahran, sat on some of the early exploratory wells on the structure after the initial discovery in June 1948, when Aramco tested oil production at astonishing rates from the lower Arab Formation, a zone they labeled "D" and the underlying Jubaila Formation.

Aramco followed this with a similar discovery in the Haradh area in February, 1949. Then 'Uthmaniyah in April, 1951, and Shedgum in August, 1952. These isolated discoveries, dozens of miles apart, were all on the En Nala ridge.

Each of them flowed oil at rates dozens of times as great as typical new oil wells in the U.S. Seismic data had little value in locating the wells. Surface and near-surface geology, plus gravity and magnetics, provided the primary reasons for drilling.

It was a magnificently exciting time for JJ, being a part of such extraordinary drilling and testing!

By 1952, it began to sink in on the explorationists that maybe all of these discoveries were possibly the same field! And, indeed, by the mid-fifties, it was fairly certain. In the late fifties, it became recognized that Ghawar, as the long ridge was now known, was one productive field, over 140 miles long, and covering some 3300 square kilometers, or 1200 square miles, with Jurassic oil pays making a total oil column reaching as high as 340 meters or 1100 feet above the contact of the oil with the underlying salt water.

The top of this massive accumulation of oil was a little over a mile below the *jibehl, sabkha,* and *dahna* that marked the surface of this desert Kingdom.

Except for a small structural saddle, or low, just south of the 'Ain Dar closure, the oil pay zones were continuous from south of Haradh, to northwest of 'Ain Dar townsite, a total distance of about 160 miles.

These pay zones were mainly in the Arab D limestone, but also in the overlying B and C zones of the Arab Formation, and the underlying Jubaila limestone.

The rock layers had all been deposited in shallow Upper Jurassic marine salt waters, mainly from shells of various small marine animals, some 140 million years ago. In addition to the shell fragments, some calcium carbonate precipitated out of the water to form tiny balls of muddy limestone in the shallow, agitated water, called oolites; along with a hodgepodge of other largely calcium carbonate materials, with some of it being reef fragments and some clays. All in all, it was not so very different from the present Persian Gulf.

But sea level did not remain constant. And the land elevation rose or fell from time to time. This caused cycles of deposition, with the end stage of each cycle occurring when the water body was cut off from the oceans, and the water evaporated at much faster rates than the supply of new meteoric (rain, hail, snow) waters. This caused the water to get saltier and saltier, but the main salt was calcium sulphate, not the sodium cloride salt we use on our eggs in the mornings.

This salt precipitated out in layers of gypsum and, after burial and pressure, turned to anhydrite through loss of water. Both these minerals are calcium sulphate; gypsum has molecular-bound water that, when subjected to heat and pressure, dissipates and anhydrite remains.

Then, the area would get flooded with sea water again as relative sea level changed, and a new cycle of carbonate deposition got under way. Thus were formed the Arab Formation zones D, then C, B, A, and finally the Hith Anhydrite Formation that put a stop to this cyclical business. The Hith is a massive anhydrite, some ninety meters, or 290 feet thick. The

Arab D is about fifty-five meters (178 feet) thick, and the overall Arab Formation, 124 meters (403 feet) thick.

Since original deposition, the sediments were tumbled about, broken in various ways until, finally, before burial by later sediments, much of the Arab Formation, was granular, like sand or gravel. Then it got covered with Hith anhydrite, then later sediments over the next 140 million years or so, with some of the original sea water still in the spaces between the grains of carbonate.

One final act of nature created some slightly different rocks interlayered with the granular limestone: As magnesium in waters percolated through some of the porous layers, some of the magnesium left the water and bound or replaced some of the calcium in the rocks. This formed dolomite. The process of formation is referred to as diagenesis, a good old Greek derivation. This is also granular for the most part, with good porosity and permeability.

And the exploration continued over the years. To JJ, it was a great privilege to be a part of the exploration and then the development of this unique giant. He could remember so well the long days of flying sand and dust in the open desert, the long camel rides and open car trips, the measuring, walking, climbing, all the work and discomforts to develop the first exciting, yet ghostly, elements of major oil exploration. After World War II, he had come back to find so many projects under way, and he could be a small part of it. Over time, the glow wore off somewhat as work became more routine, more mundane. But there was always that big, big satisfaction. He had helped find and develop the largest oil field on planet Earth.

JJ retired in the seventies. While more discoveries in this desert country were yet to be discovered, he was a part of the biggest! And he knew it!

The most significant find since the fifties occurred in the late eighties when the Saudis developed an entire new producing province in the Paleozoic Permo-Carboniferous section in central Saudi Arabia. These were high-quality crude oil discoveries with thick pays and high producing capacities; not so thick or high capacity as Ghawar, but quite high by world standards. Wells were capable of producing in the 4,000 to 10,000 barrels of oil per day range, compared to rates above 15,000 barrels per day at Ghawar.

This new trend of large fields, with old Paleozoic reservoirs, was just southeast of the capital at Riyadh. But there would not be another Ghawar.

- - - - - - -

Jon learned pretty early in his career that there would come a time when most oil might be found where it already was mapped; that is, find ways to get part of the 30 to 80 percent of the original oil in place that was bypassed and left in the reservoirs when fields were abandoned. This is what Jon and many other oilmen worked on, mostly in the United States.

It was called many things: Pressure maintenance, secondary recovery, tertiary recovery; flooding by water, carbon dioxide, fire, gases, polymers, and whatever might be imagined. Jon's main efforts were directed at careful well locations, sometimes as part of water or polymer floods, and the producing rates monitored to provide a most efficient drainage sweep.

His current project was studying the movement of low salinity vadose waters near high salinity connate waters in the vicinity of Ghawar and Abqaiq fields in Saudi Arabia. He was contracted by Aramco.

The morning after he finished his Kuwaiti book, he was abruptly awakened by a telephone call.

"Hello?"

"Hi, Buddy. Are you out of bed yet?"

Jon immediately recognized his old Aramco-days friend Rashid Ben Rimthan. "How in the world are you doing, you old desert rat? Where are you?"

"Right here in Houston. Jon, we've had a pretty bad 'quake and aftershock with a lot of destruction, and I'd like to visit with you a bit. I'm working on the reservoir aspects; Achmed is coordinating the cause study."

"I know, Rashid, it's all they have in the papers these days."

"It's pretty bad, Jon. The destruction is widespread, but what we are most concerned about right now is possible reservoir damage in the Ghawar-Abqaiq area."

"OK, Rashid, where and when do we meet?"

"Jon, I'll be here for just a few days, not over four. How about tomorrow at your office, late morning?"

"That's fine. I have a lunch meeting with a friend, but it's purely casual, and can easily be rearranged. No sweat."

Jon's mind was on little else for the rest of that day. Even while he was out Christmas shopping on this cool but pleasant December day. The only gift he was concerned about was one for Lee-Anne. She took care of all the rest. But he did have to get this one, and with Christmas only three weeks away, he had to hustle!

As Jon went to bed that night, his mind drifted back to a meeting he had attended the previous spring. Once his mind locked in on it, the details came back in vivid detail.

- - - - - - -

It all started with an awakening telephone call one March morning.

"Jon, I have something of interest to tell you. Tell me when you get awake enough to understand!" It was his dad, JJ.

"Okay, I guess I'm about as ready as I'll get for the next hour or so."

"Jon, I had a visitor yesterday from our Chamber of Commerce who would like to have a combined clubs luncheon where speakers could present ideas about the terrible state of affairs in the oil and gas business in the United States."

"So...what does that have to do with a Saudi reservoir man?"

"Just listen, my young whippersnapper, and you will see. These people, men and women, are not only interested in what's happening to our U.S. business, but they are interested in why it is happening. My visitor was a young lawyer man by the name of Fred Willis."

"You mean Fred III, son of Fred, Jr.?

"You got it. I thought I recalled that you were friends with his dad. Anyhow, Fred III came to me because some of the organizers remembered I had worked in the Mideast and might help them develop some appropriate speakers. Such as you!"

"Dad, you know that I'm not real hot on that sort of thing, but I'll cooperate if you want me to. Maybe I could get a little help from Aramco or somebody here in Houston."

His dad replied, "I think it is a helluva opportunity to get out some word on our industry's situation. Most people have no idea just how thin the ice really is."

"Okay, I'll do a little figurin' and get back in a few days."

"Well, don't let too much grass grow under you feet. The meeting is planned for April 4th, a Thursday, I think."

"Will do, father of mine. Take care. And, don't get so wrapped up in this thing that you have Thunder on your back for inattention!"

With that, they said goodbye and hung up.

Jon was able to get an Aramco speaker, an engineering supervisor by the name of Tony DeRocca, an old friend of Jon's who headed a group of engineers and who had some experience doing this sort of speaking for Aramco. Also, he found that his old friend from Saudi Arabia, Rashid Ben Rimthan was temporarily in Houston and he, too, would be glad to say a few words at the same time and, as a real Saudi Arabian engineer, lend a touch of authenticity to the talks. Between them, they worked out a forty-five minute presentation, with Tony doing most of the talking. That, added to about fifteen minutes for JJ's comments, made an hour; which was the amount of time set up for the luncheon talks.

By the time the project was set, a Houston reporter for the Chronicle learned of it and, thinking it might present a few newsworthy thoughts, decided to attend. Reporters from Nacogdoches and Lufkin also would be there. As would several people from Stephen F. Austin University, including the head of the geology department, Dr. Martin Booth. It was turning into a real wingding.

"Ladies and gentlemen, even though many of you have not finished your meal, in fact, I see there are a few who are just now being served...but, regardless, I think we should get started. We have an hour presentation, and there might be a few questions afterward." The Chairman of the clubs' joint committee, Fred Willis, Jr., was anxious to get the talks underway. He described the speakers and their individual backgrounds, and smiled at his old fishing buddy, Jon Burke.

"So, with no further talk, I give you one of our wise men in Nacogdoches, James Jonathon Burke or, as we know him, JJ."

To a polite, but enthusiastic applause, JJ stepped up to the podium, paused a moment, took a sip of water, then, "Well, if wise means old, then I oughta be mighty dam' wise!"

As the shower of laughter quieted down, JJ started his talk.

"My friends, the oil business is pretty sad. You all know that. But it may be that you don't really know how bad it is. Maybe by the time we're through, we'll all have a bit better understanding. These other men can talk better on most of the things of interest to us today than can I, but we all felt you might want a little background for our business, and at least for a part of that, I can help. I'm one of the few old hands left who explored for oil in Saudi Arabia in the thirties."

JJ continued to talk, briefly describing the early years when Aramco was born.

"In the thirties, we worked on an unusual prospective area we called En Nala. The man who found some older rocks exposed on the surface, surrounded by younger rocks, was Max Steineke.

"In addition to this inlier, he observed some flat topographic ridges, forming sort of a plateau, that was capped with limestone and cut here and there with dry washes we learned the Saudis called *wadis*. He put these things together, and suggested they probably indicated an uplift, perhaps a large anticline.

"Several geologic parties, including mine, worked on areas around Max's suggested area, finally extending over a hundred miles northerly from the original inlier. After several years, assisted by gravity measurements, shallow core or structure holes drilled to find near-surface layers we could map...contour just like one of those topographic maps you've seen...and some rather poor seismic data, we developed a feature.

"We mapped this feature as a long structural ridge, well over a hundred miles long, and thought it might have several sizeable oil fields on it.

"When I say sizeable, I mean maybe five to ten miles long and perhaps three to six miles wide. Possibly fields with as much as one or two hundred million barrels of producible oil; maybe even a billion or two barrels.

"At that time, the largest field in the United States, was East Texas Field, about sixty miles north of where we are sitting, around Longview. At that time, around 1940, East Texas was thought to have about five billion barrels of oil. My partner, Huey Larsh, and I thought it unlikely we'd ever find a field on En Nala that large.

"We originally expected the best structure on En Nala, on the southerly end of the ridge, near the town of Haradh, to be drilled in the early forties. World War II changed that. Finally, In June, 1948, the first oil well was completed on the northern part of the ridge in what was called the Ain Dar area, not far from the known Abqaiq Field.

"A second oil discovery was made near Haradh in February, 1949. Development wells were drilled around these two discoveries, and additional wells were drilled on other structures on the ridge. Production started in 1951, but it was the mid-fifties before it was realized what existed: One giant field over one hundred and forty miles long, and up to about seventeen miles wide.

"This is Ghawar Field. The largest oil field in the world. By far. One of the beauties of this immense field is the uniformity of the reservoir and the absence of significant faulting that could alter the overall trap. The few faults are mostly near the northern end of the field, and relatively small.

"It's just one huge elongate bowl turned upside down with oil floating on water that fills the reservoir below the bowl, or as we call it, below the dip closure. And the funny thing is, the oil extends down below the dip closure on the northeastern end of the field; a seeming impossibility: an oil-water contact that is not flat! How can that be?

"If oil is to float on water, when all is stabilized, the contact between the oil and water must be flat. But it isn't at Ghawar. It's tilted to the north such that the contact at the northeast end of the field is some six hundred feet lower than at the southwest end.

"We have an answer for that, called hydrodynamic entrapment. Also, there are other explanations having to do with original entrapped position versus present-day structure. But we'll leave all that for another day.

"The main thing to do here is explain just how important this structural complex, which includes its sister field called Abqaiq, is to the world. Actually, Abqaiq was discovered first, in 1940. If not for World War II, Ghawar would probably have been discovered in 1942 or thereabouts.

"For the past several decades, Ghawar and the adjacent Abqaiq fields alone, had more proven and economically producible total oil reserves than the entire United States. More than Texas, California, and Alaska combined. More than Oklahoma, Louisiana, and Colorado with their major fields, than Pennsylvania where Drake really started the oil business for the whole world in 1859, more than all these states and their thousands and thousands of fields combined. If we include Abqaiq and the Safaniya-Manifa producing complex, just these two Saudi Arabian producing complexes, just two, have more oil reserves than the entire U.S. and Canada put together.

"There are reported to be some thirty-nine thousand oil fields in all of the United States, with over half our total oil coming from only six-tenths of one percent of them. Just one Saudi field complex exceeds the whole works, all thirty-nine thousand of them.

"If you include the top twenty or thirty fields in Saudi Arabia, their total oil reserves exceed any other nation on our planet. Within 300 miles of those wells Saddam Hussein set on fire in Kuwait in 1991, there are more oil reserves than the rest of the world combined. Including all of South America, Russia, you name it. The gasoline you burn: over half of it is directly or indirectly attributable to the area within that 300-mile radius. A distance about like from here to San Antonio.

"Another example is the original large producing well in Saudi Arabia, the Dammam #7, completed in March, 1938. This single well, that is *not* in one of the largest Saudi fields, produced 28 million barrels of oil up to the time it was shut-in after forty-four years of production. And, it could still flow oil at 1,800 barrels per day when it was shut in. This single well produced more oil than the vast majority of the *fields* in the United States.

"The attraction for petroleum investment dollars no longer lies in our Texas, our United States. That attraction is foreign, where there are still huge areas that have never been explored and exploited to the extent of, say, New Hampshire. And the targets are big. None of this half-million barrels field stuff we are most likely to find, if we find anything, in new exploration in the United States. With our oil and gas prices basically controlled by Mideast production rates, there is no way our oil and gas business can compete in an open world market. But now, I'm gettin' into another speaker's territory, so I guess it's time for me to quit.

"I think you get the idea of how important Saudi Arabia is to the world as to oil supply. Maybe you also get some idea of the small role I played, along with the great names of original Saudi exploration, like Max Steineke, Tom Koch, Krug Henry, Doc Nomland, Fred Davies, Soak Hoover, and other real explorers. There were only a dozen or so of these men who started this colossal ball rolling.

"Thank you for your patience in listening to my ramblings!" And, JJ sat down. Many in the audience either knew JJ, or knew of him or his family. All was quiet for a few seconds, then a little clapping grew to a standing ovation. The old man felt his eyes beginning to burn...and he had to blink his eyes to keep the moisture spread so as to avoid tears...

Fred Willis came back to the podium. "Well Nacodochians, that wasn't too bad a start, was it?" He was answered with more lively applause. "Now, we go to our Aramco engineer, Mr. Tony DeRocca, who also has a good grasp of, and will touch on, international petroleum economics."

Another round of applause greeted Tony, and he commenced his talk. He mainly discussed the role of Aramco in continuing the exploration for, and exploitation of, oil in Saudi Arabia, the tremendous costs to do that, and the lead times required to reach specific production objectives. By the time he finished, it was clear that even with the massive resources of the Mideast, it still took equally massive quantities of money and years of lead time to meet increased demands.

It was also equally clear that the availability of oil and natural gas is directly related to its price.

Following Tony, Jon Burke came on with his talk aimed at enhancing the production from oil fields everywhere. He had many questions from individuals who had family members employed in some part of the oil and gas business. These people were quite interested in learning that as the real price (as related to say, a pound of potatoes) of oil and gas reached new highs, additional oil and gas reserves in the United States became available. Jon gave an example:

"Ladies and gentlemen, as an example of what oil price can do, I'd like to tell you about an old, old field that most of you know something about. About fifteen miles southeast of where you sit, on Texas Highway 21, El Camino Real, is the Oil Springs marker. Indians knew about the oil seeps in this area long before the Spanish came. Then the Spanish learned about it, then the settlers from the United States. Well, by the time of the Civil War, lots of people knew about these seeps, including a man by the name of L.T. Barret. He is credited as the principal force in establishing the first oil production in Texas. Records indicate the work for the well started in 1865, very shortly after the end of the Civil War, but it wasn't completed until 1866.

"This was the first Texas oil well. And it came to pass less than ten years after Drake's first oil well in the United States in Pennsylvania. The Oil Springs discovery didn't result in much of a field, but it *was* an oil field. The production was reported in the late 1880's to be 'maybe enough to oil the pistols of the Texas Rangers,' actually a few tens of barrels of oil per day. That field later became known as Nacogdoches Field, and is still making a little oil now and then today. It has produced only about a half-million barrels of oil, very small compared to many other oil fields in the United States.

"The small production wasn't because there was not quite a lot of oil there. Actually, the production comes from a depth of only about 400-feet depth, and extends over a sizeable area. Many good oil fields have produced maybe 100 times as much oil from an area that size. There are millions of barrels of oil here also. Why is the vast majority of that oil still there after drilling dozens of wells, many only a few hundred feet apart, and produced for over a hundred years?

"It's because it is heavy oil, that is, very viscous. And the price has never justified really trying to get most of it out. So, a great deal of recoverable oil still rests there. But it would take state-of-the-art technology to get it, and it's too little to fool with unless the price of oil gets to where a barrel is worth, say, a barrel of milk.

"Here we sit in our country, with literally billions of barrels of similar shallow, heavy oil and tar in east Texas and north Alabama alone, not counting many other places in the United States and Canada, where even more massive quantities exist."

Jon pointed out that, including Rocky Mountain shale oil, and heavy oils, there were enough total oil reserves in the United States, Canada, and Venezuela to supply the needs of the Western Hemisphere for at least two hundred years. At a price. Maybe about the price of milk per gallon, or barrel, surely if oil were priced volumetrically the same as beer.

He continued, "but the vast majority of this oil will never be developed as long as massive Mideast productive capacity holds out and is available to us in an uncontrolled market. And, if oil should get to the price of beer, additional huge volumes of Mideast oil would become available. Thus it seems likely that our huge heavy oil reserves will stay about like they are, unless some unpredictable force cuts us off from our Mideast supply. And even then, the lead time to develop our heavy oils is so long that we would see little effect for probably ten years or so."

Then, he briefly discussed the increasing role of natural gas in the world, especially for the rapidly developing vehicular uses that were aimed primarily at pollution reduction. This natural resource was actually less plentiful in North America than oil, if heavy oil, tars, and shale oils were included.

"But, the thing about natural gas is how plentiful the key component, methane, is. We can make methane from coal, corn stalks, manure piles, and even garbage! Again, though, it's at a price. Today, a natural gas producer sells a gallon of gasoline equivalent in natural gas, about 120 cubic feet, for about one-sixth of the price you pay for that gallon of gasoline. Even allowing for transportation from the wellhead to your station, a methane producer could not get as much as the price of gasoline equivalent unless the buyer was mandated to do so...as our state has done for bus and truck fleets. So, again, supply is not the basic problem. The real problem is price, compared to the cost of milk and beer!

"Well, ladies and gentlemen of Nacogdoches, I've taken enough of your time. I've enjoyed this chance to tell someone else about my concerns, and I hope it has been of some interest to you. Thanks very much for your time. I'm grateful that only a few of you fell asleep!"

After his presentation, the questions from these East Texas professional and business people indicated their understanding and concern. Considerable discussion centered on environmental and pollution concerns, particularly the low pollution of almost limitless methane supply. Jon emphasized that the all-controlling factor was price. If the price were high enough, people would use less oil and gas, use it more efficiently, design more efficient engines, and most of all, acquire and use it in a more environmentally safe manner. Much as has been done in Europe for decades.

A young woman rose and asked, "Jon, we all know about the gas-powered vehicles that are gradually becoming more prevalent. Is this really new technology?"

"Not at all," replied Burke. "Before the auto industry settled on gasoline in the 1890's for mobile engines, several of the early cars used 'coal gas' for fuel. And, during World War II when gasoline was simply unavailable to many people in Europe, they commonly drove vehicles powered by methane from coal or charcoal, some with small charcoal burners aboard, some with large gas bags."

He wound up his talk pointing out that, all in all, meaningful development of our own energy sources could never happen in the United States as long as someone could supply our oil needs at a price less than one-third the cost of milk, as was currently the case.

Jon walked away to strong applause, and turned the podium back to Fred Willis.

"Well folks, even though this is one of the most interesting get-togethers we've ever had in Nacogdoches, we've run over our planned time limit and it's nearly eleven o'clock! Time this boy got to bed! And from some of the nodding I've noticed, it's past the bedtime for more than me."

"However, I have one closing comment. One thing has come home to us all: Our present oil and gas business in the United States is little more than caretaker status. And a second prime conclusion is that the driving force for energy supply is price, not availability, and that force is driven by those who can control the price."

"Now! Unless someone feels they just must make one more comment, let's call it quits, and go home!"

One jokester got up, "Fred, I do have a comment."

"Yes?"

"I agree!"

And so ended the meeting that was to prove rather prophetic for these good folks, as well as a few others.

- - - - - - -

Jon drifted off to sleep after lying there for over an hour thinking about that meeting last spring, and how meaningful it was in light of his meeting tomorrow with Rashid about the Saudi earthquake destruction.

The next morning, he pulled out his old Ghawar trend maps and wondered what his friend had to tell him. About ten-thirty on that December 12th, in walked Rashid.

"Well, old buddy, tell me all about it," were Jon's first words.

"Jon, it's a pretty long story, but I'll describe everything the best I can."

Rashid then told the story of the last two weeks, after which they discussed possible subsurface damage to Ghawar, what the signals might be, and what they might do about it.

"In a couple months or so, after we've gathered and studied well production and pressures," said Rashid, "I might be back to talk about a consulting job. If so, would you be interested?"

"Could I keep my work to about half time on average?" asked Jon.

"Sure."

"Then we'll do like we've done before: I'll schedule my other work around your projects and meetings, and plan to start in late February?"

Rashid replied, "OK, Mr. Jon. Deal!"

The two old friends had lunch together, and then parted to their separate paths for a while.

~ ~ ~ ~ ~ ~ ~ ~ ~ ~ ~ ~ ~ ~

CHAPTER 5

Breaking The Link

It had only been a few weeks since the earthquake, now commonly referred to as the Sirr 'quake, because the epicenter was beneath the broad desert valley called Nafud As Sirr, and Rashid and Yasmeen had largely forgotten about it. It had caused relatively little damage, although to those whose mudbrick homes in that area had crumbled, it was not little.

However, from time to time, Rashid remembered his conversation with seismologist Achmed Asker, and imagined that another quake could follow. He had written to, and heard back from, his friend Jon Burke. Jon had no words of wisdom other than to remind Rashid that his homeland, Saudi Arabia, occupied sort of an island in the Earth's plates, with the major African and Asian plates on either side.

That, too, caused Rashid some concern, but he had pretty well put it out of his mind. The main thing now was the week off back at their country home, *Ehleebeyt*, Arabic for "high home." It was a delight to make their trips home, but since it was a good five-hour drive each way, it was best to do it only when they had a week to stay. And this time, they were going to jog south for a few hours in Hofuf, and on into Haradh for the night. In all their years, they had never visited the rather spectacular Haradh farms, and decided this was the time!

They left Dhahran on a bright Monday morning in December, the second day of the month according to the calendar the Americans used, the Western calendar.

The Eastern, or Arabic, calendar was younger than the Western calendar, starting with Mohammed's trek from Mecca to Medina in 622 AD of the Western calendar. The Arabian calendar also consists of twelve months, but each one is a lunar month, that is, one complete transit of the moon, about 29 days. This results in the seasons shifting. The twelfth Arab month, *Dhul Hija*, was winter in the mid 1970's, but summer in the late 1950's.

By the Arab calendar, the current year started the previous May 19, and was now in its sixth month, *Jumada Thani*. The last year when the Arab and Western calendars closely coincided for the beginning of a year was 1976, when January 3 marked the first day of *Muharram*, beginning the Arabic calendar year 1396. It would take about 33 years for that event to reoccur.

Whether the Eastern or Western calendar was used, this day the weather was just about perfect.

Rashid and Yasmeen drove southwest out of Dhahran, then south toward Hofuf, and were parked in a park area near one of the ancient springs some two hours later. They spent the rest of the day and night visiting the Roman ruins, the springs, both hot and cool, the old town, an old *soukh*, or bazaar, then some light shopping in a more modern shopping center.

Hofuf was an oasis in the Arabian desert, visited and used by desert nomads and their herds of goats, sometimes camels and other animals, before the Sumerians and Egyptians learned to irrigate their crops thousands of years before Christ. The springs had existed long before humans found them, and would probably exist long after this ancient city ceased to exist. And it was a city during Roman occupation in the first centuries after Christ, a few hundred years before Mohammed wrote the Koran.

In the thirties, when Socal and Aramco geologists visited it, Hofuf had a population of around 80,000 souls. Now it was a little over 100,000. It had seen little of the growth attributable to the vast increase in Saudi wealth created by the development of petroleum reserves and production. Hofuf had grown little compared to other Saudi Arabian cities.

During the same period, population of the Holy Moslem city of Mecca increased over six-fold from about 60,000. The Holy city of Medina, a modest 30,000 or so in the thirties, had grown about the same. But the real urban grown occurred in the western port city of Jiddah, from about 40,000 to over a million and a half, and the capital city of Riyadh which grew from around 50,000 to slightly less than Jiddah.

Percentagewise, the greatest growth from the early days of the oil search occurred on the eastern coast. Though these towns and cities had populations much smaller than the old cities, these sites were developed for the handling, refining, and shipping of petroleum, and most of the locales had grown from nothing, or from small fishing villages. Oases were rare in the eastern part of the country.

Dhahran, the headquarters city for Saudi Aramco, was populated by about 50,000 people, with a very high per capita education level. This was to be expected where there were many kinds of geologists, geophysicists, and engineers, as well as the many other professionals required for teaching, designing, and developing the wealth of the country.

But Hofuf was a famous old city, and a present agricultural, clothing, and tourist site. Its first name is lost in antiquity, but its first recorded name was *Hasa*, at *al-Hasa* Oasis. Dates and rice had been grown for centuries, dates for millennia. Weaving had been a productive industry indefinitely, and cement production had thrived in recent decades.

The Rimthans stayed the night in the old town area, in an old, but modernized small hotel, or *fundu*. They spent another day and night looking at the evidences of Roman occupation as well as other occupations such as its use as a Turkish headquarters for over forty years around the turn of the century. They visited the royal horse stables and admired the outstanding quality of these magnificent animals.

Late in the day, they visited the nineteenth century mosque that was thought by some to occupy a religious site many centuries old. That evening, they found a recommended *matam*, or restaurant, that specialized in grilled fowl, chicken, pigeon, and other game birds. This night, *houbara*, a grouse-like bird from the Haradh area, was the special. Served with rice, dates, and other fruit in the old manner, it was delicious. Then back to their *fundu* and a good sleep before driving on south to the Haradh oasis of Saudi historical fame.

"Wake up, my husband! Do you wish to sleep the whole day?" Yasmeen was gently shaking Rashid as she spoke.

"We don't have to leave at dawn!" complained Rashid.

"The sun is already high in the heavens, and the animals are gone to graze," said Yasmeen, quoting a saying of her Bedouin grandfather.

"Doesn't look high to me! It is barely above the horizon!"

"Yes, husband, but I've been waiting for years to find a time to quote my grandfather, and this seemed close enough!"

"Okay, you win. Couldn't sleep any more in this madhouse

anyway!"

After a quick breakfast of coffee and cereal, the Rimthans were on their way before nine o'clock that morning. Haradh, about eighty miles south, was their next port of call.

They drove west out of Hofuf for a few miles, then turned south off the highway to Riyadh, toward Udayliyah, and much further, Haradh. It was a rather unimpressive drive through mostly flat, sometimes sandy, sometimes hilly, but always dry, terrain. For about an hour. Then as they approached Haradh, the colors changed from drab grays and browns to many shades of green.

Among the many other ways the Saudis had used their petro-wealth, they had set up systems to provide food and comfort to their peoples long after the oil was gone. One of these was the irrigation and farming project at Haradh. This had been an oasis, formed by fresh water springs older than any records revealed.

As the many other springs in the Saudi regions lying east of the western mountains, these springs were fed by water that had traveled a tortuous path from its western meteoric source to these life-giving desert islands.

The Saudis had found ways to use every drop of this God-given water supply, and through sewage and other processing, even ways to recycle used water. Limited irrigation had been practiced here for millennia, but in the last few decades, major expansion took place.

It was a very efficient use of a limited natural, but ongoing, resource. If the water was preserved, stored, carefully used, and re-used, it would last as long as humans were here to consume it. Allowing for some years when the supply was weak, and others when it was strong. At this time, the springs were more active than at any time in the memory of Haradh inhabitants.

Most of these inhabitants did not know it, but this excessive current supply was directly related to the very unusual heavy rains in the mountains to the west the previous spring. Again, there had been unusual rains the last few weeks. Allah Akbar!

There, the rains fell on the surface, then drained into the normally dry wadis, which carried the water, both on the surface, and beneath the surface in gravel layers, to fault fractures that extended deep into the earth. Having no better place to go, the water left the wadis, and entered the fractures.

Down it went, until it found layers of porous rocks. Into the darkness of the small cavities in limestone or dolomite rocks, or between grains of sandstone, the water coursed easterly following the pull of gravity along these east-tilted beds. Finally, some of it found fault fractures again, and traveled up these fractures, pushed by the head of water from the much higher elevations to the west, to the surface to feed life on the desert above.

And Haradh was a world-class example of water conservation and use. These people made the desert bloom. Even more than nature had done it alone. Here they could produce two, even three, crops a year of some vegetables. Clearly, this was a classic example of the way to use petro-wealth over and over, for this and future generations.

It was here, at the Haradh oasis, in November, 1901, just before the Islamic celebration month of Ramadhan, that Abdul Aziz, the future Kind Sa'ud of Saudi Arabia, made the decision to continue his effort to overthrow the Rasheed occupancy of the old Sa'ud family capital of Riyadh.

From Haradh, with no more than seventy in his "army," Abdul Aziz traveled south some fifty miles through the desert to the Yabreen oasis. Here they spent Ramadhan, and launched their successful surprise attack the following month in January, 1902. This was the beginning of the present country of Saudi Arabia, formed from many sheikhdoms or city-states, by Abdul Aziz of the Sa'ud family and his followers.

Haradh might be called a 'desert delight.' Like a super oasis. But all visits must end, and after two nights in the area, the Rimthans had to leave. They were looking forward to the next three days at Ehleebeyt. This country home grew ever more important to them as a place to read, to take walks, entertain company, take horseback rides, hunt, and do so many things that were relaxing and undemanding.

In Dhahran, they had picked up some of the bad habits of the Western and Asian worlds: Work and strive to get more, all the time. The two lifestyles engendered many discussions between Rashid and Yasmeen, their children, and their visitors.

They discussed the shortest way, and the best roads to get to Ehleebeyt, and finally decided to take the long way and drive northward toward Hofuf for some distance before taking an unpaved desert crossroad that connected to the main Hofuf-to-Riyadh highway. It was shorter to go due west out of Haradh toward Riyadh, but Rashid wanted to show Yasmeen a striking hillside campsite near the Al Hunayy spring used by his friend Jon Burke's daddy some six decades earlier. Then they would drive westward to Riyadh and on to Ehleebeyt. They left Haradh on Thursday.

Rashid was relaxed behind the wheel, about ten minutes out of Haradh, chatting with Yasmeen about their visits over the last few days. As they always did, their speech was a mixture of English and Arabic, mostly Arabic, but with many American slang words or contractions thrown in. It was the way of talking for two persons who were completely fluent in both languages.

Rashid suddenly became aware that all was not right with the car, then sharply interrupted Yasmeen's conversation...

"Yasmeen, something is happening..."

The highway seemed to be moving slightly, up and down, maybe sideways. Rashid had some difficulty controlling the car as it seemed to be mounted on some kind of very soft wheels. It seemed to roll and wallow as if the shocks and springs were very soft. He had experienced such wallowing at very high speeds, but this was happening at only 100 km/hr. As he peered ahead, he saw an unbelievable sight.

"Yasmeen, get ready...we have something terrible coming..."

They both stared at what appeared to be a very low ridge racing directly toward them. In the approximate two seconds they had to observe and decide, they could discern that the ridge extended some indefinite distance to either side of the highway, and crossed the highway to form a rise perhaps the height of a small child...maybe a little more. It was all happening so fast, neither of them could be sure exactly what they saw.

It was a fleeting scene that lasted some three seconds from the time Rashid's first suspicion of what appeared to be a ridge, until it was upon them. Rashid started braking abruptly, but still was traveling at a good rate of speed. The ridge was suddenly there, simultaneously with a deep low-volume boom, and the car was violently slammed upward, then fell abruptly.

Just as Rashid got control of the wildly swerving car, they

sensed a second low ridge racing toward them...then another, and another, as they were successively slammed and bounced up and down and sideways. Before the second earth-wave hit, Rashid had slowed down to the point that the wave caused little swerving. The second ridge seemed slightly higher than the first, then the height diminished on subsequent waves. They counted three specific waves before all form was lost in severe shaking and vibration.

By the third wave, Rashid had stopped the car, and they tumbled out of it on the run to get away from it and better observe what was happening. Without seat/shoulder belts holding Rashid in place, the car would have been wrecked. Even so, they were both severely jostled by the sudden impacts of the waves.

They staggered and stumbled away from the car and sat down on the unstable ground so as to avoid being hit by the car if it moved, and to avoid being knocked off their feet. The car was jarred and shaken like a child's toy rattle, and bounced, jerked, forward and sideways perhaps a meter. The Rimthans were holding hands and just trying to bounce and shake in the same direction, actually only a few inches.

As the earthwaves passed under them, neither the Rimthans nor the car suffered any real hurt or damage, even though the lead waves and energy were moving at a speed of several hundred miles per hour. Each wave, as witnessed on the earth's surface, just consisted of earth being very suddenly raised and lowered, with secondary waves and energy making a jumbled mass of primarily shaking and vibration within four or five seconds after the lead energy struck. Within an instant after sensing the first movement of the car, Rashid knew what was happening.

It was a substantial earthquake. More specifically, they had been buffeted by P waves, then slammed by S waves that radiated out from an epicenter perhaps five kilometers or so below the surface. Probably not too far below the base of the sedimentary rocks if, as flashed in his mind, it was caused by fault movement. He had no idea of the size or epicenter of the quake, but there was no mistaking what it was or the general direction it came from.

They were in wide open country, with no trees or buildings to register the effect of the temblor. They could feel the waves and the associated shaking and trembling of the ground they stood on, but because of the semi-arid, open countryside, they saw nothing fall or break.

The earth did not crack; at least, here. It was just a feeling of being shocked as the rapidly traveling waves and energy hit them, at such speed that it literally knocked them off their feet. Then shaking, another shock, trembling. They thought it would never end. But it did. The heavy movements lasted only about three or four minutes, with small trembles off and on for another few minutes.

About twenty minutes after they fell out of the car, they opened the doors and got back in, and sat quietly for a few moments, just staring at the road ahead. Every few minutes, there was a mild shaking. And after some thirty or forty minutes, they were aware that everything had been quiet for over ten minutes.

"My lady, do you realize what you have just experienced?"

"An earthquake?"

"That's right. I think it must have been a very large one, based on those obvious earthwaves. And all of a sudden, our plans are changed. We must get back to Dhahran. This thing has to be centered northward of us because of the orientation and direction of the waves. And since this is an obviously big one, on top of the one we had less than a month ago, it means that something is pretty unstable right now. We might get another one, even more than one."

Yasmeen replied, "Now you are scaring me. Maybe our home is destroyed!"

"I don't mean to sound dramatic, my love, just thinking out loud."

"Yasmeen, did you notice the noise?"

She thought for a few moments, then answered, "now that you mention it, there was almost no noise; maybe some rumbling...but it wasn't very loud."

"That's what I meant. Almost silent. Just some deep rumbling, sort of like distant thunder. Did you notice anything about the light, or air?"

"Not really...but it somehow seemed brighter, maybe slightly bluish, but that might all be just my imagination," she replied.

"The reason I asked you, was that I wanted to see if what I thought I saw was my imagination," said Rashid, "and to me I thought I perceived a bright bluish cast that seemed to come and go during the worst part. Strange, huh?"

"It's all strange to me, my husband. Now, I am anxious to get back home and see if we still have one." Yasmeen spoke with a tinge of fright and worry mixed into her normal soft but bright manner of speech.

"Yasmeen, we witnessed the effects of a deep earth movement. You remember when I first spoke, when the car seemed to move around?"

She replied, "it seemed like it was on huge soft tires!"

"Well, what caused that were the *P* seismic waves, the small fast traveling waves that move out first from the epicenter. Then, you know, before I could get the car stopped, we were slammed by that ridge of earth that was racing across the country. Those big shocks were the *S* waves. They travel slower than the *P* waves and are the ones that do the real damage. In areas, like some places along the Gulf, where there are several meters of sands and clays that are unconsolidated, the surface becomes almost like jelly from the vibrating and shaking caused by the waves. Anything built on such ground would likely fall."

"You mean some of the piers and things for loading ships?"

"I expect so. Maybe I will be wrong."

It took about thirty minutes to reach Hofuf. But much longer to get around it. Streets were blocked with tumbled masonry, wrecked cars and trucks, fallen posts, and a maze of wires, all sprayed here and there by fountains of water from broken pipes.

Although taller steel-structured buildings withstood the violent shaking, ornamentations and accessory structures had fallen from them. This, added to the crumbled debris from low mudbrick buildings and all the other damaged or destroyed accoutrements of urban life, completely blocked some streets.

Rashid was very familiar with the highways in this region, and had pointedly avoided the parts of Hofuf that he felt would suffer heavy damage. Even so, it took some two hours of scouting, backtracking, trying new routes, until they finally worked their way around the city.

They saw many people out on the streets or in the rubble. These people moved slowly; some were just standing. Obviously, they were stunned, in a state of shock, uncertain of what had really happened, and fearful of what might lie ahead.

Mile after mile, as they approached Dhahran, destruction marked their way. Here and there, where an oil or gas line had snapped or split, the highly inflammable fluids gushed out and moved in the paths of least resistance. At the concentrations of flow lines, heater treaters, separators and tanks at some Ghawar field installations, there were fires.

At some such installations, there were no fires, and at some there was no leakage or severed lines. But at several there were breakages, and some of these had caught fire. A few massive fires raged.

The large gas facilities at Uthmaniyah, Shedgum, and Abqaiq were all ablaze. The large gas plant near Shedgum was marked by several fires, two of them massive, widespread infernos. The Rimthans had not seen smoke from fires at Uthmaniyah as they passed through only minutes after the temblor hit them. But looking back toward that large gas processing facility, they saw smoke before leaving Hofuf.

And from Hofuf on, the sky was blackened with oil and gas smoke, with occasional patches of blue to remind humanity that there was a greater world out there than this one created to supply the comforts and progress marked by plentiful energy.

It now seemed that the oil fires set by Saddam were preludes to these destructive fires. But, whereas the Saddam fires were limited to wells and a few installations, some of these fires were spread over acres.

There was wreckage at place after place on the roadways, where drivers of trucks and cars had failed to maintain control and had swerved into other vehicles or roadside construction. Some vehicles had turned over and rolled, others were smashed after head-on encounters. Every accident description imaginable was observable, in multiple examples.

There were a few vehicles working their way through the continuing barriers but, except for emergency police and ambulance vehicles, traffic was abnormally light. The Rimthans continued to work their way toward Dhahran as dark began to creep across this ravaged land. For hours, the sun had been visible only as an infrequent, hazy-orange disk that would abruptly disappear behind another black cloud.

The unfolding scenes had much of the appearance of a major war zone. The big difference was the absence here of bullet holes and explosive destruction. Instead, the vision was one of a massive shakedown. Unsupported masonry rarely remained standing, while reinforced and structured walls stood. Tall, basically cylindrical, oil and gas processing towers stood, but many attached and supportive structures were damaged.

Although the oil and gas facilities had suffered relatively little collapse, there were many, many ruptured flow lines that spewed oil, waiting only for oxygen and a spark to become infernos.

Rashid and Yasmeen had spoken little, being overwhelmed and awed by this unpredictable wrath of God. But why was he angered? Had this Arab world lived less in his light than others? Surely not. In fact, this couple, being deep, though not, devout Muslims, could probably cope with this disaster better than many Americans in Dhahran.

To those who ascribed to the teachings of Islam, the Will of God is not to be questioned, but instead, assimilated. The Americans were more apt to be emotionally distraught and disturbed. But after a period of disorientation and despair, most Americans had an expression similar to the Arab *Insha Allah*, "The Will of God."

Finally, Rashid spoke: "My darling, I believe we have just witnessed one of the most, if not the most disruptive Acts of God ever. At least as far as humans are concerned. I pray that our home is still standing."

"Husband, at this time, I have no way of expressing my feelings. Maybe in time I will. But I do have an overwhelming desire to get home."

"Yasmeen, we will get there. It may take another hour or two, but even if we have to walk the last few miles, we will get there. Most of all right now, I am so happy that we filled our gas tank before leaving Haradh. With all the maneuvering and detouring we've done, we would have been in trouble without a full tank to start."

Rashid drove around another wreck that suddenly loomed out of the darkness at an intersection near their neighborhood. Then, at last, he turned into their neighborhood. They were only three blocks from home. The moment they could see the homes in this area, they looked closely for degree of damage, knowing that this probably foretold their fate.

Some of the streets were wet, some actually flooded by broken water mains. There were a few burned homes and businesses, and some, here and there, were still burning. But overall, the extremely overworked and completely exhausted Dhahran utility departments and fire fighters had done a magnificent job of control.

All gas and water mains were closed, and electrical trunk lines shutdown well before night of this dreadful day. But fires could not be stopped simply by closing the gas supply. The firemen were still hard at work. And without substantial volunteer relief, could not have kept on. It seemed likely that all significant dwellings fires would be extinguished by morning.

Rashid and Yasmeen quickly noticed that some of the masonry chimneys had tumbled, while others still stood. How would theirs be? Here and there, a wall or roof had collapsed, but for the most part, these well-built homes withstood the shocks.

While less expensive homes for many Saudis had crumbled because of unsupported masonry construction, the framed and structurally supported roofs in the Rimthan's neighborhood were much more stable. Many of the masonry walls were cracked. The best they could tell as they drove slowly through the cluttered streets, *all* of the masonry walls had developed some kind of cracks. But underlying concrete beams had maintained sufficient stability to prevent enough wall movement to cause collapse.

Rashid turned the car onto their street. "Hang on sweetheart, get ready for the coming attraction!"

"Rashid, this is no time to joke!"

"Honey, I think we had better keep as much humor as we can, because I suspect many trials or barriers will rise before us in the weeks ahead."

There was their home. Rashid turned into their driveway, but stopped after two car lengths because of a pile of bricks in the way. The brick portico at the corner of their carport on the side of their home had collapsed. As the car stopped, neither spoke. For a few moments they just sat there and moved their eyes over all they could see.

Then, Rashid turned to Yasmeen with a slight smile, "Honey, we survived!"

"Not completely," she returned, "look at that back corner behind the carport and in front of the garage."

Rashid had already seen that collapsed corner, and the slightly lopsided breezeway from the home to the garage. "Yasmeen, those are relatively minor. We can fix them. I'm just so happy that there is no major collapse."

They both got out of the car and walked around the house, checking for cracks or other damage. Yasmeen stopped the walk rather quickly and almost ran to the back door, unlocked it, and entered the house. She was frightened and fearful that her china and other fine things might be broken.

After a complete inspection, as complete as they could tell by flashlight and candles in the exceptionally dark night, they found only relatively minor home and contents damage, and only two broken crystal glasses among the fine articles.

It was now near midnight, and they were both exhausted. Using some water from the commodes, they managed to wash up a bit. There was no water, no electricity, and no gas supply. They knew these would present big problems ahead, but were too tired to care. They were just happy to be in one piece, with a home the same. Within minutes they were both asleep.

For a while.

At 4:47 a.m. the next morning, a rather cold December Friday, the Rimthans and many thousands of other people were rudely shaken from their sleep. Yasmeen was bounced off the edge of the bed, but Rashid grabbed the headboard and hung on.

Yasmeen cried out in a high pitched and frightened voice, "My God, my God, not again!"

Rashid grabbed her, pulled her back on the bed, and held her close. "Hang on, Honey. We'll make it." Even though he also was frightened by now, his deeper senses told him what was going on, that it was not overly unlikely, and would probably be of lesser danger than the earlier temblor.

Almost as quickly as it started, the shaking subsided. The entire episode lasted for less than two minutes, perhaps a minute and a half, after the first awakening shock. Minor tremblings continued off and on for several more minutes. Rashid walked through the house with a flashlight, and could see the outside lawn through a crack in a front bedroom wall. Well, he thought, best not tell Yassy about this right now. Looks like the roof is still OK. He continued down the hall.

After several minutes checking, during which time Yasmeen's first concern was her tableware, Rashid found nothing else other than several wall cracks of unknown significance at this time. He walked back into the bedroom to find Yasmeen sitting on the edge of the bed crying.

"What is it, baby," said Rashid softly as he gently picked up her hand.

"My china and crystal," she said as she quit sobbing, "at least four of the plates, three cups, and six pieces of crystal are broken."

"It is OK my darling, we will replace it."

She nearly shouted in reply, "you cannot replace the china pieces...it is too old...my mother's!"

"Yasmeen, it can be replaced somehow. Through those trade outfits, or someway. And it will be alright. Anyway, let's be grateful we still have our lives and our home!"

"I know, I know, but it is so sad..." she said as she started lightly sobbing again.

"Honey, tomorrow is going to be one long day. We need to try to get a little more sleep if we can," said Rashid gently.

As so very many others, the Rimthans tried to go back to sleep after this terrifying experience. Many could not find sleep again. Neither could Rashid.

He lay there with his mind literally racing. Even though he still felt weary, there was no doubt about it: sleep is over for this night. But I have to lie still and let Yasmeen rest. Only about another hour until daylight.

Lotsa fires...no water to fight with except as hauled...broken mains, wires, etc., etc. Rashid's thoughts became more jumbled as he drifted between exhausted sleep and concerned wakefulness. Finally, the room light revealed the first rays of sunlight. Well, at least these earth destructors don't affect the sun! Rashid swung out of bed.

"Yasmeen, Yasmeen, are you awake?"

"I am now," she muttered sleepily.

"I am going outside and check around the house and neighborhood. Also, I'll take one of those two big cans we have in the garage along in case I find any good water."

"Please don't be gone very long."

"I won't. Maybe you can throw together some breakfast without any water or electricity. Use refrigerated stuff as much as possible. It will all be ruined anyway, if we don't eat or drink it right away."

"Alright." Yasmeen spoke in a rather small, dejected voice. It was very hard to feel or talk in a normal way when her very home and security were crumbling around her.

Within two blocks of his home, Rashid found a broken water main with gushing water. All else was secondary right now to water. Simply water. He filled his can and returned home for the other can. He rushed in the house and called out. "Yasmeen?" And continued on into the bathroom.

"Yes?" she quickly answered.

"Honey, I found a broken water main. Take a little of this water and wash out the bathtub while I grab the other can and go back for more." He was already across the living room headed for the garage as he continued, "I'll keep on until we get a tub full."

"Okay, husband. I'll be ready before you get back." Yasmeen was now feeling better about coping with the situation, perhaps numbed by it all.

Back and forth for four trips, the last two with both cans, Rashid had the tub nearly full. By the time he got back to the broken main the first time, there were two other men doing the same thing. Then, there were twenty, and a line was formed. As Rashid rushed up and got in line for two more cans full, suddenly the gushing water stopped. Within no more than ten seconds, it went from a full forceful geyser to a slight trickle. Somebody had managed to cut off the supply.

None of the men were overly worried. They knew there would be tank trucks with water within a day or two at the most. They just needed enough to do a little washing, cooking and drinking for that time.

Electricity was another thing. It might be several days, even weeks, before that was available again.

Knowing that, Rashid rushed back home to drop the cans immediately after the water stopped flowing. Now, he wanted to get to a store before all the batteries were sold out. The closest was only four blocks away, a small convenience outlet. He hurriedly walked there and found a short line had already formed just inside the door. Maybe, just maybe, they have a good battery stock.

While he was waiting, he looked around for other things they might need. No, nothing except batteries. They had plenty of canned food. Might get some more bread, and peanut butter! Finally, Rashid got to the head of the line and then was allowed to join the other shoppers who crowded the aisles.

He needed both regular flashlight batteries and a lantern if possible. He worked over to the crowded battery shelves, picked up six flashlight batteries, and reached toward the last battery lantern on the shelf. A young woman reached it first. Well, thought Rashid, so much for the lantern.

He worked around to the other shelves, picked up two loaves of bread, a jar of peanut butter, and started out. It took a while to get checked out, but once he got the batteries, he didn't mind a few more minutes waiting in line to pay for them.

As he walked back home, Rashid noticed smoke in a number of areas, and a great billowing mass of black smoke coming from the huge refinery and shipping terminal complex at Ras Tanura, about fifteen miles across the bay to the north. He saw fallen chimneys, power lines down, and a few damaged cars as he walked along.

He saw very little that could not be repaired without major problems. Some of the homes showed cracks, or had some part sitting a bit askew. But, all in all, at least this neighborhood survived fairly well.

The following day, Rashid worked his way through occasional tangled wires, road debris, and damaged cars in the streets, to his office. It was Saturday, the seventh, but he thought there might be a few people there and, besides, he wanted to see the damage on that building. He drove carefully to conserve both tires and gasoline. Might be a while before he could get more.

As he drove up to the building that stood perhaps forty feet high, he noted surprisingly little damage. Apparently its structural skeleton held against all the shaking and rolling motions. At the office, he was advised that the best thing anybody could do for the next few days was to take care of personal problems and needs.

The only employees asked to work were two of the

seismologists that were working with the seismometers and equipment set up to monitor and measure earthquakes and their effects. One of these seismologists was Rashid's friend Achmed Asker, whom he particularly wanted to visit.

He walked in Asker's office: "I suppose these happenings have gotten your attention?" As was usually the case with most of his U.S.-trained friends, he spoke in English, with an Arab word now and then for emphasis.

Achmed looked up and smiled. "Hello, my friend. Looks like you had to quit your vacation a little early!"

"Sure did. But that's a pretty small item. Tell me a little more about what has happened."

They continued their conversation in English.

"Rashid, we have only estimates now, until we compare with measurements at other places. But the first earthquake was at least Richter 8, probably higher. The second one was a six-point-something. We know that damage is widespread but, the best we can tell, nothing that cannot be repaired, at least at this point. It is uncertain how long it will take, but probably several months at least until things are back about normal."

"I picked up on that 'at this point,' what do you mean by that?"

"The odds are pretty good it isn't over." Asker paused, then walked over to a large map on the wall. "We know the epicenter for the first quake day before yesterday was somewhere in the Shedgum-Uthmaniyah area, probably associated with basement faulting. There are some ground cracks reported across the main Riyadh highway, north of Abqaiq.

"And there may be more cracks in places so far unseen. But the main thing is, after one Richter six-plus quake in the mountains, followed by an eight-plus, then another six-plus, a whole lot of stresses must be built up in this general area. It is entirely possible that we'll have another good-sized one, number four."

"When?"

"Who knows? But quite possibly within days. For that reason, I'm to leave here this afternoon and go over to Bahrain and set up camp. They have more complete and sensitive equipment there, plus a laser setup with a target across the Gulf on one of those reefs near Jabrin, just off the Iranian coast. That thing can pick up a centimeter of relative movements between the two coasts."

"Pretty impressive. Would you call me in a day or two if you see anything unusual?"

"Sure. But I'll be back in a week or two with all the scoop."

"Well, Achmed, I guess I'll get on back home for the rest of the day and see what all we have to get done, and try to get it started. We'll have to do some wall work at least. Meanwhile, you take care of Achmed in that strange land!"

As Rashid started out, Achmed replied, "You take care also, my friend. But if I were you, I'd wait a few weeks to do repairs."

Rashid stopped, "That bad, huh?"

"Who really knows?" returned Asker.

"Well...so long, buddy," said Rashid in his best Texanese.

"OK, pardner!" replied Asker in the same language.

It was early the following Tuesday morning, the 10th, that Rashid left for Houston to go over the quake data available at this time with Headquarters. While there, he reviewed all he knew with Jon Burke, and they discussed it. They decided it was too early to do any meaningful work now. It would be best to wait a few months to give the fluids time to do whatever they were going to do in the subsurface rocks.

Rashid was back in Dhahran late Friday, and near sick from the jet lag and fast pace of the past few days. He went to bed with a slight fever, and felt lousy for the rest of the weekend.

During that week, while Rashid was gone, there were numerous minor temblors, with two of them reaching Richter 2-plus in size. These did nothing but further frighten the people of eastern Saudi Arabia who were understandably on edge already.

Monday, the 16th: Nine days after Rashid's visit with Achmed Asker earthquake number four hit. It struck during the morning rush to get everybody to work or to school. This was another big one. Not any simple aftershock. And it seemed to the people along the east coast of Saudi Arabia to come out of the Gulf.

By this time, massive government help was underway for all the stricken areas, with temporary water supplies set up, emergency generators in many areas, streets cleaned up, and vast repair work underway.

This quake, which came to be known as the Gulf quake, was

the most devastating for the coastal area. Not only did it cause collapse of the many weakened structures such as bridges, piers, refinery stacks, buildings, and the massive petroleum processing and handling facilities, it wrecked part of the things already fixed. Water damage from huge Gulf swells that struck all along the coast topped off the misery.

Numerous ships were severely damaged by being tossed into piers, other vessels, or offshore facilities and shoals. True *tsunami*, or tidal waves, could hardly be formed in the Gulf with average water depths of seventy-five to one hundred feet, but if the earth beneath rises, then the water also rises, regardless of depth.

This action in the central part of the Gulf with water depths a little over 200 feet, generated thirty- to fifty-foot swells that raced toward shore at speeds of over three hundred miles per hour. Such swells slammed into vessels which, if near any other object, would tend to be tossed or smashed into such other object, such as a pier, another vessel, a reef, or a shoal.

Since the Persian Gulf has many reefs that either break water or come close to the surface, there was considerable shipping damage, even for vessels in the open water. Many smaller vessels, such as fishing or packet boats, were smashed and/or swamped, and sunk.

The two earlier December temblors had caused damage to shipping and waterfronts, from the "tidal waves" as well as destruction from the shaking and rolling earth, especially in the areas where fill material was placed in the water to support piers or other construction. But damage from those quakes, especially to shipping vessels and facilities, was minor compared to this one.

Within hours after this "seaquake," oil markets all over the world shot upward with no limit in sight.

Within two days, the first American aircraft carrier passed through the Strait of Hormuz.

On the third day, Saudi Arabia stopped all air travel into the country except for specific approved landings. At the same time, the Saudi government censored all outgoing messages, and allowed no unapproved news dispatches.

Massive destruction had been confirmed, but its effect was still unknown. Earth cracks had been confirmed, but size, lengths, and positions were unknown or, if known, censored.

Seismic stations in Europe, Africa, Russia, the United States, and other places confirmed four major Saudi Arabian earthquakes over a period of forty-six days. There was no question of damage, of restricted oil supply. The only question was how much and how long. There was no question that oil supplies would be restricted in some amount for some time.

Laser measurements, confirmed by satellite, showed that, relative to Iran, Dhahran was now two feet closer and one foot more northerly.

Again, there were aftershocks, but none of consequence. The damage had already been done. Additional minor quakes could not destroy more.

But, it was not over. The chain continued to move to the east, with another earthquake a few days after the vicious "seaquake," centering in the Zagros Mountains of Iran. This was a relatively small one, only 5.3 Richter.

And, it occurred in an area where temblors were common, there were no major cities or facilities and, best of all, the people were prepared. The people here were subjected to earthquakes of one kind or another, almost every year. Sometimes more than once per year. They could handle a 5.3 shake rather well.

Geophysicists were sought and questioned by the news media time after time, with no end in sight. How did this happen? Will it happen again? What do we do now? These scientists explained time after time the basic facts of Planet Earth. Some reporters understood, some were merely confused. For most of them, eyes glazed over in boredom within moments after explanations began.

- - - - - - -

The rocks that geologists and other earth scientists map, measure, explore, and find oil and gas in, are that great group of rocks referred to as 'sedimentary.' These are the limestones, shales, sandstones, and many combinations and variations of these basic types, that were laid down by sedimentary processes during the last half billion years or so.

These rocks reach an overall thickness up to perhaps thirty kilometers, or eighteen miles; but mostly less than ten kilometers, (six miles, or about 30,000 feet). In some areas, usually mountainous, there are no sedimentary rocks, and here the basement rocks are exposed at the surface. For example, in the mountains west of Riyadh.

Basement rocks are composed of igneous and metamorphic rocks that are derived from heat and pressure, or a lack thereof, from early more elemental and basic rock forms. These are the granites, basalts, lava, pumice, marble, and many other rocks often mined and used in building.

Finally, at great depth, the basement rocks that form a significant part of the earth's crust, come in contact with the earth's mantle, a poorly known portion of the Earth's sphere that may grade into iron-rich, probably fluid, at least plastic, material that grades into the earth's core.

The zone between the crust and mantle is referred to as the Mohorovicic discontinuity, or, simply the "Moho," named after a Yugoslavian geologist who first described this vague boundary layer of unknown thickness that seems to alter or change seismic energy reaching it.

The Moho lies at depths some eight to forty kilometers beneath the earth's surface, being shallowest below deep oceans. Earth movements that cause earthquakes occur in the crust, above the Moho.

The basement layers, below the sedimentary rocks, are very strong, and relatively thick. Such layers will take a great deal of stress, or force, before they break. But when they break, that is, release the built up stress and exhibit strain, the results are extraordinary. In strict engineering sense, to apply the force is to exert stress; strain is that which occurs when the material breaks. These words are sometimes used interchangeably, especially by newsmen, with resultant confusion as to their meaning.

Regardless of words used, a stable sub-continental plate such as Saudi Arabia, can take a great deal of basement stress buildup over a long period, before the basement layers finally break. But when the break comes, it is usually with more strain, and substantially more force, than that which occurs when sedimentary rocks alone slip along a fault plane.

In this Saudi disaster, basement rocks moved. The Saudi Arabian sub-plate moved. To humans, the results were awesome. To nature and the earth, it was simply normal readjustment.

The vast majority of earthquakes have power designations less than Richter 6.0, but under some circumstances, even Richter 5.0 temblors can be very destructive. For example, a house constructed with walls consisting simply of bricks stacked one atop another, while having substantial vertical strength, has little lateral strength. Even a child can push a pile of bricks over.

But above Richter 6.0, so many factors come to bear, such as soil types and moisture content, that even stout construction may fail. Of course, in earthquake-prone areas, construction is designed to withstand such forces, and has commonly proved reliable. Significant damage more easily comes to those places where such forces are unexpected.

Perhaps the largest of all earthquakes during recorded human history was the Richter 9.2 that struck southern Alaska in 1964. This produced massive damage, massive earth movements...up to 38 feet of vertical earth movements measured along faulting, and complete destruction to many hillside homes and other structures. The great San Francisco quake of 1901 is reported, by analogy, to have exceeded Richter 8.0, and it did practically destroy the city...largely by fire burning out of control for three days because of inadequate water supply.

- - - - - - -

The Saudi earthquakes occurred where they were relatively unexpected. Human history has seen little earth adjustments here, even though geophysical data and plate positions indicate rather constant movements.

That is, in geologic time: tens of thousands instead of tens or hundreds of years.

The results were predictably powerful. Such earthquakes were sure to occur. Not if. Just when.

~ ~ ~ ~ ~ ~ ~ ~ ~ ~ ~ ~ ~ ~ ~

CHAPTER 6

Sea Trial

He left his desk and walked over to the window. Looked OK. No rain likely. It was Friday, and he had a weekend coming up without his family! Achmed Asker had now been over at the Bahrain office for a week, and it was very boring. He had been monitoring the instruments along with the staff seismologist in this monitoring station. Basically, just noting the shakes when they occurred, their intensity and, if it was important, make a printout of the charts at that time and FAX them out.

And his next glorious job was to take the data just received from some seventy-five stations around the world, check the epicenters recorded on the incoming charts, then re-do them all. The re-computation was a check on precision, because it was very important to localize the epicenters of the three earthquakes as precisely as possible. It could affect later decisions on possible well re-drills, or new well locations, or other subsurface interpretations related to the oil fields.

This re-do job required precise positioning of each of the recording stations, their precise measured intensities, and multiple triangulations of all data. A computer could do it all in a matter of moments. The time consumption was in the interpretations of specific records and trace intensities on the charts, recording all the input data, and properly booting it into the computer. Then let the software make the hardware do its job, maybe several times, after readjustments of interpretations.

Achmed felt he was wasting his time here. He could do the re-work just as well on his office or home computer, and the software was rather simple; all on a single 3-1/2" disk. Why not take one of the regular packets back to Dhahran. Yes, why not?

He called his Dhahran office and presented the situation. Could he just do his work there, and return here for possible later actions that might be months, or maybe many years, before the anticipated additional earth movement might occur? They agreed. He immediately started planning. Maybe he could get out tomorrow?

Normally, it was a simple matter to catch one of the shuttle flights across the bay inlet to Dhahran. But now, the Dhahran airport had damaged runways and building, and the same was true to a lesser extent here on Bahrain Island. Normal air travel was temporarily suspended. Only helicopters were in current use, and he could not get that transportation. He had only water travel available. And these were small vessels that carried a few passengers, mail, and some supplies.

After several telephone calls, he found he could not make a connection until early Monday morning. So, he was stuck here for the weekend after all! Well, he had that new suspense novel he had wanted to read and this would be the time.

Early Monday morning, December 16th, Achmed was on the pier, waiting for his boat. The craft was at the pier, and supplies were being loaded. The most significant operation was the loading and tying down of a bulky skid-mounted electric generator. Several of these were in use on the Saudi coast, and Achmed was sure several more could be used.

Finally, it was time for the passengers. There were eight in all, but three stood out: one heavy man who Achmed judged to be British, an authoritative-looking Arab, and a young Arab woman in her abayah. She wore the proper all-concealing dress, but wore no veil, so it could be seen that she had a rather pretty and delicate face. The third standout was a tall Arab with a heavy beard, and flowing mishlah, or robe. The others consisted of three children with, apparently, their parents, a rather ordinary looking Arab couple.

The packet was a common vessel, about 24 meters in length, with a small passenger cabin built onto the deck, with a second deck above it for the ship's master. The passenger cabin was extended forward to provide storage compartments. The ship was built with considerable open afterdeck for placing and transporting larger, bulky cargo. Smaller cargo could be loaded through covered hatches into the shallow hold below. Achmed observed a lifeboat secured just above the starboard gunwale, and a number of life preservers hanging on the aft cabin bulkhead.

It was scheduled to leave at seven a.m., and was not over five minutes late in casting off. The trip was to take less than three hours from cast off to walk off. With no fanfare, the vessel pulled away from the dock on its own power.

It was slow sailing through the reefs on the northwesterly side of Bahrain Island, as well as near the Saudi coast. But these were well charted and presented no problem other than slightly delayed travel the first half hour.

Achmed opened the door, stooped slightly to keep from bumping his head and entered the passenger cabin. Low ceiling, not much above his head. Achmed was a fairly tall man, slightly over six feet.

He observed the seating choices. Not much variety. The cabin consisted of a spartan set of wooden benches, with wooden backs, on either side of a narrow aisle between them. Each bench could seat three comfortably, four if crowded, and there were five on either side. The other passengers had remained on deck to watch the early morning develop over the Persian Gulf.

The only entry was through the aft door. The forward cabin wall was curved and solid; no windows or portholes. There were four small, sealed windows on either side, leaving solid wall for about three feet, both fore and aft. There was a single, fixed ceiling light fixture a few feet forward of the cabin door. After observing his quarters, Achmed sat down on the fourth starboard forward bench, adjacent to a window. Not too bad. Actually, more comfortable than they looked.

He had not quite finished his novel and thought this was a good time to do so. He was shortly lost in the very suspenseful final chase part of the book about Turkish drug runners in France.

About fifteen minutes later, Achmed became aware that the boat had started rocking. Perhaps close to a reef. He glanced out the window and was startled to see a huge wall of water that, less than a second later, slammed into the ship. This sizeable vessel may as well have been a straw, the way it was handled. It was slammed upward, then carried several hundred feet portside and at a high velocity, and smashed into a reef that was normally slightly exposed at low tide. Achmed was thrown violently out of his seat, and his head came into direct contact with the window edge. He was never aware of losing consciousness. One instant he was reading, looking, the next he was flying about, and the next he was out. From the time he looked up, to the point of unconsciousness, hardly five seconds passed.

Achmed awoke in stages. He had a vague sense of darkness,

wetness, then fade out. His head throbbed. Another fade out. Gradually, over several minutes, he had no idea how long, he developed full awareness. It was rather dark, not enough light to see clearly, but he could discern shapes. Absolute silence, except for an occasional loud scraping, grinding sound. His head was throbbing, and when he felt of the left side, it was painful. He was in water, nearly to his waist, yet he was lying on the floor. Where were the benches? He moved a leg around. Nothing! Had the benches broken loose?

What has happened? How could this be? How can I lie on the floor and be up to my waist in water, but none over my upper body? Slowly, it began to soak into his addled mind. The boat had been swamped and it is lying on its side. It must be resting on one of the reefs. That accounts for the repetitive grinding noise. But, why is it so dark?

He raised up, stopped to grab his pounding head then, as he began to feel the effects of gravity better, it was evident that the floor was slanted, maybe 30 or 40 degrees. As he moved into a sitting position, he started slowly sliding down the floor, farther into the water. About the time the water reached his chest, his feet bumped into something. Wall? No, it's not flat. Seating bench? He felt around with his feet, but could find no other bench leg.

He moved his feet up a little, and felt something that quickly fell off this thing. What is it? He held his breath, ducked under the water, and felt of it with his hand. It was a pipe of some kind, with...a light bulb! The answer flashed into his mind. He had knocked the shade off the ceiling light fixture. He was on the ceiling! Not the floor! The boat is upside down!

About that same instant he realized the boat was upside down, he became aware that the water was now up to his neck. He realized immediately that he was in some kind of trapped air pocket. If this was the surface of the water, there would be normal light. By now, with his eyes adjusted, it was too dark to clearly see. He should be able to see something. He looked up, and could make out the shape of the benches overhead, and could make out vague dark shapes at water level. Must be things floating, he thought. Luggage? Bodies? He was lying on the ceiling, with his feet pointed aft, toward the door.

The boat must be completely submerged and I am in an air pocket that is gradually closing as the air escapes upward through the floor or forward bulkhead.

Allah Akbar! What do I do? Panic, and there's no chance. Reason, and there might be a way out. At this point, his state of mind was such that the throbbing injury was unnoticed. His mind was working furiously. Where are the windows? He peered to either side, noticing in the process that the vessel was slanted from his left to his right as well as strongly tilted aft. There, he could make out the windows, and the ones on the left, the ship's port side, are fairly light. He became aware that the water had slowly crept up to his neck.

Well, first things first, he thought. Somehow, I must get higher in the cabin. Closer to the floor. Closer to the forward bulkhead. He reached around in all directions with both arms, and after several interminable moments of increasing panic, he found nothing. Maybe I can grip the floor, no, the ceiling, with the rubber heels on my shoes. He moved slightly, standing with the toe of his left shoe against the light fixture, and pulled his right foot up under him. Maybe I can stand up. He applied pressure against his right foot. It held! He pulled his left foot up under his seat, and slowly worked himself into a squatting position. The water was back to chest level.

Great! Now at least I'll have air for a while. And, if worse comes to worst, I can always swim and float for as long as the air lasts. Obviously, I cannot stay here. He rose from the squatting position and then he started slipping. He lunged upward and grabbed at the seat shapes with both hands. Left hand found a seat back and held on! Now he could...suddenly, there was a bump on one of the port side windows. Bump, Bump...pause...bump, bump, bump. Somebody's there! He squinted his eyes and, there...a moving shape. Achmed moved quickly toward the window, walking with both hands and feet, then reached out and did the same two...pause...three knocks. The shape quickly returned the knocks, then disappeared.

Achmed understood. Someone had dived to look for him, or possibly others? And had to return to the surface for air. But what can he do? At this point in time, probably less than half an hour since the ship went down, the others were at the surface, but without any equipment. Besides, this water has moved into the air pocket at least a foot since I came to. I don't have all that much time. What to do? He decided the first thing was to check the cabin door and see if he could get through it and see anything at all.

He removed his shoes, socks, jacket, and shirt, leaving him dressed in only shorts and pants. Then he gulped a chest full of air and dived for the door. The light was so poor, he could see nothing with sureness, but felt around and found the door. Then, holding the door facing, quickly stuck his head out, looked around, ducked back in, and returned to the air pocket.

Outside the door, the light was somewhat better, and he could make out the uptilted portside gunwale, and grayish rock below. Basically, the ship must be resting on its pilot house and stern. He began to lay his plans. The rock is probably very light colored, probably reef, even though it looked dark gray to me. Since the diver came down and stayed a while to exchange knocks with me, the water must not be very deep. Achmed knew the Gulf was rather shallow, and around these reefs, probably not over forty or fifty feet deep, and this boat may not be all the way to the bottom. He guessed it was about thirty feet from the windows to the surface. Okay, I'll count on that, and move ahead.

The plan: Get a lot of air, dive through the door, then work through the rough reef front and remaining deck cargo over to the port side, under the portside gunwale, and to the surface. Simple. The only real uncertainty: could he get through the possible maze of rock and cargo? Must try. If I can't find an opening right away, observe, come back here, and re-evaluate. Then do it over again.

Achmed breathed deep several times, noting that he seemed to be working a little harder to get a deep breath...maybe the air is beginning to get foul?...then inhaled strongly, and dived. He was out the door in about five seconds, then swam and crawled through rock protuberances and around two cargo masses, then began to worry about his ability to go on without more air. He kept crawling and stroking along, feeling the bottom and reaching toward dark shapes. Twenty-five more seconds went by. I can't hold out much longer.

He knew that he should be able to get by without air for at least two minutes, if he didn't work too hard, or lose his composure. He had been working his way along the cabin wall, then aft, then back forward. No lighter water ahead. Can I find my way back? Must get air. He fought back to the door, gratefully found it, and swam back into his air pocket.

After several moments gasping, Achmed calmed down, and

did his best to relax. Then, he reasoned that the best hope for an opening under the gunwale was toward the aft end, downward. Remember, dammit, remember. How was the cargo stored? He closed his eyes and recalled coming up the gangplank and stepping down the steps onto the main deck. What lay ahead? Solid cargo along the gunwale. No openings. But wait, this boat is resting on the pilot house, and the cargo was surely not piled all the way to that height, and even if it was, it was probably dislodged by the reef crash. An opening near the base of the pilot house should exist. OK, that's the plan. Out the door, up and over to portside, and out! By all reason, it should work!

He oxygenated his lungs, then one last deep breath, and down he went again. Out the door, down and across the reef and back toward the pilot house from one of the cargo masses he had previously worked around the other way, and there it was! Lighter water! He felt his way along, and after a few more feet of groping, found a gap between a canvas cargo cover and the reef! He wiggled into the gap, his hips caught, thought for a few seconds he couldn't get through...trapped!...then squirmed, bit by bit, until...he broke free! He stroked strongly for the surface, and when he reached it, he felt like he shot five feet into the air! Actually, it was closer to one foot.

Achmed looked around. Just as he caught sight of several people, and the lifeboat, he heard a shout.

"Over here, over here. We have preservers. I will bring one."

It was the helmsman from the boat, he swam toward Achmed, holding a life preserver over his head. A few moments later, Achmed grabbed the preserver, smiled at the man, and said, "I have never been happier to see someone than you with that preserver!"

The helmsman replied, "My friend, we are all so happy to see you too. Especially after I dove down and found that you were alive. We were trying to find a plan to get you when, suddenly, you jumped out of the water!"

They spoke Arabic. During his ordeal, Achmed had thought in Arabic, English, and even a little French. Like many of his British- or American-educated friends, they were quite comfortable in at least two languages. For the next few hours, all conversation was Arabic.

Achmed swam over to the lifeboat and found that they were all in it. Passengers and crew alike. They had been hit by a tidal wave. He was the only one in the passenger cabin, and the only one who had been knocked out. The others got off safely. One of the children went under, but the helmsman went after him and pulled him up, then held him, treading water, until the captain had gotten the lifeboat. As planned by the way it was secured, the lifeboat broke loose and floated when the ship capsized.

The captain had managed to send a distress signal before the ship sank, and the lifeboat had an emergency kit that included a small transmitter that was steadily beeping out a distress call.

There was much conversation about the wave and what caused it. After finding that Achmed was a seismologist, he was overwhelmed with questions. He described the event as best he could, but explained that he did not know how powerful or damaging the earthquake was, but suspected it was both. But after a few moments, Achmed's only concern was keeping warm. The whole group had varying degrees of chill from the cool morning air on their wet clothes and bodies, but Achmed was bare from the waist up. He was cold, but he was safe! He could handle the chill!

He did know and explained that this was the fourth in a series that were probably related. He also felt that this one was rather strong, and probably destructive, based on the strength of the wave that wrecked their ship. This was true even though, as the captain explained, the ship would not have sunk except that the wave threw it into the reef, then the extreme water turbulence capsized it.

They were investigated by a helicopter about two hours later. And were picked up by a fishing *dhow* shortly thereafter.

Before his wife and children knew anything was wrong, although they were more than a little concerned at his delay of half a day, Achmed was at home, calling out, "Anybody home?"

- - - - - - -

In the years ahead, Achmed thought many times about the gift of air. Simple air. How good it is to simply be alive and well. *Allah Akbar! Allah Kareem!* God is Great! God is Kind!

~ ~ ~ ~ ~ ~ ~ ~ ~ ~ ~ ~ ~ ~

CHAPTER 7

The Trail Forks

It was now January, usually a good time of year in most of Saudi Arabia. Although the nights could be downright cold, with temperatures occasionally below freezing, the days were just right. Cold mornings and evenings, but balmy during most of the day. Unless winds were blowing and trying to transport large parts of the country to some other part of it; or so the people thought, based on the huge volumes of sand, dust, dead plants, and other clutter that rode piggyback on the masses of moving air. But this was normally a time of much pleasant weather, at least relative to the months when the Scorpion, Scorpios, rode high in the sky, with bright Antares as a reminder of his sting.

The seismologists had by now collected all the measurements, the descriptions, and some of the interpretations and opinions. A basic interpretation had evolved as to what happened to cause this series of mammoth destroyers.

Achmed Asker was still having bad dreams about his overturned boat experience, but the dreams were getting milder and more infrequent. He never lost his sense of the terror. And he never lost his sense of gratitude to Allah for his Will.

The first earthquake, referred to as the Sirr quake, was a Richter 6.3 that occurred in mid-November, with its epicenter west of Riyadh. Then came the big one, Richter 8.7, on Thursday, December 5th, called the Hofuf earthquake because the epicenter was just west of that city; followed by an aftershock of 6.0 early the next morning. This was followed by the destructive Richter 7.6 earthquake that came to be known as the Gulf quake, or the Seaquake, on Monday, December 16th, with an epicenter near the center of the Persian Gulf east of Dhahran. Finally, there was the Zagros Richter 5.3 earthquake the following Friday, with the epicenter in the Zagros Mountains of Iran.

The primary cause of the movements were major stresses that built up in the outermost part of the earth's crust, the lithosphere, until strong and massive layers of heavy basement rock finally gave way and fractured. The forces had been building up for centuries, and while such massive earthquake destruction has rarely been witnessed during the history of man, such movements are common in geologic history.

Perhaps the best general description of this series of events was one given by Aramco seismologist Achmed Asker during an interview with reporters in Houston in mid-January. By this time, a great deal of interest had been building in the news media regarding the possible effect of the earthquakes on oil production, as it appeared more and more certain that Saudi Arabia would be unable to deliver the major share of American imports, as it had before the quakes. At least until they repaired the damage. The main concern of the rest of the world was simply, will it be months or years?

Mr. Asker was in the city, after a trip to the Berkeley, California seismic center, to discuss the findings with Aramco management. He was permitted to grant an interview and explain the causes but, at this time, not the possible longer term effects.

A reporter from Dallas started the interview: "Mr. Asker, could you explain to us what happened, and what will be done?"

Achmed realized that it was going to be difficult to stay away from effects, but he could at least delve into the causes and plead ignorance on the destruction of the cities and oil facilities. "You must all understand that I am a seismologist, trained for petroleum industry work. I am not really a quake expert. You'll have to go to others to get formal answers, but I will try to give you a fairly good picture of things, if you wish."

The Dallas reporter replied, "We understand your background, Mr. Asker, and we also know that your company chose you to decipher and describe the event for their management, so you must have more knowledge than you say. We'd like you to go ahead."

Achmed looked at the reporter's name tag, and started his talk. "Thank you, Mr., Charleston, I believe. This major rupture, as the series of quakes has come to be known to those of us working with it, might have been called a 'ten-or hundred-thousand year event.' Such ruptures have happened, and will happen again. There is no doubt as to 'if.' It's only 'when.' But the odds are pretty low that it will happen again like this for perhaps several thousand more years...but that doesn't mean we won't have more quakes in this same area; just not major ruptures for a long time. Probably."

"But, there were several quakes," said a lady from the Houston Post. "Why did you have five of them so close together, and so large?"

"The main cause of major earthquakes is the shifting, crushing, and thrusting of earth plates. To compare them to something we can see and comprehend better, you might think of these plates as thick crusts of mud resting on heavy, but not crusted, mud, and which, in turn, is resting or floating on light, watery mud. The heavy crusted mud at the top could develop breaks and cracks, forming sections or plates of the crusted mud. Then, if pushed with a stick, one of the plates could slide on the less viscous mud lying below, and strike or grind against an adjacent mud plate. If you pushed hard enough, the plate you are pushing might go under the other mud plate it's against. That's called subduction".

"Earth plates are roughly similar to that, but on massive scales of size and strength. And, instead of a stick pushing a plate, internal pressure and temperature changes supply the pushing forces".

"In the case of our temblors, the major plates involved are the Asian and African plates, with the Arabian plate, or as it is sometimes called, sub-plate, in between. The Asian plate includes most of Asia, and continues westward into Europe and, as a result, this plate is sometimes referred to as the Eurasian plate. The southerly boundary of that plate is marked by a huge basement fault zone that trends east-west through the Mediterranean Sea, then swings south into and through western Iran. It is marked by the northwesterly trending Zagros Mountains in western Iran".

"This mountainous trend is sometimes called the Zagros Fold Zone, or Zagros Crush or Suture Zone. It is the contact of the Iranian sub-plate, a small part of the Asian plate, with the Arabian plate. This contact is almost constantly shifting a bit, the western plate downward, or northward, or both. On average, for centuries, probably millennia, there are some ten or twelve quakes a year in this trend that extends on into Iraq. All of which causes a lot of suffering to the people in that area; but these hardy people have pretty well learned to live with quakes in the way they build and react."

"What happened in our Hofuf major rupture was that stresses, or forces, had been piling up on the eastern part of the Arabian plate, until finally, it began to break along an old major north-south fracture zone that extends from near the Iraq-Iran border southward well into Saudi Arabia. It is surmised by some researchers that there is occasional, that is geologic, not human time, sideways slippage between the basement blocks adjacent to this regional basement fracture. For reference, let's call this major feature the Hofuf fracture, which is what we call it, because the epicenter was just west of the ancient Saudi city of Hofuf".

"As forces built up, first there was movement along basement fractures beneath the western Saudi mountains about 75 miles west of Riyadh. While these fractures were separate from the Hofuf fracture, all are part of the gradually moving Arabian plate and, if forces build up on one part of the plate, the first movement will occur in the weakest place. I guess that was the weakest place. The west Riyadh slippage produced the first quake, 6.1 Richter, as I recall. The epicenter was relatively shallow, about five kilometers deep."

"Then what happened," asked the Post reporter.

Asker looked at the lady's card. "Well, Ms Collins, is it?"

She smiled and replied, "That's close enough, Mr. Asker." Actually, it was Cotling.

Asker continued. "Now, what I am about to say, is our interpretation. It is not certainly correct. But it is one reasonable interpretation of all the measured data we have at this time.

"After the western slippage occurred, it loaded more stress on the Hofuf fracture, which finally broke with a real bang, a powerful release of energy. Somewhat like a dozen hydrogen bombs going off at one time. That was the 8.7 Richter quake; not too much less than the largest ever recorded, I think. The next one was a Richter 6.0 aftershock to the 8.7 one. The next two quakes were adjustments to the major movement, wrought by stresses built up on other basement blocks by the big movement.

"The first of these, at 7.6 Richter, had a movement and epicenter beneath the Persian Gulf, and this quake caused a lot of damage. This is the one referred to as the Seaquake. The last one centered beneath the Zagros Mountains of Iran, in the Crush, or Fold, zone and registered 5.3 Richter. There were several small shakes after and related to each of the main movements.

"The timing of these events is significant. Earthquakes such as these, two of which centered on a relatively stable plate, do not occur often. In the Zagros Mountains of Iran, earthquakes occur every year, most relatively small. Those mountains are part of the boundary area between the Arabian sub-plate and the huge Eurasian Plate. But in Saudi Arabia, the substantial earth movements we have just witnessed are relatively infrequent, perhaps occurring only once in several thousand, perhaps tens of thousands of years. That makes it uncommon when we think in terms of human history as opposed to geologic history. But it did happen. It was predictable. The timing was not predictable. It will happen again. But when? No one can say."

Another reporter, too far away for Asker to read his card, spoke up, "Tell us about the effect of this major rupture on the oil fields."

Achmed Asker knew this was coming. And knew he could say very little. By this time, the oil companies involved knew quite well that there were problems, but they also knew that it was clearly the best route to break this news gradually. And, they truly did not know the full effects on the fields.

"We simply do not know the effect of this rupture at this time," answered Achmed. "We anticipate there will be some well work needed, but do not know details." He did not lie, but he also avoided the full truth.

The reporter asked, "Will the oil supply be reduced?"

Asker had to be careful here, but had a prepared answer: "It will probably be modestly reduced for a short time. To say more is pure speculation."

There was a momentary lull in the conversation, then a reporter asked, "Do you know the seismologist who was trapped in that boat that sank? We never got all the details, but it seemed scary."

Achmed thought for a moment, then replied, "You can be sure it was scary. I doubt that word is quite the one. Blind terror is more appropriate. You see, that man is me."

This started a new round of enthusiastic questions and conversation, and Achmed was glad to get off the oil business for a while. The questioning and answering went on for some time, but Achmed Asker successfully avoided any sensationalism, kept the conference directed at the scientific factors and causes, and pretty well stayed away from effects. He knew that Saudi damage was severe and production was off by nearly twenty percent. The oil world knew it was down, but had no idea how severe.

But what anyone outside a limited few in Aramco did not know, was that they kept the production as high as they did by maximizing all wells, and using all available storage. And some of the Ghawar wells were not holding up as well as expected. One or two dropped off every day....

- - - - - - -

The field foreman, speaking in Arabic, called an operations man: "Abdul, go out and check well A-16. The monitor indicates pressure has dropped and flow has nearly stopped."

Abdul had just reported to the field office for work, and had been relaxing with a small cup of typically strong and sweet Saudi Arabian coffee, and reviewing the recent destruction with his co-workers. This was a Ghawar Field field office just out of Haradh. It had been here for decades, being one of the first established for the field, in 1949.

Abdul got up, stretched, picked up his work ticket from the foreman, and started on his way. He was soon bouncing over the rough field road headed for the assigned well. This was routine. Well site electronic sensors monitored flow rates and a few other functions, which were radioed by a small transmitter to the field office monitors. One person could keep a pretty good watch on dozens of wells. If trouble was indicated, the field operations men were sent out to look for the problem.

Abdul arrived at A-16. All that was visible on the surface here was a steel well head with several valves, and a large flow line. Normally, the well flowed several thousand barrels of oil each day.

As he strode up to the well head, he noticed that the pressure on the flow gauge was near zero. Why? He went back to the pickup, got a bucket, returned to the well, opened a valve off the flow line, and watched the small stream of fluid. Ordinarily this would have been utterly impossible. If Abdul had tried the same thing a few weeks ago, oil flow would have knocked the bucket out of his hands, and he would have had trouble closing the valve.

Obviously, something was wrong. As he looked at the flow of

fluid, his experienced eye discerned water. The fluid was oil and water, but mostly water. He did not know much about the structure of the field, or of the oil column in the reservoir, but he knew that the wells that produced water were farther off structure than A-16, and in his twelve years in field operations, he had never seen a well go to water like this before. Usually, it took years for a well in this area to change flow from 100% oil to 20% water, and there had been very few such happenings.

He picked up his bucket, placed a newspaper over it, put the bucket on the floorboard, then drove away from the well.

Abdul walked in to the field office, handed the bucket to his foreman, and said, "Ajab, we have a problem. Notice how much water is there."

"Abdul Aziz al Qurishi, what do you mean...water?"

Abdul responded, "Look at it."

Ajab Ben Jamban got a glass, dipped it into the bucket, well down into the fluid, and withdrew it. There was about two centimeters of oil in the glass, the rest water.

Later the same day, well A-12 monitors indicated the same slow down. Then the next morning, it was A-7. Then A-14. Within two weeks, sixteen oil wells on the southern end of this unbelievable oil field went to mostly water production, and very little at that. Most of these wells had been on the lower southwestern flank of the giant structural ridge trapping Ghawar, and several had been producing some water for years.

Still further down the flank of the structure, there were injection wells where produced water plus makeup water was pumped or gravity drained back into the massive Arab D reservoir. This injected water helped maintain reservoir pressure and make the oil flow better, and at the same time get more of the oil. The field had been closely monitored for decades, and all reasonable engineering and operations precautions were taken to maximize ultimate oil recovery. Some of the injected water flowed faster through one part of the reservoir than another, called channeling, and thus caused some of the oil producing wells to make more water than others.

But this sudden shifting of oil to water, especially in three formerly strong oil wells, was highly unusual and, at this time, unexplainable. The only thing that could be associated with this sudden change was the major earthquakes. But how, or why, was unknown.

Ajab talked to his boss, the field superintendent, who discussed it with the reservoir engineering section in Dhahran. After some study, the engineer called back and asked that several samples of the new water production be sent in. The field office obtained new samples in sterile glass jugs, capped them, and shipped them to Dhahran. The samples were delivered to the lab where the first determinations were chloride content. Although the samples were tested for potassium, Ph, and a few trace elements, it was immediately obvious that the chlorides were anomalous. By the time the lab had analyzed the third sample, the results were unusual enough that the reservoir section was called.

Later the same day, the engineer who handled this section of Ghawar Field reported to Rashid Ben Rimthan, head of reservoir engineering in the Dhahran headquarters office.

"Chief, I just received some water measurements from the lab on Haradh area wells that are unusual."

"How is that?" Rashid said.

"Too low. Normal chloride values for any connate water with the oil range around 200,000-plus parts per million. These values are less than half that. On seven samples from nine wells, the range is 72,000 to 88,000. Looks like water is breaking in somehow from off structure to the south."

Millions of years ago, probably at least 60 million, oil had migrated into the Arab D reservoir, millions of years after the reservoir had been formed by deposition of shells from various marine animals, and other calcareous sediments that became limestone and dolomite. Many of these layers were very porous and oil or water could easily move through them and collect in high places on the giant structural ridge, where oil could float on water in this reservoir. In that manner, huge quantities of oil migrated in and through this and adjacent similar zones and became trapped.

Trapping of the oil was aided by thin layers of anhydrite within the Arab formation, as well as about ninety meters of anhydrite in the Hith formation overlying the Arab formation. When water comes in contact with anhydrite, it changes to gypsum, which acts like a sealing wax to oil. Thus oil trapped in the Arab formation, of which zone D is the thickest and lowest member, could not escape upward because of the seal, nor move laterally because of water surrounding the oil at the top of the anticlinal fold.

But then an unusual geologic event developed. This Arab formation was very widespread, and because of the east dip on the formation, the continuously connected porous and permeable layers extended all the way up to the surface, hundreds of miles to the west. In that area, many drainage channels, dry most of the time, crossed these outcrops that cover thousands of square miles. Those drainage channels, or <u>wadis</u> collected rainwater runoff from an even greater area.

Thus in a year's time even two inches of rainfall could place many trillions of gallons of water into the Arab formation. Provided the water had some place to go. And it did. Dozens of springs, such as Haradh, and Hofuf yield water that is probably largely derived from the Arab formation.

Some of that water passes through the formation clear into the Persian Gulf region, and up fault fractures to feed shallower reservoirs, and to make surface springs of slightly salty water.

Because of the vast area covered by the thick Arab formation, even trillions of gallons of water would move quite slowly downdip in the formation. Probably a few hundred centimeters, maybe a foot or so, per year at most. Over hundreds of years, this fresh water moved downdip in the Arab, mixing with the old original connate water, and diluted it until the salt content measured less than 15% of the original. South of Ghawar, the water has as little as 30,000 parts chloride per million parts of water, compared to about 240,000 parts per million for the water that was there before the fresh water migrated downdip. In the field itself, water with as little as 38,000 ppm chloride occur on the southwest end of the field, and gets more and more salty to the north and east in the field.

At this time, in January, the rainfall in the west had been

unusually high over the past year. It had been estimated that as much as 250 centimeters, or ten inches, of rain had fallen over most of the region of the Arab formation outcrop and the higher area to the west that drained into that large outcrop.

The reservoir engineers and geologists familiar with the formation were well aware of these phenomena. The presence of water that was distinctly less salty than the connate water trapped in the oil-filled part of the reservoir indicated that, somehow, water had moved in from elsewhere.

The overall Ghawar Field had what was called a "tar mat" at or near the oil-water contact. This was a zone of oil up to 500 feet thick that had been oxidized enough over millions of years to remove some of the lighter constituents of the oil and leave heavier oil, even tar in some places, behind. While this tar mat phenomenon was present in many oil fields around the world, it is not common. Most oil fields had no such mat. Here at Ghawar, this mat was not impermeable. Water, even oil, could move through it. By actual test, it had been observed that injection water from flank injection wells moved through the mat zone of heavy oil and/or tar. It became important to the production planning and development of the field to recognize the permeability of this "tar mat."

"Got any ideas why that water would have moved in?" asked Rashid.

The engineer responded, "Seems to me, if water came in, some of the oil must have moved out. Maybe some excess pressures were created by the quakes?"

"Possibly," Rashid replied, "but if that were the answer, we ought to have measurable changes in the observation wells around the southerly parts of the field. Did you check that?"

"No, Chief, but I'll get on that right now!" said the engineer as he turned to leave, feeling that his boss had pointed out something that he should have already checked.

"Let me know as soon as you can, Nasir," Rashid requested as Nasir walked away, "and also, get some measure on the oil columns height where pure oil wells went to water."

Rashid pondered the problem. If the 100% oil wells that went to water had only a few meters below the base of the perforations in the well casing, down to the oil/water contact in the reservoir, then the sudden water production might not be so bad. But, if the underlying water part, or "leg," of the reservoir was considerably below the oil zone producing in the well, then there might be real trouble.

As days passed, more information filtered in. The reservoir engineering section established several key pieces of information to help solve the puzzle. Nasir's thought that there would be distinct pressure highs in the water below the oil was not correct. After corrections for depth and fluid type to get what these engineers called datum pressure, there were no measurable differences in the wells within several miles of the wells that started making so much water.

As Rashid suspected, those oil wells that went to water were indeed close to the water leg. So, the water did not have to move up in the reservoir but a few meters to significantly increase the water production in these wells that were on the flanks of the huge structure.

Another very interesting pattern developed. The most northern part of the overall Ghawar structure is referred to as Fazran Field. That field proved to be separated from the main field to the south by a structural saddle, that is, a place where the formations had been bowed down lower than to the north and south. This saddle bowed down so much that only water could be produced from test wells drilled in the middle of it. But cores on those wells showed that oil had been there. It had migrated out somehow and left residual amounts of oil behind.

The part of overall Ghawar that lay just south of this saddle became known as 'Ain Dar Field. The northernmost oil wells at 'Ain Dar had produced some water for several years. Within the last few weeks, these wells had produced less and less water, and now some of them were producing oil without any water at all.

This is almost unheard of in the oil patch. The geologists and engineers were quite puzzled, had several theories, but no proof of what was going on.

Meanwhile, some of the southernmost wells in Fazran Field, just north of the saddle, started producing more water. This further complicated the subsurface equation. And the data to help solve the equation were from points in the reservoir thousands of feet apart, with large areas yielding no useful information.

One thing was crystal clear. Ghawar oil production was down. Production was down by nearly twenty percent, and getting worse.

Many wells in the Haradh area, and to the north in the southern part of Fazran Field, had gone to water, or started making water with the oil. For mysterious reasons, some of the excellent oil wells in high structural positions started making some water. There were no obvious patterns or reasons for such high wells going to some water production.

It was indeed a puzzle, and it became apparent that some kind of unusual fluid movements were occurring in this very important reservoir. Not only important to Saudi Arabia, but important to Planet Earth, if humans were to continue having the luxuries provided by the energy from oil.

As the weeks wore on, it became more and more clear that something different, a test plan, new studies or mapping, but something, had to be done to develop a most-likely geologic and engineering scenario. And a way to attack it. Rashid felt it was time to follow up on his December meeting with Jon.

Rashid recommended, and it was approved, to hire Jon Burke as a fluid movement consultant. Perhaps his old friend who knew as much as anyone about such things could help develop a plan.

It was early March. The telephone rang. The man turned in his chair toward the phone stand, picked it up, "Hello?" said Jon Burke at his office in west Houston.

The voice was loud and clear, "Jon, how is the old Aggie these days?"

Jon immediately recognized his old friend, Rashid Ben Rimthan. "Well, I'll be damned," said Jon, "to what do I owe the honor of this call from such a distinguished member of Saudi society? You sound like you're in Houston?"

"To begin with, I am in Dhahran, and we just happen to have a super connection! As to the honor business, I would have to say it is not an honor, but then, maybe it is...for you! We have a few things to talk about old friend but, first, bring me up to date on everything. How are you, Lee-Anne, and your family?"

For the next few minutes, the two men reviewed the health and latest happenings in their families. Then, Jon asked, "Rashid, what's the story, and how may I help? Have things changed much since our December meeting before the Seaquake?"

"Jon, since the quakes, we are seeing strange things happen

as to oil and water production in Ghawar and Abqaiq. And, most recently, a new oil seep has developed in the Qatif area, if you can believe that! I finally decided, and got it approved, to see if you and I together might could puzzle it out. The plan is that we would just renew your contract that expired last summer before all this quake business happened."

"I know it's too involved to try to describe on the phone," returned Jon, "but I'm sure it has to do with water encroachment in some manner."

"You got it. Could you come over for a week or so pretty soon? Then keep up as we try to execute some test or study program? About the same approach as we've used before."

"No problem, Rashid. And a simple contract extension for whatever time you like, is okay with me. How about week after next?"

"That's fine. Any ideas on what we might do meanwhile?"

"Get all the detail datum pressure data you can. I know you have already done this. But take a few bottom-hole shut-in pressures, long enough to stabilize, even interpret if necessary, but collect data from as many wells as possible, and stick it all on one of your base maps."

"Jon, we already have datum pressure maps, but most of the pressures are pre-earthquakes. We will try to have at least fifteen or twenty new points by the time you get here. Is your passport current?"

"It's not current, but still valid, I think. If I have a problem with that I'll be in touch. And, Rashid, as to those pressure values, spot new ones beside old ones so we can see changes, if any."

"Okay, buddy. Will do. And, I'll look forward to your arrival week after next. Let me know when your travel plans are set, and I'll get your housing ready."

The friends hung up. More strange things were to occur before they were to get understanding.

- - - - - - -

It was now June. Jon had made two trips to Dhahran, and spent most of his time since the first of March working on the problem. The pressure maps showed that there were minor changes from the older data. Individual values would have been insignificant, if it were not for the fact that a pattern had developed.

From these datum pressures, Jon could map a distinct change in the slope of the pressures from southwest to northeast across the area. Even though the measured pressure increased to the northeast and east, because depth of the Arab Formation increased from the surface to over 6000 feet near the northeast end of Ghawar Field. Once depth and fluid density data were all corrected to a common reference datum, datum pressures, all referred to that common plane, could be computed. These values at the different wells could then be contoured, just like a topographic map, to produce curved and sloping surface. After this was done, there was a slight increase in the rate of decrease northeasterly.

The datum pressures had always reduced to the northeast and east but, now, the slope of this pressure decline surface had increased quite distinctly. Jon and Rashid had immediately recognized the significance of this as to the oil accumulations, but there were several other pieces of the puzzle to be analyzed and interpreted to confirm the overall pattern.

In addition to the new oil seep near Qatif on the Persian Gulf coast, the old original seep in that area reactivated. Then, just a few weeks ago, another seep had developed about thirty kilometers northwest of Hofuf.

Saudi fishermen and pearl divers had worked their trade off the coasts of Saudi Arabia for longer than any records existed. Over the last few decades, many of the sons of these skilled men left the sea for the plentiful and better paid work onshore that was created by everything from new oil exploration to trucking products, and everything in between. Entire new industries in food handling, transportation, and a host of services had developed in these decades. But there were still a few who chose the water.

These hardy few continued the work of their forefathers. Ever ready to adapt the fancy and better methods, mind you. These younger generations found sonar, computers, satellite navigation and all the other modernization quite acceptable. Except for the few remaining pearl divers. Sonar and computers couldn't find the pearls. Some of the new electronics, such as navigation and sonar search for floor irregularities, were quite helpful. But oysters had to be examined to find pearls. So, diving was still practiced by some who found this to be an exciting way to make a living.

But, in the past few weeks, these divers began to notice things that they had never seen, or even heard in their grandfather's tales of old. The fresh water springs had turned salty. Not all of them. And some were more salty than others. Then, there was the oil. A few of the springs that flowed the saltiest water also seeped oil. And the oil was not seeping in spoon-and cup-fulls, it was in buckets and barrels. With widespread surface sheens that gradually spread and turned into a discernable layer in some areas.

As the oil sheens increased, word quickly spread, and the Saudi pollution forces attacked with booms, pumps, and the other tools at their disposal. Would the seeps continue? Would they grow?

These events were not lost on the news media. Every newspaper over the globe, columnists, television personalities, radio, and mountains of mail spread the word. Exactly what the word was, had vague boundaries, uncertain facts, and speculative guesses. Yet many of the media proceeded with their normal fashion of measuring the diameter of a cloud with a three-inch hawser, with a micrometer on the end. They quoted results in precise gallons when the true knowledge could not differentiate between barrels and lakes of oil.

Information began to leak out of Iraq that destruction of producing facilities along with multi-well damage from the Seaquake had curtailed oil production more than had been stated.

The world oil market had been quite unstable before this new round of earthquake ramifications. Now it was chaotic.

Where these new events would end was unknown.

- - - - - - -

The Trail Forks...

Things were changing back in Nacogdoches. It was as if the problems and uncertainties in the Persian Gulf area had somehow transferred through the ether to strike a former soldier in the great chase of the thirties. JJ was sick. It was not something ordinary. Maybe it was the result of dormant cells that had been hibernating in his kidneys. He had cancer again. Now in the lungs.

It all started one evening the previous fall after a football game.

Just before the series of devastating Persian Gulf earthquakes. He and Ruthanne had been watching the game on television, and after the end, he got up to go relieve himself. But he could not do so. He waited at the commode for several minutes, and nothing would happen. He had noticed that his normal "slow pee" had seemed to be getting slower, but thought little of it. Just that blamed prostate gland growing, he thought. That's one of the problems old men have. If you live long enough, you are sure to get prostate cancer. But he also knew that this type cancer usually grew so slow that usually it was something else that finally got you.

Ruthanne came in to find JJ holding a wet towel against his lower regions. "What on earth are you doing, JJ?" she asked incredulously.

JJ grinned sheepishly, "Well, you know how sometimes I have a little trouble peeing, and it works a little better if you heat it up a bit with a hot wet towel."

"Is it working?" she asked.

"Let's see..." And JJ tried again. This time it started trickling. "Yep. One more small victory for mankind!"

But the problem continued the next day, and the next. So, JJ went in for a little exam by the medico.

"JJ, it's enlarged pretty good," said the doctor. "I think it'd be smart to do a little work on it."

"You mean cutting?"

"I guess that's about the size of it," replied the physician.

A week later, it was all over. His doctor had referred him to a reliable surgeon who performed the rather straightforward operation to remove most or all of the prostate. However, there was a problem: The malignant cells were not all prostate cells. This meant that some malignancy elsewhere had spread into the prostate area, and it needed to be found.

One thing led to another until the whole story, a very depressing one, unraveled. It seemed that a primary tumor had developed in his left kidney, perhaps from some dormant cell from his naso-pharynx cancer decades before. However it started, it had developed in the kidney, then spread to JJ's lung, and to other organs. It was a bad situation.

After much consultation, JJ finally decided that it really wasn't worthwhile to go through the only treatment, chemotherapy, that could help a little, but not possibly cure anything. Maybe give him a few more months of rather poor quality life, for which he would have to undergo the distress of the treatment. Just let 'er go, he thought. Won't grow too fast at my age anyhow!

While all this was going on, JJ kept up his long walks with Thunder, but it got tougher and tougher until finally, he cut down to a mile, then shortly after the first of the year, quit.

"Baby, I reckon the signs are gettin' pretty clear," he said to Ruthanne one morning after a breakfast of crisp bacon and "false eggs" burrito. "One good thing..."

"What's that?"

He answered with a rather sardonic smile, "at least our cholesterol and fats stuff paid off for me. 'Twarn't my heart that got to me. And all the dieting and exercise in the world wouldn't have staved off this thing I got."

"Yes, my dear man. And who knows? You might be around for a long time yet!"

"Maybe so. Maybe not. In either case, t'aint too bad. We got some fun left...and speaking of fun, why don't we make a trip to Lake City just one more time?"

Ruthanne thought a little, then replied, "JJ, I hadn't thought of Lake City in years and years. When were we there last? 'Seventy-five, I think."

"Sounds about right to me," he said. "It just seemed like a good idea to go back to one of our old Colorado stomping grounds to see how much it may have changed. Might even make another jeep trip over Engineer's Pass."

"Well, old Buddy, I'm game if you are!"

They did make this trip. But it wasn't as easy as they remembered. And JJ seemed to go downhill while they were gone. Two weeks after getting back, he was bedridden. Three weeks later, he started on heavy pain drugs. Now, it was all downhill. He was fully aware of what was happening, but chided his mate if and when she seemed sad. He kept reminding her all was absolutely OK. Just regular stuff!

It had seemed only a short time ago that JJ had participated in the Nacogdoches Chamber meeting. And then, in other ways, it seemed a lifetime. He arduously rolled over on his side. Now he felt strange. Weak. But, also, just peculiar. Part of the time he felt almost like he was floating. His mind drifted...to West Texas in 1934...then, it was his running in the fire to save the little boy...Udayliyah, then Cairo...the snake bite, he and Huey and the Hofuf caper. That brought a wan smile. He knew he was fading...make it through the night? What time is it? Is it night or day...?

JJ slowly reached out with his hand to the intercom monitor. He found the button with his fingers...and pushed it. He could hear the loud buzz in the kitchen where Ruthanne was doing something....

"Here I am, my thriving young scientist," said Ruthanne as she walked in the bedroom, making a distinct effort to maintain her composure.

JJ spoke softly, with pauses while he caught his breath, "...Sugar, I believe....I think...maybe you call...the kids?"

She could stand it no longer, and broke into hard sobbing.

"...No, no, my...my beloved...it's as it...should be..."

Ruthanne fought to regain her composure..."I'm so sorry I forgot our plan, my darling. I just can't always follow my programming." She was still crying, but now controlled, and gradually changing to calmness. She kept telling herself, this is normal, this is normal, I know it's so, it's part of living, it's normal. She convinced herself to the extent that there was no more crying.

Turning perkily back to JJ, with her slightly crooked little smile he loved so much, she continued, "I know what you've said, I know it's all perfectly natural as you said, and all that stuff, but my emotion isn't always the way it ought to be. My dear man, my heart's companion, I am here and will be here."

She picked up the phone on the bedside table and called Jon. Lee-Anne answered. "Hello?"

"Lee-Anne, we think you and Jon had better come home...."

Lee-Anne knew what the call was about. The whole family had been following JJ's progress day by day. "Okay, mom. We're on our way. We'll call the others...."

JJ breathed deeply, then ever so slowly, took another breath. "Baby,...won't las...won't last...just do...do the letter...my love, my love...'s been great...real grea..."

He breathed deeply again. Almost a minute passed. Then

another breath...more shallow. Another deep breath. A slight gasp. A full minute passed...then another. Ruthanne threw herself on him, sobbing, "Oh JJ, my JJ, my JJ..." But he was gone. The trail had ended.

It was a little before ten p.m., Wednesday, the 16th of July. Summertime in East Texas. A time when flowers were in full bloom, and all outdoor life was fussily, zealously, pursuing its course. But a course that no longer included the old East Texas geologist, one of that group of explorers, those tough and knowledgeable men of the thirties who laid the foundation for the greatness of Saudi Arabia in later decades.

The outside door opened, and in walked Lisa from her visit with a neighbor who wanted to know JJ's condition. Lisa had taken a week's vacation from her work to be with her grandparents. The whole family had been taking turns the last three weeks, staying at or near the Nacogdoches homestead as JJ went downhill. She came into the bedroom, saw Ruthanne sitting quietly, stroking JJ's head, and rushed over to comfort her, knowing full well what had happened. It was no longer necessary to comfort JJ, but Ruthanne was clearly distraught and in need of help.

Within nine hours, the whole clan had gathered. Jon and Lee-Anne, their children, Lisa and Nicole Brittany, and Jon's sister, Elizabeth, and two of her three children. Elizabeth's husband, Charles Munson, had, two years earlier, preceded JJ down the trail of the unknown. Cancer was his assailant. That night the family concentrated on Ruthanne in every way possible to help her adjust to the inevitable that had now happened.

The next morning, Jon called his friend and attorney, Fred Willis III. "Fred, could you come over this afternoon for an hour or so? We need you to read something."

"Sure, buddy, what time?" Fred knew that JJ was in bad shape, and that this probably meant that he had died, but he decided JJ would tell him what JJ wanted him to know, so said no more.

"How about, say, two?"

"Sure. I'll be there, Jon."

"Fred, what we have is a letter JJ wrote some time ago, that he wanted the family to read as soon as possible after he left this world. We all feel that we might be too emotional to read it very well, and know that you are pretty good at this sort of thing."

"It'll be my honor to do this, Jon. You know how deep the water flows between our families."

And so, that afternoon, Fred read JJ's letter.

"My family, I write this little note on Saturday, October 14, 1995. I've wanted to do this for a long time, and now am finally getting around to doing it.

"First, as to the event that has just occurred, you all need to remember, to know, and understand this: Death is a part of living. It's natural. All that commences life must end it. At least until some power we now know nothing of changes things. So, above all else, concern yourselves with what you can change or alter, and work on learning what that is. As for me, have good memories if you will, but smile as you have them. And let the smile sink beneath your lips, to your heart.

"I'm now on a voyage into the unknown. And it has always given me a little thrill to wonder what, or how it is on the other side. I leave you with real interest in this adventure, knowing not whether I'll be aware of who I was, what I did, my wife, my loves, or maybe, just maybe aware of all, and somehow able to observe or sense you. Right now. Maybe I'm standing here, laughing that you are all so somber. Think of the good things, the happy things, new life, the thrills of new learning. Don't brood over me, let your heart laugh at the challenge of the road, the trails ahead, until some time, some way, you come to join me in this great adventure.

"That's about all I have to say. Except for one more thought, mainly for my life's companion, my eternal love, Ruthanne; but also, for all of you: To adapt an old Indian saying,

May the winds be at your back, and the warm sun light your way, with the smell of roses to adorn you all on your trails ahead.

All was quiet for a few moments. Then Jon spoke.

"I think he said it all pretty well. So, as for me, as of now, I am sad no longer. Let's get on with the business at hand and send my dad off in a blaze of glory!"

And they did. Even with good cheer, and a few laughs at the dinner following the joining of JJ with the Earth he loved and studied and of which he felt he was a small part.

~ ~ ~ ~ ~ ~ ~ ~ ~ ~ ~ ~

CHAPTER 8

Oil and Water

Three weeks had passed since the Burkes said goodbye to JJ. Jon had great difficulty accepting that the man he had depended on, grown with, that rock he could lean on when everything went to hell, was no more. He sometimes could not prevent his eyes getting moist. But JJ's letter, which so well bespoke his philosophy, would come to mind, and Jon would smile. Perhaps, weakly and plaintively, but still, a smile. It was as JJ would have wanted: Remember me if you will, but mourn me not; you have much to do and so little time in which to do it!

In Nacogdoches, Ruthanne was undergoing the same problems of acceptance and, with her, it was more difficult than for Jon. She did not have big things to do, mind-testing questions, the opportunity to escape. So she attacked the problem another way. Everywhere she turned, she could feel his presence, and nothing could happen that didn't remind her of some past event with JJ. She accepted these things and just let that flow which wanted to flow. Which was mostly memories. Why not capture that for this expanding family of ours? Ruthanne began to write.

At first, she simply wrote notes in a notebook, thinking that someday some grandchild would find their 1941 Saudi adventure fascinating; or maybe the mixup in Temple after JJ's training for war; or maybe the meetings on old El Camino Real; or whatever. Now, after these weeks of a new loneliness, Ruthanne began to develop a plan. She would write a book. Not a fancy book; just one about the hows and whys of the Burke and Cook families. It really wasn't such a dull story, and she would publish it herself. Just for the family. After developing this plan, Ruthanne felt good about it. She talked of it with the children and they fully supported everything about it. Only time would tell if it really was a good idea.

Jon's work kept him increasingly busy and concerned about the situation in the Persian Gulf area. He had come back to Houston from Nacogdoches after his dad's funeral, and dived into the business of trying to make an accurate map of this thing that was so mysterious to so many people, even many geologists and engineers. The reservoir engineers referred to it as a datum pressure map. Geologists called it a piezometric or potentiometric map. Since there was little use for such maps in most oil fields around the world, these maps were poorly understood. But in eastern Saudi Arabia and several of the giant fields there, such maps were critical.

One example of a potentiometric surface is a water table. Farmers and ranchers have always been concerned about the location of a water table if they were to drill water wells into it. In most places, the layers of earth near the surface include layers of sandy or other porous rocks or sediments. When it rains, some of the rainfall sinks into the earth, and comes to rest on water already in the ground. The top of this water in the ground is called the water table. If it is trapped and cannot flow away, the water table will be very flat, maybe over distances of many miles.

Sometimes, in swampy and low-lying areas, the water table is at the surface. In dry areas, it may be several hundred feet deep. If this subsurface water reaches a fracture or break in the rocks someplace, or if the beds slope away as on a mountainside, the water will tend to flow downhill or into fractures, always trying to become level. Thus, if the subsurface water is flowing, then the water table will be tilted in the direction of flow. In this case, the tilt could be mapped to determine exactly how much lower the surface is in one area compared to another.

If water at the surface drains into a water-filled layer that slopes down mountains to the sea, the water will tend to move slowly in that direction, particularly if there are some fault fractures somewhere at lower elevations where some of the water comes back to the surface to form springs. One way to determine the true potentiometric surface for this moving water would be to drill a number of holes down to the water layer, then let the hole fill up as much as it would, then measure the depth from the surface down to that water top in the hole.

This level of water in the hole is called the *head* of water for the deeper water layer at that location. By correcting all such heads to a common datum, such as sea level, the geologist can contour those heads and he has a potentiometric map. Topographic and geologic structure maps use sea level as a datum so that the elevation in one place can be compared directly to that in another. If this potentiometric map is anything other than flat, the water in that reservoir is moving, in the direction of decreasing head values.

This map, which Jon and the other engineers often called a *P-map*, was Jon's current and critical problem. When water is moving, and the P-map slopes, or is tilted, then the contact between oil trapped in an anticline on that water will also be tilted in the direction of the water movement. This is called a dynamic oil entrapment; not static. The mass of oil floating on moving water in an upfolded layer can change in configuration if the underlying water movement is increased or decreased.

Ghawar, giant Ghawar, is a dynamic entrapment. The recent heavy rains in the Saudi mountains west of Riyadh had filled the Arab D reservoir unusually high. And the earthquakes near and in the Persian Gulf had formed new fracture pathways for the water to flow back up to springs at the surface. This increased the movement of the former rainwater now in the Arab D from westerly to easterly toward the Gulf. The movement increased only few inches per month, but this caused dramatic change in the P-map Jon was constructing, and he suspected this was the explanation for some of the southwestern Ghawar wells going to water.

Jon Burke and Rashid Rimthan used every trick they knew to compute head values at different locations. They used information from the many springs, shut-in bottom hole pressure measurements, recent water well data, and anything else from which they could make corrections to arrive at the all important head numbers. By this time the engineers were convinced that a good quality and current Arab D P-map was critical to the establishment of new wells to replace those that had gone to water.

The new oil seeps near the coast and in the Persian Gulf indicated that not only was the Ghawar oil-water contact northeasterly tilt increased, but some of the oil was probably spilling out of the structure and floating on the water in the reservoir into fractures that offered escape to shallower beds that actually were the sources for most of the surface seeps.

It was Monday, August the eleventh, and he felt he was about as ready as he was going to get. Jon picked up the telephone, and dialed the fourteen-digit number he needed on his long distance service. In a few moments, the telephone rang on the other end. "<u>Aloh</u>," said a female voice on the other end.

"May I speak to Rashid Rimthan, please?" Jon replied.

"A moment please," came the heavily accented answer.

Now a man spoke: "Hello, who is calling?" This voice was not so heavily accented, but still obviously Arabic.

"Jon Burke."

"Ah yes, Mr. Burke, you hold a moment?" The man spoke with courtesy, indicating he recognized Jon. In just a few seconds, a familiar voice came on the line.

"What do you have to say today, oh great and wondrous one. To what do I owe the honor of this most distinguished privilege?"

Jon replied, "I grew lonely to once again hear the voice of the remarkable Prince of Arabia!"

"Shhhh, Jon, if somebody heard that, I might be in trouble."

"Well Rashid, you are as close to an Arabian Prince as I've been, so...I hereby designate you as true Prince of Arabee."

Rashid, chuckling, "OK, so I'll be a prince for the next few minutes! How's the map going?"

"That's why I called. I reckon it's about as good a time as any for us to get together and have a go at finding that oil-water contact."

"You have the P-map done?"

"All but getting prints. Do you think it might be best to meet at the Aramco offices here...or me come there?"

Rashid thought a bit, then, "Jon, let's meet there. Tony DeRocca and his people are very interested in what we come up with and, besides, we might get a quicker recommendation decision."

"OK buddy. When?"

"Right away. Let me think a minute...I can be there on Thursday of next week. Is that OK?"

"No problem for me, Rashid. Does Tony have the latest pre-earthquake oil-water contact?"

"Sure does. And I'll bring the latest production data."

"All right. I'll be in Tony's office next Thursday morning."
"That's a deal. So long, partner."

"Adios!"

By ten in the morning of Thursday, the 21st, even before the first contour was struck, when Jon overlaid his new P-map over the pre-earthquake Arab D P-map, and then the structure and oil outline map of the Ghawar complex, an answer was obvious. There was no doubt that there should be a tendency for the oil mass to move somewhat to the north-northeast. It would take several days to make an estimate of the amount.

Tony looked at the maps without saying much, then went over to a chair and sat down. "Boy, we've got our work cut out for us. Jon, how long would it take for you to make a new set of maps for the whole Ghawar-Abqaiq complex?"

Jon replied, "Tony, the first thing I'd say, is it to be me by myself, or can you provide some help, say three developmental geologists who are at least a little familiar with hydrodynamics?"

"Hydrodynamics, moving water. You know, Jon, there are not over two or three men in all of Aramco who really know how to make all those tricky maps. But we have a lot of people who know the fundamentals. Sure, we can provide help."

"That'll speed things up a lot. Rashid, could you get me a new reproducible base of the whole area with all key well data spotted?"

"No sweat. We already have a current base. It will just take a day or so to spot whatever additional data you need. Heads, and recent production tests, I presume?" Rashid knew that Jon needed the head values he had computed for his own P-map on the new updated base, probably plus definition of exactly which wells had started making more or less water with the oil production.

"Rashid, the only other thing that would help is a water salinity map, with new values highlighted someway."

"Of course. That's another basic. OK, Jon. You'll have the whole business by the end of next week."

The three men and the other engineers and geologists attending the meeting continued the discussion as to who would do what. Then they broke for lunch, and all were the guests of the Production General Manager, Gene Light, who wanted to be brought up to date as to their findings, and discuss another thing or two.

During the luncheon meeting, oil production in general in the Mideast came up. GM Light brought a staff specialist along and, after a few broad comments, it became clear to all the reservoir people that this staff man, David Roady, had a lot of information that was rather restricted, if anyone was interested.

"Any of you guys interested in knowing a little more about Gulf area production in general?"

Jon felt it was not his place to comment, but Tony immediately replied, "Gene, I think it would be useful information for us all." Actually, Tony was already aware of the latest production research, and knew that what appeared in official reports did not tell the complete story.

Light introduced David Roady, and told a little about his background. Roady was a geological engineer out of Colorado School of Mines, with special post-graduate training in finance and statistics. For several years his principal job had been world oil production analyses and projections, with emphasis on the Mideast.

Over the next twenty-five minutes, he reviewed Mideast production and responded to numerous questions. The overall picture that was painted was grim.

Even before the earthquakes, a number of problems had begun to develop in this oil-rich part of the globe.   O v e r a l l production had climbed in the last few years, but the costs climbed faster; reducing overall profitability to the Gulf nations.

Roady pointed out to the group that sustainable Kuwaiti production had never been regained after the 1990 Iraqi destruction. As the years went by, it became increasingly evident that the giant Burgan Field reservoir had, indeed, suffered irreparably. The oil people knew it, but the controlling politicians forced new drilling, massive workovers, anything to keep the production up, regardless of exacerbation of the reservoir damage.   In that manner, Kuwait expanded its production almost back to 1988 levels, and kept it there. But this procedure hastened the certain decline to come.   Roady's research indicated that Kuwait's twelve-to fourteen-percent share of the Gulf production would have definitely diminished within two or three years. But since the massive earthquakes of last year, now commonly referred to as The Gulf Disaster, did little damage to their production, Kuwait's share might actually increase, even though their actual production would go down.

Iran was squeezing its relatively old fields as hard as possible during the Iraqi probation period when Iraq sold little or no oil on the world market. The last year, Iran had averaged about eighteen percent of the Gulf's 18 million barrels per day average, compared to as much as twenty-two percent only four years earlier. Iran had suffered substantial earthquake damage, but Roady could find no evidence of major reservoir or well damage; it was mostly surface facilities, and a few wells. The Iranians could overcome their share of damage within two years at the most.

The Gulf Disaster was substantially destructive to Iraq. The damage was known to be somewhat similar, but not so extensive, as that in Saudi Arabia. Roady's research indicated that the Iraqis were reporting surface damage as well as could be done, but they were saying very little about serious reservoir damage. Their production had dropped nearly twenty percent from its pre-quake level of 2.6 million barrels per day. Their embargo had ended nearly three years ago, and they had brought their production up dramatically within three months time.

Including their newly developed Paleozoic field inland, Saudi Arabia had brushed ten million barrels per day many times over the last two years prior to the Disaster. They were now going all out to average six million per day. It was clear that this rate could not be sustained without significant new drilling, workovers, recompletions, and surface facility modifications.

In the Ghawar-Abqaiq-Dammam area, all major refinery, gas processing, and petrochemical activities were shut down by colossal destruction. For several months, major production cutbacks were caused by heavy damage to the major Ras Tanura and Qatif port facilities. Some of these facilities were now partly back on stream, and within two years would be back to full stream. If a full stream of oil production was available.

For the incredible quantities of oil produced by Saudi Arabia in the last half-dozen years, production handling facilities had to be massive. There were water treatment plants, gas-oil separation plants, heater treaters, huge flow lines pumping into even larger cross-country pipelines to deliver a dozen or more super-tankers their cargo every day. Many of these elements of the system had been built during the boom days of the early eighties, then mothballed later in the eighties. Demothballing started in the early nineties, and were in maximum use these past few years.

As world production stabilized or started declining in Alaska, the North Sea, Russia, and other non-OPEC countries, OPEC had increased its efforts in every way possible to meet the gradually increasing demand. The demand had been met, with such efficiency that a modest excess capacity existed. Until the Gulf Disaster. Now, with so much in shambles, energy was becoming a crisis. Particularly in the United States, but only slightly less critical in western Europe.

The highest priority now for Saudi Aramco were the ports and the gas plants at Shedgum and Uthmaniyah westerly from Hofuf. Within the next eight to ten months, the gas plants and ports would be back to at least 50% functional and would allow an important increase in Saudi production. It would take some months longer to get to normal 90% or better.

In the last few years, Saudi Arabia, even with its massive oil reserves, had to exert ever-increasing effort to maintain its high rate of production. Massive producible reserves were still there in the giant fields, but more and more water had to be injected to maintain pressure and reservoir sweep efficiency. One pipeline delivering seawater to inject into just part of Ghawar Field, was five feet in diameter. Such a line was necessary to inject the massive quantities of water to keep the oil flowing.

Replacement wells had to be drilled. Only ten years earlier, Saudi Aramco had drilled less than 20 wells per year in the entire country. Starting in the early nineties, more effort was needed to maintain production. The last few years, over two hundred wells were being drilled per year. By U.S. standards of many thousands of wells in most years of the eighties, 200 was small. But when the oil production per well was measured in thousands of barrels per day instead of tens, 200 wells was an impressive effort.

Major workovers were needed to replace old and heavily used casing and tubing. Total costs per barrel produced climbed steadily. Yet, in the world oil surplus of the early to mid nineties, price continued to dance rather wildly around the $20.00 per barrel level. Not much above 20% of the price for a similar quantity of milk, and only a little above 10% of the cost of that much beer.

The other Gulf nations had been experiencing the same sort of problems. Fighting to maintain production share in a fixed price market and ever-increasing costs.

But now, the past problems seemed minor. Those needs for all the Gulf nations to work like fury to stay in place, were now just a dream. Extraordinary, total, even absurd, efforts would now be required to get back to position zero before world standards were altered forever. Even then, this could only happen if God had not ripped the subsurface asunder. And that was still an unknown in so many fields. Including the giant of them all, Ghawar.

Roady, with occasional input from Gene Light or others at the luncheon continued to paint the overall oil supply and demand picture. Light had an underlying purpose for this discussion that he intended to bring out later in the meeting.

Roady quoted from and referred to published research papers from around the world in some of his comments. Particularly the more interpretive opinions that touched on politics more than science and business.

This cost-price squeeze had long since pretty well killed the oil business in many parts of the world, especially the United States and Canada. The great domestic oil business crash of 1992 sank the U.S. oil exploration and production business to its lowest level since the original build-up of the industry in the thirties.

But it was good politics to keep prices low, regardless of the building deficits of production versus consumption. Most of the countries of the world saw the impending price/supply collision, and in the seventies and eighties imposed heavy taxes on petroleum, particularly gasoline, consumption. This encouraged more efficient vehicles and use, moderated consumption, and provided funds for society's energy use needs, such as roads and expressways.

But U.S. politicians were determined to meet the demands of the majority of its citizens, regardless of the outcome, and regardless of the ultimate price that would have to be paid. These men felt that in order to be elected or re-elected, they must consider their welfare first, pleasing the voter second, and the good of the country a distant third.

Congress fought mightily to deny any encouragement to exploration, enhanced production, or anything else that might cause an increase in the cost of oil, or possibly harm the slightest fragment of the environment. Regardless of domestic need for adequate self-sufficiency to prevent chaos in the face of import deficiencies.

The unusual situation developed where gasoline in many other countries cost up to four times that in the U.S., even though the U.S. was using much the same supply sources as these other countries.

The world was far more interested in the Persian Gulf area now than just fifteen months ago. The Gulf Disaster saw to that.

Roady discussed Saudi development, markets, shipping and, most important, prices. Even with sharply reduced Gulf production, total oil sales income was up. The difference between $20.00 and a sudden change to volatile $40.00 to $60.00 per barrel, made a remarkable change in Gulf income. It was a time of great emotional swings between despair on one hand, for the uncertainty of ever regaining productive capacity, and elation on the other, wrought by the huge positive cash flow.

But this group of oilmen knew these times would not last. And as Roady seated himself, and the questions died down, Gene Light decided it was time to present his underlying purpose for the luncheon meeting.

"Well, boys and girls, I guess we need to get a little deeper into the reason for this meeting." Light smiled as he spoke, and looked directly at the two women in the meeting, before glancing around at the nine men. The women were both geologists by training, but working strictly on production and development problems and opportunities. Most of the men were engineers, but several were trained as geologists or geological engineers.

Light continued, "As of this morning, the number of wells with severe downhole damage is over four hundred, counting the Ghawar-Abqaiq complex, Qatif, and several fields in the Gulf. There are something like six hundred and fifty that have some amount of downhole damage in all the fields. We currently have very little oil production from some three hundred pre-quake key producers that made over 5,000 barrels of oil per day.

"You can see the significance to production. Even if all our production and handling facilities, pipelines, shipping, docks, and plants were in normal condition, our production would be nearly two million barrels less than before the Disaster.

"But these supportive elements of our overall business are by no means in normal shape. It will be nearly two years before everything is completely back 100%. Even before the quakes we had various restrictions cropping up because we had been working everything at full tilt for the last two or three years, not taking time for preventive and, in some cases, even normal, maintenance. Without our relatively new Paleozoic production in the overall Riyadh trend, we would be in real trouble. Fortunately that area escaped damage.

"We all know that some of the wells that have started making water may have been altered simply by the oil tilting more off structure. But some of the new water production may be the result of sheared casing, and the opening of water reservoirs. Or, new fracturing may have provided routes for water channeling from deeper or lateral zones.

"We have many wells that suddenly dropped dramatically in producing anything. That is most likely caused by sheared casing or tubing. But which of these kinds of wells should be redrilled? We sure don't want to redrill one that will make water because of the oil-water contact shift.

"As has already been discussed, we've been pushing to keep our production up for several years. Without the Disaster, we would have reached the point of overall decline within another few years. It would have been a very slow decline, but unless the exploration people come up with something new, that decline is as sure as death and taxes. The only uncertainty is exactly when and how much.

"With the quake destruction, we may be in real trouble right now. A very big question is, 'How much is irretrievably lost?' How much can we get back by redrilling?

"Another question: 'did the quakes and possible increased reservoir water movements cause tilts or lost oil in the Gulf fields? Particularly in the Safaniyah-Marjan complex?'

"What I'm building up to is this: We are in desperate need of the P-maps and the subsequent oil-water contact map. For all of the possibly affected fields. Without these maps, we're shooting blind on redrilling operations. We must do whatever is needed to get data to construct these maps. I repeat, not only for Ghawar, though that is most important, but also for all the fields that might be altered. We start with the biggest, and work down. We'll even drill wells for data if need be. Not oil, just data...pressure, chlorides, whatever.

"So, my friends, you see, we need to dramatically increase the level of this project. Where is the oil? Where is the water? Field by field? Where do we drill? Where do we redrill? What say you? How do we do it?"

As Light had been talking, and the subject got more and more complex and critical, absolute quiet crept into the room, and prevailed. When he stopped, there was dead silence for several moments as each person tried to grasp the full significance of what this all meant to Aramco, to Saudi Arabia, to the entire world. And to themselves.

"Gene, I believe you have gotten everyone's attention." It was Tony DeRocca, speaking quietly and slowly, with strength of purpose increasing in his voice as he formed the thoughts in his mind. "Since Jon Burke, our reservoir dynamics consultant, is leading this key mapping, I'd like to know what he has to say."

Jon had been thinking deeply as Light addressed the group, and readily spoke up, "Tony, once we get all our salinity data on newly recovered versus old produced water, and get it mapped, that should go a long way toward identifying water sources. I think that such maps, plus our planned theoretical current oil-water contact map, will be of substantial help.

"We have all been directing our work toward the Ghawar-Abqaiq area. I did not realize the scope of the damage until a few minutes ago. Basically, we can enlarge the effort by getting more people involved. At least in theory, with enough man- and woman-power, we should be able to investigate all the major fields within a few months. But to do the work with maximum reliability, we may need to drill a few data and observation wells. And we will surely have to spend some money on bottom hole pressures, water sampling, et cetera, as soon as preliminary work indicates where and how much."

"Jon, I can tell you this," said Gene Light with determination, "the resources of the entire Aramco Production Department are available to this operation. I will look to Tony and Rashid for recommendations. I hope you and all the others involved will keep them busy handling such recommendations."

All was quiet for a few seconds, then, "Well, boss, I guess we better get cooking' on who, what, where, when, with, and how!" said Tony DeRocca.

"One last thing, people," said Light, "please get an attack plan to me tomorrow. Detailed planning can follow. But try to address those five 'W's' pronto!"

With that, the meeting broke up. Tony released everyone except Rashid and Jon, with notice that another meeting of this working group would be held in this same conference room the next morning at seven a.m. It was now 3:20 p.m.

"Rashid, how many people can you put on this, assuming maximum effort?" asked Tony.

"As you can imagine," replied Rashid, "I've been thinking about that for the last half hour. One thought I had was to ask Exploration for some temporary help. If they go along, we should be able to put at least twenty-five people on the project."

"Good idea. I'll try Exploration here. Jon, what do you think?"

"There are two main considerations: We need a lot of data, and we have a lot of ground to cover. I would like to have an hour or so to think about the data approach, then get together with a plan. Could we meet here again about five?"

"Five is fine," said DeRocca, "but let's do it in my office. Meanwhile, Rashid and I'll do some planning."

Promptly at five, Jon walked into Tony's office. "Are we ready?"

"You bet," replied Rashid. "Tony and I have a few thoughts on the who, with, and when parts!"

For the next three hours solid, the three men discussed, argued, and reviewed the many sides to the question. They talked about the damaged Burgan Field in Kuwait, the possible water channeling in some parts of the Arab D and other reservoirs that might have resulted from the heavy Saudi production during the last few years. How the reduced Iraqi production would impact. How the current high prices would hold, and what they would engender elsewhere.

They were particularly concerned about the new faulting that had displaced the Jurassic Hith Anhydrite overlying the Arab D in the Ghawar trend. This sealing wax material would probably reseal in a few months if it had not already done so. None of them really knew how fast anhydrite would meld back together after being fractured, nor how much the melding would be enhanced by the introduction of water from below along such fractures.

But as long as the new faults did not completely displace the anhydrite beds to a position opposite other beds, they believed it would reseal quickly. Jon remembered a paper he had read on this subject long ago...he couldn't remember much about it except that anhydrite would rapidly fuse back together under subsurface conditions of pressure and heat, once broken...and that the presence of water hastened the process. He just couldn't remember if 'rapid' was minutes, hours, or weeks, but it surely was not years.

This defined a new problem: Study existing and new faults with great care to see if the throw, or displacement of beds along the faults, exceeded 75 meters, or about 230 feet. This was the minimum displacement that would likely create an ongoing escape for underlying oil into overlying Lower Cretaceous Sulaiy limestone beds. Of course, the many thinner anhydrite beds in the Arab B and C zones that overlay the Arab D, would have sealing effects in addition to the massive Hith anhydrite. But since these Arab anhydrites were rarely over two or three meters thick, it wouldn't take much of a fault to completely displace them.

Another thing to research: Anhydrite resealing.

They made notes about how teams would be formed, what they would do, who would lead them, and where each team would work.

There would be salinity teams, bottom hole pressure teams, data computerization teams, and detail structure/faulting teams. Finally, Tony would assign a single literature research team of two young, bright geologists.

The data would all be computerized so as to combine maps most rapidly and effectively. Jon had long ago developed a particular contouring program that was ideal for the construction of potentiometric, or P, maps, as well as the intermediate hydrodynamic and structure maps required to get to the all-important oil-water contact map.

Computerization provided for automatic head calculations with variable salinity, pressure and other data. Then, automatic posting of the data to maps, and the contouring of the data. One of the neatest computer programs would subtract one map from another, and contour the resulting map!

But computers could not get and interpret the data. Or tell whether it was pre- or post-Disaster. This would be a grinding, time-consuming job.

A main concern was obtaining data in critical areas near the fields. The only way to do this was to drill investigation wells. Then, in some selected wells, it would be desirable to case and perforate the wells so as to observe possible changes in head, salinity, or fluid type. Oil might move into water zones, or vice versa. This was an enormously expensive way to get mapping data. There had been very little of this sort of drilling anywhere in times past.

But this unique time required unique effort, and that was what Aramco was prepared to do, with the full support of the Saudi government.

An underlying, but widely recognized among the technical people, purpose of all this massive effort, was the desire to appear to the world that 'all is well; nothing we can't fix right away.' And to thereby diminish the effort of others, especially in the Western Hemisphere, to find or develop new production. The current heady oil prices were sufficient for Americans to go after heavy Canadian, Venezuelan, or Alabama heavy oil; Utah shale oil, Canadian tar sands, U.S. secondary and tertiary reserves, new high-risk exploration, very deep waters, and all the other places where oil was available. At a price.

The Gulf Disaster had created massive stirrings of oil and water. Water in oil. The old nemesis of oilmen everywhere.

But, in problems lie opportunity. At the right price, high as possible, especially if the world markets could be fooled long enough, Saudi Arabia could come out of this Disaster making money!

The only dilemma was the risk to planning. If plans were made to make major expenditures based on the assumptions of continuing high oil prices and they did not hold, disaster could be waiting around the corner. If such expenditures were not made, it would be difficult to maintain sufficient production rate to keep the world from knowing the degree of the production shortfall.

~ ~ ~ ~ ~ ~ ~ ~ ~ ~ ~ ~ ~ ~

CHAPTER 9

Uncertainty

It was now October, a little over ten months after the Disaster, and things were in turmoil in the upper Gulf. Iraq had suffered more production loss than Iran, and had unused shipping facilities. Iran had also suffered severe production loss, but a good part of the damage was not in the subsurface, it was instead in the handling and shipping parts of the business. Their ports and storage had been severely damaged, to the point that only lighters, or small tankers, could be loaded. Their sales had dropped nearly three million barrels of oil per day, but they could sell more if they could only develop a way to get it out. Overseas shipping with loads of only ten or fifteen thousand barrels of oil per shipload was highly impractical.

Iraq had surplus major ship facilities at this time, but were not inclined to allow Iran to deliver small vessel loads to their super-tanker docks and storage for trans-ocean shipping.

Discussions led to anger, and anger led to threats. Iran let it be known that if Iraq would not make a reasonable deal with Iran for the use of their idle, or near idle, Iraqi shipping facilities, then Iran would see to it that Iraq would not have them either. Iraq, being filled with pride, would take no such threat without proper rejoinder. This led to Irani raids with small arms, to which Iraq responded with larger arms.

Finally, after three months of such minor skirmishing, Great Britain and France, along with some aid from others, managed to calm the hotter heads, and develop a mutually advantageous plan. Britain and France were not being exactly benevolent in the operation. They needed the oil.

So it came to pass that here, near the end of October, Iran was about to deliver its first of many lighter-loads of oil to Iraq's super-tanker outlet, and pay Iraq a two-percent royalty on every barrel so shipped. Iran was losing money compared to what they could do with their own port outlets, but this way they could take advantage of the current high oil prices to hasten their reconstruction.

It was a good deal for both countries. Good Arabian and

Persian logic finally prevailed. With a little steering from the outside.

Jon punched in the 14-digit number. The telephone rang. "Hello?"

"Hello yourself, Rashid. This is your Houston analyst."

"Glad to hear from you. Got all those numbers from last week crunched?"

"Yeah, and Rashid, it ain't too good."

"Thanks for the warning. Lay it on me."

"Well, you remember we talked about those three structurally high wells in the 'Ain Dar part of Ghawar that had started making a lot of water? When you put in all the new measured data you guys got on the wells in that area, I get a local anomaly on the P-map. It's a clearcut pressure sink. We have a leak."

Rashid Ben Rimthan was shocked. "Jon, are you sure? That's very unexpected."

"Old friend, I know that. I ran parts of the data three times, and contoured it both by hand and computer program. There is simply no mistake. Oil has moved into that sink, probably mainly from the southwest. The sink elongates in that direction. My present interpretation is that the cross fault juxtaposes Arab B to the overlying Cretaceous Sulaiy, fractures tie Arab D to B, and oil from all Arab zones is leaking into the Sulaiy."

Silence. Neither man could think of anything to say at the moment. In a subdued voice, Rashid said, "Jon, I think you should gather all your work and come over for a few days. Don't tell Tony the full story until... well, maybe you should... I really don't know. Maybe it's best you tell Tony what you know, then tell him you're coming over for all of us to check and review, before making a firm interpretation."

"I kinda thought you might say that, so I checked schedules. I can be in Dhahran late Thursday, day after tomorrow, the 16th. Before I come, I'll finish the Udayliyah-Hofuf maps so we can tie it all together better."

"OK Jon, see you Thursday. Take care and try to sleep some on the way!" They both knew Jon had a jet lag problem going from Houston to Saudi Arabia that usually left him feeling rather rough the first day or so there.

"Will do," Jon replied. "I'll rent a car in Riyadh, and show up at the office so's we can get a little done on Thursday."

The previous week, Jon had received six 3-1/2" disks full of data in individual well format. Most of the data was already on his hard disk, from prior work. But, as a check, the Dhahran office had rechecked and reloaded all the data they had in the entire Ghawar-Jubail trend and easterly to production and dry hole information on Bahrain Island.

Since new data was intermixed with old on many of the wells, Dhahran had just copied it all, including production histories, core data and much more, in addition to the pressure and salinity data. It was enough to fill several large books. But Jon was interested in only a part of it all at this time.

Later, they all planned to make various interactive maps combining elements of several sets of information, such as production rates versus salinity changes, etc. This was the sort of thing Jon anticipated Rashid had in mind to do when he arrived in Dhahran.

Jon had replaced his hard disk files of the Saudi data with the new files. Then he booted his potentiometric map (P-map) program and withdrew selected data from the files. His P-map program almost immediately created a "true head" set of data for the many wells. He then saved that file, booted the first of his contour map programs, a geologic structure template, and proceeded to make the first of several contour maps, a current structural contour map.

After getting the contour map on screen, he used a mouse to make revisions of faulting and contours to fit human rather than machine concepts, and saved the map.

Altogether, considering the large area involved, and the numerous mapping templates to be used, Jon made thirty-six maps. With his computer, he did in six days what would have taken six months back in the days when Dr. King Hubbert first developed some of these fundamentals at Shell's Houston Research in the forties and fifties. The basic concepts had not changed. The way of doing it had changed drastically.

The first P-map spelled trouble in capital letters because it showed an area of relatively low pressures. Fluids would tend to move from surrounding areas into this low, or "sink." Jon knew immediately that this indicated a leak into overlying formations. He also knew how disastrous this could be.

Such an escape route could drain the entire 'Ain Dar part of

Ghawar Field. The sink was only a few tens of feet head at most, but it was distinct. And it had not been there prior to the Disaster. To Jon it was no longer a matter of leakage, the only question was, how much?

An additional startling result of the P-map and Jon's first effort at the new and current oil-water contact, was the effect at the structural saddle that separated the 'Ain Dar and Udayliyah parts of the giant Ghawar ridge. The map indicated that the oil mass had been tilted more to the northeast than prior to the Disaster. Enough so that the low point of the saddle might now be above the oil-water contact. If a well were drilled now in that saddle, it would probably make oil instead of water as in past wells drilled there.

This continuous oil linkage across the saddle could increase the 'Ain Dar leakage loss by causing part of the Udayliyah oil to move into the pressure sink. Jon had not covered this point with Rashid in the telephone call. It would be better to discuss it in person. There could be ways to combat this possible loss, by drilling more wells in and near the saddle.

But, Jon thought, all this can wait now 'til Thursday. I gotta finish the Udayliyah work today, then come by here and pick up my files in the morning.

He decided to tell Tony DeRocca that he had talked with Rashid and they thought they should study the data together first before presenting him with an interpretation and recommendation. He called Tony, and the plan was approved.

There was no quick and easy way to get to Saudi Arabia. It just took the better part of two days, even with the recently improved flights that involved only one airline change, in Cairo, Egypt. What with the one flight change in the U.S., plus the airline change in Cairo, plus flying time, and lost time flying eastward, then a drive from Riyadh to Dhahran (or another flight that gained little time), it took over thirty hours from Jon's home in Houston to the office in Dhahran. Then, allowing a few hours of sleep at Dhahran to adjust for jet lag, nearly two days were gone. But Jon was accustomed to the trip and had it worked out pretty good.

He left Houston early on Wednesday morning and, as planned, asked the receptionist in Dhahran for Rashid Ben Rimthan at 3:35 p.m. Thursday. Jon sat down to wait. The door into the reception area burst open in slightly under two minutes, and Rashid strode over with his hand out in greeting.

"Jon, I'm sure glad to see you. The last two days since our talk I've been imagining all sorts of things. Let's get to the conference room. I asked my secretary to round up the others right away."

They shook hands as Rashid talked, then started for the door while their hands were still grasped.

"You know Rashid, I almost get the feeling you are in a hurry!"

"You got that right, Tex."

"Wow! Any time you call me that, things are about to pop!"

They continued down the hall. "Jon, do you have all the key maps?"

"Oh yes, all folded neatly in my bulging briefcase. Of course I couldn't bring everything, but I have the disks so you can print out anything you like."

There were three men in the room when Jon and Rashid came in. Within thirty minutes, there were twelve men and three women, all geologists or engineers. Clearly, all the teams were vitally interested in the P-maps and oil-water contact maps Jon had made.

As Jon displayed the 'Ain Dar area maps, nothing was said. All eyes were on the lazy contours that curved into an elongate pattern displaying a clearcut pressure sink on the P-map, with similar contours on the oil-water contact map showing a local slight rise. The maps showed an existing situation as if there was a very large well in the south central part of 'Ain Dar, producing oil at a very high rate.

"The basics are very clear," muttered Rashid, "from here on, we're just detailing. There is a leak. And, looking at the structure over here, it is associated with the west Hofuf area faulting." As he talked, he pointed to a particular northwesterly trending fault in that area. "And this is the one that our before-and-after data indicates at least ten meters vertical movement during the quakes."

Jon commented, "that's what I figured. The additional movement on that fault was just enough to place the upper Arab Formation beds opposite basal Sulaiy, with each of the Arab Zones being juxtaposed to overlying Zones."

Jon was describing a scenario where Arab D oil could move across the now-increased fault into overlying Arab C or B Zones, then from there on up through that porous Zone, or along the fault plane, into successively shallower Arab beds, past the Hith anhydrite, and finally into the Lower Cretaceous Sulaiy porous limestone beds. Once in that formation, the direction of migration was speculative, but probably mostly horizontal in that formation.

"I think it would be a good idea if each team, Jon, and I, all independently, would make an estimate of the leakage rate," said Rashid. "We all know that is like measuring mountain heights on the far side of the moon, but we have to try. With several independent approaches maybe we can get some idea of the parameters, if nothing else."

"Also," he continued, "make estimates of where the oil might go after it gets in the Sulaiy calcarenite." They all knew that the calcarenite, or granular, sandy-like, limestone, layers would provide good migration routes for the leaking oil. Provided the newly increased faulting did not provide still further upward outlets to younger, overlying layers.

"And finally," Rashid said, "we must develop a specific plan for development. Take all the time you need to do these little things, just so you have your answers by Monday afternoon at 1600 hours! That is the time of our next meeting. Here. In this same room."

The group then quickly departed to get to work, knowing that there was no way to be ready by Monday afternoon when it was now Thursday evening.

After three and a half days of intense research and computations, involving both daytime and night work over the weekend, the teams stumbled to the Monday meeting as planned. All were rather tired, and a few were obviously near mental exhaustion.

Observing the general lack of alertness, Rashid spoke, "seems to me we are all pretty beat. So, let us make general comparisons, outline our next step, then all go home for a good night's sleep."

For the next hour, they made comparisons of the many estimates. These proved to be surprisingly similar, and a crude pattern began to take shape. Almost all the leakage computations were based on best estimates of the cross-sectional areas through which oil was moving, along with permeabilities of such areas, and head drops across the flow channels. Since the head drops were low, the main leakage driving force was gravity: the tendency of less-dense oil to rise through water.

The leakage was probably between twenty and one hundred thousand barrels of oil per day. Where this oil would finally trap was speculative. Being lighter than water, it would tend to migrate upward in the water-filled formations, provided sufficient permeability existed. Either in porous rocks, or along the fractures or faults.

It might move laterally some distance, perhaps less than ten kilometers, and trap in the upfolded porous Salaiy calcarenites. But, since these beds had no capping seals of massive anhydrite such as the Hith Anhydrite overlying the Arab Formation, the leaking oil might escape along fractures and the new or pre-existing faults into ever-shallower beds until no traps existed.

In such case, the leaking oil might eventually find its way to the surface, as seeps, or be lost in many minor traps here and yon along its migration paths.

When compared to the overall production from Ghawar, this leakage loss was relatively small. But it meant huge volumes of wealth would be lost over a period of months and years.

There were some compensating factors. As some of the oil leaked off, and as the regional northeastward water movement in the Arab D Zone decreased back to a rate comparable to past decades, oil would cease moving across the structural saddle from the Udayliyah area to the 'Ain Dar and a good part of the leakage would stop. This was so because at least two-thirds of the leakage was in the 'Ain Dar area, with the rest being south of the saddle.

Of course, these geologic events would transpire slowly, and it could take years before final adjustment.

The primary course of action the teams developed was to do heavy additional drilling in the 'Ain Dar area so as to produce that area at maximum rates and thus distort the pressure sink and perhaps reduce the leakage. Or, if nothing else, get as much of that oil as possible before it leaked out.

All in all, they concluded that with massive effort, including perhaps a hundred and fifty new wells, total production from the Ghawar complex could be worked back to around seventy, possibly eighty, percent of the pre-Disaster production levels. It would take at least two years and very heavy expenditures. But if prices remained high, it would ultimately be profitable to do so, and leakage losses would be minimized. Even so, at best, leakage losses would mount into a few billion dollars at current oil prices.

And, this massive effort was only to minimize the Ghawar leakage. In addition, to get total production back to near pre-Disaster rates, the teams all concluded that dozens of additional wells would have to be drilled on the north and easterly flank areas of both Ghawar, Abqaiq, and possibly a few other of the large Saudi fields. This drilling was required to minimize oil losses caused by the dynamic effects of increased regional northeasterly water movement in the Arab Formation.

The increased northeasterly slope of the oil-water contacts in the several major fields, wrought by the increased Arab Formation water movement, caused huge quantities of oil to move downdip on structures into upper flank positions where the reservoirs formerly contained only water.

Over several years, perhaps tens of years, as the temporary northeasterly regional Arab water flow diminished to the normal rates during pre-Disaster decades, the northeasterly tilting oil-water contacts would move back to the vicinity of pre-Disaster positions. But at least half of the oil that moved down-structure on the fields would stay there as residual oil, or left-behind oil after depletion of an oil reservoir. Only a large number of new wells in these flank positions could minimize these losses.

The next morning, Tuesday, the engineers and geologists reconvened for orders.

"I think we can wind up our work to a recommendation stage by tomorrow," said Ben Rimthan to start the meeting. He briefly outlined the conclusions that best fit all their work, then divided the people into two groups: one to do economics, and one to summarize their findings and technical recommendations of actions needed. He called for a meeting at 4 p.m. the next day.

Neither of the groups was to work on timing of the actions, or expenditure recommendations. Rashid, with Jon's assistance, and the help of their accounting and economic groups would prepare a specific recommendation of action.

During this entire evaluation period after the first day's explanations, Jon Burke had been called from group to group to explain or discuss reservoir dynamics. His was a position of consultant and advisor, and he was accepted as the final authority on all matters involving the movement of oil and water in the reservoirs. He had little to do with economics and recommendations, except of a general nature with his friend, Rashid.

On Wednesday, the teams, along with Rashid and Jon, reviewed their work and developed final interpretations, conclusions, and recommendations. The next morning, Rashid organized the voluminous reports and files, and started his report that summarized findings and recommendations. While he worked on his report, others assembled the backup maps and reports for presentation to Houston.

Rashid's biggest job was to try to reach the balance between desirable development work, and economically feasible recommendations. He obtained voluminous cost and price data from the teams and company finance experts, then assembled the possible different courses of action as well as his own specific recommendation based on the tons of work done.

Individually and together, the teams concluded that there was no evident way to economically bring total Saudi production rates back to pre-Disaster levels, at current or reasonably projectable oil prices.

But most of it could be recovered. Of course, with sufficient expenditures for new wells and processing equipment, production could be brought completely back to pre-Disaster levels, but it was not economically sound to do so.

In the economic evaluations, it was necessary to consider the present value of oil that could be produced in the future with existing wells if new ones were not drilled. Even though barrels produced ten years in the future were worth less than half as much in dollars or reichmarks as if produced now, considering the value of interest on money, there was a limit to available money to spend now. Also, other variables such as oil prices under different conditions of supply, the cost of borrowed money, and other things, got involved in the economics of further drilling.

The operations plan they developed considered the necessity of recovering oil that would otherwise be lost, as a first priority. Then, as to efforts to get production back to pre-Disaster amounts, economic feasibility was the governing factor.

By late afternoon on that Thursday, Rashid started his report. It took only a few hours to prepare his conclusions and recommendations regarding the geological and engineering work; each of those reports summarized the findings and recommended corrective actions. His major effort was directed at that ever-controlling factor: How much can we spend to get what back?

A very large factor in the evaluations were future price predictions. The people on the teams were geologists and engineers, not soothsayers. No person knew for sure what oil prices would be in one year, let alone ten years. If prices in ten years were still comparable to about half the price of milk, as now, the projected amount and rates of expenditure on development and re-development of the rich reserves was economically feasible. If prices drifted back to a quarter or less that of milk, as they were before the Disaster, the re-development pace would have to spread out over tens of years.

For their recommendations, the reservoir and development people assumed that prices would continue at current rates with two percent annual inflation escalation. Among their many different evaluation scenarios, they developed programs with pre-Disaster oil prices, with two percent inflation escalation, as well as programs assuming the above base case, and another using five percent annual escalation rather than two percent. All in all, they developed four economic program scenarios, each with three different production and three different cost variances. Overall, the presentation yielded a good picture of investment and profitability.

Rashid worked into the night trying to evaluate the economics presented in the reports, then assemble them all into a coordinated, economically reasonable plan. With two variations to the plan: worst probable, and best probable. By 9:20 p.m., he was completely punchy in his thinking, and realized it would be best to refresh his mind before continuing.

Within thirty-eight minutes, he had driven home, eaten a fish dinner Yasmeen had kept warm for him, brushed his teeth, and was in bed, drowsily considering the morrow. He had set his alarm for five a.m.

At ten minutes before six the next morning, Rashid opened his car door at the office building, and stepped out into the quiet beauty of a still, October day in this ancient land of Arabia. He had a fruit and bran breakfast at home, took the last sip on his cup of coffee, and placed the cup back in the car before closing the door. Within five minutes, he was correcting the last page of his report from the evening before.

He worked without letup. His secretary was immensely helpful. She too had arrived early in anticipation of his rush. She typed, ran errands for more information, got help to make additional computations, researched a few pieces of data, brought coffee, and prepared his sack lunch when the time came.

Rashid had asked Yasmeen to make him a lunch, as he had done many times when time was critical. She always came through with a tasty sandwich, chips of some sort, a few cookies, and fruit...usually a banana. That way, Rashid could work non-stop, right through his lunch. He didn't do this often, but still often enough that he and Yasmeen were quite familiar with the routine.

Late that Friday afternoon, after everybody had time to get to work in Houston, some nine hours earlier, Rashid called Tony DeRocca. They arranged a meeting there on Monday. He suggested that Tony might be sure that General Manager Gene Light was available for a second presentation.

Within a half hour after the meeting in Houston got under way on Monday morning between DeRocca, Ben Rimthan and Burke, Tony said, "okay, men, let's stop right here. This is too big for me. Let's get Gene in on it right now."

He called Gene and told him that the research teams had developed important information, and perhaps we should all meet in the fifth floor conference room.

Gene responded, "Tony, I'd like to do it, but could it wait until tomorrow morning? I have a budget meeting with two other department heads in ten minutes."

"Gene, I think you better come," Tony said quietly.

"That big, huh?"

"Yep."

"Okay, I'll be there in ten minutes."

And so began what would later be looked back on as the beginning of the most dramatic operation changes in super-giant Ghawar Field, by far the largest single source of oil on this planet, since the early days following its 1948 discovery.

By now, approaching eleven months after the Gulf Disaster,

the oil supply situation was becoming critical in many parts of the globe. In most countries, refiners and suppliers kept a bare minimum of twenty days storage, often double that. That is, they had sufficient storage available to handle most supply deficiencies created by political concerns, ship damages, strikes, weather, or other problems. But the storage planning did not include wars or other major catastrophes. As a result, spot shortages of gasoline, lubricants, and petrochemical feedstocks were widespread. It was approaching general shortage.

Although the news media highly dramatized the oil shortages, in reality, no real suffering existed. There were inconveniences, but no pain.

The news media did have one story essentially correct. The Gulf Disaster did curtail Mideast production, and it would be difficult to get it back. Better analyses occurred in oil industry trade journals.

These publications made specific estimates of production shortages and when supply would be replenished. They pointed out the long lead times necessary to drill the many replacement wells needed in Saudi Arabia, Iraq, and Iran. At this time, they knew nothing other than rumors regarding unrecoverable losses. This information was closely guarded by the producing companies. And the only way to make up for unrecoverable losses was by new exploration. Lead time for substantial production from new exploration would be at least eight to ten years. Possibly never.

The world was being advised that OPEC was indeed unable to meet current demand, and it was best to prepare for shortages. Politicians attempted to assuage fears by promises that all would be back to normal in a short while. The companies just had to redrill a few wells here and there.

Gene Light and Tony DeRocca listened to the presentation. Light asked numerous questions as the meeting proceeded. Finally, he asked, "so what you're telling me is that overall, several hundred new wells will be required, just in the Ghawar-Abqaiq trend, to get that production back to about eighty-five percent?"

"That's about it, Gene," replied Rashid. "Other fields in the Safaniya-Marjan trend will also require considerable workovers, redrills, and a few new wells. But we believe the only place we're actually losing oil is the 'Ain Dar structure. And, we can lose more of the dynamically displaced oil on structure flanks if we don't drill and produce it before it tends to move back.

"We think the order of necessity is full and major effort in those two areas first. Then we can attack repairs to get back to normal production on the other fields. We think the only way to get our total production back to around ten million barrels per day, is to find new oil. Most likely in the Paleozoics."

"Man, that is one tall order," said Light. "Let's call it a night for now, sleep on it, and get together at eight sharp in the morning. I need a little time to better grasp the picture you've presented, and think about how to shift resources to combat it."

The meeting continued the next morning, but no new facts were developed that mollified the situation. There was no systematic approach to be taken other than something fairly close to the one recommended by Ben Rimthan. Sure, it could be modified, or shifted somewhat in timing, but bottom line, it was clear: Attack the 'Ain Dar leak first. That was oil being lost every day, not likely to ever be recovered.

Then, or within a few months after 'Ain Dar startup, go after the oil shifted off-structure. And if there's enough money available, increase exploration promptly. Only in these ways was there a reasonable chance that Saudi Arabia would be able to meet and sustain demand anytime in the future, whether two years or twenty years.

In December, a Houston financial expert, David Morse, wrote a column for the Houston *Post*, at their request. In preparing for the article, Morse called on several of his friends, including Jon Burke, for information about what was really happening behind the scenes.

"David, I can't tell you anything I know about Saudi Arabia, whether positive or negative, but I can tell you a few things I've learned from other workers as to Iraqi and Iranian problems."

"Okay," said Morse, "what's the situation there?"

Jon described what he had heard other than from Aramco sources. Most of what he recited was from *World Oil* and *The Oil and Gas Journal*.

The article by Morse pointed out that, for all practical purposes, worldwide storage was pretty well used up and, except for limited areas in and near the Mideast, a two-week delay in production shipments would result in significant shortages. Of course, for a price, Mideast oil production could be brought back to normal rates. But that could result in an additional hidden price: future supply shocks. He concluded that at current oil prices, averaging nearly $50.00 per barrel in the United States, world supply could be brought back up to a point some ten to fifteen percent below that of a year and a half earlier. But it might take several years to accomplish.

At current production rates, there would be sufficient local or temporary shortages that price spikes, up to $100.00 per barrel were likely. But at higher costs, people would find ways to reduce consumption until supply and demand were balanced fairly well, at which point prices would drop back to the $50.00 area. He predicted a rather volatile price scenario. One that would put a cap on new U.S. petroleum development and exploration because of the unpredictable price. A firm could ill afford to develop new oil when the net values after operations and taxes might only balance or equalize investment.

Morse, quoting Jon Burke and two other successful oilmen he knew, stated in his article, "the great majority of oil in the world occurs above eight thousand feet. In fact, almost all giant accumulations, those that account for the stability of the world's oil supply, are above such depth.

"Another key factor to major oil accumulations, is that they are rarely subject to abnormal pressures, that is, pressures that indicate closed or confined reservoirs. Abnormal pressures, typical of depths below nine or ten thousand feet, where gas is commonly found, are a primary cause of high well costs. Thus, in normal pressure environments, wells can be drilled relatively cheaply. This is a key reason why all of the more obvious structures in the world have long since been drilled to depths normally associated with oil production.

"Even in some of the wildest jungles, or remote arctic locations, obvious structures have been tested to some degree for oil.

"In addition, any oil field that is to supply as much as only ten days of world oil demand, will cover a relatively large area. Rarely would such a field have less than twenty to thirty square miles areal extent.

"Because of the relatively shallow depths and inexpensive well costs to search for oil, in almost all of the known oil trends in the United States, there simply is not room between existing wells to fit a giant field. One needs no science or engineering to make such a conclusion...just a map that shows where the wells are located.

"The same conditions prevail in much of the rest of the world. This all leads to the conclusion that finding new super-giants, such as a few of the Mideast Fields, is highly unlikely. The largest oil field discovered in North America in the last several decades, Prudhoe Bay in Alaska, would meet world demand for hardly six months.

"The resounding conclusion to all this is that new oil supply will come mainly from known accumulations. And those that have not been fully exploited are waiting on sufficient real price to do it.

"Don't expect the Saudis, or the Iranians, or anyone else to bail us out. We must face facts as they are: Energy from oil is both limited and depletable. Our oil supply surplus may have crested. For all time. More can be developed and produced if the price is high enough, but at higher prices, other energy forms and conservation play a larger and larger role, putting an effective cap on the long term real price of oil.

"This is not to mean that 'all the oil has been found.' Far from it. There is no doubt that relatively large accumulations are to be found. Probably the largest being trapped by rocks pinching or wedging out in some fashion to trap oil. These are called stratigraphic traps, and do not require faults or anticlines to form traps and oil fields.

"But these are very much more difficult to find. Under some conditions, new seismic techniques can find these obscure traps that otherwise are mostly found by serendipity. That is, through random drilling, or accidentally found while looking for something else.

"The overriding factor in all new major oil exploration is cost. The new seismic procedures are very expensive compared to the old ones. Deep water drilling is very costly. Remote operations in undeveloped regions of the arctic and jungles carry a huge price tag up front.

"Nonetheless, new fields will be found. Some of them quite large. Huge quantities of oil will flow from them and yield vast fortunes to the hardy and fortunate.

"But the quantities of production, the reserves, will with relative certainty, be minor in relation to world needs.

"Oh, and by the way, don't expect to be bailed out with methanol, alcohol, or other substitutes to any large degree. In general, alcohol costs at least 50% more than gasoline, even at present prices; unless government picks up part of the bill with our taxes. Since methanol can be produced from natural gas, it is cheaper. Automotive natural gas itself, being almost all methane, is still cheaper, and cleaner burning.

"But there are limits to natural gas, or methane, availability. It costs more to prepare vehicles to burn methane, as compared to gasoline. And the large increase in urban fleet use of natural gas in recent years has sopped up most of the domestic, Canadian, and Mexican supply that can be made available for those purposes. Large scale expansion of natural gas or methane in automobiles has a hard road ahead. The vehicles cost more, and the new supplies of natural gas, or methane made from coal or wood or some other organic material is available only at increased cost.

"What about alcohols? The beauty of alcohols is renewability. These can be produced from grain, grass, wood, and other renewable resources. There is an end someday to depletable oil, natural gas, and coal. But alcohol can be made so long as a livable planet exists. Again though, the problem is cost. And to some degree, pollution.

"At this time, there is no way for private industry to produce any feasible alcohol fuel cost-competitive to gasoline. But perhaps in a few years that disadvantage may disappear. As the cost of oil and natural gas increase.

"As to pollution, alcohol is better than gasoline, but not so good as methane.

"The best approach to a better supply-demand balance is to better use our fuels. This will require American acceptance of smaller cars, more mass transport, more car pools, better insulation, and the host of other things that can be done to better use what we have.

"Finally, let us hope that the American dollar does not weaken more as a result of our insatiable desire for foreign cars and a host of other products. If it does, and the Saudis shift from dollars to, for example, the more stable German mark, for their currency exchange base, our cost for oil will go up. Which weakens the dollar more, which makes Mideast oil and many other foreign products more expensive, and on and on...until we run out of money or desire..."

Evidently, Morse's article was not widely read or believed. In January, the United States Congress and a hesitant President, in response to shrill news reports, and their perception of public anger, took action. They reinstituted the Windfall Profits Tax that had been invoked in the eighties and revoked after some ten years. The oil companies were just making too much money with these high oil prices, and it was simply unfair for them to gouge and reap such resounding rewards at the expense of a suffering people.

This act convinced most oilmen that it was economically suicidal to make large expenditures with about a five-percent chance of developing substantial reserves when, if successful, would be taxed to the point that net revenue would only exceed investment four or five times. If there were no chance of getting twenty-or thirty-to-one on investment, why risk money with odds of success about one in twenty?

So, again, Mexican Standoff: just like the downfall of the industry in the late eighties. True, those who had the oil now, found and developed in years past, would make great profits at $50.00 up per barrel. But additional expenditures in, under, and around those same old fields, to get oil otherwise unrecoverable, was hardly worth the risk, at $50.00 per barrel.

The result was that, at this time, a year after the first real reductions in oil supply, oilmen were not rushing to develop more oil in the United States. To a lesser degree, the same was true in the rest of the world where most of the oil had long since been found.

Shortly before Christmas, two United States aircraft carriers and their support ships moved into the Persian and Oman gulfs. Shortly thereafter, a similar British force joined them. These were followed by French warships and, finally, a Japanese troopship. Their respective governments claimed that they were there only to maintain peace and tranquility in a volatile area.

This was truly so. But even more, they each were doing their best to be sure that their shares of oil kept flowing. In the right direction.

~ ~ ~ ~ ~ ~ ~ ~ ~ ~ ~ ~ ~ ~ ~

CHAPTER 10

Real Aftermath

It was late December, just after Christmas. A year after the Gulf Disaster. J.C. Wolfort was number nine in the gas line at his third-choice Shell station on the western outskirts of Lincoln, Nebraska. And this was after leaving home at six in the morning on this, his "get gas" day. He had already tried his first and second choice stations closer to his farm outside Beaver, Nebraska. The Exxon place he used in Beaver ran out of gasoline the day before, and they were curtailed to three tankers a week. The next was due tomorrow. Wolfort needed fuel today if possible, because tomorrow he needed to haul supplies in preparation for the coming grain harvest.

His second-choice station, in the old Milford Crossing community, had vehicles lined up halfway around a block. He was afraid that place would run out of gas before he got to the pump.

His *C* stamp entitled him to fourteen gallons per week, for his pickup. In expectation of problems ahead, he had traded his older dual wheel-pickup last January for a smaller one. He couldn't haul the loads he could handle with the old truck, but he could manage fairly well on the *C* stamp ration. He had found that he could get some of the occasional larger haulings done by truckers, and even rail.

Wolfort was by no means convinced that this supposed world shortage was anything other than a money grubbing conspiracy but, he felt that it was probably somewhat true. And it really didn't make too much difference either way. Gasoline was for sure short around here, and he just had to learn to cope with it.

Damn, it sure is gettin' cold. Wish they would hurry up before I freeze!

At the same time, after working most of the day in his machine shop in Biarritz on the Bay of Biscay, Charles Fortier found himself number 14 in line for 30 liters of petrol. He didn't need much for his small truck, but his business would fail if he was unable to make scheduled deliveries of his mostly farm and dairy machine replacement parts. He heard from one of his customers less than an hour ago that a tanker truck had just delivered to a nearby tire and auto repair store that also sold petrol. Fortier immediately drained fifteen liters of his truck's tank into a storage can, so as to make room for a full allotment, and left for the store.

A little after five a.m. the next morning, Dr. Georg Goepfert pulled up in his BMW at the super pump in Heilbronn for his 30-liter allotment. He found only two others getting benzene at that early hour, both at other pumps. And he would not be here except that this was his day for Emergency Room calls, starting at six a.m. At least there were some benefits to this early hour business.

It was much the same in most of Europe and North America. It became apparent some six months earlier that governments would have to take some kind of rationing action to prevent doctors from finding all the fuel gone to joyriders. It was the same as during World War II. When there's not quite enough to go around, at least make sure there is some for those who need it to keep the wheels of business, commerce, and medicine turning.

Gasoline, whether called gas, gaz, petrol, or benzene, was often gone within hours after tanker deliveries to regular retail outlets. The United States had gone back to the old World War II rationing stamps system until things could be sorted out.

At least that was what the government said. Actually, government had no magic answers and knew full well that the rationing was unpredictable. It might be over in months, or it might take many years. All depended on how easy it was to get fuel, and how much of it we demanded.

As had been the case for several months, there was no effective storage; perhaps three days here, three weeks there, maybe two months in a very few places. All the major urban areas were in short supply, with little more than emergency storages.

But the general feeling was that, with care and good fortune, the shortages would cause little more than inconvenience for the time being. It would all be alright in a few months. Just adapt.

Persian Gulf oil production was slowly climbing, but still down by nearly a quarter, and world production down by nearly ten percent, compared to pre-Disaster. The Saudis found that the Paleozoic fields, mainly in the general Riyadh area, while very good, are giants only by normal world standards: a few billion barrels in the best fields.

These reserves were nothing like the older Mesozoic and

Tertiary fields that are now in irretrievable decline unless many more wells were drilled to get reserves out faster.

New finds in South America, and major Russian development provided local surpluses and some relief on world scale. However, the decline in U.S. exploration and development in the last ten years because of the low prices of oil, world abundance, and increased demand, was now felt. There was no excess production.

U.S. oil production was well under half its demand in the last year before the Gulf Disaster. And, in the U.S., it was now clear to all but those with their heads in the clouds that substitute energy from alcohol, water, coal, wind, and the sun could hardly dent the heavy demands without substantially increased energy costs.

The big question all across the world, but particularly in the United States, as New Year's Day approached, was "how long will it last?" The general feeling was it would all be back to normal in a few months.

The old 'Trickle Down' theory was now in full force. In reverse.

Reduced oil and gas production made gasoline and natural gas supplies more expensive but, even at the greater costs, there were not enough energy supplies to meet demands. Reduced vehicle operations wrought reduced vehicle sales. This cause plant suspensions and layoffs. Which reduced purchase of parts and basic metals and plastics. Which caused more layoffs, plant mothballings, reduced imports, and less of everything all around.

There was an ample supply of one thing: Finger pointing. Politicians were busily engaged in blaming each other and various 'foreigners' for the strong economic downturn. It was not depression yet. Nor economic collapse. Too many people were quite busy shifting gears in new directions. All aimed at managing lives without quite so many cars. Making refrigerators, roofs, air conditioners, and a host of everyday machines last longer. Changing jobs. Moving.

They were finding all the ways to meet this energy dilemma that had been thrust upon them unexpectedly early. It was known to be lurking in the shadows of an unknown future, but so soon?

Of course, these copings further depressed the economy. But there were some offsetting elements to the overall picture. People began to look for country homes, farms, places where living costs were less, where food could be raised, where a family could manage to survive without so many urban luxuries. This added new jobs, new ventures for those who would furnish these needs.

Industries aimed at repair and maintenance thrived. Whether it was automotive parts, refrigerator repair, or heater replacement, there was a strong demand.

Service industries never skipped a beat. Drugs and medicals continued normally. Only basic industry, steel, aluminum, manufacturing, chemicals, were hit; some worse than others.

Most people kept their jobs or adapted successfully when laid off. Some looked to welfare from overstressed governments. There was indeed a lot said and to be said about how such a small thing as six to ten percent sustained reduction in world oil supply could have so much effect. But there it was. The effect was real. Perhaps one should be grateful the supply loss was not fifteen percent. Or twenty.

One industry that was sleepily arousing was the United States oil and gas business. Many independents foresaw long delays in plentiful oil supplies, and believed that the $5.00 per MCF of natural gas was here to stay for a long time. One of these was Jon Burke.

It came upon him in a rush, as if being slapped. Jon was sitting comfortably, reading a historical novel about a Virginia family during the American Revolution. It was a cold, rainy evening in December, just before Christmas, at the old Cook farmhouse just off old El Camino Real east of Nacogdoches. He and Lee-Anne came to the quiet beauty of this woodland retreat at least once per month. Sometimes for a week or more. It was rather cozy to be so comfortably ensconced in the big platform rocker Jon had place in the alcove off their bedroom.

Bon Tierce. It hit him suddenly, and was immediately followed in his mind with a jumble, a chaotic assemblage of words: gas and condensate...left behind...$5.00 dependable...pressure maintenance...secondary recovery...would sell now. How much worth? Maybe five, ten million...net half million, maybe million to Lee-Anne and me. Why not? This is the time. Need to call John Venable and see what he thinks.

But it was too late tonight. It was now nearly eleven. So Jon just turned in his chair and gazed into the pitch darkness outside his window.

"Hello?"

"John, this is Jon Burke, even though it's Sunday..."

"Well, Jon! You surprised me. I'm sure glad to hear from you, what in the world are you up to?"

"First off, forgive me for calling you at home on Sunday..."

"Jon, we've fought too many problems together to let Sunday bar our talk; go ahead!"

"I'm not sure at this point whether it's all good, or just a dream, but I had a flash! You remember Bon Tierce?"

"How could I ever forget it. You struggled to get it put together, agreed to take a piece of it and could never get anybody to take the last third. 1991 as I recall."

"Yeah, it was 1991. John, do you remember the deal's details?"

"Oh, yes. Indeed I do. Going back into an old field in Colorado County to develop secondary recovery of Wilcox gas and condensate left behind after fast production and near-hole condensate blocking."

"You got it."

They discussed the deal and Venable agreed that the timing was good to try it again. He also agreed to take about twenty percent if Jon could get it and carry it off.

Immediately after hanging up, Jon called a key friend.

"You have reached the Welker abode, and you may address your wishes if you so desire!" This was a typical phone answering for Don Welker, an old landman friend of Jon's who lived in partial retirement at his lake home near Conroe.

"Well, Don, I see you haven't changed too much since our last talk, even though it's been over two years!"

"Hello yourself, Nacogdoches whiz. To what do I owe the distinction of such honor as you bestow on this poor soul?"

"Poor soul, hell. You're the original artist himself in exciting lessors in their contribution to oil finding!"

"I know, I know. But what's up, old buddy? Tell me about yourself, Lee-Anne and, finally, whatever is really on your mind!"

Don Welker was a petroleum landman who Jon had known and worked with many times over the years. During the last ten years or so, between contracts, Jon occasionally generated drilling prospects and turned them to others to prosecute. While employed with Mosbacher Exploration, Don worked with outside independents to obtain drilling deals suitable to Mosbacher. The two got together on a deal and became friends. Don had retired to his lake home some seven years ago, and occasionally brought a deal to Jon, or helped him on a prospect.

It was Welker who brought Bon Tierce to Jon shortly after he left Mosbacher. Don came in on through a friend who was a lease owner there. The group that had the marginal field had insufficient funds to redevelop the deep zones there, knowing that their leases would eventually die from non-production if nothing was done to develop additional production. They were anxious to farmout their rights, keeping a small interest after full payout to new investors.

Jon Burke described his intent to resurrect Bon Tierce if it was still available. Welker asked him to hang around an hour or so, and he'd find out. He called back within an hour. The deal was still just as it was. Don agreed to secure the farmout agreement and do the necessary land and legal work in exchange for $10,000.00, payable if and when drilling commenced, and one-half percent overriding royalty.

Thus it came to pass that within twelve hours after his flash, Burke had an old deal revived and underway.

In the late 1870's, a Frenchman moved into this Colorado County area and selected an area that he felt would yield good grapes for wine. He planned to produce wine and sell it by the tierce, or 42-gallon barrel. It would be good. So he named his farm Bon Tierce. The label stuck, not only for his farm, but for the creek that flowed through it, and the oil and gas field that straddled the creek.

Coincidentally, it was that same barrel, the tierce, that was adapted by the U.S. oil industry as their standard measure for oil.

In many reservoirs below ten thousand feet, high gravity oil, or oil-like liquids that condense out of solution in a gas, called condensate, fill part of the pore spaces in sandstone or other porous layers. This is particularly true in the Texas and Louisiana Gulf Coast region of the United States.

In sandstones, the sand grains are normally coated with connate, or original, water that also fills about twenty-five to forty percent of the pore space. The remaining pore space is filled with hydrocarbons that migrated into the reservoir and displaced part of the water. Sometimes in these deep sands, the hydrocarbon is a gas, with considerable liquids in solution. Sometimes it is liquid, with considerable gas in solution.

When drilled, cased, perforated, and produced, the main production is gas. With attendant condensate or oil. If the original reservoir fluid was liquid, gas breaks out as the fluid enters the hole and finds ever-decreasing pressure as it flows upward. If the reservoir fluid is gas, it flows out and up the borehole, dropping out liquid as it approaches the borehole and journeys upward in ever-decreasing pressure.

In either case, if the reservoir is subjected to strong pressure reduction because of fast gas production, so much condensate collects around the borehole that it becomes more and more difficult for the gas to flow through it.

Finally, the gas back in the reservoir, well away from the borehole, does not have enough remaining pressure to force it through the condensate around the hole, and the well gradually dies down to a very slow production rate of mostly condensate. This is called condensate blocking. There are various ways to overcome it, but if prices are too low, it's not worth while to do anything.

Over the next few weeks, Jon spent most of his time on Bon Tierce. All he had to do was review his maps, check back with the lease owners to see if the deal could be reconstructed, then check with some of his friends who had formerly had an interest in the deal. The owners were happy to have Jon come back in and try to develop the property that was now kept alive only by the high oil prices.

The old gas wells were dead, but two oil wells, some forty years old, were still making a few barrels per day, along with several dozen barrels of salt water that they let flow downhill to an abandoned well that gravity drained the water back into the formation.

There had been no new drilling anywhere in the area, so the maps were still valid without correction.

It took three full weeks to do all the telephoning, faxing, re-drafting, economic evaluations, get drilling bids, and update the original report and recommendation to the new economics. What had previously been an iffy deal was now clearly profitable.

Basically, the deal was to drill a well, take pressures in the multiple sand reservoirs between ten and twelve thousand feet depth, produce virgin stringers or layers, and analyze and evaluate gas cycling potential. If the measured pressures proved to be at least forty percent of original as Jon computed and expected, in one or more layers at least fifteen feet thick, Jon's analysis indicated such a reservoir was worth gas cycling.

Since three of the sands were over twenty-five feet thick, and covered at least eight hundred acres, such gas cycling could recover perhaps a few million barrels of condensate or oil.

As planned here, the gas cycling consisted simply of pumping gas down one or more boreholes into the cycled sand zone, let it move through the reservoir, collecting and pushing the condensate and oil left behind, then producing it from other boreholes into the zone. Such cycling required buying gas to supplement produced gas. But most of the injected gas would be recovered and sold some five to ten years later.

It was a costly operation, but if oil prices stayed at $50.00 per barrel, or thereabouts, Jon figured his investors could get their investments back at least three times within seven to nine years.

By New Year's, the deal was set. Jon had no trouble getting North Ventures, a large independent in Houston, to take forty percent of the deal and operate the project. John Venable took twenty percent, Jon kept two percent plus one-and-a-half percent override, and Jon's other investor friends took the remaining twenty-eight percent working, or participating, interest.

If the deal was as successful as Jon's median projection, he would end up making a half-million dollars, his buddy Don Welker would make a hundred thousand or so, and his investors would make over a million dollars per ten-percent interest.

In this event, the field would average about 1200 to 1800 barrels of condensate or oil per day for the first five years.

All over the oil patch in North America, similar ideas were being developed...many to be prosecuted. Based on past history and odds of success, it was reasonable to expect a hundred or so such additions, maybe even a few hundred, every year in the United States. If so, such new production might offset part, possibly even most, of the domestic natural decline, and keep it to only a few percent per year.

It was now winter time. The dramatic reduction in world oil supply had commenced only a little over a year earlier.

~ ~ ~ ~ ~ ~ ~ ~ ~ ~ ~ ~ ~ ~ ~

CHAPTER 11

Finality

It had been a hard winter. December and January saw a total of sixteen days in New York City with temperatures equal to or below previous lows. Gratefully, snows were infrequent and light. But fuel was inadequate. This winter had started only a year after the Persian Gulf Disaster, but massive oil storage had long since been effectively depleted to only a few days' supply.

By mid-January, heating oil cost was double what it had been the previous winter, triple its cost three years earlier. Of course, the cost had been driven up by the unusual cold weather demand, but there was the other factor also: Supply was about five percent below normal, and all local storage had been used up by shortly after New Year's. This left suppliers dependent on incoming shipments only.

Natural gas was also a problem for much the same reasons, but the shortage was manifested differently. Pressure was so low that many residential units were either automatically shut down, flames went out, or the fire was so low that thermostat-controlled blowers ran continuously, putting out heat at a rate below heat loss from the outside cold. This occurred most frequently at night, with the result that families often arose to a house that was colder than when they went to bed, and well below freezing.

An unexpected dilemma was electricity. Everybody knew extended cold brought heating problems. But rarely did electricity ever fail during winters, and even when it did, it was restricted in areal extent. Now, the plants fired with gas began to have severe problems with resultant brownouts, and some blackouts. Urban electric heat became undependable, whether it was furnaces or hot plates.

Colder homes meant plumbing problems. Each new day in late January brought a new set of water restrictions. Families would wake up to find no water. Pipes, somewhere, were frozen, or burst. Or exposed city mains were broken and with the unrelenting cold, anything frozen stayed frozen.

Even water previously drawn by families who prepared ahead, froze in bathtubs, buckets, and other containers inside the house.

Fortunately, this kind of ice was usually not very thick and could be broken to get at the precious water.

Still, even with all the personal and public planning, the frozen environment resulted in multiple obstructions and, after a few days of no bathing, heavily restricted basic water supply, and continuing inadequate heat, serious health conditions developed in the urban areas, especially in the sorely deficient housing of the poor.

Day and night, city officials and crews struggled to solve the water supply quandary. For each barrier removed, new ones developed. They steadily lost ground in face of the persistent freezing weather. In most of New York and New England, the temperature never rose above freezing from Christmas to the end of January. Then, another specter crept upon the frozen cities.

Inadequate medical aid. Hospitals and medical facilities were overloaded by frostbite and hypothermia victims. Then they were further restricted by inadequate heat, reduced electrical supply, and insufficient fuel for emergency generators.

February brought the heavy snows that had so far been missing in this "hundred year" winter. It hit the northern US but was particularly heavy in the across Ohio and western New York State.

Fortunately, temperatures were not abnormally low, but stayed below freezing for most of the month in many areas, preventing snow melting. Perhaps the heavy snows were caused by the unusually low temperatures of the previous two months.

The streets and roads, even major highways, became clogged. City personnel could not keep up with snow removal and after two weeks of February, began to run out of fuel. New supply was restricted significantly to pipelines because tanker trucks and trains were limited by uncleared snow and ice.

Coal-fired electric power plants ground to complete shutdown by mid-February as all storage was consumed and new supply was inadequate to operate turbines.

Reduced fuel supplies further hampered snow removal until, finally, by the third week of February, over two-thirds of all activities in the northeastern United States had been brought to a halt. In many places, people were in a rigid survival mode.

Now, there was a general shortage of food, as well as water and heat in any form. Even funerals were unavailable to those who succumbed to this horrid winter. To add to their misery, the many affected families had to endure the temporary storage of their departed members in unused cold rooms, hallways, garages, or wherever/whatever available. From western Ohio to the New England coast, there were eight thousand, six hundred and fifty-six deaths attributed to the dreadful cold and fuel shortages. Most of these were elderly, quite a number in nursing homes or special-care apartments.

The greatest sadness came from the many deaths of very small children who could not cope with ongoing cold with resulting hypothermia. Most of these tragedies were suffered by the poor.

But, as has been said in so very many ways in so very many languages, over eons past, all things must change. And in this case, for the better.

In March, temperatures climbed to normal levels and changes, but with some flooding resulting from unusual snow melts. However, modest flooding, even that wrought by residential broken water pipes, could be handled. Perhaps there were inconveniences, but at least trucks could roll, trains could rumble. Heat was available. Food and medicine, services and care, all the other pieces of a complex society could move back to that wonderful "normal!"

Many of the dead were not buried until March. There were thousands. The poor of New York City and Boston bore the brunt. The United States Congress passed special legislation in April providing seven billion dollars aid to the heavily stricken areas across the northern part of the country, a goodly part of which was designated for those who had lost family and had little or no money. Many wage earners had a forced, unpaid vacation of several weeks.

April brought a beautiful and bright spring, as if to say, "here, miserable people, look at my delightful gifts!" Spirits rose with the good weather and plentiful supplies of all kinds. People found a myriad of ways to get their lives back on target after this winter that came to be called the Winter of Disaster. It was so called not only because of its disastrous nature, but also because it had been harshly worsened by the Gulf Disaster.

In June, the Iranian Oil Ministry advised OPEC that they would reduce their production by five percent. Their explanation was that they needed more time to complete their upgrading, and did not want to create reservoir damage by over-production. Actually, this was not the case.

Because of their relatively minor subsurface damage from the Gulf Disaster, Iran was able to get their production back to near their pre-Disaster levels quicker than Iraq and Saudi Arabia.

By this time, it was widely known and publicized that Saudi Arabia would probably not exceed eighty, maybe eighty-five, percent of their pre-Disaster production for several years, if then. Iraq was expected to reach about ninety percent, perhaps more.

But Iran was now back onstream with nearly four million barrels of oil per day. At a price. The Iranian oil-production people resisted the sudden major production buildup, but the politicians enforced it. These men, partly driven by personal rewards, maximized production in every way they could. The leaders explained to the ordinary Iranians that if ever there was a time to capitalize on good prices, this was it. Even in the face of warnings of water channeling, gasification, and other reservoir damage, the politicians said, "we will not be curtailed by these old wive's tales. Modern needs and common sense dictate taking advantage of our unusual opportunity." Plus their own pocketbooks.

So, in these very old fields, the larger of which had been producing since the second and third decades of the twentieth century, production was wide open. Pumps, power lines, pipelines, supplies, and men were pressed to maintain, exceed if possible, production. This had invoked irreducible decline in most large reservoirs. It had caused widespread reservoir and downhole damages.

The high production levels could not be maintained and, instead, certain reduction would prevail. It could be predicted that Iranian production would sink steadily over ensuing years, probably averaging some five to 10 percent per year over the next ten to twenty years, then perhaps at a lower rate. Provided major efforts were maintained to keep production up. Without such efforts, the decline would be steeper.

It was the story of the United States production decline that started in the seventies. In another language, with different parameters, but just as certain.

Without still-higher prices, perhaps until the price of oil per volume compared to the price of drinking milk, Iran would now be a lesser force in OPEC.

The announced June reduction was not to "preserve capacity." Iran simply could not continue their high rates.

Even with the sharply higher oil prices now available, where crude oil in the United States had climbed from a quarter of the cost of similar volumes of milk to over half, supply was short. OPEC could not meet demand; the North Sea was in decline, along with the United States and much of the rest of the world.

Even the spate of large, new reserves developed in the former Soviet Union, after Western oil technology was applied, could not stem the tide. The increase in all Eurasian oil fields outside the Persian Gulf made up for less than half the Gulf Disaster reduction.

There were natural declines in Alaska, Asia, everywhere. Some new oil was required to just keep even.

Current prices would indeed generate more discoveries, more development, more of everything that promotes more oil. But, mega-giants, such as the top dozen or so fields throughout the world, could probably never be duplicated. Too many wells had been drilled in too many places to allow more than a few, if any, additional such finds.

As early as 1960, a few researchers who applied a great deal of geologic research, along with a generous dosage of common sense and sophisticated projection methods, had predicted a diminishing number of really meaningful new discoveries, anywhere on Earth. They were right. The total reserves of the dozen largest oil fields discovered in the world in the last forty years did not equal even a quarter of that from the same number of fields in the prior forty years. Yet during that same period, demand saw multifold gain.

Large oil reserves now could only be created from expensive, often environmentally unsafe, attacks on heavy oil, tar sands, and oil shales.

The Gulf Disaster did not cause this developing energy change, it simply triggered it.

By summer, oil supply had crept up to a fair balance with demand in most places. The Mideast was down only about twenty percent, and because of price-encouraged additional drilling in known productive areas, world supply was down only five or six percent compared to pre-Disaster.

Oilmen knew that much of the world increase had been from

known reserves; relatively little of total world demand came from new discoveries. We were just using up what we had at a faster rate. Pass the problem on to future generations!

The big unknown was the next winter and heating oil needs, with crude availability for storage essentially non-existent.

How can a worldwide loss of only five or six percent of world production cause such problems of supply and cost? Because supply/demand had been on thin ice for the last 3-4 years before the Gulf Disaster, caused by increasing world demand in the face of slowly eroding supply via old fields depletion and declines without sufficient resupply. New discoveries were held down by low prices, and ever-compounding political and environmental restrictions.

Actually, in the year before the Disaster, oil prices, after inflation, were considerably lower than 20 years earlier. It had the effect of making other sources, such as alcohol and methane, even more difficult to develop economically. And all this in the face of bigger cars, bigger engines, more controls on development of reserves, and less interest in conservation because gasoline was so cheap.

Environmental activists blamed pollution as the cause of the previous hard winter. They now proclaimed lurking disaster as a result of continued loading of the atmosphere with CO_2. These proclamations were often made from a standpoint of ignorance of the past. The activists were concerned only with present conditions they were convinced were adequately and properly measured, and pushed hard for CO_2 controls. They pointed to computer analyses which proved that carbon dioxide in our atmosphere created a blanket below which our planet would become increasingly hot. If we didn't stop such pollution, we would wipe out life itself!

Unfortunately, the computers suffered somewhat from GIGO, "garbage in, garbage out." As had been recognized by some researchers in the last two years, more carbon dioxide in the atmosphere is not by any means all bad. In fact it might be good!

Geologists knew all along that the earth's atmosphere in times past had CO_2 levels several times the present, during periods of prospering plant and animal life probably similar to the present, with probably less desert areas. In fact, with or without mankind, atmospheric carbon dioxide content would naturally cycle up and down over time. For tens of millions of years in the past, atmospheric

CO_2 levels were much higher than in the present. The dinosaurs breathed air that was much richer.

Some research physicists and chemists had now shown by actual testing, that with increased atmospheric carbon dioxide, plant life would tend to flourish and water would tend to be conserved. Biologically induced, cooling, cloud cover would tend to increase. And perhaps have the opposite effect of that predicted by some environmentalists wearing knowledge blinders. Such increased clouding would tend to reduce daily maximum temperatures which, when combined with the tendency for night-time temperatures to increase, would create an improved environment.

Based on the most recent worldwide glaciation cycles, our planet is apt to be within a few thousand years of the commencement of another such cycle. A little extra heat might help.

Even though some of the governmental and environmental controls forced on industry, including oilmen, were questionably founded, they were nonetheless there. These, when added to the natural market limitations, were the causes for U.S. shortages in these latter years of the twentieth century.

Analysts and businessmen could see the handwriting on the wall. It was quite evident that the United States could not continue to sell gasoline for a quarter to half the price of the same fuel in Europe. That led to many conclusions: Energy prices were sure to increase as government gradually recognized and accepted that as the only way to engender efficiency, conservation, and the creation of new supplies. Manufacturers knew that the wave of the future would be transport in the mode of Europe and Japan: More public transportation, and more efficient vehicles.

In October, these factors began to soak in on business, and the response was strong in that area which first recognized big changes ahead: The New York stock market. It dropped nineteen percent in one week, followed by a slight increase the following week, then an eighteen percent crash the following week.

The Depression was on. It would take several months to recognize it, but the basics were now quite evident. Wholesale reductions and changes in automotive construction caused plant closings, massive layoffs, and heavier governmental welfare programs. These would have ripple effects through the steel, plastic, chemical, tourist and, finally, all major businesses. Then it would spread overseas, if it had not already set in there. Higher energy prices, massive negative balances of trade (meaning fewer U.S. jobs), ever-increasing demands of governments, schools, medical care, insurance, and inflation heaped additional burdens on the ordinary American.

The only business that resisted the stock selloff and work onslaught was, ironically, the energy business. Next to food, shelter, and medicine, this was the next most important necessity. Though stock prices were off, the days of massive energy layoffs were over, at least for this time.

There would be heavy U.S. oil field workover and development work, but little growth in U.S. exploration until the risk investors could believe that prices were fairly stable. Only heavy and very high-risk exploration, for the more hidden traps, or very high-cost operations, could meet long-term oil and gas needs.

The preacher described his life, his recent despair as his body became more racked with pain and deterioration. It was Jon's old college buddy, Dr. Michael Randolph Williams. Cancer had finally claimed this old Marine. Jon and Mike roomed next to each other in the Corps dorm at A&M. Mike studied pre-med, Jon geology. Mike worked to get his medical degree, then externed, interned, and finally was a doctor! Then he began his struggle to reach his life goal: to be a GP in the old sense.

He was a good doctor, didn't hesitate to go to the home of his regular patients when they were really sick. He not only understood medicine; he understood human nature and common sense. He had a good practice; made a good living. Until he failed to recommend an MRI for a new patient with a back problem.

That patient's back problem got worse. He took workman's compensation from his employer...after suing for it, and got $4000.00 per month for the rest of his life. Then he sued Dr. Williams for malpractice and won a five million dollar claim. Against a doctor whose insurance paid half, and left Mike with nothing but a home and practice, plus one car. At age fifty-two. Mike then contracted cancer and hung on for the three years it took to kill him.

Jon could not help but compare the fall of this old and dear friend to the oil business. They both worked so hard and so long to build something good. Then through the acts of others, timely aided by an act of nature, came the sudden demise.

The Burke family was fortunate. Jon was now in demand for about as much contract work as he wanted. And the first well at Bon Tierce found a new ten-foot pay as well as two zones totaling forty-eight feet that were almost ideal for gas cycling. He had plenty of income now. Sufficient that he and Lee-Anne made significant contributions to their favorite charity: Education.

They didn't choose the brilliant to aid. They found a way to encourage the ordinary to seek skills and a better life through the use of their hands.

For most, times were hard. There were real concerns that the US might collapse under massive new welfare burdens on top of a huge debt, and deficits that could no longer be reasonably controlled. Or at least, Congress and the Administration certainly lacked the courage to try to control even the deficit, much less the debt.

People were moving back to the land in droves. Unemployment approached the twenty-five percent of the Great Depression of the thirties. It was 1932 all over again. To millions the basics became paramount: Food, clothing, shelter.

No longer was truck driving demeaning. Or farming not cool. Nearly half of the population sought work in any way, any form.

Massive mortgage abandonments created numerous bank failures. With deposits in danger of no government protection. So the Federal government pushed bank mergers and other temporary approaches to the basic problem of unsecured debt. Their objective: any delay in meeting these cash demands was better than trying to satisfy them now.

Governments could hardly find funding for basic security and entitlements. Even some of the entitlements were in jeopardy.

The people would survive. Just how was uncertain. Some might not make it. But all in all, with increased efficiencies of food and other basics production, coping would not be so bad as it was for the dust-destroyed Okies of the thirties.

The politicians, the news media, and a great part of the people, looked for and found the bright spots, the happy affairs, the positives. The cheerful music, the cheap entertainment, the togetherness so evident in the thirties, was found again. This too, they said, shall pass.

There was general acceptance now that cheap energy was probably a thing of the past, although it was expected that after readjustments, new design, added efficiency, most of the old luxuries would be recaptured for the "common" man. It would take time. But it could be done. And there would come a time, maybe only a few years down the road, when energy might be inexpensive. Not cheap, but not expensive. And definitely more variable.

Alcohol would become more and more useful in automotive fuel mixes. If gas prices held firm, the domestic oil and gas industry would find ways to supply enough gas for the ever-increasing demand for compressed natural gas, liquid petroleum gas, and liquified natural gas, better known as CNG, LPG, and LNG. CNG and LNG were preferred because these were nearly pure methane, which save, hydrogen, were the least polluting of all automotive fuels. LNG was a tad better than CNG because it was essentially all methane.

Clearly, the day was close when very little gasoline or diesel fuel would be used in urban bus and truck fleets.

By the fall of the year, it was no longer difficult to refill automobile tanks. Things were back to normal so far as gasoline lines were concerned, but less gas was being bought. And more CNG, or other fuels were being used. It was the major increase in automotive use of the new fuels that kept U.S. demand about in balance with supply. Except for these non-gasoline fuel additions, there would be shortages.

It was a cold Sunday evening, November 29th, at Woodland, the old Cook farmhouse in the woods near the Oak Ridge country store on State Highway 21, El Camino Real, east of Nacogdoches.

Lee-Anne came in bearing two brandy glasses, each with a carefully measured one and a half ounces of liquid. One was cognac, with a touch of drambuie, the other amaretto and cognac.

"I thought you'd never make it!" Jon said as he laid his newspaper down. "Did it take that long to put the dishes in the dishwasher?"

"Well," returned Lee-Anne, "there's just a bit of other work I have to do to clean up after dinner. You'll survive!"

"Maybe so, but I'll survive a lot better with this. Prost!"

Lee-Anne replied, "Prost!"

Most evenings the Burkes had a drink together after dinner. It seemed to help with their stomachs and sleep. Or so they were convinced. Besides, it felt good! They had learned the "Prost!" from some German friends many years before. It meant about the same thing as "Cheers!"

This particular evening, they were sitting in the alcove off their bedroom. They had a light mounted on a pole about fifty feet from the house back in the woods, behind their bedroom. As they sipped their cognacs and talked, they kept looking out into the beautifully lighted woods.

Occasionally a deer could be seen. Sometimes a squirrel, or raccoon, with his mask making him look like a bandit. One time they saw a skunk, with the clear white stripe down his back. Gratefully, nothing excited it before it left the lighted area. Often, at the far edge of the lighted area, only eyes were seen. If the animals were looking toward the light, eyes were always the first marker to Jon and Lee-Anne that another being was nearby.

Actually, they didn't know if many of the animals they saw was "him" or "her," but out of habit, ordinarily used the masculine designation unless they knew the sex. Which in the case of birds in this area, Lee-Anne usually knew. Sometimes, Jon knew. But not as often as Lee-Anne.

"How's things going at Bon Tierce?" Lee-Anne asked.

"Pretty good. Our net income is up to nearly $3,000.00 per month for both our small working interest and override. If the cycling works, after a lotta expenditures, the net should be two or three times that. For a while! Maybe three or four years."

"Infinitely better than nothing!" she replied.

"You know, honey, we're fortunate. I'm so grateful that we have enough money to pay our bills, live pretty much as we want, and still have some left over to give away."

"Well! If I had my way, we wouldn't have so much to give away. All you wanta do is save money to give away!" Lee-Anne smiled as she repeated her little tease she used occasionally at appropriate times.

"Okay, but I'd rather give it to some pore sufferin' kid than bet it on horses!" he teased back.

"How about buyin' gold?"

"Well, I had sense enough to sell it. And besides, that's not as bad as the horses!"

Back in 1990, Jon had bought ten ounces of gold as a hedge against severe inflation. After about three years of no gain and storage costs, he decided this wasn't much of an investment, and sold it.

Lee-Anne looked out into the woods for a few moments, then said, "you know, Jon, we talked for years about how tenuous total oil supply was. We just thought war would be the stifling force, not earthquakes. And now, all this depression that it triggered."

"You got that right. Triggered. The forces had been building up for years for an old-fashioned depression. The Arabian Gulf earthquakes and resulting shortages weren't the total cause. They just triggered something that was gonna happen sometime anyway."

"Yes, we know that. We also know that the feds couldn't keep on spending the way they were, that so much company and personal borrowing created weakness. But I think most people didn't know or didn't care."

Jon thought a bit, then said, "yeah, you and I can sit here and make our wise statements, nod back and forth affirmatively, but it doesn't make the slightest difference. We are in a small minority. I think most people are too interested in what they can get from the government for nothing or, who make money, like some lawyers, at the expense of other's sufferings, instead of creating it through invention, ingenuity, or jobs. Like auto manufacturers or drillers. Or lawyers who shape their deals, their agreements. It doesn't help for you and I to agree, or to even see things the way they truly are. Something has to happen to alert the masses. Unfortunately, it's only when we have chaos that governments and the people see what they have done."

"So what do we do, mighty warrior?" said Lee-Anne perkily.

"First, get off my soap box!" laughed Jon. Then more seriously, "spread the word, honey, I guess that's about all we can do. It's finally up to the masses. The same masses that need chaos to engender enough selflessness."

"There just are no easy ways," replied Lee-Anne. "It's hard to expect anyone to place the good of the community above themselves."

"Only through education. Maybe," said Jon. "At least that's my hope. And I personally think we have to learn how to educate more of those who work with their hands. The brainy kids have no problem getting scholarships. It's the broad average who have the problem."

Lee-Anne turned and faced Jon. "And you know what, my husband, maybe some day more people will realize that there are no free lunches. Somebody has to pay. Some way."

"Oh, I think there is one more major element to reaching Utopia," said Jon.

"Yes?"

"We humans have to recognize that we don't all have to have three-bedroom, brick, air-conditioned, homes with built-ins, and two or three cars, to make it."

"You did a calculation on that here a while back," said Lee-Anne. "Let's see. If we were to live just the same as most farmers did in the thirties: Frame house, no electricity, no plumbing, no built-ins, no medical insurance, no car, no fancy clothes, plain food, 100-pound sacks of wheat flour, a hog and a cow, and no honky-tonkin', what was it you came up with?"

"In today's dollars, starting tomorrow, a small family could make it pretty easy on a hundred dollars a month. 'Course, they'd hafta do a little gardening and cannin', do their own house building over several months, maybe a year, but a good, steady hundred dollars would do it."

"And laugh just as much," said Lee-Anne.

"And play cards and eat divinity or chocolate candy every once in a while!"

"And play music with neighbors for entertainment."

"And have just as much time for reading Plato or funny books as now!" Jon said with a chuckle.

"Maybe more time!" laughed Lee-Anne.

"And you know what else, my Queen?" said Jon.

"Yes, my lord and master?"

"Let's go to bed!"

"Oh, do you have funny ideas?"

"At our age? Who knows... sweetie-pie," whispered Jon.

Twenty minutes later, they were in bed. Jon was lying on his back, just about to doze off.

Lee-Anne whispered, "Honey, in a thousand years, do you think anybody will know this Depression even existed? Or have the slightest care if they did?"

"I doubt it," said Jon sleepily and he rolled over and began to drift off into fantasy land.

A thousand years. About like one page in five hundred encyclopedias of Earth's history.

End Of Book Two

It had been six years. Rashid carefully guided the old horse around the larger rocks that lay scattered in the trail leading around the rocky, sparsely vegetated *jabal*. Wundeen enjoyed the rides out from his home, the canyon corral. He was not quick to gently allow anyone to mount him except his lord, Rashid. For his lord, he trotted readily to be saddled for an outing. And tried to not to betray his advancing years.

Rashid looked around him carefully. Yes, this was about it. He worked his way through the rocks down into the *wadi*. It was quite dry. No water this time. No spring. All was quiet with Allah. He was at rest.

Rashid Ben Rimthan remembered the visit here six years ago quite well. That had been the beginning of a marked change. Oil was his life now, just as it was then, but he, as well as others, had to adapt to changes. Both in his science and his personal world.

Allah had been kind to him and his beloved Jasmeen. They had their home in the city, and also their Ehleebeyt, their "high home" in the mountains. He suspected that Ehleebeyt would become even more important as they grew older.

Well, nothing had changed here in these six years. It is just like it was then. Probably just like it was sixty, or even six hundred years ago.

Rashid dismounted and walked up the *wadi* toward the spring of six years past. It was not necessary to hold Wundeen's reins. Rashid simply draped them over the saddle horn and Wundeen followed along just like a boy might have done.

There is the outcropping, and...there is the fracture, the spring. And it is damp around it. No moving water, none even visible, but clearly, it was not very deep. Maybe only a few feet.

About an hour later, after more walking, contemplation and looking at the geology, the story in the rocks, Rashid mounted up. Wundeen worked his way slowly down the wadi, past the damp earth at the old spring site. Looking back at the damp earth as Wundeen walked away, Rashid thought, you look so bland, so quiet, yet in you lurks an unusual capacity.

A capacity to make that which provides life sustenance. And a capacity to announce change in the land, this world of ours.

And change would come again. Not if. Only when.

End of Epilogue

APPENDIX

THE ARABIAN LINK

PRINCIPAL CHARACTERS:

(In approximate order of appearance).

All characters are ficticious unless specifically noted as "Real", who are actual persons.

James Jonathon Burke: Geologist, b. 9/15/10, called JJ.

Charles Homer, his father, b. 1883.

Alma, his mother, b. 1887.

Mary Jane, older sister, b. 1908.

Elizabeth Ann, younger sister, b. 1914.

Ruthanne Cook, b. 5/12/15.

Bill Stroud: Socal Field Coordinating Geologist.

Suzanne Stuart: Train pal and girl friend of JJ.

Huey Lyman Larsh, JJ's mapping partner.

Yahiya Ibn Rimthan: Fictitious younger brother to **Real** Khamis Ibn Rimthan; guide to JJ and Huey.

Fuana: Yahiya's wife.

Rashid Ben Rimthan: Yahiya's son & friend of Jon (Book 2)

Yasmeen: Rashid's wife.

Abdul Jamban: Young driver for JJ.

Zaki Ahmed Khaled: Sheik and friend of JJ.

Askra: A falcon.

Al Clark: A District Geologist in Houston, 1937.

David Hatcher: Seismologist, work w/JJ on fictious Dulce discovery.

Dewell Davis: Rig pusher, Dulce discovery.

Henry & Flora Khulen: Land owners, Dulce discovery.

Spartan James: Black yardman/painter...well-read. B1c13.

Sam Swartz, B1C14, Core driller for JJ.

Elmer Roach and Roger Evans, geologists, JJ's core drill (CD) crew.

Bob Killgore, geologist on Larsh CD crew.

Charlie Dye, Seismic plotter & radio/instrument repair specialist.

Captain Del Roca: Captain of *El Caballo*, 1/42 to Cuba.

Jaimito Azul: Cabin boy on *El Caballo*.

Continued

*Some of the following very real exploration
pioneers are mentioned in the story:*

Doc Nomland: **Real** Chief Geologist, Socal.
Fred Davies: **Real** Socal geologist; in Bahrain 1930.
Robt P. (Bert) Miller: **Real** Socal/Casoc/Aramco (SCA) Jubail District Geologist.
J. W. "Soak" Hoover: **Real** SCA geologist in Saudi Arabia, 1934 on.
Dick Kerr: **Real** SCA Engr & jack all trades; also ran 1st seis in 1936.
Hugh Burchfiel: **Real** SCA leader geologist, 1930's.
Other **Real** SCA geologists 1934-35:
      Schuyler B. (Krug) Henry, Art Brown, Fred A. Davis (Manager), Felix Dreyfus,
      T. F. Harriss, Tom Koch, Karl Twitchell, G. C. Gester (leader), Mex Rodman,
      Heinie Hawley, Allen C. White, Ken Crandal, Allen Weymouth.
Max Steineke: **Real**, and Key SCA leader, later chief geologist; important man in
    solving the geology of Eastern SA. Partner: **Real** Tom Koch; and guide was
    Real Khamis Ibn Rimthan.
Charles Rocheville: **Real** SCA pilot 1934-35.
Ajab Ben Thanian: **Real** soldier's Amir for some of the geological crews.
Khamis Ibn Rimthan: **Real** and unusually outstanding guide.
R. A. Bramkamp, **Real** paleontologist, Chief Geologist 1947-48.

BOOK TWO:

James Jonathon Burke, Jr. (Jon): JJ's son, b. 7/14/43. Geologist
    and Engineer. Called Jon.
Lee-Anne Gardiner: Jon's wife, b. 7/12/48.
Mary Ellen Burke: JJ's daughter, b. 6/40 in San Francisco.
Elizabeth Anne (Lisa) Burke: b. 6/16/72; dau of Jon & Lee-Anne.
Nicole Brittany Burke: b. 9/12/75; dau of Jon & Lee-Anne.
Thunder: Black Lab dog of JJ's.
Rashid Ben Rimthan: Son of Yahiya Ibn Rimthan; Jon's comtemporary & friend.
Yasmeen: Wife of Rashid.
Achmed Asker: Seismologist in Dhahran & Jon's friend.
Fred Willis, Jr.: Jon's old fishing buddy & Nacogdoches lawyer; his son Fred III.
Woodland: Old Cook farm, near fic. Oak Ridge village.
Virgil Kapsinger: Geological engineer and good friend of Jon when both young.
Ehleebeyt: "High Home" mountain place of Rashid & Yasmeen:
    built by his father Yahiya.
Liz Simpson: Roommate of Lee-Anne when she met Jon.
Martin Booth: Head of Geology Dept @ Stephen F. Austin.
Tony DeRocca: Engineering supervisor in Houston. Jon's friend.
Gene Light: Production General Manager in Houston.
David Roady: Staff analyst to GM; Geological Engineer.
John Venable: Investor pal of Jon Burke; from Ft. Worth.
Don Welker: Independent Landman buddy of Jon Burke.

BIBLIOGRAPHY
(See Preface for use of bibliography)

ARAMCO HISTORY:

Aramco personnel: Tony Delay, Abdul Aziz Alhusain, Melody Morningstar.
Aramco And Its World.
Hoover, J. W. "Soak": Retired geologist, ARAMCO. Diary and personal interview.
Lacey, Robert: The Kingdom; Arabia & The House of Sa'ud. Avon Books, February, 1993; Library of Congress Card #8183741. House of Sa'ud.
Stegner, Wallace: Discovery. Export Book, January, 1971: Library Congress Card #74-148026. (Several Book 1 references).

SAUDI ARABIA CULTURE AND HISTORY:

Aramco personnel: Tony Delay, Abdul Aziz Alhusain, Melody Morningstar, et al.
Aramco And Its World.
Doughty, Charles Montagu: Book & Videotape re: Saudi Arabia 1887-88. Book used by Lawrence of Arabia in WW1.
Encyclopedia Americana.
Hoover, J. W. "Soak." Ibid.
Lacey, Robert: Ibid.
Lawrence, T. E.: Seven Pillars of Wisdom, London & Garden City, N.Y., 1935. National Geographic, May, 1988.
Philby, H. StJ. B.: Arabian Oil Ventures; Washington, 1964.
Stegner, Wallace: Discovery. Ibid.
U.S. Department of State: U.S. Policy in the Persian Gulf.

TECHNICAL REFERENCE; ENGINEERING AND DRILLING

Delay, Tony: Engineering Supervisor, ARAMCO. Personal interview.
Uren, Lester Charles; Petroleum Production Engineering, Third Edition; McGraw-Hill Book Co., Inc., 1946.

TECHNICAL REFERENCES;
EARTH SCIENCES AND PETROLEUM STATISTICS

Powers, R. W., Ramirez, L. F., Redmond, C. D., Elberg, Jr., E.L.: Geology of the Arabian Peninsula. U.S.Geological Survey Professional paper 560 D.
Arabian American Oil Company Staff: Ghawar Oil Field, Saudi Arabia: Bulletin, Am. Assoc. Petroleum Geologists, v.43-2, February 1959, p. 434.
Idso, Sherwood B: "Carbon Dioxide Can Revitalize The Planet, The Opec Bulletin, March 1992 Opec Bulletin, March 1992. Research Physicist, U.S. Water Conservation Laboratory, Phoenix, AZ.
Nelson, T. H. and Temple, P. G.: Mainstream Mantle Convection: A Geologic Analysis of Plate Motion: Bulletin, Am. Assoc.Petroleum Geologists, v. 52-2, March, 1972, p.226.
Oil and Gas Journal: Petroleum statistics, various issues.

Continued

Oliver, Jack: Contributions of Seismology to Plate Tectonics, Bulletin Am. Assoc. Petroleum Geologists, v. 522, March, 1972, p. 214.

Roach, J.W.: How To Apply Fluid Mechanics to Petroleum Exploration, World Oil, March, 1965, p. 71.

Roach, J.W.: Biogenically Formed Petroleum Should be Considered, World Oil June, 1987, p. 84.

Scott, R. W.: World Oil, June, 1991; Editorial Comment, p. 5. World Oil. Petroleum statistics, various issues.

ILLUSTRATIONS

Most photographs are courtesy of
J. W. "Soak" Hoover and ARAMCO. Other sources listed.

1. Cable Tool drilling rig. Uren, Ibid, p.157.
2. Saudi Field Geologist's dress, Saudi Arabia 1934: J. W. "Soak" Hoover.
3. Camel supply train coming into camp: 1934-5.
4. Field Camp scene, 1934.
5. Airliner, 1935.
6. Fairchild field observation aircraft, 1935.
7. Rotary drilling rig, 1937 vintage: World Oil.
8. Rotary drilling rig, 1990's vintage: World Oil.
9. Borehole electric log, 1937 vintage, Chambers County, TX: Cambe Log Library.
10. Basic borehole electric log, 1990's vintage. Does not show various porosity, hydrocarbon, etc. detail logs.
11. Seismic Record, 1937 vintage: Society of Exploration Geophysicists.
12. Seismic Record, (Section), 1990's vintage.
13. Structure Contour Map with Fault.
14. Map of Saudi Arabia and surroundings.

REAL EVENTS

1933: Standard Oil of California (SOCAL) makes deal to explore Saudi Arabia for oil.

1934: Socal exploration commences, with surface geologic crews, initially ten geologists.

3/39: Initial working seismic and gravimeter; Dick Kerr in charge of seismic.

5/39: Original ten geologists gone, including the last one, Krug Henry. Now all replacements; Dhahran Camp underway. First American woman, Anita Burleigh; will live in Jiddah.

5/39: Ibn Sa'ud turned valve at Ras Tamura terminal to load the first tanker, *D.G. Scofield*. Socal and Texas Co. management plus Saudi royalty present. Oil went to Bahrain refinery.

5/39: Huge increase in Saudi Arabia concession to Socal

7/39: Dammam 12, spudded 10/23/38, while at 4565' TD, was perforated
in Arab D zone and exploded (Stegner, ibid, p.127). Finally shut in and filled with mud (Stegner, ibid). This well was the foreteller of major discoveries to follow.

Continued

9/39:	Germany invades Poland; starts World War II.
10/39:	Air raid by Italians who dropped 50# bombs on Bahrain and Dhahran; no real damage, inept raid. Italians announced Bahrain destroyed. Major exodus of Socal American personnel starts right after bombing. (Stegner, ibid).
12/39:	By now, the largest Saudi Fields, Abqaiq, parts of what will be Ghawar, and the onshore part of Safaniya structures are mapped and recognized as favorable geologically.
2/40:	371 American employees, 38 American wives and 16 children, along with 3300 Saudi, Indian, et al, employed at Dhahran. (Stegner, ibid).
3/40:	Abqaiq discovered.
6/40:	Italians mass 250,000 troops versus 36,000 British preparatory to invasion of Libya.
9/40:	80,000 Italians invade Libya. Invasion fails, almost all Italians lost, most as prisoners. British race across Cyrenaica (Central north coastal Africa).
11/40:	Abqaiq discovery confirmed: Tested 405 barrels of oil per hour from Arab D. First giant Saudi Arabiaian discovery. Discovery based on surface Tertiary inliers, followed up by core (structure) drilling and seismic.
12/40:	226 American employess with 19 wives and 5 children left at Dhahran (Stegner, ibid).
3/41:	Rommel attacks British with his German Panzers at El Agheila, and rapidly pushes British back across Libya. British forces weakened by troop movements to Greece. British fooled by Rommel's fake tanks.
4/41:	Germans push British out of Greece.
5/41:	Rommel takes Benghazi and seiges Tobruk after heavy fighting; British hold. Rommel succeeds partly because British fooled by fake German forces.
6/41:	Wavell attacks Rommel; loses, relieved of command.
6/41:	Germans invade Soviet Russia.
6/41:	Saudi Arabia activity near shut down; some drilling, some production and shipping to Bahrain, but now have 3000 BOD refinery near Ras Tanura. Nearly all employees, wives and children gone home for duration.
1941:	British Malta is constant thorn to Germans who bomb it incessantly without conquering it.
12/7/41:	Japanese bomb Pearl Harber and make WW II global. Dhahran Camp: 2 American women, nurses, left, one of them gone 12/15/41; other marries soon thereafter (Stegner, ibid).
11/41:	British under Auchinleck attack Rommel; lose initially, then push Germans back to El Agheila, Libya.
1/42:	About 100 Americans left at Dhahran; skeleton crew only, for standby operations until end of war. Dick Kerr, Floyd Ohliger, and Floyd Meeker stay. Continue to drill a little, mostly at Abqaiq to determine size and shape. Use camels more for transport. Develop dairy cattle and gardening during war. Aramco now virtually a reclamation bureau for water wells, pumps, gardens agriculture, insecticides, medicine, schools, etc. (Stegner, ibid, et al)
1/42:	Rommel pushes British back across Cyrenaica (northern Libya), takes Tobruk, and invades Egypt to within 100 miles of Alexandria. British dig in at El Alamein.
8/42:	Montgomery takes command of British 8th Army.
11/8/42:	U. S. forces land in French North Africa.

END OF REAL EVENTS THROUGH BOOK ONE

- - - - - - - - - -

REAL EVENTS - BOOK TWO

1945:	World War II ends.
6/48:	Ghawar, `Ain Dar area, discovered. (Source: AAPG Bulletin v43-2., op. cit.)
2/49:	Ghawar, Haradh area, discovered. (Source: AAPG Ibid).
4/51 & 8/52:	Ghawar, additional areas discovered. Production started in 1951 (AAPG, Ibid).
1957:	Ghawar Field averages 600,000 barrels of oil per day (AAPG, Ibid).
9/90:	Iraq invades Kuwait.
1/91:	U. S. and U. N. forces attack Iraq army in Kuwait.
2/91:	Iraq expelled from Kuwait.
1992:	Saudi Arabia oil production averages 8.2 million barrels per day, versus 7.1 U.S.A, and 60.1 worldwide. (Source: Oil and Gas Journal, 12/28/92)
1/92:	Saudi Arabia estimated proved oil reserves 258 billion barrels of oil, versus 25 U.S.A., 662 total Mideast, and 997 worldwide. (Oil and Gas Journal, Ibid).

The setting for Book Two is post-1993.
Real Events after 1992 are unknown.
Above listed events bear on Book Two.

ARAB-ENGLISH DICTIONARY FOLLOWS

ARAB-ENGLISH DICTIONARY OF KEY WORDS

(Phonetic only; Alphabets different; different kinds of words)

Arab	English
abayah	dress, head to toe, loose
Abdul	servant of
abu	father, father of
ad, il, an	the
aghal	headdress cords, double
ahlan!	Hi!
ahwa, gahwa	coffee; liquid, v. sweet, tiny cups
ain	well or tank
Akbar	Great
akhiwiya	slaves (up to 1962)
Al	Family, as Al Sa'ud, Family Sa'ud
al, an, as	the
Allah Akbar	God, Great
Allah kareem	God, kind
Amir, Emir	Commander; chief
Anisah	Miss
Araif	camels lost and recovered by raids
Ardha	sword dance
askaree	policeman, local
askra	soldier
at, ath	the
Aziz	attribute of God
Bahr	sea
baksheesh	bribe, gratuity; way to get things done
bayda, baydah	egg
Bay'ah	oath of allegiance to authority
Bedouin	nomad
bin, ben	son of
bint	girl, daughter of
boum	boat; most with two masts; shallow draft, pulls up on sand
bukra	tomorrow; put off to another day
chador	dress, head to toe, loose
chai	tea
cobra, black	snake, v. poisonous but v. rare
dabb	lizard, spiney-tail, large:20"; edible
dahna	desert, sand
Dahna	sand belt inland
Damoosa	lizard-fish, lives in sand
dhelul	camel, riding
dhib	hyena? maybe coyote
dhow	boat w/ lateen sail; single mast; shallow draft
dibdiba	desert, flint
dihn	butter
dikaka	plain, sandy, level to rolling, with stunted shrubs
eed	feast

Continued

Arab   English

Arab	English
fok	up
gazelle	antelope w/goat-like horns
ghazzu	raid; old Bedouin way of building herds; usually no killings
ghirba	water bag; sewn skins - camel or goat, etc.
ghutra	headdress
hadhar	settled farmers, merchants
hadhdh	luck
Hajj	pilgrimage, one of five pillars of Islam
Hajji	pilgrim
higehb	scarf for woman's head
Hofuf	city; capitol of Eastern Province
houbara	bird, bustard, edible, grouse-like
ibex	mountain goat
ibn	son of
Ikhwan	brothers
Iman	leader of prayer
insha	if wills, if is to be
Insha Allah	If/As God wills
ishbickah	snare for falcon
jabal, jebehl	hill, hills, mountain, mountains (also called gabal, gebehl by some)
jeddah	grandmother
jemel	camel; many other words for camel
Jihad	holy war
Kafiya	headdress for men
khu-daar	vegetables
Koran	Muslin bible, 114 suras or chapters
mah'rook	congratulations
majlis	room, reception/sitting
min	from
mishlah	robe or cloak, outer
mohandis	geologist
Molia	snake, cobra-like, not dangerous to man
Nafud	a desert area
nahr	river
Najd	sand area, central SA
naseeha	advice
nigga	sand hills in jDhana, to 800' high
Quadi	judge
Qateef	oil seepages, oasis, sometimes sand covered
Qateef	region; east coast Saudi Arabia
Ramadham	fasting month of Islam
rim	gazelle, one of three types
riyal	currency unit for Saudi Arabia
Rub al Khali	desert, great of SE SA; empty quarter/barren land
sabkha	flat, hard, either salt or coastal plain, usually with gravel
Saker	falcon for hunting; prized
salaam	greeting, peace be upon you
Saudi Arabia	830,000 sq. mi. vs 815,700 for Western Europe; created 9/'32
Sayyid	Mister
Sayyidah	Mrs
scorpion, black	fat-tailed, bite painful, not normally fatal

Continued

Arab	English
selugi	dog
shabath	spider, hairy 6" sun or camel, aggressive non poisonous
shamal, shamehl	storm, sand; norther
Sheikh	elder, literally; tribal leader; boss
shozen	shotgun
sirr	secrets
soukh, suq	market, bazaar, meeting place for people/animals
thobe	full length shirt, men's inner garment; not underwear
thub	wolf, small,
tuhayhi	lizard, small; disappears into sand
Ulema	religious scholars; holy men; issue religious interpretations
umm	mother
Umm Abdul	mother of Abdul
uruq	sand ridge
viper (sand)	poisonous snake, not normally fatal to man
wadi	dry wash, draw
wajid flus	much money
Wallahi!	By God! (common exclamation)
waral	lizard, small, fast
weled	coffee boy
wudayhi	oryx, rare antelope-like animal
yimkim	maybe
zakat	religious tax
zawba	storm, sand